CITY LIMITS

Wild Woods,
the sequel to *City Limits*,
is expected to release in the
summer of 2019. There is more
to the story of Gee yet to come.

OTHER TITLES BY NATHAN EVERETT

For Money or Mayhem

COMPUTER FORENSICS DETECTIVE Dag Hamar is pulled from behind the safety of his computer and takes to the streets when he discovers a link between an online predator and real life kidnappings around Seattle. His fledgling romance is threatened when his girlfriend's daughter is suddenly among the missing.

For Blood or Money

COMPUTER FORENSICS DETECTIVES Dag Hamar and Deb Riley discover secret files and hidden code can be as dangerous as dark alleys and flying bullets as they track a missing man and the billion dollar fortune that went with him. Fourteen years after *For Money or Mayhem*.

The Gutenberg Rubric

TWO RARE BOOK librarians race across three continents to find and preserve a legendary book printed by Johannes Gutenberg. Behind them, a trail of bombed libraries draws Homeland Security to launch a worldwide search for biblio-terrorists. Keith and Maddie find love along the way, but will they survive to enjoy it?

Steven George & The Dragon

Steven has always known he was a dragonslayer, but on the day his village sends him to slay the fearsome beast he realizes he doesn't know what a dragon looks like, where it lives, or how to kill it. His quest is facilitated by the exchange of "once-upon-a-times" with the people he meets on the endless road. Think Grimm. For young adults, not children.

The Volunteer

JOURNEY INSIDE THE head of a chronically homeless man--a man that in a less politically correct age we might have called a hobo. Gerald Good, known now only as G2, volunteered to take the place of a homeless man, believing he would work his way back quickly. Ten years later, twenty... thirty years, find G2 alone in his head, his memories, and his boxcar.

CITY LIMITS

NATHAN EVERETT

ELDER ROAD BOOKS
BELLEVUE WA

A special thank you to my editors and advisers who stuck with me through this entire project. Your help was immeasurable.
Kathryn McCullough
Michele Palmer
Lyndsy Fernandes

CONTENTS

1

POPULATION 4190 (+1)

Crossing the Limits

HE SHOULD have passed up that last lift but there weren't many trucks that took the state highway east—especially on a holiday. Four hours of bouncing on a poorly maintained two-lane left him in serious bladder pain. When he arrived at the crossroads, the driver didn't even pull over to the side. He barely stopped in the middle of the inter-section long enough for Gee to jump down from the cab.

"Town's about five miles south," the driver said as he ground the gears.

"Thanks for the lift," Gee yelled back.

As soon as the truck started moving, Gee ran to the ditch to relieve himself. He was about to burst, but having clamped down so tightly for so long, it took a minute to relax and let his stream flow. He sighed deeply. Five miles. There was nothing he could do but start walking. He shouldered his backpack and headed south on the narrow road. This one was in even worse repair than the previous, but at least he wasn't being bounced along it.

The sun blazed near its zenith and the sweatband on his baseball cap was wet and sticky. He hadn't eaten since midnight and had noth-ing to drink since five in the morning. He knew he was dehydrated and woozy, but the nearest place he could eat and drink was the town. He just needed to keep walking.

———————◁◆▷———————

AN HOUR AND a half after the truck dropped him off, he could see the first sign of habitation. His eyes played tricks on him and the town looked like it was getting farther away until he nearly ran into a sign suddenly in front of him.

"City Limits, Rosebud Falls," he read aloud with a cracked voice. "Population 4,190. Looks like this is it." His spirit quest had shown him the vision and Gee followed it. He reached deep into one of the pockets in his cargo pants to find a black felt tip marker. He used it to X-out the zero on the sign and draw in a large '1.' "Population four thousand one hundred ninety plus one," he said as he walked past the sign. Another wave of disorientation and dizziness swept over him. He needed food and water soon.

An Instant of Foolish Heroism

THE FIRST SIGN of life he came to was a working-class bar called the Pub & Grub. Its flashing sign advertised 'Eat Here.' When he reached the door, he found a sign that read 'Closed for the Holiday.' He tried the door anyway, but it was locked tight. Gee pulled off his cap to mop away the sweat with a handkerchief. He turned away from the pub and continued into town.

Fifteen minutes later, he saw tents along the river walk where an Independence Day celebration was being held. It was the first life he'd seen in the town. Apparently, folks here went all out for the holiday and Gee was certain he could find food and drink there. He'd take anything at this point.

He limped onto the bridge with the roar of the waterfall behind him. He'd picked up a stone and slumped down to take off his shoe and shake it out. It felt so good to put his sock-clad foot on the cool shaded pavement that he took the other shoe off as well.

Rosebud Falls glistened with the distinctive pink-tinged water that gave the river its name. The falls was the culmination of over half a mile of rapids that plunged seven feet onto more rocks just below the con-fluence of the Rose River and the West Branch. It was beautiful and horrific at the same time—mesmerizing in his current mental state. He stood with his backpack and shoes by his side as he wished he was drinking straight from the mineral-laden water.

"Devon! No. Stop!" a woman screamed from beyond the other side of the bridge. Gee ran across the roadway and looked down on the celebration. A young woman rushed toward the water, which poured swiftly through scattered rocks on this side of the bridge. Gee traced the trajectory of the woman and saw a toddler near the water's edge. He was gleefully tossing sticks up the river and then leaning out to capture them as they floated by.

The mother was still twenty feet away when the toddler overreached and tumbled headlong into the rushing water. Gee jumped to the railing of the bridge without thinking and arched into a long dive beyond the turbulence of the falls. He was only feet away from the little one when he emerged.

Welcome to Rosebud Falls

WHEN HE MANAGED to get to shore, he let the mother and a crew of emergency techs take the child from his arms and didn't complain when they loaded him in an ambulance to rush to the hospital. A swipe at the water on his face told him his head was bleeding. The EMT applied pressure to his head with a soft cloth. He coughed up some of the water he'd inhaled, but it relieved his parched throat and mouth a little.

At the hospital, a young doctor put six stitches in Gee's forehead and ordered more fluids when he complained of thirst. An attractive, dark-skinned nurse named Ellie was fussing at the IV when a man wearing an open-collared shirt with a mustard stain on the front entered the room. His khaki shorts went poorly with the sandals and black socks on his feet. A straw hat crowned the ensemble. Gee wondered if this was the child's father. That thought was dispelled when the man fished around in his pocket and produced a badge and ID.

"Hello, hero," the guy's rough voice said. "I'm Detective Mead Oliver. Just spent some time with the Panzas to make sure everything was okay with little Devon. You made quite a splash with that family." The detective chuckled at his own joke and Gee saw the nurse roll her eyes. "How's everything in here, Ellie? Is our hero in good shape?" he asked the nurse.

"Detective, you know I can't comment on a patient's condition. You have to ask Dr. Poltanys about that. From *my* perspective, the patient didn't run from the room screaming when you walked in, so I suspect his condition is serious."

Gee watched the friendly banter between the two and waited for his turn to speak. Finally, Detective Oliver turned back to Gee.

"It's nice to meet you, Detective."

"It's not every day we have a genuine hero walk into town and save the life of one of our kids. What's your name?"

"George Evars, sir. I usually go by Gee. 'Cause my middle name is Edward. G-E-E."

"Sounds like something you got tagged with in grade school and never lost," Mead continued in good humor. "Where do you hail from?"

"I'm from…" Gee stopped as his brow furrowed. It was right on the tip of his tongue, but he couldn't remember. "I'm from, uh… that way, I guess. I can't think of it right now." Ellie looked at him with concern written on her face.

"Is there someone we should call to let them know you are here?" Mead asked.

"I… um… don't know anyone."

"We need to have the doctor come back in," Ellie said. She stepped to the doorway and spoke toward the hall. "Mary, please have Dr. Poltanys paged to room 1108. I think we have an issue."

"Memory problem?" Mead said. "You got a big cut on your head. How did you know it was safe to dive off the bridge?"

"Was it safe?"

"Well, no. It's posted at both ends of the bridge, but under the circumstances, I'm not going to charge you. You dove a long way out. Marian said it looked like you were flying—came out of the water almost in reach of little Devon. Seemed like everything was fine until you slipped as you handed off the boy and fell on a rock at the shore. Were you in the Coast Guard?"

"I… That doesn't sound familiar to me. Maybe. I don't know." When Gee thought back on his life, he drew a blank. Dr. Poltanys came into the room and took the chart from Ellie.

"What seems to be the problem?"

"The patient seems unable to remember certain things," Ellie said. "I thought you should know."

"Right. Could you repeat your full name for me?"

"George Edward Evars."

"And how old are you, George?"

"Thirty-four. Thirty-five on September 24."

"And what is today's date?"

"July fourth. It's Independence Day, isn't it? I mean, I wasn't unconscious or didn't sleep through it, did I?"

"No. You're answering just fine. What are you unable to remember?"

"I… uh… don't remember…"

"He couldn't remember where he's from. Didn't know if he'd been in the Coast Guard," the detective volunteered.

"Ah. I see. Under interrogation, the witness failed to respond with details the officer wanted to hear," Poltanys answered.

"I wasn't interrogating. This was a friendly visit," Mead answered. The left corner of his mouth pulled back as he scowled. He folded his arms. Poltanys smiled.

"Let's try it this way," the doctor said, examining Gee's eyes with a small light. "We'll do a little test and see if we can spot anything. Do you want me to send Detective Oliver out of the room?"

"No. He's fine. You three are the only people I know here. I think."

"I'm going to give you four words and ask you to repeat them back to me. I want you to remember the four words and I'll ask you to repeat them again when we're finished. Got it?"

"Got it."

"Apple. Television. Lamb. Camera."

"Apple. Television. Lamb. Camera."

"Good. Remember those words." The doctor looked back at his chart before continuing, giving Gee a chance to repeat the words to himself. "What is the sum of seven and twelve?"

"Nineteen."

"Touch your left elbow with your right hand." Gee did so without disturbing the IV. The doctor handed him a clipboard and pen. "Draw a clock face with the time set at a quarter past seven." Gee drew a rectangle with the numbers 7:15 in it.

"A.M or P.M?"

Poltanys laughed. "That will do. What year was the Declaration of Independence signed?"

"1776."

"What were the words I asked you to remember?"

"Apple. Television. Lamb. Camera."

"Where were you born?"

"In... I... It was..." Gee struggled. He should remember this as easily as he remembered his own name. Poltanys nodded and jotted something down.

"What was your mother's name?" Gee just shook his head. "It seems that you have some long-term memory loss," the doctor said. "I want an MRI, but the technician isn't available today. Let's make sure you get it in the morning, shall we? I doubt that it is too serious. Your head injury is not significant enough to warrant memory loss and there is no sign of concussion. When you came in, you were suffering from dehydration. When was the last time you drank water?"

"A... um... long time ago. I was really thirsty when I got here and was hoping to get something to drink at the celebration."

"I think you just suffered traumatic shock, probably from a combination of dehydration and hitting the river. Your body hasn't had a chance to regain its equilibrium. The drip in your arm should have your fluid levels back up soon, but keep sucking on the ice cubes Ellie is bringing for you. We'll keep you overnight and get that MRI first thing in the morning."

Dr. Poltanys turned to the door but stopped before he left. "I don't suppose you have insurance, do you?" Gee opened his mouth and then shrugged. "I thought not. Don't worry about it. I'll bill the City's hero fund. Go easy on him, Mead."

"Rosebud Falls has a hero fund?" Gee asked as the doctor left.

"No. Private joke," Detective Oliver responded. "Poltanys Memorial Hospital has never in its history turned away a patient. They aren't likely to now."

"Poltanys? Like the doctor? He owns the hospital?"

"The hospital has been here a lot longer than he has, but for some reason there has always been at least one Poltanys on staff, either as a doctor, nurse, or administrator. They're one of the seven Families," Mead said obtusely. "Now, let's see if I can help you. Do you have any next of kin that we should notify? Wife? Girlfriend? Parents?"

Gee just shook his head. "I really don't remember."

"How about ID? Do you have a driver's license?"

Gee reached to his hip for his wallet and found it bare. "I don't have pants on."

"You wouldn't want them on, believe me," Ellie said. "We got you out of your wet clothes as soon as the doctor verified that there was no sign of neck or spinal injury. Sorry about the shirt. We cut that off so we could do the x-rays. Let me get your trousers. They're hanging in the bathroom." She opened a door across the room and reached for the cargo pants. "You reached for your left hip, Gee. I don't feel anything in that pocket. Here, you'd better check." Ellie brought Gee his trousers and he searched the pockets. He went so far as to check the leg pockets as well. The nurse was right, he didn't want to put them back on in their soggy condition.

"I'm sure I had a wallet. I always carry it in my left hip pocket. I *think* I had a wallet. Everyone carries a wallet, don't they?"

"I suppose we'll find it washed up on the shore someplace. What was in it?" Mead asked.

"A-uh… little money. Not much. ID. A driver's license. I think. That doesn't sound quite right."

"Credit cards?" Gee shrugged and shook his head. "Membership cards? AAA? Health Insurance?" Gee put a hand on his forehead, clearly in distress.

"I just… don't remember."

"Okay. They brought a backpack and shoes in from the bridge. First off, if you were thirsty and headed to the festivities for a drink, why did you have your shoes off?"

"I got something in my shoe. It was driving me crazy. I kind of collapsed there to get it out. Felt so good to have my shoe off that I took the other one off and decided to walk barefoot."

"Walk a long way earlier?"

"I guess. I know my feet were tired."

"Let's look through your belongings and see if there are any clues to your identity and who to contact in an emergency."

"You can't do that, Mead," Ellie insisted immediately. "You know you can't do that without a warrant and I won't let you." The corner of Mead's mouth pulled back toward his ear as he gritted his teeth.

"Ellie, this isn't New York City. And I'm not one of the police bullies you were used to seeing there. I'm just trying to help," Mead said. He turned to Gee. "You aren't suspected of anything and I'm trying to get you help. Will you give me permission to search your pockets and bag for information regarding your identity?"

"He means well, Mr. Evars," Ellie jumped in, "but if he finds anything illegal in your bag he can still use it to arrest you because you gave him permission to look. You should have a lawyer present or he should have a search warrant."

"Ellie, where am I going to get a search warrant on the Fourth of July? And under what pretenses? We're on the same side here, trying to help this guy."

"Wait." Gee's voice stopped the sparring between the two. "I don't know *who* I am. Not really. I know my name. But more importantly, I know what *kind* of man I am. Maybe it's not the kind of man I've always been, and maybe I broke a law before I got here. Or maybe a lot of laws. I don't know. But the man I *am* says if I did then I should go to jail. I just don't feel up to pawing through stuff myself."

"Then let *me* look through your things," Ellie said. "Mead can sit there with a piece of paper and inventory what we find. We can all sign the sheet."

"You make such a big deal out of it," Mead sighed. "Does that suit you?"

"That's fine," Gee answered the detective. "I don't know what good it will do, but maybe I stuck my wallet in the pack. And if someone is waiting to hear from me, maybe there's contact information. I just hope I have clean underwear."

The Ingredients of Life

"FRONT RIGHT POCKET: Cash. Two fives, seven ones, a quarter, a dime, and two pennies. Seventeen dollars and thirty-seven cents. One Swiss Army knife. Not a big one, but a lot of gadgets on it."

"We don't need to itemize every blade and gadget," Mead interrupted. He could already tell this was going to delay dinner.

"Right," Ellie answered. She didn't have any other patients on this hall and didn't mind taking her time at all. "Left front pocket: Handkerchief. And a stone. What is this, Gee?" She held out an oblong white stone, a little more than an inch long and an eighth of an inch thick. Scratched deeply into the surface was a single vertical line crossed by five horizontal lines. It looked like they had once been filled with black paint, but most of it was chipped or worn away. He reached for the stone and closed his fist around it. He felt a sense of calm wash over him—as if he'd been reborn.

"I don't know," he said. "But it's important to me. I... I like to hold it."

"Woowoo shit," Mead grunted. "Maybe just a worry stone."

"Yeah. That's probably it." Still, he breathed more easily holding the stone.

"Hmm. That's all," Ellie said. "Wait. In this cargo pocket there's a Magic Marker. Nothing else."

"What else were you wearing?" Mead asked.

"Jockeys. Socks. T-shirt. Belt. Of course, I'd just taken off my shoes. Hey! So that's something I remember from before I hit the water. That's good, right?" Gee reached to his head. "Um... I was wearing a cap, too."

"Probably halfway to Palmyra in the Rose River by now."

"The rest of your clothes are drying in the bathroom," Ellie said, "but I'd get them washed before I put them on again if I were you. Sorry about the t-shirt."

"Okay. Let's move to the backpack," Oliver directed. Gee shuffled the cash, knife, and marker into a pile beside him, but kept the stone in his hand. Ellie put the damp handkerchief in the bathroom along with the trousers before she brought the backpack to the bed.

"You sure you want me to do this?" Gee nodded and slid over a bit so Ellie could lay his possessions on the edge of the bed. "Okay. Sleeping bag." Mead had her unroll it to confirm there was nothing rolled up in it. She sighed but complied, finding nothing. "Pack main compartment" she said. She began laying clothing on the bed in piles. They were all clean and neatly folded.

"No dirty clothes?" Gee asked.

"Looks like you just did your laundry," Ellie responded.

"Pockets on the bag?" Mead asked.

"That's next." Ellie itemized basic toiletries. "Right pocket: Shaving mug, brush, and a straight razor."

"A straight razor? Who shaves with a straight-edge razor these days?" Mead asked.

"I could use a shave," Gee said, stroking his stubble.

"How do you sharpen it?"

"I use my belt as a strop."

"Is that it?"

"No. There's a front pocket, too," Ellie said. "A book. *The Odyssey* by Homer, a Signet Classic."

"That could hold a clue," Mead said.

"How? That I read old Greek myths?"

"That might say something, too. What I meant was, look inside. Any inscriptions? Notes? Bookmarks?"

"Oh, sure." Ellie opened the book. "Bingo! 'To Gee, Here's to your journey. Love, Rae.' How sweet."

"Who's Rae?" Mead asked.

"She's um... I think... like I know her. She's my... I should know who she is. I'm... I hope she's okay."

"Any reason she wouldn't be?"

"I just don't know."

"There's a bookmark, too. I'll try not to lose your place."

"Bookstore marker?" Mead asked.

"No. It's a... Hmm. It's a free admission pass to the Elmont County Fair in Rosebud Falls, August 15-18. Present at the Whirl-a-Gig for a free ride."

"So, you were here at the fair last year," Mead said. "That's something. Someone will know and recognize you in town then. We'll just have to put a bulletin in the *Mirror*."

"That would be good, except this isn't for last year's fair. It's for this year's," Ellie interjected.

"This year's fair isn't for…"

"…six weeks. Mid-August."

"Have they even started selling tickets?" Mead asked.

"There's nothing else on the ticket," Ellie said. "A picture of the ride. I wonder if they'll even accept it. It doesn't really look official." Gee took the ticket and looked at it, shaking his head. He handed it to Mead. The detective looked it over and gave it back to Ellie, who carefully replaced it in the book. She looked through the backpack and then handed it over to Mead to examine. He felt around it but found nothing else.

"Well, that didn't help much," Mead said. "I don't see that we even need the list." He handed it to Gee and gave the clipboard back to Ellie.

MEAD HAD BEEN excited to meet the hero when he got to the hospital. He was intrigued and puzzled as they tried to figure out Gee's identity and discover his memories. Then he got tired and a little grouchy. He'd left his family at the celebration by the river and they were staking out a spot to watch the fireworks at night. He wanted to be there with his kids while they were still willing to associate with their parents.

He pushed his hat back on his head and scratched. "One more thing. Where do you live, Gee?"

Vagrancy

THERE WAS A long silence. Mead started to turn away in frustration when Gee finally spoke.

"Here, I guess. I mean, not here in this room, but here in Rosebud Falls. I just don't have an address yet," he whispered. Mead and Ellie looked at each other.

"I should have thought of that," Mead sighed.

"I didn't mean to create a hardship when I came to town."

"Are you sure?"

"Mead, why don't you get back to your family," Ellie said. "Things are quiet here and Dr. Poltanys wants to run an MRI on Gee tomorrow. I'll get someone to bring him a hamburger."

"Well, technically, he's vagrant," Mead said. "Can't do anything about it while you are in the hospital, but when you are released tomorrow, come by the police station. You don't have enough cash to pay for a room and you have no lodging. Our policy is to put you up for a night at the jail—unlocked cell—and then buy you a bus ticket in the morning. Seems like a harsh way to treat a hero, but I don't know what else I can do."

"That won't be necessary, Mr. Oliver," said a woman from the doorway. Gee looked up to see an attractive young woman holding a toddler followed by a man who could only be her husband. He almost felt like he should know her, but it was the toddler who held his eyes. "We have a room where he can stay."

"We heard Mr. Evars lost his memory when he saved our son," the man said. "It wouldn't be right to just cut him loose and say goodbye. We'd be planning a funeral now if it weren't for him."

They came farther into the room and the toddler set up a squeal when he saw Gee, stretching his arms out to his rescuer. Gee held out his arms in return.

"Are you sure?" asked the woman. Gee nodded, and Devon practically leaped from his mother's arms. "I'm Marian Panza. Thank you so much for what you did for Devon!" Marian collapsed on the edge of the bed and hugged Gee and her son together. Gee could see her husband hovering over her shoulder and reached out his hand.

"I'm George Evars. Just call me Gee. Everyone does."

"Nathan Panza," the young man said, shaking his hand. "I can't believe Devon got so far away from us. We were all on our blanket getting ready to picnic and the next thing we knew he was in the water. Thank you. All I can say is thank you." There were tears in the young man's eyes. Marian loosened herself from hugging Gee and Devon and stood beside her husband.

"It looks like Devon knows his savior," Ellie said. "Is he that friendly with everyone?"

"Hardly anyone," Marian said. Devon giggled as Gee tickled him.

"Gee!" the toddler said. "Call me Gee!"

"I am Gee. You are Dee," Gee laughed.

"Dee! I am Dee!"

"Um… Mr. Evars… Gee… we heard you didn't have a place to stay. We have a spare room you are welcome to," Marian said.

"It isn't much—just the attic, really—but it has a bed and there's a bath at the foot of the stairs. You can eat with the family. Just until you get on your feet and have a place of your own, you know," Nathan said.

"Are you sure about this?" Mead asked.

"I'm sure," Nathan answered. "He saved Devon. What kind of man would I be if I didn't do this little bit to help him in return? I need help down at the market, too. I'm sure we can get him a job. Then he won't be vagrant."

"Hey, that would be great," Gee responded. Devon finally squirmed back to his mother as she held out her arms. "I appreciate your offer and I promise I'll work hard and contribute. I don't want to be a burden to anyone. Whatever I earn, I'll use to help with expenses."

"Then consider yourself to have a home in Rosebud Falls," Marian said. "Ellie, can you call us when he's released? We'll pick you up and show you your room, Gee."

"Thank you. It means a lot to have a home to go to," Gee said.

"I hope you don't regret this," Mead said. Nathan, Marian, and Devon all wished Gee a good night and left. "I'm leaving, too," Mead continued. "With luck, I'll still have a family on the riverbank for the fireworks. I'd like you to come by the station after you're released tomorrow and let us get your fingerprints to run. There's close to a hundred million fingerprints in the national database. We might find a match."

"I'll do that," Gee responded. "And if I'm in the wrong database, I'll willingly become your prisoner."

"I doubt we'll see that, but I appreciate the offer of an easy arrest," Mead said. The left corner of his mouth pulled back and his left eye squinted. "Uh… just one more thing. Where do you work?"

Gee cocked an eyebrow at the detective. "If I understood Nathan correctly, I work at the market. He hasn't told me what I do yet."

"Oh. Yeah," Mead sighed. "See you tomorrow." Gee and Ellie watched his back as he disappeared through the doorway.

"Let's get the IV out of your arm and see about getting you that hamburger," Ellie said, moving efficiently to remove the cannula.

Praise the Lord

"THANK OUR MERCIFUL God that you arrived when you did," a man said as he entered the room. "I came as soon as I heard, but stopped to pray with the Panzas on their way out. As Jesus said to suffer the little children to come unto me, you have given a child the opportunity to know the Lord. A child who might otherwise have perished."

Gee and Ellie were surprised by the effusive visitor.

"Do you know me?"

"I know that today you became a messenger from God. He used you as his outstretched hand to scoop a child from the raging waters. He blessed us with your presence. I am Pastor Lance Beck from Calvary Tabernacle. I've come to pray with you that you might receive the blessing of God's healing grace and that you might always walk humbly before the Lord." The man wiped his sweaty palm on his pants before offering to Gee to shake.

"Uh… thank you for your concern, Pastor."

"Let me ask you, young man, do you know Jesus as your Lord and Savior? You acted courageously in the face of danger this day, and God used your courage to fulfill his purpose. But have you accepted his grace and salvation into your heart? Have you been washed in the blood of the Lamb?" He didn't let go of Gee's hand after the shake and Gee could feel it getting slipperier by the second.

The preacher had an overbearing presence that swept all resistance before him. The sheen of sweat on his forehead seemed out of place in the cool atmosphere of the hospital. Gee had an instant distaste for the man and struggled to sit up straighter in the bed.

"Thank you again for your prayers, Pastor. Now if you will excuse us, I was about to get dressed."

"Of course, of course. I'll just wait outside and we can have a long chat."

"That won't be necessary. Why don't I look you up in the next week or two and we'll *chat* then? I'm sure you appreciate the fact that I have a bit of a headache right now and can't focus on your message."

"Let me pray for you healing," the preacher insisted.

"Reverend Beck, you've been warned before about ignoring a patient's wishes," Ellie said. "Mr. Evars has made it clear that he doesn't want you here. If you wish to continue access as a chaplain in the hospital, you *must* respect the patient's wishes to be left alone."

The preacher glared at Ellie, but nonetheless moved away from Gee's bed. He drew himself up to all of his five-and-a-half feet and smoothed his salt and pepper hair with the hand that wasn't holding his Bible.

"I answer only to God, nurse, and one day you will be called to answer to Him as well. Pray that on that day Jesus does not cast you aside for preventing the salvation of this wretched man." The preacher spun without another word and left.

Gee sighed and flopped back against the pillows. "Thank you, Ellie. I hold you blameless in preventing the salvation of this wretched man."

"The only thing worse than a cop in the hospital is a preacher. And that one is the worst."

"I don't much care about religion. It has its place, and as long as they are doing good and helping others, I have no problem." He fingered the stone that was still in the palm of his left hand. He realized he hadn't let go of it since he plucked it from the change that had been in his pocket. It calmed him.

"Were you serious when you said you had a headache?" Ellie asked. "We should watch for that."

"Not much. I can tell I hit my head, but it doesn't really hurt."

"Well, as Dr. Poltanys would say, 'Take two aspirin and call me in the morning.' Why don't you get dressed in something comfortable while I see if I can order you a hamburger? I'll see you after a while."

The Man in the Mirror

GEE FACED HIMSELF in the bathroom mirror. Following Ellie's instructions not to get his bandages wet, he managed to scrub the river residue from his body in the shower. He was no longer light-headed, but was extremely hungry.

Who am I?

The reflection was silent as he lathered his face and began meticulously shaving with the straight razor. *Tap water is never really hot enough for a good shave.* His beard wasn't heavily grown, so he must have shaved that morning. Still, there was something comforting about the ritual of scraping the whiskers from his face and neck. It grounded him in the same way the mysterious worry stone did. But still the only answer he received was what he had already said. 'I'm George Evars. Call me Gee. Everybody does.'

Why am I here?

Wasn't that the question that all humanity asked? 'What is the essence of being?' 'Why do we exist?' But for Gee, the question was more immediate. He could remember stumbling into town, hungry and thirsty, but he could not remember getting to town. He must have had some reason to come to Rosebud Falls. *What was it?*

He thought vaguely that it should concern him more than it did, but when he tried to focus on it, his mind turned away. It seemed more important to determine who he was now rather than who he might have been before. He felt that he was a part of the City. He was simply supposed to be here.

He took one more look in the mirror, picked up the stone from where he laid on the sink, and turned to the main room to pull his sweats and a t-shirt from his bag.

Love at First Sight

"Knock-knock. Is this the hero's room?" a cheery woman called as she pushed his door open and marched across the room to his bed table with a bag. Gee held his sweats in front of him as he straightened up. She turned and giggled at his predicament. He held his breath as he looked at her, convinced she was an apparition.

Perhaps I should pay more attention to Pastor Beck. I've been visited by an angel.

It wasn't that she was the most beautiful woman in the world. He had just enough objectivity to recognize that it wasn't physical beauty that had captured him. She was pretty enough for his tastes. Her mocha-colored hair framed a perfectly oval face and fell in waves just below her shoulders. The pale blue tunic blouse, belted at her thin waist, highlighted the deeper blue of her eyes. The shorts she wore stopped just above her knees and showed golden tanned legs and feet encased in leather sandals.

Gee finally remembered to breathe.

"I… uh… 'm not really a hero. I just didn't have sense enough to stay out of the water."

"I'm Karen Weisman of *The Elmont Mirror*. Reporter. You're news. May I have an interview?" Her eyes hadn't wavered from his, even while he seemed stunned by her presence. There was a glint of merriment that played about them and tickled at the corners of her mouth.

"I… uh… don't have my pants on."

"Yeah. Awkward. I don't usually get that far on a first interview," she laughed as she turned her back. "Go ahead and dress. I met Nurse Ellie on the way up here and she was being called by someone else. She asked me to bring you this food. Don't know what she got you, but it smells good."

Karen began unpacking the bag while Gee hurriedly stepped into his sweats and pulled them up. She laid a wrapped burger and a huge basket of fries on the bed table and helped herself to some fries.

"Oh, it's a burger and curly fries from Zeigler's stand. They're the best if you don't have a cholesterol problem." She turned back to him just as he was pulling a t-shirt over his head. "Ooh. Nice. You're in good shape. Is that why you felt confident in diving off the bridge to save that little boy?"

Gee got his head through the neck and blushed as she looked at him appreciatively. He spotted the hamburger and made a dash for it. He couldn't open the wrapper fast enough. The burger was covered with the works—cheese, bacon, lettuce, tomato, grilled onions. He suddenly knew where Mead got the mustard stain on his shirt. He had a second bite before Karen continued.

"You must be really hungry!"

"I haven't eaten since… in a long time," he answered. He was unsure of exactly when his last meal had been.

"Well, let's get this started," Karen said. She snagged a fry from his basket. "Axel says he can get the story into tomorrow's edition if I get it to him by ten tonight. It's already after eight." She flicked on a small recorder and began. "This is Karen Weisman, reporter for *The Elmont Mirror*. I'm talking with George Evars who rescued three-year-old Devon Panza from the rushing waters of the Rose River this afternoon."

"I prefer to be called Gee," he said.

"G-e-e? Got it. Where are you from, Gee?"

"Uh… up north. Somewhere." He remembered walking up to the Pub & Grub on the way into town and continuing south until he reached the river.

"Okay, man of mystery. Let's get right to the point. Why did you take that impossible leap from the bridge into the river?"

"Well, obviously, it wasn't impossible. Improbable, maybe, according to what I've heard." Karen nodded and motioned for him to continue. "When I got to the railing, I saw Devon tumble into the water. Everything else was automatic. A child was in danger. You have to respond to that."

"Just like that? No moment of hesitation? No evaluation of the situation to determine the best available action?" Karen asked.

"There was a baby in the river."

"Wow!"

"I saw other things—was aware, I guess. Marian was screaming and running toward the river. That's little Devon's mom. I met them a while ago when they offered me a place to stay. But little Dee…"

"Dee?"

"He heard me say I am Gee and he tried to copy it. We settled on Gee and Dee. He'll be a force to reckon with in the future."

"And little Dee?"

"He was already downstream of them when I saw Marian and Nathan running to the shore. I just jumped."

"That's a very selfless attitude. Have you done things like this before?"

"I… don't know." He hesitated, unsure of how much he wanted to tell Karen. "I… lost a bit of my memory, apparently. The doctor says he thinks it's temporary—a kind of post-traumatic stress condition. I'm having an MRI tomorrow."

"I had no idea! Someone should have called me up here a lot earlier," Karen barked. She opened her purse and grabbed a notepad, on which she began furiously scribbling things that didn't seem to have anything to do with the recording. "How far back can you remember?" she asked.

"I was thinking a bit ago, and the first solid memory I have right now is seeing the Pub & Grub. I was hungry and thirsty and felt disoriented, but it was closed. I kept walking into town and heard the celebration by the river. I stopped on the bridge to dig a stone out of my shoe."

"So, you don't remember anything else? Nothing before that?"

"I seem to have all my cognitive faculties. Dr. Poltanys gave me a memory test and I was able to answer a math question. I have a book that I can read. I know what year the Declaration of Independence was signed. Pretty much anything except about myself."

"So, you could be a serial murderer or a rapist and just don't know?"

"If I am, I've promised Detective Oliver that I'd turn myself in at once," he laughed. Karen made a note and reached for another of his fries. He considered whether there was anything in him that felt like an evil man. *Evil.* He knew that concept and what Karen mentioned was evil. "It's like this," he began. "Imagine you are reading a history book. The book has everything that happened for the past thirty years and you can call out every tiny little detail. But the book doesn't have anything about you in it. If you read about a person, for example, you might imagine that you were once friends or enemies or lovers. But the story doesn't include that. It only includes the other person, but nothing about how you know her or what kind of relationship you did or didn't have."

"You know everything in the world?"

"No. I was just using it as an example. I think everything I know is what a normal person my age would know. Like the name of the president or of the river that runs through town. There are some things I feel like I *should* know, but I can't quite bring them into focus." Gee poured himself a glass of water and drank deeply. Karen reached absently for another fry as she jotted down notes. "Have a French fry," he chuckled. She snatched her hand back and blushed.

"Sorry."

"I'm serious. Have some more. Fries always taste better when shared with a beautiful woman." She looked up into his smiling face and grinned back.

"Glad you put your pants on," she mumbled as she plucked up another fry. "Can you give me an example of the kind of thing that you think you should know but can't quite grasp?"

"Um… let's see." He reached for the book from his backpack that was still sitting on the table with the things from his pockets. "Like this." He opened the book. "I know the story generally, and specifically, I know where I stopped reading, though rereading passages isn't a chore. But I don't remember the act of reading, I just remember having read it. And here, inside the cover, there's an inscription. It's obviously from a friend who knows me well. She writes, 'To Gee. Here's to your journey. Love, Rae.' I *know* that I know her. I can feel it. But I can't see her. Is she my sister? Friend? Wife? Co-worker? Schoolmate? She sounds supportive. It doesn't mention when I got the book. It doesn't look new. But does that mean that I've had it for a long time or that she gave me a used book? I… I just don't know."

KAREN DIDN'T WANT him to stop talking and kept thinking up new questions to ask, even as her deadline drew nearer. She'd thought she was just reporting a quick news brief of a man diving off a bridge to save a child. Instead, she found a man with a missing piece of his life—maybe his whole life up until today.

And when she asked about meeting little Devon, the joy he had in talking about the little boy was contagious. Maybe he was a man who just rescues children. If so… *Maybe he can help me. If…*

The real story, Karen decided, was not that he dove into a river, but who he was. Strangely, he didn't seem concerned about that. He talked about what he could and couldn't remember and Karen ran her own series of little tests with questions about politics, religion, current events, and the world situation. But it was obvious that he talked for her benefit and not his own. She decided that this deserved an in-depth search of the Internet. Everyone could be found on the Internet.

She clicked off the recorder and started putting things away, including taking the empty burger wrapper and fry basket to the trash.

"I NEED TO get the story filed so it will make tomorrow's paper," she said as she grabbed her bag.

"I enjoyed talking to you, Miss Weisman," he said. "And sharing my fries."

"Puh-lease. I'm embarrassed. They were just so good… But if you want me to call you Gee, you'll have to start calling me Karen," she laughed. "Tell me, though; you came to Rosebud Falls from somewhere and lost your memory. Why are you here?"

Because of you.

Gee didn't speak the words aloud, but after the hour they had spent together, he could think of no better reason to be in Rosebud Falls. Before he could form an answer, a boom shook the windows of the room.

"Oh, look," Karen said. "You can see the fireworks from your window."

"Why don't you stay and watch them with me? There's really nothing important about me that merits a newspaper article." Karen turned to find Gee very near to her, looking out the window at the display. She bit her lip before answering.

"I'd like to do that, but I really need to get going." She offered her hand to shake. A magnetic force seemed to hold their hands together when he took it. Both struggled to regain their composure when they finally unlocked their hands, and their eyes. "I'll… uh… contact you at the Panzas' in a few days to schedule another interview."

"Should I wear pants?"

"Uh… yeah… Until at least the third date… interview. I'll be in touch."

CLUTCHING HER BAG beneath her arm, Karen left the room without a backward glance. She didn't dare. She wasn't exactly fleeing, but something told her she needed to be out of the room and out of Gee's sight before she made a professional error.

GEE WATCHED HER go and exhaled. It seemed like he'd been holding his breath the entire time she was visiting. Karen was captivating. He might have had any reason for visiting to Rosebud Falls; Karen was all the reason he needed to stay.

He brushed his teeth and spent another minute looking in the mirror, trying to see what other people saw in him. He didn't see a hero. His black hair was closely cropped, accenting the hairline that had begun to recede. His ruddy face was plain, marked by a furrow between his eyebrows. He was in good shape but, by Hollywood standards, he wouldn't call himself handsome.

I'm just me.

He settled into bed and picked up his book, opening again to the inscription. He could almost picture the person writing it, but the image fled. He wondered again if someone was waiting for him someplace out in the world and if he would ever find out who he was.

Who is He?

"So, WHAT DO you think, Detective?"

"You know I'm not very good at this. He just seems like a common ordinary guy. Except he lost his memory."

"Could he be faking it?" the voice on the other end of the line asked.

"That's what I thought, but Poltanys thinks not. He's cleverer in his questioning than I am," Oliver said.

"I want to know who he is and why he is here. Especially now. Is he a stabilizing influence or disruptive? I'm thankful that he saved that kid, but I don't believe in coincidences. Why was he on the bridge at exactly that moment? Keep an eye on him. I want to know as soon as you have an identity."

"Yes, sir."

2

HICKORY ROASTED COFFEE

Brain Scan

"I DIDN'T REALLY expect that we'd find anything," Dr. Poltanys sighed as he pointed out the topography of Gee's brain to him. "There are no signs of brain trauma. Frankly, you are a picture of both mental and physical health. Any new memories that have cropped up?"

"I remembered walking into town from the north and seeing that bar out on the edge of town, the Pub & Grub," Gee said. "I remember feeling disoriented and thirsty, but the pub was closed. I don't remember a lot of what I saw as I walked through town. Houses, I guess. A library. The next clear thing was the falls. I wanted water and didn't feel like I could move. Then Marian, little Devon's mother, screamed and I ran to see what was happening. I guess we've covered everything else."

"Okay. Let's count that as a slight expansion. And you mentioned an inscription in the book, but it didn't trigger a real memory. Try to be aware of images that flash through your mind. Don't focus on words or what you think of as memories. Just things that seem to be automatic for you and any images that appear. I see you shaved. Ellie told me you use a straight razor. Any problems?"

"None. I was thinking that tap water was never hot enough."

"Hmm. How would you get it hotter?"

"I suppose I'd put a wet towel in a microwave."

"That's good. Something inside has told you how to get your beard softened. Our physical bodies are often triggers for memories. Things that smell familiar. Favorite songs. Whatever feels familiar," Poltanys said.

"I'll try to stay aware. It seems simple. Could I ask one more thing?"

"Sure."

"Is it important?"

"What do you mean?"

"This is hard to explain. I know I must have had a life before Rosebud Falls. I'm thirty-four years old. But, I don't feel like I've really lost anything. I'll stay aware because everyone seems to think it's important, but I don't feel incomplete. Does that make sense?" Gee asked. Poltanys looked puzzled.

"I'll have to do some reading about this. Most of our scientific studies have been about disease-related memory loss. Sundowner's syndrome, Alzheimer's… that sort of thing. There aren't really that many cases of trauma-induced memory loss. Most of what people know about it is speculative or outright fiction. Looking at it from this side of the equation, we think how terrible it would be to lose our memories and how much we'd miss them. But maybe from your side it doesn't seem so bad because you don't know what you're missing. I'll let you know if I find anything else."

"Thanks, Doc."

"I'm going to release you. I understand you'll be staying at the Panzas' house. Please don't hesitate to contact me if there are any developments or if you experience discomfort. Give us a call in ten days and Ellie will take the stitches out."

"Um… How do I pay? I don't have any money, but Nathan says I'll have a job next week. I can bring some money when I get paid."

"I'd say not to worry about it, but you seem to be the type who would. We're a non-profit hospital, funded by various charities and grants. We charge for services, but when we have treatments that can't be paid for, we have funds to cover them. If you want to pay for your treatment and last night's room, do some volunteer work. We can always use help. Until then, live your life." Poltanys scratched something on his clipboard and looked back at Gee. "If you have a headache from the blow, take an aspirin. I'm not prescribing any painkillers. Go."

"I'M SO GLAD there are no other problems, Gee," Marian said after she met him in the hospital lobby. "I'm sure you'll recover your memory soon. In the meantime, let's get you home and settled in your new room."

"Thank you, Marian," Gee answered as he took a squirming Devon from her arms.

"Gee!" said the little boy.

"Dee!" he responded. "Let's get you in your car seat, little buddy."

"I some buddy!"

"You sure are." Gee finished stowing his pack and fastening the seatbelt on Devon's car seat before sliding into the passenger seat of the Prius. Marian stopped to check Devon's belts before she started the car.

"You did that like an old pro," Marian said. "Do you have children?"

"I wish," he laughed. A puzzled look crossed his face. "That's like one of the things Dr. Poltanys said to watch out for. I knew how to buckle a child into his seat, but my automatic response to you was that I wished I had children. That tells me I don't. I wonder why. Children are important."

"Maybe you were a teacher."

"Hmm. Say, do you mind if we stop by the police station? I promised Detective Oliver that I'd come in after the hospital to get fingerprinted and photographed. He's going to see if he can find me," Gee said.

"We can do that. Doesn't it make you nervous?"

"Why?"

"I don't know. Most people try to keep their fingerprints out of public records. They feel the less the government knows about them, the better. Here you are and no one knows anything about you and you are willing to be fingerprinted, photographed, and have your information put through all the government databases."

"I didn't even consider that. Here's what I think. I'm a stranger that you invited into your home. If I was some kind of criminal, would you still be comfortable with me living with you? Wouldn't you want to know?"

"You're doing this for us?"

"For everyone. I... It's funny. Maybe I should care about staying hidden, but I don't. Today, I feel blessed. I have new friends. I have a new home. I have…" he almost said *a girlfriend* but he could scarcely claim his instant infatuation with Karen Weisman put her in that category. They hardly knew each other. "I have possibilities. I don't care who I used to be."

"Then for everyone's peace of mind, let's get you fingerprinted."

A Trustworthy Tenant

"THANK YOU FOR coming in, Gee. Sorry about the mugshot. I know it looks like you are a criminal," Detective Oliver said. "The height background helps to refine a match, but most of the actual work is done by facial recognition software these days. It's a long time since we had to sit a person down with a book of mugshots to try to get them to identify a perp."

"I don't mind. I know everyone will rest easier if they know who I am."

"Then there is one more thing we can do, but you need to sign a release in order for me to take and submit a sample."

"What's that?"

"We can run a DNA test against CODIS, the US national DNA database. It will turn up any match to a known criminal. If there are no matches, the DNA is destroyed."

"Let's do it. Do you need my blood?"

"No. It's called a buccal smear. Basically, I use a cotton swab to wipe the inside of your cheek, drop it in a sterile container and ship it to the lab. There are about ten million samples on file in CODIS, but they are all of convicted or suspected criminals."

"If nothing else, it would eliminate ten million possible people I could be," Gee laughed.

"I'LL ASK YOU again, Mrs. Panza. Are you sure you want to do this?" Detective Oliver said. "You've got a kind heart, but we don't know anything about the man you are inviting into your home."

"Yes, we do," Marian responded. "We have twenty-four hours of evidence that he is a good man, selfless, and a keeper of promises. He didn't have to come in to get fingerprinted, photographed, and DNA tested like a common criminal. He did it because he told you he would. And because he believes that if he is a danger to anyone, we should be told."

"Okay. I'll buy that. George Edward Evars, in care of Nathan Panza, 683 Joshua Street. You now have an address." The detective stood and pulled Gee with him a few steps away from Marian. The left corner of his mouth pulled back slightly and he squinted. "Let me tell you, son," he growled quietly, "if you betray the trust of these people or harm them in any way, I will hunt you down like a rabid dog. I'm watching you."

"You have my word, Detective."

<hr>

MEAD OLIVER WATCHED Gee leave with Marian and reached for the phone.

"He's on his way to the Panza house. There's still no sign that he's a danger to anyone," Mead said.

"I'm not as worried about him being a danger to any particular person as I am that he's a danger to the City. Until I meet him myself, I need your eyes, Mead. Follow them and just make sure you can respond in an emergency for the next hour or so. My gut tells me it will be a boring hour."

"As you wish. I'm on my way."

<hr>

THE ATTIC ROOM was partitioned with a door that separated it from the stairway. He could stand up straight in the center of the room, but the ceiling sloped down on either side. Against one wall, a mattress and box springs sat on the floor, neatly made up with a bedspread and matching pillow covers. A table and chair claimed the space under the window at the end of the room and the bureau against the left wall was as tall as the half wall itself. Braided rugs were tossed casually around the room on the pine floorboards.

"It's not much, but I hope you will be comfortable. I'm afraid there's no lock on the door, but I promise no one will come up here without your permission. I have a baby gate that latches across the bottom of the stairs so Devon can't start climbing. Don't trip over it when you come down the stairs. Especially at night." Marian bounced Devon on her hip, not letting him down to run around the room.

"It's really lovely. Thank you, Marian."

"When you're settled, come down and we'll have some lunch. Nothing fancy, just a sandwich and soup. Devon is going to get testy if I don't get him fed."

"I'll be there shortly."

MARIAN HIT THE speed dial on her phone as soon as she set Devon down at the foot of the stairs.

"No problems, honey," she said cheerfully when Nathan answered the phone. "Gee was fingerprinted and submitted DNA for testing. He's putting his things away upstairs and I'm preparing some soup and sandwiches. Devon adores him."

"I worry about you," Nathan answered. "I'm all in favor of helping the guy out, but he makes me nervous. Don't… you know… get in any compromising positions, okay?"

"Nathan, honey, there isn't even the slightest spark between us. Not on either part. He'll be like a brother to us both. Or maybe a visiting cousin," Marian assured her husband.

"I love you," Nathan said.

"I love you, too. And so does Devon. I'll have a nice dinner ready when you get home this evening."

After she disconnected, Marian went about the task of getting lunch. She wished Nathan wasn't so insecure, but at the same time she was soothing her own doubts about having the strange man living in her attic.

It was so easy to trust him.

One Eye on Main

GEE SKIPPED DOWN the front steps of the Panza house after an early lunch, intent on exploring his new 'hometown.' Within a block, sweat began to trickle down the back of his neck as the July temperature rose into the eighties. A quick three-block walk took him to Main Street.

Main Street, USA. It was almost a cliché. Businesses lined the east side of the street while the west side had just enough room between the street and the railroad tracks for the post office and old depot. The stores and businesses shared common walls between them, but each business was painted a different color. Names on the upper façade declared enterprises founded in the 1800s. The store windows seldom bore the same name.

He stopped to pick up a newspaper just outside the office of *The Elmont Mirror*, and glanced through the window, hoping to see Karen. He did, but when he saw the expression on her face as she apparently argued with an older man in the office, he moved on without interrupting her day.

Music filled the street outside the local radio station. He looked through the window, directly at the broadcaster sitting behind his desk and microphone. The man waved a friendly salute and Gee returned the gesture. He stepped back toward the curb to get a better look at the broadcast studio.

"WRZF Radio, Rosebud Falls," read the lettering on the window. At the bottom of the window, Gee read aloud, "With One Eye on Main." Next to the door was a picture of the announcer and broadcast schedule. The door of the station opened and the broadcaster stepped into the street.

"Hi. Don't recognize you," he said. "I'm Troy Cavanaugh. I broadcast the morning show and get out of there as soon as my shift is over." Gee glanced back at the window to see a young woman settle in behind the microphone and position her headset. She smiled and waved. Apparently, that was standard for the broadcasters who did their shows directly in the public eye.

"Uh... Gee."

"Don't be awed. I'm just like everyone else," Troy said as he held out his hand.

"Oh. Sorry. My name... is Gee."

"Really? Very interesting. Oh! Wait." He took the newspaper from Gee's hand and looked at the front-page article about the daring rescue. A grainy photo, probably taken on someone's cellphone, showed a man diving off the Fairview Bridge. "That's you, isn't it!"

"I… uh… I guess so."

"You need to come in for a live interview. Can you stop in tomorrow morning? You're more of a celebrity than I am," he laughed.

"Not really. I just…"

"I'll bet Karen wrote this and that slime editor dropped her byline. By nightfall he'll have convinced half the town that he was the one who saw you, took the photo, and wrote the story. He'll get his eventually," Troy said. "I'm heading down to Jitterz. Let me buy you a cup of coffee."

"That would be great," Gee answered. "I'm just trying to get acquainted with the town a little."

"Well, next door to the station here is Citizens Bank, the oldest of our financial institutions. Are you staying in town long?" Troy asked.

"I guess. I live here now."

"Well, not that I'd ever say this on the air, but rather than bank here, I'd go a block over to First Rose Valley Bank. It's locally owned and operated. Karl Nussbaum is a good guy and a member of one of the Families. You'll learn all about the seven Families, I'm sure. His daughter, Krystal, is an absolute knockout. Former Miss Teen Elmont County and first runner-up in the state competition. If she could sing as well as her cousin, she'd have won," Troy said as they headed south on Main. He seemed quite happy to pass on tidbits of town history and local gossip.

"This is where to come for a great cup of coffee," Troy said as they approached the complex of shops south of Fourth Avenue. An ice cream shop on the corner connected inside to a lounge with lots of tables where people sat with laptop computers. Large ceiling fans gently stirred the air. The heavenly smell of roasting coffee led them on into Jitterz, the coffee shop and bakery. Beyond, Gee could hear the sounds of an arcade.

"Give us a couple short Americanos, please, Elaine," Troy said. "Do you need room for cream, Gee?"

"No. Just black." The response was automatic and an alert went off in his head. *I like black coffee.* Dr. Poltanys had told him to investigate things that came automatically. His taste buds came alive with the thought of black coffee. He sighed.

"Our coffee isn't that bad," the barista said, handing Gee a cup. "You don't need to be so mournful about it."

"Oh! Sorry! I was thinking about something else. The coffee is fine."

"Gee, this is Elaine Nussbaum. She will never forget what you drink. Elaine, Gee is the guy who jumped off the bridge to save that kid yesterday." Elaine was pleasant enough. She was a bit overweight and spoke softly, but there was a musicality in her voice that belied her looks. "Elaine is one-fourth of the Nussbaum Quartet," Troy continued. "She has the voice of an angel."

"No, I'm still not going to sleep with you, Troy," Elaine giggled.

"That you could think such a thing of me," he laughed placing a hand over his heart. "Take care of yourself, Angel." They found comfy chairs in the lounge and Troy watched Gee take his first sip. Gee's brows went up in surprise. He curiously took another sip and his expression changed again—this time to utter bliss.

"This is amazing."

"I love watching a person's face the first time they try Birdie's coffee," Troy laughed.

"Birdie?"

"Birdie Lanahan owns Jitterz. And all the other shops in this little complex. Don't let the name fool you. She's black as coal and claims to be from Jamaica, mon. But she talks like an Irishman. She got that from her husband, Red. She tells everyone that the coffee is Jamaican, too, but I doubt that as much as I doubt her origins. I'd guess Haiti based on her reputation for voodoo," Troy said conspiratorially.

"The flavor is incredible. If it's not Blue Mountain, she must have a secret of some sort."

"It's the roasting. Birdie has an old wood-fired roaster that she feeds with our local Rose Hickory. In addition to the flavor of the dark roasted coffee, you get the smoky flavor of our number one resource."

"The hickory?"

"Yes. A third of our town is covered by the Forest. If you haven't been out to it yet—and since you've been in town only a day, I'd guess you haven't—you need to make a trip out there. Wood for smoking and roasting is strictly allocated by the foresters. Birdie gets her share," Troy said.

"That's amazing. And the coffee is great!"

Grimm's Market and Meats

FRIDAY, GEE ROSE early to walk to work with Nathan. Halfway there, they stopped for a cup of Birdie's coffee, then crossed the river at the southern bridge. South Main was more industrial than the business district.

As far as supermarkets go, Grimm's was a step above most family stores and perhaps a step below the big chains. It had long been their policy to handle only food and kitchen supplies. People didn't go to Grimm's for greeting cards and magazines, but rather for fresh-cut meat and produce.

Nathan led Gee through the store to a stairway at the back. "Rupert is kind of an old-world butcher. He doesn't want anything on the main floor that isn't food related. You should have seen the arguments when we added toilet paper and facial tissue to the paper goods aisle," Nathan laughed. "So, the offices are located up here above the stock room, refrigeration, and receiving. This office is Frieda Grimm's. In case you didn't catch it when we were talking at dinner last night, Frieda and Rupert are Marian's parents—my in-laws. If anything, their divorce clarified the roles within the store. Frieda is CEO and handles all the administrative details, including new hires. I manage the operations below."

"What about Rupert?"

"He's the butcher. Much happier slicing meat than he is thinking about how to run a grocery store." Nathan opened the office door and Gee met an imposing woman he guessed to be in her early fifties. "Frieda, I'd like to introduce George Evars. He prefers to be called Gee. This is the guy who saved Devon's life Wednesday. He needs a job and I need help with stock downstairs."

"Of course you do," Frieda sighed. "Welcome to Grimm's, Gee. Have a seat and let's get you ready to work. We'll be less than an hour, Nathan. Clock him in now."

"Thank you, Frieda," Nathan said as he backed out. He acted just a little afraid of his mother-in-law.

"Mrs. Grimm…"

"We're informal here, so I'm just Frieda. Let's get the application filled out." She pushed a form toward him and he quickly filled out two lines before pushing it back. She looked a question at him. "Your name and my daughter's address. What about job experience? Social Security number?"

"I don't remember."

"Identification?"

"I don't have any."

Frieda contemplated how to handle this with one hand against the side of her head and her eyes closed.

"BANK ACCOUNT?" SHE asked. Like every other question, Gee just shook his head. If it weren't for the fact that he saved her grandson's life, she'd send him on his way, maybe with lunch from the deli. Maybe not.

It wasn't difficult to hire an undocumented worker for a day or two, pay them cash and bury the expense. Even before she took over the business side of the operation, Rupert had often enough done that with high school kids and transients. But to have one on the long-term payroll was a special kind of problem.

Her husband and high school students. Frieda shuddered as she glanced out at the front of the store and saw Onyx Grimm walk in. To be fair, Onyx was out of college when she made her play for Rupert. He'd been clueless and easy prey. The horny old goat.

At least I don't have to put up with that anymore.

Still, she missed some of the good things. They were just so long ago.

Frieda tapped her little finger against her forehead, returning to the matter at hand.

"OKAY, HERE'S HOW we'll do this," Frieda said, getting another form from her drawer. "This is a Form I-9. All official documents from the Immigration office say that a business is only audited if it is near a nuclear or national security site, or if the employer is suspected of abusing undocumented workers. The truth is that it's easy money for the government, so they routinely investigate small businesses just to collect a hundred to a thousand dollars per illegal employee. Then they run the scam again the next year. It's pretty much like a protection racket."

"Perhaps I should just work odd jobs around town," Gee said. "I don't want to put you at risk. That's certainly not why I'm here."

"Why are you here?"

"I guess I'm only one of several people who want to know that."

"Well, odd jobs won't keep you off the police blotter. Fill out the I-9 first page. Name, address, and birthdate. The second page is where I'm supposed to examine your proof of eligibility to work. What I'm going to do is make a note here saying, 'Identity documents withheld pending police investigation.' You need to visit Detective Oliver and get a copy of his investigation report so I can attach it to the I-9."

"I can do that. Detective Oliver has been very helpful."

"I don't expect there to be any problem with authorities. Rosebud Falls is a… very tight community. You arrived and became a hero. As long as you don't mess that up, the whole town will do its best to protect you. However, if you *do* mess it up, the least of your problems will have to do with the government of the United States."

"Frieda, I don't know who I really am, but I know I'm not the kind of person who will intentionally cause harm to this town or anyone in it."

"Good. You'll be paid seven-fifty an hour to start. I'll withhold taxes based on zero deductions, including withholding Social Security and Medicare payments. I will also deduct and escrow a portion of your pay, up to one thousand dollars total over the coming year, to pay any fine levied by ICE. You can expect take-home pay of about two hundred fifty dollars per week and I'll cash your paychecks since you don't have a bank account. We pay on Fridays for work done on Friday through Thursday. Nathan will show you how to clock in and clock out. Welcome to Grimm's Market and Meats."

"Thank you, Frieda. I'll work hard to show I deserve your trust."

A Walk in the Woods

"WE'RE NOT REGULAR church-goers," Nathan said, blushing. "I'm not really that interested. If you'd like to come, it's okay, but don't feel obligated."

"Like we do," Marian sighed. "That minister, Beck, caught us at a vulnerable moment in the hospital. We were worried we'd miss you and sort of promised we'd come to church this morning."

"To express our thanksgiving," Nathan sighed. "I really don't want to do this, but we promised."

"I'll pass, thank you," Gee said shaking his head. He remembered all too well the overbearing minister at the hospital. He couldn't blame Nathan and Marian for succumbing to the pressure. "Do you need someone to take care of Devon?"

"No. That, at least is covered. No matter what the preacher wants, I don't feel comfortable taking Devon there. But Mom has a standing date with her grandson on Sundays," Marian said.

"It usually gives us some alone time," Nathan added. He looked longingly at his wife. Gee was about to leave them alone when Marian's cellphone rang.

"Yes? Oh, hi. Sure, he's right here." Marian turned to Gee and giggled. "It's a girl!"

"For me?" Gee squeaked as she thrust the phone into his hand. "Hello?"

"Hi! It's Karen Weisman, your trusty news reporter. How are you settling in?"

"Oh hi, Karen. Pretty well. I have a job and have already worked two full days. My boss is pretty tough, but he gave me today off." Gee winked at Nathan.

"I thought we might continue our little interview this afternoon. Maybe I can show you a little more of our town." Gee's heart began racing.

"Tha... that... would be great," he said. He could feel the color rising in his cheeks. *Karen wants to get together!* Well... for an interview. "Where shall I meet you and when?" They concluded their arrangements and Gee handed the phone back to Marian.

"A date?" Marian sang.

"Um... Just another interview. I guess I'm not old news yet."

"Right," Nathan laughed. "I'm sure you'll have more fun than we will. Oh. Frieda's here."

AFTER THEY'D EATEN at the Golden Dragon, Gee was more than willing to join Karen for a walk. He'd been a bit embarrassed that she'd snatched the bill away from him at the restaurant, proclaiming that it was a business lunch. He'd borrowed twenty dollars from Nathan so he would have enough cash.

Karen led him across town, first stopping by Memorial Park in front of the statue of the Seven Heroes. "The story behind this monstrosity is far too long to tell at one sitting," she said. "But a lot of our town's history and not a little bit of our tension are woven into it. I just wanted to point it out so you have a landmark when you visit the courthouse and police station over there. Even a little town like ours can be confusing to a newcomer."

"Thank you. I remember the police station, but I wasn't paying too much attention to exactly what was around it," Gee acknowledged. "And I remember this... clearly," he said as they approached the bridge over the Rose River.

"Are you... Will you be okay crossing it?" Karen asked. "You didn't exactly get to the other side the last time you were here."

"Do you mean, will I dive off the bridge or have some kind of PTSD flashback? I don't think so. I'm not sure I want to look over the edge at what I dove into, though."

"This is the quickest way to get into the Forest. There are a lot of access points, but they are all on the east side of the river."

"Several people have mentioned the Forest," Gee said. "I'm looking forward to seeing it."

They crossed the bridge without incident and continued on to the entry.

"THIS IS BEAUTIFUL." Something about the Forest kept Gee's voice hushed—a tone that was almost reverent. "It's not like a wild forest. But it doesn't look planted in rows either. It's just so... neat."

"I've been learning a lot about you today, Gee," Karen said. "I've learned you are a hard worker, a kind man, and you have a nurturing spirit. I wanted to share with you a bit about what makes our little City of Rosebud Falls unique. The Forest is inside the city limits and is open to everyone to walk and explore. But it isn't owned by the city. It isn't a public park."

"Who owns it?"

"Mostly, the Families. The seven founders of Rosebud Falls laid claim to all the land around here and then sold portions to new settlers. Every landowner in the city owns a share or part of a share of the Forest, proportional to the amount of land owned. As the shares were sold, though, most of the Families retained the voting proxies for them. So, the founding Families still control and maintain the Forest."

"Why? I mean, it's beautiful, but why the... uh... fanaticism? I don't know. It just seems like a lot of complications over a few trees. No matter how beautiful they are."

"There would be no Rosebud Falls without the Forest," Karen said. "It is a rare type of hickory... Never eat the nuts; they're poisonous. Its wood is beautiful; the smoke is what makes Birdie's coffee unique, and even though they are poisonous, the nuts are the main ingredient of a wide range of products from lotions and creams to pigments to chemical products. A small army of foresters patrols and maintains the grounds while every person in the city helps during Harvest when hundreds of tourists descend on our little burgh. The Forest is our lifeblood."

"So that's how these seven Families became rich, I suppose," Gee sighed. "They exploit everyone in order to profit from their private Forest."

"Oh, no. I wish I could describe this better," Karen said. "They own it to protect it. Everyone in the city profits from the Forest."

"A bucolic paradise."

"I'm not saying everything is perfect about either the Forest or the Families. Believe me, I've uncovered some dirt that would make your stomach turn. But what I'm trying to say is that there is a powerful connection between the people of Rosebud Falls and this patch of woodland. You're new here. You'll have an easier time relating to people if you understand that connection."

"What's this?" Gee and Karen stopped at a chain link fence and looked at the buildings beyond.

"This is Lazorack Lumber Mill. The Lazorack Family started it to process the timber coming from the Forest almost two hundred years ago. It's still the only place that our Rose Hickory is processed, but of course, that's a small part of its total output. Logging trucks from the hardwood forests up north bring in raw materials all summer long. Keeps the mill working year-round."

"What do you want?" They spun to see a thin man with short, graying hair approaching them.

"I was just getting a tour of the Forest," Gee said. "I'm new in town and was told it was important." The man looked past Gee and fixed his eyes on Karen.

"Oh. You." Gee could hear the disdain in the man's voice.

"We…"

"You look strong. We'll have work for you at Harvest," the man said.

"I… My job is at Grimm's."

"Everyone works Harvest."

"Mr. Lazorack, Gee hasn't had a chance to get oriented yet," Karen said. "This is just a get-acquainted tour."

"Get-corrupted tour is more likely. You stir up enough trouble. There's no reason for you to be fixing things that aren't broken, Miss Weisman."

"Only when there is an injustice that we can still remedy, Mr. Lazorack. The embarrassment will be short-lived compared to the honor that will evolve."

"Just stay away from the Mill," Lazorack grumbled. "The Forest continues over there." He pointed across the road before turning to unlock the gate to the mill and locking it again after himself. He didn't turn back.

"Um…" Gee started as Karen took his arm and guided him across the logging road.

"David Lazorack," Karen said. "Head of the Lazorack Family and Chief Forester."

"One of the seven Families?"

"Yes. But he's not happy about it. Don't judge the Families by his attitude. His father was killed in a Harvest accident less than a year ago and David was forced into leadership he didn't think he'd have to assume for years. He's mostly a good man, but he has his issues, too," Karen said. They continued through the quiet woodland.

"Gee," she said, "the DNA test Detective Oliver gave you… you know there are other tests that might reveal more."

"What kind of tests?"

"Well, the same ones, really. It's just that the swab he took will only be sent to the criminal databases for a match. There are services though that do family analysis and heritage testing in the same way. For example, it would tell if you were part French and part Zulu—not that I believe you are either," she laughed. Gee raised an eyebrow at the odd combination. "They were just nationalities I thought of that were extreme," she explained. "But these tests are voluntary. They are non-government and retain the DNA signatures. People even volunteer family history to go with their DNA sample. If you submitted a sample, they might find a close enough match to identify at least a potential relative."

"I'm willing to do that, Karen, but why?"

"I chose to become a reporter because it allows me to stick my nose in everyone else's business," Karen said. "In another life, I was probably Nancy Drew. You are a mystery I want to solve. If you'll let me. More than anything, I want to know why you are in Rosebud Falls. Especially now."

"Why especially now?"

"The City is on the verge of a crisis. A lot of people will be upset. Maybe even the Families. We don't have such a huge population that one person can't make a difference. Sure, Detective Oliver wants to know if you are a criminal. I want to know if your influence will affect the outcome of our changes."

"Wow. That's heaping a ton of expectation on a guy who just wandered into town and can't remember more than his own name. I'm not here to change things. I just want to settle down and be a productive citizen." Gee paused and tried not to look directly at Karen as he added, "Maybe get married and raise a family."

Perilous Times

"OUR READING THIS morning is from the Gospel of Matthew, chapter five, verses ten to twelve," intoned Deacon Stewart.

*Blessed are they which are persecuted for righteousness' sake: for
theirs is the kingdom of heaven.*

   *Blessed are ye, when men shall revile you, and persecute you,
and shall say all manner of evil against you falsely, for my sake.*

   *Rejoice, and be exceeding glad: for great is your reward in
heaven: for so persecuted they the prophets which were before you.*

"May God add his blessing to the reading of his Holy Word."

"Amen."

"The Word of God can be difficult for mere men to comprehend.
Even when we believe we understand the words, we may not know how
they apply to our lives. We are blessed to have called into our service
a great interpreter of the Word of God—a true shepherd of his flock.
Let us empty our hearts and our minds and prepare to receive God's
blessing. Pastor Beck." Stewart moved aside as Lance Beck strode to the
pulpit and mounted the step behind it so he could see over the top.

"Brothers and sisters, we live in perilous times," Pastor Beck began.

"Amen."

"You might think I refer to perils of the flesh—to Islamic terrorists,
pornography, homosexuals, illegal aliens, and government infringement
of our God-given rights—but I speak not of physical danger. Our bodies
are temporary vessels. What matters it if we die in an auto accident on
our way home this afternoon? What matters it if a terrorist's bullet finds
my heart? It will do naught but liberate my soul from this mortal flesh.

"No, my brothers and sisters, it is not peril to the body of which I
speak, but peril to our souls. For we as a church—as children following the
Lord—will be reviled, persecuted, and falsely accused. We cannot hope to
escape this peril. If we are doing the work of the Lord then we can expect
it! It is guaranteed that people will hate you for your faith. We can expect
persecution around every corner, for the world is not a Godly place.

"But how, my friends, will you respond to that persecution? If you
were put on trial for your faith, would there be enough evidence to con-
vict you? That question spells out the peril to your soul. Will you rejoice
and be glad—stay faithful and true in the face of revilement, persecution, and false accusations? Or will you, like an undisciplined child, pay
no heed to the frantic calls of your Heavenly Father, and instead plunge
into the turbulent rapids of damnation?"

DEACON WATCHED THE congregation attentively. He'd held this office and run the church so long that even people unassociated with the church called him 'Deacon'. The name was his identity. The church was his domain.

Pastor Beck continued his moving sermon. They'd chosen the pastor well. For years now, he'd been building the congregation with many families from outlying farms and communities—a dynamic engine of evangelism. And each new family brought new children.

They would not, of course, siphon off the children of locals. They needed the testimony of the families to show how effective the church's training in obedience was. Beck's reputation as a deprogrammer of homosexuals, potheads, and rebellious children was a draw across the nation. Their children's 'camp' was full. And with the discoveries they'd made over the past few years, the programming success was deemed irreversible and undetectable. Perfect little boys and girls who did whatever they were told. *Whatever.*

His eyes fell upon the couple who had nearly lost their child this week. They squirmed in their seats. *Becoming convicted of their sins.* He could see that soon, they would come to Pastor Beck for counseling on how to discipline and train their son. There were so many good examples of obedient children in the congregation. And the generation of adults who had been through childhood programs in the church were easily used. Like the pink-haired space cadet. She'd been carefully groomed over the years to look rebellious and dangerous. But in truth, all he needed to do was suggest something to her and give her a communion wafer. *Go and sin some more, my child.*

There was always a place for obedient, unquestioning children.

"I COULDN'T STAY and listen to him any longer!" Marian fumed. "I'm sorry if you think I was rude. Did you see the rest of those children? I have never seen a bunch of kids who looked so cowed. I will *not* have Devon brainwashed of all his creativity and intelligence!"

"Honey. I agree. I'm not as bold as you are, but I'd never let our family return to that awful place," Nathan tried to calm her.

"He implied that Devon falling in the river was *our* fault for not being parents who could *make* their child obey and that he should have been *spanked* soundly as soon as he was pulled from the river!" she continued as if he had objected to her viewpoint. "I feel guilty enough about letting him out of my sight. But he wants us to beat Devon for it. 'Spare the rod and spoil the child,' he said. That's not even what it says in the Bible. Not that I'd give any more weight to a biblical proverb than to any other aphorism. He might as well have said, 'A stitch in time saves nine.' It's not about sewing."

"We'll never go back, sweetheart. You and Devon are all there is in the world for me. I'm not going to go get religion somewhere and destroy our home. I love you."

"If I ever see that man again, I'll... Oh, Nathan. I'm a mess. I love you, too. I'm just so angry... All the smug parents' faces... All those cardboard cutout children... We have to do something, Nathan. What can we do?" Marian demanded.

"First, we care for and protect our family," Nathan said softly. "*Our* family, Marian. We can't go out and launch a campaign against parents because their children are too well-behaved. But we should let our friends know. Warn them. Especially those who have discipline problems. For a frustrated parent, he has a tempting message."

"But how do we give them an alternative? You know how awful it was when Devon was colicky. We'd have done anything for relief."

"Maybe we can find help—an alternative way for parents to deal with volatile children that doesn't involve programming them like some kind of robot."

"We'll do it, won't we?" Marian said, sucking in her breath and stifling her sobs. "We'll find a way." She embraced her husband, and assured of his emotional and physical support, allowed their kiss to deepen.

A Little Help

"You're not a parent, Gee. At least that we know of. You can't know how hard it is sometimes," Nathan said as they walked to work on Monday. "It's not just that we make mistakes in our parenting. We accepted that and just make it our priority to let Devon know that he's loved and cherished. And he's a good kid! We know people who have absolute terrors for children."

"Devon knows he's loved. And he listens to you. You can't train a child like a puppy and expect him to heel on command," Gee said.

"Exactly." Nathan paid for their coffees at Jitterz and they walked quietly to the bridge on lower Main. They paused to look out at the turbulent water of the Rose River. "The thing is… I don't know why I feel like I can talk to you like this… But Sundays are our day to connect. I mean Marian and me. And… Well, yesterday wasn't a good day. We had a lot of pressure built up about Devon falling into the river, you coming to live with us, and then that preacher… unspeakable. We won't get another chance to… connect until next Sunday. It's really…" Gee could hear the frustration in Nathan's voice as they continued toward the market.

"What kinds of activities are available for kids and parents in the evening? Are there playgroups? Gyms? Children's theater? Music? Art? Reading? I mean, anything where you might get *someone* to take over for a while so you and Marian can connect?"

"I guess we've depended on Frieda and Rupert as our babysitters. Frieda takes him every Sunday and that has been great, but I'm sure even she needs a break now and then."

"Well, I'm still trying to figure out what to do with myself when I'm not working, and don't want to be a burden on you and Marian, either. I thought I'd look for activities I can do after work. Troy mentioned a summer softball league and that there are often pickup basketball games at the school. I'll keep an eye out for activities Devon might like as well."

"That would be great. It's not like I'm trying to palm him off on someone else, you know," Nathan sighed. "It's just that sometimes a couple needs some help."

Easier to Get Rid of Her

DAVID LAZORACK SURVEYED the faces of the three other men and the woman seated at Heinz Nussbaum's table. At fifty-five, David was the youngest of the Family heads and was not happy to be at the table. The unexpected and shocking death of his father during the previous year's Harvest forced the responsibility on David. The fact that Jan Poltanys, just eight years older than David, had been the Poltanys Family head for nearly twenty years, did not comfort David. Jan's father was still living, even though Alzheimer's had robbed him of his rationality. And Leah Roth-Augello, six years older than David, held the place at the table on behalf of her father, old Ben Roth. She was a shrewd business woman and tended to manipulate the rest of the Families to suit herself.

David listened to Loren Cavanaugh as he covered the financial prospects for the Forest based on his projected allocation of the crop. At seventy, Loren continued to make the final decisions on the financial aspects of the Forest, though he left day-to-day business management to his son, Clark. Of course, Cavanaugh didn't operate in a vacuum. He'd walked the Forest with David in May to go over the productivity estimates. The trees were in full bloom and David used his experience as Forest manager to predict the tonnage of nuts, dry wood, and felled wood that would be available. He also proposed his budget for maintaining the Forest, his foresters, and even the cost of milling the timber. Loren was a good businessman, but David doubted the ability of his son to maintain the same level of professionalism.

Finally, Heinz Nussbaum chaired the meeting as the oldest Family head at the table. Like David's father, Heinz was one of the orphans of the Seven Heroes, the young men of the Families who went off together to fight World War II and never returned. After the general business, Heinz turned to Leah. She summarized the findings of her report.

"She refused to even let me in the house. God knows what other damaging papers my wanton aunt might have left behind, but Judge Warren agreed that the will was legitimate and binding. The house, the property, and all the contents legally belong to her," Leah said.

"She's always been a crusader," Heinz acknowledged.

"Well, now she's a crusader with access to Family secrets," Leah said. "She wants to legitimize the Ransom line as Roth Family heirs. And she wants her own proxy returned so she can 'personally vote her share in the Forest,' as she declares."

"Why?" David asked. No one ever contested the proxies held by the seven Families. As long as they got their share of the profits, that was all anyone cared about.

"To get her little nose into our business," Leah scoffed. "She wants all the inside dirt. But on the plus side, she's said she'll vote it with the majority and support the annexation. Frankly, she could be an asset this fall. I hate to admit it, but she has quite a following in the city and even circulation numbers for the newspaper are up."

"It would have been easier to just get rid of her," David snarled.

"David! The Families haven't done anything like that in over a hundred years," Leah reprimanded him.

"Really?" David scanned the faces of the others at the table. Someone had killed his father last year. He was certain the accident had been contrived and had launched his own fruitless investigation. It was his father who had led the movement to annex South Rosebud, citing the condition of the trees in the section the foresters didn't manage. "We should hope, then, that your grandfather's and aunt's notes don't show anything different."

"David, I know you're still upset," Heinz sighed. "There's no reason any of us would want your dad gone. We're all in agreement with the annexation. He was a good leader and a great forest manager. And, I'm proud to say, a good friend. I also know you didn't want all the responsibility of the Forest dumped on you yet. But you are a good forest manager and we're all proud of you. Don't hesitate to call on us when you have difficulties."

David was not comforted, though he stopped complaining. Something was going on in his town and he couldn't put his finger on it. It threatened to upset the way they'd existed for two centuries. He admitted it could be an outside influence, but wanted to believe it was the reporter. Or perhaps it was the mysterious appearance of the new guy in town. David wasn't usually a violent person, but he couldn't help the desire to lash out.

"It would have been easier," he sighed.

3

NO GOOD DEED UNPUNISHED

The Library

"YOU AREN'T having any difficulty figuring out the computer," Karen said.

"It all seems pretty straightforward. I don't remember doing this before, but it feels like I've done it. Is this my Gee-mail?" Gee asked.

"Yes. But remember that you are on a public computer in the library. You need to close your email when you are finished and make sure you are logged out after each use. And don't forget your password," she laughed. She suddenly looked shocked that she'd made a joke about his memory. Gee joined the laughter. "Are you sure you want to post pictures?"

"I don't know how else someone could identify me, do you?" They sat with their chairs pulled close enough that Gee could feel Karen pressing against his arm while she pointed things out. The computer wasn't difficult, but having Karen lean in to point things out was distracting to Gee in its own way. He paid attention to what she said, but he was constantly aware of her closeness.

"Okay, then let's snap a couple pictures and I'll send them to you. That way you'll have my email, too." Karen used her cell phone to snap the pictures and in a minute a flashing icon alerted Gee that he had mail. He opened it and looked at the pictures. "When you save the pictures, use the cloud server. That way you don't store anything on the library computer. And then we're ready to start posting inquiries." Karen pulled

46

out a notebook and began directing Gee to various websites where he could post his picture with a caption that said, "Do you know me?"

"Do you think I know people on all these social websites?" Gee asked.

"How would we know?" Karen asked. "You are very social… comfortable with people in ways I would never imagine a man without an identity to be. Not that I'd know what to expect. I can't imagine you not having friends out there who would want to help. We just have to find the right place."

"I appreciate everything you've helped me with, Karen. I haven't been a resident here for two full weeks yet and already this feels like home to me. I'm glad you're my… um… friend."

"I *am* your friend, Gee. I hope we're friends for a long time." She looked at Gee and he got lost in her eyes.

"Are you researching a story, Ms. Weisman?" a matronly woman asked, interrupting whatever connection Gee thought they might have made.

"Oh, hello, Ms. Tomczyk. Have you met Gee? We're researching his identity," Karen said.

"I saw your picture in the paper, but this is the first I've had the pleasure to make your acquaintance," Ms. Tomczyk said. "So, the story I've heard about the man with the missing memory is true? I do hope you have a speedy recovery."

"Thank you, Ms. Tomczyk. The pleasure is mine. With Karen's help, I'm getting the word out. She's showing me some of the different activities and services available in Rosebud Falls. Tonight, our investigation is the public library."

"Do you like to read, Mr. Gee?"

"Oh, yes. At the moment, I'm puzzling through Homer's *Odyssey*. I understand all the words, but getting the structure and context to make sense takes a bit of time. By the looks of it, I've been working on it for some time."

"Is there a way for Gee to check out books? I'd be happy to extend my card to him," Karen said.

"I'll have to do some investigation on that. It would be irregular not to have an ID first, but we do it for children. Hmm. For now, I'd recommend you come in and use the reading room. Just be aware that our Bookhouse meets Wednesday evenings. It can be a little chaotic."

"Bookhouse?"

"Children's reading groups. Summer is both a good time and a bad time for us. There are lots of children with nothing to do and long evenings in which to do it. But there are fewer volunteers. We're stretched a bit thin."

"I could help," Gee blurted out. "I mean, *could* I help? Crowds and children don't bother me. In fact, I've been looking for activities to get my three-year-old housemate Devon involved in. I know he likes stories."

"Really? You read to him?"

"I often read a story before dinner to keep him out of his mother's hair while she's cooking."

"Would you mind auditioning?" the librarian asked. Gee started to stand and follow her. Karen laid a hand on his to stop him.

"Log out first, Gee. Never leave your email open." It only took a moment and they followed Ms. Tomczyk. She pointed to a beanbag chair and Gee settled in. Karen folded her legs beneath her and sat nearby.

"This is our story nook. Take this book and begin reading aloud. We'll see how your voice and expression fill the room." Ms. Tomczyk smiled and handed Gee a children's book. Lacking any children in the nook, he began reading the story to Karen. She laughed as he used different voices for different characters and pointed out the pictures.

Before he was halfway through the book, two little children—maybe three or four years old—entered the nook holding hands and sat down in front of him. Gee saw a woman he assumed was a parent standing near the door. He simply included the two children in his reading and showed them the pictures. By the time he'd finished the book, two more children and another mother were in the room. The mothers sat on a sofa nearby and whispered to each other. Ms. Tomczyk handed him another book.

Gee read three books to the five children who had wandered in. They were laughing and enjoying the stories, often making the sound effects Gee suggested to go with the story.

"What does a train sound like? Woo-woo!"

"Woo-woo!" the children responded.

"Chug-chug-chug-chug."

"Chug-chug-chug-chug."

"Children, would you like to have Mr. Gee come back to read more stories one day?" Ms. Tomczyk asked the group.

"Yeah!" Even the mothers responded positively.

"How about it, Mr. Gee?" she asked. "Can you make Wednesday at six?"

"THAT WAS WONDERFUL, Gee!" Karen said. "And you just got volunteered for a new community service."

"It was fun. There is so much more to a book than the words when you have a bunch of children involved."

"I'll meet you after your reading Wednesday, if that's okay. We can do the swabs for the DNA services. I'll have all the kits by then."

"It's a date." Gee smiled at Karen and then stepped back. "I mean… I'm sorry… I didn't mean… I mean… an appointment."

"I understood, Gee. We'll have a meeting. An appointment. We've set a time. And a date."

Super Marketman

"HELLO, MRS. RESNICK. It's so nice to see you again," Gee greeted the old woman who approached him in the aisle. He'd seen her nearly every day and remembered her name.

"Young man," the old woman said, "I can't reach the corned beef hash. I don't understand why it is on the top shelf."

"I'll discuss the location with Nathan," Gee said. "In the meantime, can I reach it for you? How many and which brand?" Mrs. Resnick wanted only one can of the generic brand. Gee noted the can cost half what the name brand next to it did. The woman thanked him and collected three or four more items in her basket before she left.

"Oh, Mr. Gee," the pink-haired checkout girl named Rena panted at him after Mrs. Resnick left. "Can you show me where the tampons are?" The girl seemed to always try to embarrass Gee, but he did his best to treat it all in good humor.

"I'm sorry, Miss Rena. We didn't get a delivery today. I could get you a roll of paper towels." He looked at her quite seriously and she broke up laughing.

"I can't get one over on you. I'll come up with something. Just you wait!"

"Gee to the Deli for wet cleanup, please," a voice over the store speakers said.

"Maybe you'd better take that roll of paper towel with you," Rena laughed.

Gee hustled to the janitor closet to get the needed supplies and headed to the Deli. The cute blonde deli girl was hugging Rupert Grimm tightly with her head buried against his chest.

"I'm sorry. It just slipped," she said. It took a moment before Gee remembered that the young woman was Rupert's second wife. They made an odd couple.

"It's okay, sweetie," Rupert soothed her. "Accidents happen and help has arrived." He looked up at Gee. "The minestrone soup got away from Onyx, Gee. Do you have the right supplies for cleanup?"

"I've got it, Mr. Grimm. "This will only take a minute, Mrs. Grimm. Nothing to worry about."

"Please, Gee. No formalities," Rupert said. "It's Rupert and Onyx."

"Yes, sir."

"Perhaps you could make part of your mid-morning routine picking up the soup kettles and putting them in the warmers for the lunch crowd," Rupert said. "I nearly dropped one myself and it's silly to have Onyx trying to lift a full kettle like that. Do you mind?"

"Of course not. I'll plan on it for about ten-thirty daily. Does that work?"

"Thank you, Gee," Onyx said. "I'm not really a klutz, but they are heavy."

"No problem!"

Gee finished the spill and returned to stocking canned goods. He greeted several more customers during the day and they all called him by name. Gee was feeling at home.

The Head of the Family

*Wives, submit yourselves unto your own husbands, as unto the
Lord. For the husband is the head of the wife, even as Christ is
the head of the church: and he is the saviour of the body. Therefore
as the church is subject unto Christ, so let the wives be to their
own husbands in every thing.*

*Husbands, love your wives, even as Christ also loved the
church, and gave himself for it; That he might sanctify and
cleanse it with the washing of water by the word, That he might
present it to himself a glorious church, not having spot, or wrinkle, or any such thing; but that it should be holy and without
blemish.*

"What a terribly misguided world we live in and how simple the
remedy, brothers and sisters," Pastor Beck intoned from the pulpit. "I
said 'simple,' not 'easy.' For God gives us the solution. It is all laid out in
His holy Word. But it is not easy for us to set aside the burden of this
world and abide by His Word.

"We are confronted on every side by the seductive voice of Satan.
Satan twists the blessed words of the prophets and the apostles to make
us believe that what he is offering is what God wants. Remember his
first words to Eve were, 'Has God indeed said 'You shall not eat of every
tree of the garden'?' He subtly twists God's Word and entraps his prey.
And he tries the same thing on you and me today. 'God,' says Satan,
'wants every person to be treated equally.' 'God,' says Satan, 'wants us to
give welfare to those illegally in our country.' 'God,' says Satan, 'thinks
deviant lifestyles are okay.' But let me tell you something, my friends.
Satan is a liar. And he is good at sounding so reasonable.

"I am here to tell you today that God is *not* on the side of Satan!
God has told us that there is man and woman and the two shall cleave
together and be of one flesh. Believe me, cleaving together and becoming one flesh is one of the great blessings God gave us. He did *not* say
man should cleave to man nor woman to woman. He made it clear that
he *created* male and female, not that there was a choice in the matter.
God doesn't send men into women's restrooms. God doesn't make mistakes about gender. God has shown us the way, the truth, and the light,
and He is unchanging."

Heads were nodding in the congregation. Roxanne agreed with the preacher. Faggots weren't part of God's plan on earth. If Larry found one, he'd beat the crap out of him like he did that disgusting old man, Jig Riley. Of course, her husband wasn't in church to hear the lesson. Sunday was his day of rest. Besides, he was hungover like on most Sundays when he was home.

"Wives… oh, most precious of all God's creation… submit yourselves to your own husbands. I can see that makes some of you uncomfortable. Bear with me. You *chose* a man to stand beside you through your life. Men like to think they had a choice, but you women know that you are the ones who made the decision. And what were the criteria you used in that selection? A good lover. A good provider. A good father for your children. A good-looking huuunk." He dragged out the last syllable until the congregation started to laugh. Several women nudged their husbands and nodded.

"And yet… All too often I counsel with married women who have made it impossible for their husbands to be the men they said they wanted when they married. How can he be a good provider when he is too tired to go to work because he spent the night listening to the complaints of his wife? How can he be a good father if his authority in the home is undermined and his children see him as a second-class citizen? How can he even be a good lover if you withhold your body from him as punishment for an unseen slight?

"Satan would have you believe, sisters, that you should be free and independent, equal in pay and equal in rights. Equal in the bed and equal at the table. But God says that the husband is the head of the wife, just like Christ is the head of the church. God says to submit yourselves to your husbands *in every thing*. Was God unclear in what He said? Do we question Christ as head of our church? Do we prance around saying, 'I know you said this, Lord, but I think it should be this way'? What kind of church would we be if we called into question every word of our Lord?

"And yet, that is what the feminazis would have you do, women. They would have you leave your homes and labor as a man while you give your children to heathens to educate, their knowledge prescribed by State Boards of Education. *They* would have you earn money to pay someone else to cook for you, clean for you… What next? To mate with your husband for you? Submit yourselves, I say again, submit yourselves to your husbands as the church submits to Christ. For in that submission, you will find peace, happiness, a growing family, and a great love."

Roxanne shivered. She always had difficulty with that part. She needed Larry to keep her in line. At five-eleven and a hundred ninety pounds, she was a big girl and it was easy to get out of control. Raised in South Rosebud, she earned the nickname 'Timex' because she could take a licking and keep on ticking. Her father and her brothers proved it time and time again. She wasn't abused. They just wanted to make sure she knew her place and could tough out the hard times.

Her husband, Larry was a hard-drinking, hard-fighting trucker and loyal member of the church. He'd smacked her butt as she waited tables in the truck stop and she'd slapped his face. It was love at first fight. Larry needed a tough woman and she could take it.

"Husbands, love your wives," Pastor Beck continued. "I want to clarify what that means. It is not merely remembering her birthday and your anniversary. It is not about flowers and candy. Yes, those are all good things, but loving your wife goes much deeper than these trappings. How can you claim to love your wife if you do not nurture her in the way of the Lord? If you do not value those characteristics that make her lovable, how can you profess your love?

"Popular society, feminism, liberals, would all have you simply give in to her whims. But that is not how Christ treats his church and it is not how you should treat your wives. With your love… With your wife's submission… comes your responsibility to keep her and your children pure in the sight of God. Even if it pains you to see that look of submission in her eyes, you must overcome the desire to let her get away with that little slight. The fear of the Lord is the beginning of wisdom. Not an irrational fear that you will capriciously knock her around a little to keep her in line. If that is how you love, you need to spend time in prayer considering how Jesus loves you.

"But, you must lead her as your head leads your body. Exercise self-discipline and let your family see by your example that you are no easier on yourself than on them. That you expect perfection. That your heart's desire is to present her to your Lord and Savior glorious, not having spot or wrinkle, holy and without blemish. You must discipline her, your children, and yourself. Let this message weigh heavy on your hearts, husbands. Like the man with the one talent, you could be judged and damned if you dare present your wife to the Lord and He is not pleased."

The Good Samaritan

GEE HOPED THAT Karen would want another 'interview' over the weekend, but she'd been called out of town to follow up on a story she was working on. She'd hinted at exposing sex traffic in Palmyra, but working in Rosebud Falls had slowed her research.

"Trafficking?"

"Sex and drugs," Karen said. "I just can't get a handle on where they come from. I talk to prostitutes and even some drug dealers. They all end up being normal people who do whatever is necessary to survive. Not *nice* people, but normal. They all point vaguely at an underground traffic that is much harder to see. No one will say anything about it. It could take me years to uncover enough evidence to begin to understand what is going on."

"If there is anything I can do to help, let me know," Gee said.

"I'm sure there will be."

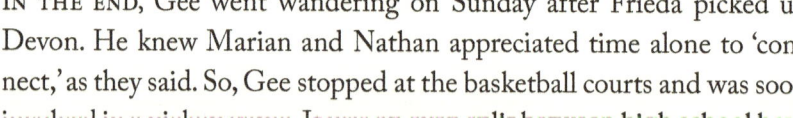

IN THE END, Gee went wandering on Sunday after Frieda picked up Devon. He knew Marian and Nathan appreciated time alone to 'connect,' as they said. So, Gee stopped at the basketball courts and was soon involved in a pickup game. It was an even split between high school boys and older men. Troy Cavanaugh was on the court along with a couple of other 'older guys.'

"Hey, Gee!" Troy said. "How about the old men take on the kids?" Gee agreed and shook hands with the other men. "Luke Zimmer, Zach Poltanys, and Ken Probst," Troy introduced the older men. "This is Gee, our local hero."

"I think that qualifies as 'old news,' Troy," Gee said. "I'm just a stock boy at the grocery store." The guys welcomed him as he was just what was needed to round out the teams.

On the boys' team, Gee was introduced to Ryan Moffat, Barrett Zimmer, Victor Nussbaum, James Nussbaum, and Drake Oliver. The boys quickly proved to the old men that they could run longer and harder. When they finally gave up the match, they'd lost track of how far ahead the boys were.

For Gee, playing in the pickup game opened a door for new friendships and a wider circle of acquaintances. He promised to return regularly. Feeling invigorated by the game, he jogged north along the river trail and cut west toward the fairgrounds. The West Branch was turbulent in this area, but a hundred yards upstream it flattened into a glassy calm marked by a low dam. From the north, the canal was separated by a lock from which daily barges emerged to cross the river to the coal yards.

Gee was in the narrow section of the trail between the river and the fairgrounds fence when he heard a cat yowling. He hurried along to see if he could help the distressed animal, first looking toward the river and then toward the fence. When the yowl came again, Gee started running. This was no cat.

Leaning against the fence next to the parking lot, a woman wept, periodically releasing a long wail. She struggled toward the road, using the fence to support her. Her face was bruised and she cradled her left hand between her breasts as her right supported her against the fence.

"Can I help you?" Gee panted as he ran up. The woman startled and cringed against the fence before nodding slightly. She pointed toward the road.

"Hospital."

Gee slipped under her right arm, replacing the fence as her support and gently circling her waist with his left arm. She winced and he did his best to support her without causing more pain as they worked their way toward the street.

She was a big woman, nearly as tall as Gee and weighing at least as much. Tears flowed down her bruised face. Gee spoke soft comforting words as they struggled slowly toward the hospital. He didn't try to find out what had happened. It didn't seem to be his place. After struggling a few minutes, the woman collapsed and Gee caught her in his arms before she hit the ground.

He couldn't think of anything else to do, so he carried her. As he got used to the burden, his pace picked up until he was running toward the hospital emergency entrance.

When Gee appeared at the entrance, he was spotted by the receptionist who pressed a button and requested assistance. Two EMTs rushed to his side and eased the woman to a gurney. They disappeared into the hall and Gee sank to the floor in front of the reception desk. He could hear the receptionist on the phone, and a minute later, a nurse arrived.

"Are you also injured?" the nurse asked. "Where was the accident? Are there others?"

"No accident," Gee gasped as he caught his breath. "Found her down by the river near the fairgrounds."

"Why didn't you call for help?" The receptionist showed up with a glass of water that Gee gulped gratefully.

"No phone."

"You don't have a cell phone? You don't look like a Neanderthal." Now that it was clear that Gee wasn't injured, but was just out of breath, the nurse eased up on her interrogation.

"I... I uh..."

"Relax. Let's get you to an examination room where I can take your blood pressure and vitals. I don't want to risk an incident in the waiting room. You can walk?"

"Yeah." He stood and followed her into the hall. "Will she be all right?"

"We'll know when Doctor Poltanys is finished with his exam. You know her?"

"No. I just found her by the river. I was out for a run after playing basketball."

"Hmm... You're the new guy in town with no memory, right?"

"Gee."

"Yeah. Adam told me about you. I mean Doctor Poltanys. I'm Julia. I'm sure the doctor will want to check you over, if for no other reason than to find out if you remembered anything. I'll get him as soon as he's finished with the emergency." With that, Julia left Gee sitting in the exam room with a fresh glass of water.

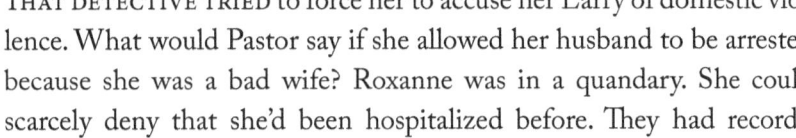

"I'M FINE, REALLY," Gee said to Doctor Poltanys as Julia hovered nearby. "Just a little more exercise than I'm used to. It was quite a run."

"You ran with her?" Poltanys asked. "I thought you brought her in a car. How far?"

"The other side of the fairgrounds near the river. I don't have a car."

"Roxanne weighs a good one-ninety," the doctor said. "You must be strong as a horse. You might be sore tomorrow but no permanent damage. Get out of here and be useful."

"I was going to stop by to see about volunteer work," Gee said. "Hopefully not as a horse."

"There's always grounds maintenance to do. A volunteer coordinator is here from nine to five weekdays. Give her a call and she'll tell you about orientation. I hear you're good with kids. We always have a few who could use someone to come in and read to them. Talk to Sofia tomorrow."

THAT DETECTIVE TRIED to force her to accuse her Larry of domestic violence. What would Pastor say if she allowed her husband to be arrested because she was a bad wife? Roxanne was in a quandary. She could scarcely deny that she'd been hospitalized before. They had records. She'd really pushed Larry this time, though. She'd needed to be punished and he wasn't rising to the occasion. She'd badgered him about his manhood. That did the trick.

The detective showed up before the doctor had even finished his exam. He wanted a rape kit done as well and she'd violently refused.

"Roxanne, why are you protecting Larry? If I put him behind bars, he won't be able to touch you. Where is he?" Detective Oliver demanded.

"He's out of town. It wasn't him. It was someone else. I don't know who. I didn't see."

The doctor interrupted to order x-rays, and the nurse readied her to be rolled down to the x-ray lab.

"This can all be stopped, Roxanne," Oliver tried once more as she was being rolled out of the room.

And then her salvation appeared. The man she met by the fence. She could sacrifice him to save her husband.

"That's him!" she screamed, pointing at Gee. "That's the man who beat and raped me." Then she let herself lapse into hysterical screaming. It wasn't difficult. She hurt so badly she needed to scream.

ALL HELL BROKE loose when Gee left the examination room. He saw Detective Oliver standing next to the room across the hall and had just raised his hand to wave when the woman he'd brought in started screaming and pointing at him. Oliver dropped his head and shook it as Roxanne was rolled away, still screaming.

Mead Oliver turned to have a quiet word with Poltanys and Nurse Julia. Gee just stood there in shock. Why would the woman he helped accuse him? Oliver laid a hand on Gee's shoulder. "You need to come with me, Gee."

"Mead, I didn't..."

"Shh. It is better right now that you don't say a word. Come with me." Mead followed Gee outside and pointed to his car, opening the back door. "Watch your head," Mead said automatically.

They drove to the police station in silence. Once there, Mead pointed to a chair next to his desk.

"Don't say anything. I haven't read you your rights. Just sit, damn it."

The tone of voice took Gee more off guard than the bizarre arrest. He wasn't even sure if he'd been arrested. Mead wasn't angry—not at all what Gee would expect from a policeman running in a suspect. It was more like frustration. Mead went to a large coffee urn and poured two foam cups. He set one in front of Gee.

"It's not Jitterz, but I'm a public servant. I can't afford the best," Mead said. Gee took a tentative sip and decided on the spot that if it wasn't Jitterz, he wasn't interested. *When did I become a coffee snob?*

"Uh..."

"Not yet," Mead said holding up his hand. "My son says you played basketball this morning and weren't bad. Good to know. I don't get down to the courts as often as I'd like. We try to encourage a few adults to play on Sunday so the kids have good role models. Not muggers and rapists."

"Mead, I..."

"Shh." The phone rang and Mead pulled it to his ear.

"This is Oliver.— Yes, he's with me.— No charges. He hasn't said a word.— Send Ellie down with the affidavit, would you?— No, he likes her.— Right. Thanks." Mead hung up the phone and grinned at Gee. "That was Dr. Poltanys. Ellie Smith is on her way here with a signed affidavit from Roxanne Syre saying she was confused and disoriented when she saw you and only remembered you picking her up. She apologizes for the inconvenience and smirch on your character and thanks you for helping her."

Gee nodded.

"You can talk now."

"Um… Thanks. I… I didn't assault her, you know."

"Yeah. I know. She's been in that hospital or a doctor's office a dozen times in the past twenty years. It's not the first time she's pointed out someone and retracted her statement an hour later. Now she says she didn't see her assailant. Everyone knows it's her husband. But unless he beats her in public, it's just our word against his and she won't accuse him. One day it will go too far, and I'll have a murder case to solve. She won't be able to testify then."

"That's really sad."

"Most people in Rosebud Falls are just normal, mostly happy people," Mead said. "But we have our share of nuts, and they aren't all in the Forest."

Ellie arrived with the affidavit and handed it to Mead.

"Are you okay, Gee?" she asked. "If he has threatened or harmed you in any way, I will testify against him. You just say the word."

"It's nice to see you, too, Ellie," Gee grinned. "We had a pleasant Sunday afternoon conversation."

"Hey! What's the story?" another voice said from the doorway. "Do we have a serial rapist loose in Rosebud Falls or a false arrest?"

"America's favorite snoop," Mead grumbled.

"Detective Oliver! I'm flattered. I'm glad to see you free and apparently unharmed, Gee. No story of police brutality?"

"None at all, Karen. I thought you were…?"

"Why don't we take a walk and maybe have dinner, Gee. Detective? Is he being held? Do you have a statement?"

"If I say, 'no comment,' you'll make something up, won't you? How does this sound. Mistaken identity resulted in confusion when a Rosebud Falls woman identified local hero George Evars as her assailant instead of her rescuer. Following proper protocol, Evars was escorted to the police station for questioning. The mistaken identity was quickly corrected, and no charges were filed in the case. How does that sound?"

"You should be a journalist. How about we just say that continuing his quest to recover his identity, George Evars stopped by to chat with Detective Oliver Sunday afternoon. Doesn't really sound like news to me. Come on, Gee, let's take a walk."

"How did you find out I was here?" Gee asked. "Not that I'm complaining."

"I have sources!"

"Julia Poltanys," Ellie snickered. "Those two are thick as thieves."

"I understand you are one of the Family now," Mead said to Karen.

"Always have been," Karen answered. "But, since Mom and Grandma are gone, Great-grandma left the estate to me. Your sources of information seem to be pretty good, too."

"You're a Poltanys?" Gee asked.

"No. A Roth. Poor old Uncle Ben is apoplectic about having no male Roth as heir. Made Leah hyphenate her name and the kids all take it so it wouldn't die out. I'm hungry, Gee. Aren't you taking me to dinner?"

"You bet I am."

Seven Heroes

"WHAT DOES IT mean to be one of the Family now?" Gee asked as they walked away from the police station. They were headed for the parking lot, but Karen took his arm and redirected their walk toward the Memorial Park in front of the courthouse.

"I guess this is as good a time to educate you as any other. Let's go sit in front of that grotesque statue in the park. I know you've got the basics of the story," Karen said.

"Seven friends, comrades in arms, who went off to fight in World War II and all died at Omaha Beach," Gee said. "I read that on the plaque."

"Right. But who were these comrades in arms?" Karen said. "That is, in one question, the key to the history of Rosebud Falls. And history is the key to understanding the city."

"Please tell me." Gee was acutely aware that Karen did not release his arm as they sat to look at the statue.

"The years 1918 to 1933 were a hard time for Rosebud Falls. People were moving out of the big cities and found small towns like ours weren't as idyllic as they thought they would be. Prohibition was strictly enforced. The seven Families that founded the city were competing for loyalty and control of the Forest. But by some miracle, there were seven boys born within five months of each other in 1924."

"The Seven Heroes."

"The Families put all their efforts into grooming the boys to unite the city and the Families. They were leaders in school, the front line of the football team, and genuinely good friends. But no one counted on Pearl Harbor. As soon as they could volunteer, they left to defend democracy. They all died on Omaha Beach."

"And I suppose that ended the hopes of unifying the Families."

"Almost, except for one little thing. The boys had left behind seven pregnant teens. Even though they were overseas already, they wrote to their families acknowledging their offspring and promising to marry the mothers as soon as they returned. Most of the Families accepted the mothers and their children. In fact, all except one. My family. My great-great-grandfather refused to acknowledge his granddaughter. I'm going to change that."

"And why is this all important to me?" Gee mused. "I appreciate knowing more about the city, but I'm not sure how it's relevant."

"The seven Families—Nussbaum, Poltanys, Lazorack, Cavanaugh, Roth, Meagher, and Savage. The head of the Meagher family is a crazy old coot who lives alone in a barn full of antiques. No one has heard directly from the Savage family in years, but they are still considered full members and their Forest voting rights are held by their company, Savage Sand and Gravel. I guarantee you that all seven Families are interested in you and who you are. You could find yourself memorialized up there with the Seven Heroes one day. Or you could find yourself buried under them."

"That sounds ominous."

"I like you, Gee. In fact, I'm becoming quite fond of you. Maybe because I have LPS—lost puppy syndrome," Karen said.

"I'm a lost puppy?"

"More like a strange new breed that I'm fascinated by and strangely attracted to."

"I think you are calling me a dog, Karen."

"No, but it should explain to you why the pack is interested. You are new in town. Maybe in fifty years, you can claim not to be an outsider. But when a new person enters the territory—especially a *mysterious* new person—everyone wants to sniff around and find out if he's a threat."

"And am I?"

"Maybe to some. Maybe not to others. I just thought you should have some background about who was sniffing."

"TAKEN TO JAIL, were you?" Ms. Tomczyk glared at Gee over her glasses when Gee showed up for Bookhouse Wednesday evening.

"It was a mistake. No charges."

"I'm sure. We have to be very careful about who comes in contact with children in the library. I'm not saying you did anything inappropriate, but if you get taken to the police station enough times people will begin to think there is a reason."

"I assure you, I have a clean record."

"Keep it that way. We have a nice group of kiddies in tonight and I've stacked your books next to the beanbag," Ms. Tomczyk said, the event apparently forgotten. "Oh, and you wanted one of these." She handed him a library card with his name on it. "Now what kind of books do you like to read?"

"That's a very good question. I've not read anything since I got to Rosebud Falls but the newspaper and Homer's *Odyssey*. How about local history? Any suggestions?" Gee said.

"Hmm. I think I can come up with something. Go do your story time and I'll see what I can come up with." Gee went into the story room and settled into the beanbag. A small bundle of boy energy tumbled onto him before he was fully settled.

"Gee!"

"Dee! How's my little buddy?"

"You didn't have dinner with me."

"I met Karen for dinner."

"She's nice."

"Yes, indeed she is."

"Gee, can I impose upon you to bring Devon home after story time tonight?" Marian asked as she followed her son.

"Certainly, Marian. You want to stay with me for all of story time and walk me home afterward, Devon?"

"Yeah. I walk you home."

"Thank you. Nathan and I need to um… discuss some things. Uh…"

"We'll be back in a couple of hours."

Gee began his story reading to over a dozen kids. Ms. Tomczyk was a master at choosing stories and putting them in an order that settled the children and held their interest. The first couple of books were short and had lots of pictures so the younger children got involved. The stories grew progressively longer until he read just a chapter of the first Harry Potter book for the last story. This enthralled the older children, but by that time most of the younger children had either left with their parents or, like Devon, had curled into a ball next to Gee's beanbag and gone to sleep.

"One time I saw magic," a seven-year-old girl declared to him when he'd put down the last book. "It was different than that. There was a lot of sparkly stuff."

"Well, Sally Ann, I'm sure that real magic is not the same as book magic. When did you see magic?" Gee asked.

"At Disneyland."

"Of course."

"I have to go now. Thank you for the story, Mr. Gee."

"Goodnight, Sally Ann."

Gee picked up Devon and the two books Ms. Tomczyk selected for him before carrying the sleepy boy home.

Confidant

OVER FIVE HUNDRED dollars nestled with his library card in the new wallet Gee purchased. He had very little to spend money on after giving the Panzas his rent, other than a morning cup of coffee. He was recognized and called by name in Jitterz, but most of the people he knew, he had met at Grimm's Market.

Gee's duties at the market expanded until he had a hand in just about everything. He was quick and efficient at stocking shelves, sweeping floors, helping customers to their cars with bags of groceries, or reaching cans off high shelves for Mrs. Resnick. He helped with the soup at the deli, much to Onyx's relief, lifting the heavy pots and placing them in the steam table for the self-service lunch crowd. Onyx asked him to sample them and give his opinion on the seasonings. Gee considered her a good cook and said so.

After he stocked bakery items in the morning, Gee moved whatever large carcasses of beef or pork Rupert needed to or from the meat locker. Rupert showed Gee how to slice bacon and cold cuts, and gave him the responsibility of making sure that part of the butcher's case was stocked. Customers commented that they liked the new thicker slices.

"MR. GEE?" A teen boy said softly when he stopped Gee in one of the aisles.

"Oh, hi, Ryan. No need to be formal, it's just Gee, same as on the basketball court. How can I help you?" Gee said brightly. The boy put a finger to his lips and looked around nervously. A girl at the end of the aisle turned her head with a hand at her mouth and giggled. "How can I help you?" Gee repeated in a whisper.

"I need... I mean... Where do you keep... Rubbers? Condoms? You know?"

"Oh, yes. Of course, I know," Gee answered conspiratorially. He glanced at the girl at the end of the aisle. "I'm glad to know you are thinking ahead and being prepared. Unfortunately, I can't help you. We don't have a pharmacy section. You'll need to go to one of the drugstores." The boy moaned and squinted his eyes.

"No… I can't do that."

"Why not?"

"My dad owns one and her family owns the other," he said. "We can't just walk into one and buy something without everyone in town knowing. I was hoping that… since you are sort of new… you wouldn't tell anyone."

"Oh, I won't tell anyone."

"What am I going to do? We know we… I mean… We're a little scared… But I love her," Ryan moaned.

"How old are you?" Gee asked.

"Sixteen. Please don't say we're too young. This is for real."

"I don't doubt you at all, Ryan. Do you have a driver's license?" Ryan shook his head.

"I have to complete Drivers' Ed this summer before I can get a license."

"I understand there's a Rite Aid Pharmacy next door to Walmart just south of town. It's not so far that a guy couldn't ride his bike there. For love."

"I could just sneak into the Pub & Grub. I hear they have a vending machine," Ryan suggested. Gee sat down on a box of canned goods he was getting ready to shelve.

"Ryan, I'm not an expert on these things, but hear me out. You are a young man and a young woman you care about is interested in you. Interested enough, by the way, that she's still waiting for you at the end of the aisle even though she knows what you're asking. There will be enough uncertainty and tension when you become intimate that you don't want to add to it by not knowing if a condom is dependable. Do you want part of the memory of that very special time to be you sneaking into a bar to get some unknown brand of condom?"

"I really want to… to show her how much I love her." Ryan looked at his girlfriend once more and a smile crept across his face. "What kind should I get?"

"A top name brand with a spermicidal lubricant. Remember, you are going to take good care of your girlfriend. Nothing but the best."

"Thank you, sir. Um… Just thank you." Ryan turned and walked swiftly to where his girlfriend still waited. She immediately took his hand and the two left the store.

"That was so sweet," a voice said behind Gee as he watched the couple leave the store. Gee turned to see the wild-haired cashier behind him.

"Rena, you shouldn't have been eavesdropping," Gee reprimanded her.

"But it was so… He could treat *me* like that. I want a boyfriend who adores me like he adores her."

"I'm sure there is one out there for you someplace."

"Pastor Beck says he'll find someone for me. He teaches our young singles class in Sunday School. You'd think that a guy who has so much fire and brimstone in him during the sermon would be that way in Sunday School, but he's really good and kind. He takes time with us like you just took with that young man. Of course, he'd tell him to stay pure until marriage and not to go get condoms," she snorted.

Gee hadn't been impressed when he met Pastor Beck. Nathan and Marian had been furious at the preacher. It was hard to reconcile their experience with Rena's. He wondered that the minister even tolerated her. She sported the most unnatural shade of pink hair he had ever seen. Her face was so pale she might have been wearing clown white, with lips colored the same shade as her hair and black eyebrows penciled into a permanent look of surprise.

What was more disturbing, however, were her eyes. Not the fact that she was wearing blue tinted contacts over her normally brown eyes, but the glassy look that told him that whatever drug she was using was fresh in her veins. People were such a contradiction at times. How did she reconcile her religion and her drug use?

Pressure Points

"Your great-grandmother never wanted her proxy revoked."

"Great-grandmother didn't need to cast her own vote," Karen said. "She knew everything before the votes were cast. I have to build from nothing."

"I could just tell you what is planned," Leah responded. "Or is that too easy for you?"

"Oh, I appreciate your confidence. I'm sure you will tell me exactly what I *should* hear. Leah, I'm not planning to bring down our family, even in the midst of righting some wrongs. But something is not right. We're going to inherit a lot of problems when the annexation goes through. Problems for the city and problems for the Families," Karen said.

"The plan to annex South Rosebud has been in the works for fifty years," Leah said. "The time is right to implement it. Everything indicates that we have seeded enough votes in the residential area to carry it without a problem."

"Mmmhmm. So that's why you've been buying up houses and changing tenants."

"How did you…?"

"I won't upset things. I have a story ready to run the day after Labor Day that announces the planned annexation and supports the vote. We'll have two months of campaigning. I just hope we don't run into problems with the special interests."

"They'll campaign against it, but they don't have a vote. They aren't actually residents."

"Thank you, Leah. The information you brought me will help me write a convincing story. We're on the same side, you know."

"Yes, cousin. Come for dinner sometime soon. We should become a closer family."

Leah left Karen's office with a wistful look at her aunt's former possessions, the Rose Hickory desk, and the stacks of her grandfather's journals. Inviting her to meet here had been like rubbing salt in her wound. Karen knew her cousin felt the contents of this room should have been her property. But the deeper she got into the family history, the more convinced she was that Leah would never be granted access to what was here.

Karen settled back at her desk to go over the details of the planned annexation and to identify the problems she knew lurked there.

--------⊰◆⊱--------

THE MUSICAL CHIMES of her cellphone startled her back to reality. She'd been so immersed in the papers that she'd missed dinner.

"Weisman."

"Karen, you don't need to be so curt with me."

She sighed, unsure of why she didn't block his calls. "What do you want?"

"I sense a disturbance in the Force."

"Get real."

"I'm serious. I'm not sure what's going on, but there's an undercurrent. I've always been sensitive to these things, Karen. Someone is planning something and people in Rosebud Falls are in danger. I don't think it is directly related to the annexation."

"How did you know about that?"

"I'm Family, Karen. I might not hold my own vote, but my Family doesn't hide secrets from each other."

"So, if not the annexation, what is the threat?"

"From my window, I see parents hanging on to their children more tightly. I see cars coming through town I haven't seen before. A policeman walks by every morning. We've never had police on foot patrol. People are like animals preparing for a storm."

"I think you're crazy, but I'm not discounting what you say. You watch out your window every day. I won't deny that you see things changing," she said.

"You've changed."

"No doubt."

"You don't really want him, do you? Come back to me, Karen. We were always good together. Gee's a nice guy. I can't help but like him. But he's not made of steel. He won't be able to stand up to your heat. Not like me."

"We broke up long before he came to town. Don't interfere in my relationships. You and I are not together. Understand?"

"Anything you say, Karen. But be careful out there. It's a cold cruel world."

She rolled her eyes and hung up.

4

WHIRL-A-GIG

First Date

"NEXT WEEKEND is the County Fair," Karen said over dinner. She looked uncommonly excited to Gee. But her enthusiasm always affected him positively.

"It must be a big thing here," Gee said. "I see signs and posters up all over town." Karen looked at him questioningly.

"Gee?"

"What? Did I say something wrong?"

"Of course not. I just thought you'd be excited."

"Why? I mean, it does look like a big deal to the town, but I don't have a proper context for what that means. Tell me."

"The ticket," she said in exasperation. "Have you forgotten that you have a ticket? This could be the clue we've been waiting for. The clue to who you really are."

"Oh! You know, I completely forgot. I use that little slip of paper to mark my place in *The Odyssey*, but the past couple of weeks, I've been reading other books from the library and hadn't thought about the ticket," Gee said. "I suppose it's important, huh?"

Karen shook her head and smiled at him. Her eyes sparkled and he lost himself in them.

"You really don't care, do you?" she whispered. "Mead has exhausted his DNA databases and we've sent samples out to seven commercial

DNA services. We've posted your picture on over a dozen social media and missing persons websites. You're everywhere but on a milk carton, but you don't care."

"I *have* gotten some interesting responses to the ads on Craigslist. I don't dare open them in the library, though," Gee laughed. "Apparently there are a lot of people who 'would like to know me,' as they say."

"Ugh. You can come over and use my computer if you'd like. We can sift through the responses together. I should have known there would be a lot of crack-pots wanting to take advantage of you," Karen sighed. "But that brings us back to the one solid lead we have about who you are. The Fair."

"It really doesn't sound like that much fun to me."

"It's not for fun. Gee, that ticket is a clue to who you are. There is a reason that you acquired it and a reason you are supposed to go."

"What reason?"

"That's the point!" Karen said, frustration creeping into her voice. "We don't know the reason. You have to promise me that you'll go to the fair and even go to that ride. Just look around and observe. There's a reason for you to be there. There has to be a reason."

"I see your point, and I'll go. I just don't feel compelled about it. It would be easier if you'd go with me."

"I…" Karen stopped and looked at Gee in silence for a minute. "That sounded an awful lot like you were asking me out, Gee."

"I guess… um… We've been meeting together once or twice a week for the past six weeks, Karen. I'm sorry if it's not appropriate, but I feel that meeting with you is a lot more important than working out who I am. Would you go out with me?"

"I would. But…"

"That sounds ominous. Please continue."

"It's just that next weekend I'm supposed to be in New York. It's the Society for Professional Journalism Conference. I'm attending a track on investigative reporting and its relation to law enforcement and police investigation. It's a pretty hot topic and relates to my effort to dig into trafficking," Karen rushed on. "So, even though I would be willing… I would like to go out with you… to the fair… I can't because I won't be in town."

"Oh. I see. Of course. That makes sense." Gee was dealing with simultaneous attacks of encouragement and disappointment. She couldn't go to the fair with him, but she did want to go out with him. He felt a little like an infatuated teenager.

"Gee? If you'd like… I mean since we've broached the subject… We seem to both be interested… Well… We could drop the professional nonsense this evening and consider this a date. Sort of. I mean, just getting to know each other socially. I promise to stop investigating for the next hour or two. I mean…" It was obvious that Karen was having as much difficulty sorting through her feelings as Gee was. A blush crept across both their faces.

"Um… Wow! What's a good first date?" Gee asked. "I'd ask you to dinner, but we've already finished eating. I guess that was a business meeting. Now, it no longer is. Could I… uh… interest you in a walk? Maybe for ice cream?"

"That sounds very nice."

GEE FELT HE got to know Karen beyond her professional life, and she got to see that he was more than a man with no history.

"Take the idea that all people are created equal," Gee said. "Does that mean that every person in every stage of his or her life is equal to every other?"

"Doesn't that require a definition of 'equality'?" Karen responded. "People can be created with and have equal value without having equal economic or social standing."

"Does that mean a military action is an inherent violation of equality? Not just that the enemy is of less value, but that the lives of front line soldiers—cannon fodder—have less value than those of their officers?"

Poaching

GEE STRODE ALONG briskly on Sunday, still slightly euphoric over his date with Karen the night before. He'd been happy to drop the probing questions about his background and transition into more revealing conversations about what they felt and believed. They didn't get together on Sunday, but Gee was still stoked about the relationship.

Determined to explore more of his adopted city, Gee took a new route, entering the Forest on the southern edge near Aldo Lake, where the public beach was. A fence at the end of the beach marked the city limits. A stark contrast divided the neatly groomed nut orchard on one side of the fence from the wild woods on the other. Gee walked some way along the fence, finally shifting north into the Forest.

There weren't as many people in this section of the Forest as he'd seen in the central part, nearer to downtown. Gee soon had his shoes off and tied to his belt as he walked among the trees. A broken branch lying nearby looked like a perfect walking stick. Gee picked it up, trimmed a couple of twigs from the branch and began swinging it with each step. He even whistled a little tune as he hiked.

To him it was a tune. Gee wasn't certain if anyone else would be able to tell. He had a feeling the tune he was hearing in his head was not what was coming from between his lips.

"Stop where you are and drop the stick," a young but authoritative voice said behind him. Gee froze and let the stick fall to the ground. "Turn around, poacher," the man commanded. Gee turned to face a man in the obvious dress of a forester. He wore a pith helmet, short sleeved khaki shirt, cargo shorts, and hiking boots with over-the-calf socks. Gee supposed he could be a Boy Scout.

"I don't think I've poached anything. I haven't even seen any animals in the woods," Gee said. "I'm Gee, George Evars. I'm new here."

"Oh, you. Sorry, I'd never met you. Have you had an orientation session on the Forest yet?"

"Orientation?"

"I swear, people can be so negligent when it comes to protecting our resources. That's why there are four times as many foresters as there are police in Rosebud Falls. I'm Jonathon Lazorack. If you don't recognize the outfit, I'm one of forty foresters who manage this area. Since you haven't been through orientation, I'll let you off with just a warning," Jonathon said. He reached in his pocket for a small booklet titled 'Rules of the Forest.' "Okay. You'll get one of these at orientation. You've been here a month already, haven't you? I can't believe no one gave you a rulebook. Here we are. 'Poaching is defined as moving or removing any resources from the Forest proper, whether living or dead, plant, animal, or mineral, unless directed by an active duty forester or his agent.' That stick you were carrying toward the edge of the forest is worth thirty days in jail."

"Wow! That's pretty extreme."

"Second offense is a felony conviction. The law is patterned almost word for word after some of the countries who have had problems with their antiquities being stolen. It's proven enforceable in local courts, as well. Did you know there was a twelve-year-old boy who served a week in an Athens jail last year for picking up a pebble on the Acropolis and putting it in his pocket?"

"And you treat the Forest like they treat the Parthenon," Gee breathed. "I had no idea."

"Yeah. I get that. There's no orientation this week because of the fair, but I'll expect to see you at the library on the Saturday morning following the fair. Believe me, you don't want to be stopped a second time," Jonathon said. Just as quickly as the surprising warning, Jonathon's persona changed. Now that he'd done his job, it seemed he was curious about the new guy in town. "Tell me about yourself, Gee. What do you think of our Forest?"

"It's really beautiful, Jonathon. I've never been in a forest where there was no undergrowth."

"We call it Forest, but in the strictest sense you could say it was an orchard. There is only one kind of tree in the entire 1,200 acres and we care for them like the lifeblood of our community that they are."

"And you keep the whole area mulched?"

"People like to walk out here in their bare feet—like you. We do a lot of sawing up at the mill, so all the sawdust comes to the Forest. It makes it easier to pick the nuts, too," Jonathon said. "Since we keep the undergrowth down, the mulch also helps prevent runoff and erosion."

"I heard everyone works during Harvest. When is that?"

"Sometime in September or October. We make the decision based on the nut-fall from the trees. It's exciting, but it's also when the problems start. We double the number of foresters with trained volunteers and there's an equally big squad of security people. The north, east, and south sides of the Forest are fenced, but there are only intermittent fences on the town side. We have to balance protection with access and there will be a thousand tourists flooding into town that week as well. The fair next weekend is miniscule compared to the one during Harvest."

"You are really enthusiastic about it. You must love your job," Gee said smiling.

"I do. I love this old Forest. All I ever wanted was to be a forester. It was a pain to go to the College of Forestry. They have some strange ideas about forest management out West. Different kind of forests. Mostly about managing fire threat and logging. Here, we're more like arborists. I was also away from the two things in life that I love most and couldn't wait to get back."

Jonathon liked to talk and while they walked through the forest he led them to an old tree.

"I want to be like this tree," Jonathon sighed. "My grandfather wanted to *be* this tree. It has stood here for 150 years. Look how straight and tall it is. Over a hundred feet. The bole—that's the trunk, really—is a yard wide. The canopy shelters an area of fifty feet. It will be the last tree harvested this year with a big celebration and will drop between ten and fifteen bushels of nuts. But that's half of what it dropped when I was little. This old tree is dying. When the nuts have been gathered and the deadwood harvested—around the first of November—forty foresters will gather around this old man. We'll scale, lop the limbs, and bring him down in twenty-foot sections. He'll go to the mill and be dried and turned into high-grade lumber that will go out to furniture makers around the county. In another 150 years, some little kid will be sitting at a table made from the wood of this old man, coloring in a book about trees, and dreaming of becoming a forester. That little kid's great-grandchild might sit at the same table. These are our trees. These are our life. Growing up in the Forest is only the beginning."

Free Ride

I'M STALKING HIM. Rena had to admit the truth. She'd become fascinated with the newcomer in town and eventually infatuated with the mystery man who had no memory. She flirted shamelessly with him, but he just took it in good humor and let her suggestive remarks slide.

She'd talked to Pastor Beck in the Young Singles class at church. It was easy to talk to the minister. He seemed to understand her desires and fantasies.

"God gives us our desires as well as our intelligence," he said. "Our desires make us aware of opportunities and our intelligence helps us discern God's will regarding them. Explore what it is that attracts you to this young man and invite him to join you in fellowship here in church. Perhaps you are an instrument of God's grace to bring him to salvation."

Pastor Beck had prayed with her and given her communion. She always felt filled with the Holy Spirit after communion. When he placed the wafer on her tongue, her fantasies burst forth in a way that could only be inspired by the Spirit. She was determined to entice Gee to join her at church.

"Hey, handsome," Rena said when she saw Gee on Friday morning. She'd just applied a coat of bright red lipstick that matched the new bright red hair color she was sporting. It had been so much work to get just this shade of red. She'd dyed her eyebrows the same color. Gee looked up from the bacon he was slicing and stopped the spinning blade.

"Rena, you've outdone yourself," he laughed. "Does the fire department know you stole their paint?"

"The fire department wants to hose me down because I'm so hot!" she fired back at him. "How about you, Gee? Do you want to hose me down?"

"That's not something that crossed my mind," he said. "Oh, listen! They're doing an interview with Troy on the radio." That change of subject was too obvious for even Rena to miss. She wanted to storm off and let him regret what he was missing, but she wasn't sure he'd regret it.

"This is Leslie Lake filling in for Troy Cavanaugh on the morning show. And I have Troy on the line with me. Good morning from your hometown, Troy," the announcer said.

"Good morning, Leslie. And good morning to all the fine folks in Rosebud Falls."

"Troy, how does it feel to be presented with a peer award for your radio broadcasting?"

"It's really an honor, Leslie. When I came to New York for the joint Radio Television Digital News Association and Society of Professional Journalists Conference, I really had no expectation of receiving an award. I credit the people of Rosebud Falls for keeping life interesting outside our window on Main Street. That's really what the morning show is about. The people of Rosebud Falls."

Rena wanted to pull Gee's attention back to her. She had worked hard for this look. But Gee looked like he was a million miles away. He looked… troubled. Maybe she could help.

"Are you going to the Fair this weekend?" she asked. "I plan to spend the rest of the weekend there as soon as I get off work tonight."

"Uh… Oh… yes. I'm going to stop by tomorrow."

"I'll watch for you. You can buy me cotton candy."

"Sure. I'll see you there." He sounded so vacant. But meeting at the fair was good. She could almost convince herself it was a date.

Maybe.

ON SATURDAY, GEE worked his usual morning shift at the market. It was only when Nathan and Marian packed up Devon in the stroller that he decided to join them on the walk to the fair. He showed his pass and the ticket-taker merely waved him through. She didn't collect the pass, stamp his hand, or ask any questions. It was as if she didn't really see him.

"We're going to get Devon a balloon and some frozen yogurt so we can spend some time seeing the exhibits," Nathan said as soon as they were through the gate. "Catch up with you later!" With that, Marian, Nathan, and Devon were off on their own adventure and Gee was alone. Food booths lined both sides of the passage and he stopped for a sausage at Zeigler's, remembering the excellent hamburger he'd had his first night in Rosebud Falls. Somehow the sausage fell short of his expectations and the curly fries were dripping in grease. He dumped half the meal in a bin and continued on. He was sure the fries he shared with Karen had been much better.

At the end of the aisle, a long line marked the location of the Jitterz coffee stand. He joined the line and finally made it to the front.

"Well, Mr. Gee, how are you doing today," said Violet Lanahan, the owner's daughter.

"Miss Violet, I'm better for seeing you and knowing your fine coffee is soon to be in my hands," he answered. Violet smiled at him, stunning white teeth contrasting with her caramel skin. She had dark eyes that darted around her surroundings, always on the move. Most striking, however, was her red hair—not bottle red like Rena's, but the ginger hair of her Irish father. "Are you working alone today?" he asked. "With a line like this, I'd expect Elaine to be with you."

"She will be. First, she has to be a star. You should go catch the quartet. She sings with her three cousins." Violet looked at her watch. "They perform in ten minutes." Gee took his coffee with thanks to Violet and made his way to the stage where a crowd was already gathering.

Applause greeted the Nussbaum Quartet as they walked on stage but died quickly as the smallest of the quartet, a cutie in a barely legal denim mini skirt, opened her mouth to sing. She started a scat rhythm that was helped immensely by the microphone close to her mouth. She had a nice voice, but Gee wasn't sure it would carry past the first row without the microphone. Her bright blue eyes, highlighted by dark liner, were enough to light up the stage.

Her vocalese was joined by a young man's baritone. He towered over his cousins and looked like he just walked off the cover of *GQ* magazine. He had chiseled good looks and a presence that said he knew he was handsome.

When the third member of the quartet joined in, Gee remembered Troy Cavanaugh's comment the first day they met. Krystal Nussbaum, beauty queen, could have won the state pageant if she had her cousin's voice. She began a counterpoint singing in a higher range than the other two.

Elaine, the only member of the quartet Gee met previously, looked sad and out of place at the right end of the quartet. Her mike was a little farther from the others, which only served to accent the fact that she carried several more pounds than her female cousins. When she opened her mouth, though, nothing else mattered.

Troy had described her as having the voice of an angel, but it was more than that. When she began to sing "The Sun is Rising," the three individual voices of her cousins suddenly gelled around her. The change that came over Elaine when she sang was heart-stopping. She glowed as the notes poured forth; she was what made her cousins beautiful.

AFTER THE QUARTET'S performance, Gee moved away from the crowds toward the mercantile building. Amidst the typical demonstrations of blenders, vacuum cleaners, cookware, and cutlery, the mercantile at the county fair included exhibits by several of the local furniture craftsmen. Slater Craft exhibited a new stain derived from the bark of the Rose Hickory applied to a white oak table. It was among many furniture offerings attempting to get the look of the Rose Hickory without having access to the wood.

Gee stopped abruptly in front of Forest Custom Furnishing's booth. The furniture exhibited was exquisite. Several different styles were represented. Gee could see instantly the difference between the stained oak furniture up the aisle and the genuine Rose Hickory. It was beautiful and begged to be touched, stroked along its satin finish.

"That's genuine Rose Hickory, Gee. There is no finer furniture wood in the world and we at Forest are the premier craftsmen in its use." Gee smiled at the thin man and recognized him from basketball.

"Luke! Is this your company?"

"It is. Please forgive my pride and bragging about it." Luke was several inches taller than Gee, but probably lighter in weight.

"There is no question about what a difference there is between this and the look alike up the aisle here."

"There's nothing at all wrong with what Slater produces. It's good quality furniture. It just isn't Rose Hickory. Some people can't tell the difference. I'm glad to see you can."

"I suppose it could be your stain and finishing technique. It brings out the color. I didn't realize what a beautiful grain the hickory has."

"You are right about the finishing technique. Good eye. But there is no stain applied to this wood. And the finish is created here in town at Larue chemicals. It is regulated and won't be available outside Rosebud Falls for at least five more years. The finish is an oil distilled from the nuts of the Rose Hickory. It penetrates the wood and hardens, giving this satiny hand," Luke said.

"Just for curiosity's sake, what does a table like this cost?" Gee could already see a table like this in Nathan and Marian's dining room. Perhaps a little smaller than this one.

"This table? This would sell for about five thousand dollars new. This one is old, so it would probably go for twice that. Of course, this table isn't for sale. All our work is custom. We build the furniture to match the customer's exact specifications."

"Thank you for the education. I'd love to visit your shop sometime."

"I'll see that you get a good tour. There is a limited amount of wood available to craftsmen each year, which is what keeps the price high. That, and we care about what we make. This table will be around for hundreds of years. In fact, it is already nearly a hundred years old."

Here Now

GEE CONTINUED THROUGH and out of the mercantile building. He let his feet take him where they would and wandered onto the midway. He spotted the unmistakable fire engine red hair of Rena and turned abruptly away, hoping she hadn't noticed him. He found himself looking up at a frightening ride. It was like a Ferris wheel, but this was no ride for romance. Passengers stood in cages located at intervals around the standing wheel. Instead of riding straight up and maintaining their orientation to the ground, though, these cages flipped over randomly. Extremely boisterous teens could rock the cage, pumping it like a swing until it rolled over. Bright letters in the center of the contraption advertised the Whirl-a-Gig.

"I knew you'd get here eventually, Gee," the ride carny called. Gee looked at the bald man operating the ride and taking tickets. "Going to go around a few times?"

"No, I don't think so. You know me?"

"Well, *know* might be a bit of a strong word. You always show up at the right time, though."

"What do you mean? Where have I shown up at the right time?"

"Think about it, Gee. You got to Rosebud Falls just in time to rescue a little boy from drowning. You walked along the river just in time to get a beaten woman to the hospital. Even when you walked down Main Street, you arrived just in time to meet Troy Cavanaugh. You showed up at the library just when they needed someone to read to the children. You were in the grocery store just in time to advise a young man about how to treat his girlfriend. You got to the fair just in time to see the Nussbaum Quartet. Everywhere. Always right on time."

"Those are just coincidences. It's not like I go out looking for people to help or to save. Or even music to listen to. I wasn't even going to come to the fair today."

"Except you did. Gee, the possibility of a coincidence occurring at any given moment is always one hundred percent. You have your eyes open when they occur."

"You know a lot about me. Do I know you?"

"I doubt it. Bill Williams," the carny said holding out his hand. Gee shook it. "I know you have a lot of questions. Not that I can answer them."

"Who am I? Where did I come from?"

"See, like that. You think I can answer those questions?"

"But you know me, Bill."

"I know you right here and now."

"That doesn't make sense."

"Gee, are you happier wondering about who you were or being who you are?"

That stopped the conversation short. When Gee tried to remember his past, he was plagued with frustration as memories slipped just beyond his grasp. When he was just trying to be helpful and a part of the community, not thinking about past or future, he was always happy.

"I guess when I'm just here."

"Here and now, Gee. Always be here and now."

"Here and now. Just keep showing up?"

"Just in time. Like now." Bill gestured toward a young family watching pig races not far away. "That little girl is what... seven years old? The one in pink shorts and striped shirt. She wanted to ride the Whirl-a-Gig," Bill laughed. "Her parents were horrified. Don't blame them. I wouldn't get on this thing."

"I recognize her from my Wednesday reading circle. Sally Ann. I don't think I've ever met her parents."

"They've been here all afternoon. Mom and Dad are getting cranky. You know we see cranky moms and dads more than kids at fairs. Mom and Dad just reach a point where they can't take any more. They need a nap. Unfortunately, the kid has had enough cotton candy and soda to be wired for sound. They're not like that guy over there. The one in the green and white tractor hat and black t-shirt and jeans. He doesn't look like much—probably nobody here at the fair has noticed him. Funny thing, though. He's never more than fifty feet away from that family. Has been all afternoon. It's almost like he's been watching them. Waiting."

"Do you think he means to hurt them?"

"Don't know what it means. I just think it's odd that they are in those positions right when you show up at the fair."

"I think I'll watch them for a while," Gee said, starting to move away.

He almost turned back when he heard Bill say, "I'll tell Rae you're doing well." *Rae, as written in my book? This is more important than a pig...* Just at that moment, though, one of the pigs took a wrong turn and broke through the plastic retaining wall into the crowd. It was harmless, but the frightened animal darted one way and another as people either scattered or chased after the porcine fugitive. Gee laughed at the antics with the crowd. Then he caught a different movement out the corner of his eye. The little girl was standing alone on the other side of the roadway from where the pig was still cavorting. But her eyes were fixed somewhere else. Just beyond, the man in the green and white farmer's cap was approaching and talking to her.

Kidnap

GEE MOVED QUICKLY and stepped between the man and his target. He knelt on one knee next to the girl as she continued to look up at the other man, mesmerized by the piece of candy in his hand.

"Did you lose your parents, Sally Ann?" Gee asked softly. The little girl's eyes snapped down to Gee and she flung her arms around his neck.

"A bad man," she croaked in his ear.

"You're safe now, honey. Shall we go find your parents?"

"Yes, please."

"Want to ride on my shoulder? They'll be sure to see you up there." He lifted the little girl to his shoulder and began moving back toward the pig race where the competitors were being corralled and caged. He glanced over his other shoulder and saw the man in the green and white cap disappear into the crowd. Two fair security people and a police officer were managing the crowd of people, most of whom were still laughing at the excitement.

Gee scarcely heard a woman calling out, "Help! Help! My daughter. Sally Ann!" He saw the girl's father approach the police officer and started toward them.

"Mommy!" Sally Ann called out. Mother, father, policeman, and both security people headed toward Gee.

"That man is taking my baby!" the mother cried out. Others turned and started toward Gee and Sally Ann from all directions.

"Put the child down and your hands in the air," the policeman yelled. He already had his hand on his gun but was reluctant to pull it in the crowded midway. Gee eased Sally Ann to the ground and the girl ran to her mother. He raised his hands.

"I was trying to help her find her parents," Gee said calmly.

"I'm sure," the officer said. "Where's your wife? Kids?"

"I'm here alone."

"Your kind make me sick. Where were you taking the little girl?" The officer, assisted by the security men, had Gee's hands pulled none too gently behind his back and in cuffs. A sheriff's deputy headed toward them. Gee wasn't worried. He was just helping out. As soon as things settled down, he would be able to explain.

But things didn't settle down. The officer searched him and emptied his pockets, removing his pocket knife, marker, worry stone, and wallet.

"There's no ID in here. Just a ton of cash. And a library card. Where'd you get this money?" the policeman demanded.

"My job... at the market."

"Nobody earns this much money in a market. Who are you?"

"George Edward Evars. Gee."

"Where do you live?"

"683 Joshua Street."

"You better take him in and call Detective Oliver," the deputy sheriff said. "This is above your pay grade, Mac."

"County Mounties," muttered one of the security men 'helping' hold Gee. "We should just take him down to the river and drown him."

"Rick, there's a reason you aren't on the force any longer," the deputy said. "Mac, handle this by the book or I'll take it over." The two security guards assisting the officer grumbled again.

"I'm not happy about it, but you're right," said the police officer. "I can arrest him, but I don't know crap about booking him. I'll take him to the jail and let Oliver sort it out."

"I was just trying to help the little girl find her parents."

"Speaking of which, did anyone get a statement from them? Their names?" the deputy asked.

The policeman looked at the security guys blankly.

Identifying the Suspect

"WHAT THE LIVING hell is going on here?" Mead Oliver demanded when he saw Gee in his jail Sunday morning. The scene was chaotic. People had been coming and going all night and no one had thought to call him until six o'clock in the morning. Gee was fingerprinted again, put in a jail cell, and forgotten until morning. His arrest notice said, 'John Doe, alias George Edward Evars, alias Gee. Attempted kidnapping.'

"It's all a big mistake, Mead."

"It always is."

"If they'd just let me explain."

"Keep it, Gee. You need a lawyer here."

"But…" Mead turned and left the holding cell to face Nathan and Marian Panza in his office.

"Detective Oliver, there has been some kind of mistake made. Gee would never attempt to kidnap a child. He has ample opportunity to do that every day with Devon. He takes him with him to the library. He just isn't like that," Marian complained.

"Not to mention that two policemen came to our door in the middle of the night to question *us* as accomplices!" Nathan shouted at Mead. "Accomplices to kidnapping! What is the police department coming to?"

"If that man has harmed my grandson, I'll hang him myself!" yelled Frieda, Grimm banging through the front door of the little police station. "Where is my grandson?"

"Momma, he's fine," Marian called from the door of Mead's office. "I have him right here."

Mead buried his head in his hands.

"Detective, Jack LaCoe is on line one," the desk clerk called back to Mead. "He says he's been retained as attorney for George Evars and wants immediate access to his client."

"Who retained Jack LaCoe?" Mead asked.

No one volunteered an answer.

"Have him come in now," Mead yelled back at the desk clerk in front. He'd never seen so many people in the police station at one time before. "Officer McCarran! Where's the complaint? Who did Gee supposedly kidnap?"

"A little girl. It wasn't supposedly, Detective. I saw him with the girl."

"What little girl? Where's the complaint from her parents?"

"We didn't get one," the officer said sheepishly. "They disappeared as soon as they had little Sally Ann back."

"Sally Ann?" Marian said. "As in Sally Ann Metzger? If Ruth Ann Metzger started this mess, I'll… I don't know what I'll do, but it won't be pleasant."

"You know the family?" Mead asked.

"Yes. They're nice enough, but Ruth Ann is a real hovercraft and Dale is like a beaten puppy. I can't imagine Sally Ann getting out of her sight. Of course, she'd blame it on someone else."

"McCarran, look up the Metzgers and get them in here. Make sure they bring the child with them."

"Detective Oliver, Mr. and Mrs. LaCoe are here," said the desk clerk.

"Both of them? Already? Was he waiting outside the door when he called? Send him in. If we can get everyone here, maybe we can get this clusterfuck straightened out."

IT TOOK A while. In the midst of anger and accusations among the families involved, the lawyers, and the police, Gee was led into the conference room. Officer McCarran had reluctantly followed the detective's instructions not to restrain him.

"Gee!" Sally Ann and Devon both broke away from their parents and ran to Gee. He hugged them. Ruth Ann screamed.

"This is a kidnapper?" Jack LaCoe asked. "It looks like they think he's Santa Claus."

"Kids," Gee said calmly. "Why don't you go to your mommies for a couple of minutes while the nice police sort out what happened."

"Okay, Mr. Gee. Devon, come with me. I will help you find your mommy," Sally Ann said. She was easily three years older than Devon and acted like a big sister, taking his hand to lead him back to Marian. Frieda snatched the boy up. Rupert and Onyx had arrived in the meantime and Gee saw the young wife roll her eyes at Frieda's possessiveness.

"Everyone sit down or stand back against the wall," Mead said. "It's ten o'clock on Sunday morning and there is no one in this room who wants to be here."

"Has my client been charged?" Jack asked.

"No. We don't have a formal complaint. Mr. and Mrs. Metzger, do you wish to file a complaint."

"He took my baby," Ruth Ann shouted.

"You saw him take her?" Jack asked.

"I saw her riding on his shoulders."

"That's a pretty unlikely place for a kidnapper to put his prey," Mead followed up. "Sally Ann, did this man take you away from your parents?"

"Gee saved me from the bad man," Sally Ann spoke up. "He helped me find Mommy."

"She's been saying that Gee saved her from the bad man, all night," Dale Metzger said. "Uh… I thought she meant God saved her."

"Sally Ann, do you know this man?" Ruth Ann finally asked.

"He reads to us in the library," Sally Ann said.

"The library? Where Daddy takes you on Wednesday night?" Ruth Ann glared at her husband. "You knew him?"

"I didn't really recognize him," Dale confessed. "I usually read the city newspaper during story time." A storm was brewing between Sally Ann's parents. Mead moved quickly to redirect it.

"Sally Ann, was there another man? A bad man who was trying to take you away?"

"Uh huh. When the pigs got loose I ran away. I was scared. A big man told me to come with him and offered me some candy. Gee chased him away."

"Does that match what you saw, Gee?"

"Oh. Do I get to say something?" Gee asked. He'd been sitting quietly in the face of accusation and exoneration the entire time they'd been in the room.

"No one took a statement from you, Gee?" Gretchen LaCoe asked, rolling her eyes.

"I didn't have a lawyer, and no one was interested in listening to what I had to say. I told them it was a misunderstanding and they should go ask Bill," Gee said.

"Who's Bill?" Mead asked.

"He runs the Whirl-a-Gig ride at the fair. He pointed out the man who was stalking the Metzgers all afternoon."

"McCarran! Get over to the fairgrounds and find this Bill…"

"Williams. Bill Williams," Gee supplied.

"Detective, the fair's gone. Last night was the end. They were tearing down and packing up at one a.m. The whole convoy was out of here by six," the police officer said.

Mead groaned again.

"Mead, maybe we should get a description of the 'bad man' and then let everyone go home. Do you have Gee's belongings?" Jack asked. "It seems this is all a misunderstanding, and unless Gee wants to sue the city for false arrest, it looks like we should focus on finding the other guy."

"McCarran, get Gee's belongings," Mead snapped.

"I don't want to sue anyone."

"I didn't think so," Jack said.

Officer McCarran returned with a baggie of Gee's possessions. Gee emptied it and immediately grabbed his worry stone. Sensing the marks under his finger made everything he had just been through seem like a joke. He smiled as he pocketed his handkerchief, pocketknife, marker, and the somewhat battered ticket he'd shoved in his pocket. He picked up his wallet and glanced inside, looking from the wallet to the officer.

"Oh!" Officer McCarran said. "I'll call the sheriff's office. The deputy observer last night demanded that we lock your cash in their safe. It would have only been in a desk drawer if we left it here." He ran from the conference room.

"You had cash?" Jack asked.

"Nine hundred eighty dollars. Maybe nine-eighty-five. I suppose I owe it to you," Gee smiled.

"A dollar. The rest of this case is pro bono. Why were you carrying so much cash?"

"Where else would I put it? I collect my pay and give Nathan and Marian my rent. Then I have this cash left over in my wallet. I don't spend much other than lunches and a cup of coffee each morning at Jitterz. It just kind of collects there."

"Why don't you put it in the bank?"

"I don't have an account."

Jack and Gretchen looked at each other and then at Mead.

"We've been running every database we can get our hands on," Mead said. "I expected to at least get a hit from Social Security, but nothing. No fingerprint matches. No photo matches. As far as Homeland Security is concerned, he doesn't exist outside our little town."

"We need to get Judge Warren involved," Jack said to Gretchen. "Gee needs some kind of photo ID, even if it is only good within the city limits."

"Gee, I doubt that we'll be able to do anything about things like citizenship, a passport, voting, or driving, but Judge Warren should be able to get you some kind of identity papers that declare you a legitimate person. At least you could have a bank account and sign a lease," Gretchen said. "We'll go to work on it."

Just then Officer McCarran returned and placed a baggie with cash in it in front of Gee. Quickly counting out nine hundred eighty-two dollars, Gee handed a dollar to Jack and stuffed the remainder in his wallet.

"Mr. LaCoe," Mead said formally, "does your client wish to pursue any action against the Rosebud Falls Police Department or any of the other persons related to this misunderstanding?" Jack glanced at Gee, who shook his head.

"No, Detective. I will say, however, that various aspects of police training and pre-employment screening will be reviewed with possible recommendations forthcoming. We will not, however, file any direct complaints," Jack said.

"Thank heavens for small favors. Does anyone else have anything to say in the matter?" There were no responses and Mead released the group as if adjourning a social club meeting. Ruth Ann and Sally Ann Metzger headed for the door at once. Sally Ann waved over her shoulder and Gee waved back.

"Mr. Evars, my wife failed to tell you that we are truly sorry for the misunderstanding and hope you will not hold the concern of panicked parents against us," Dale Metzger said.

"Of course not, Mr. Metzger. And please, I'm just Gee. No 'mister' is required. I hope to see Sally Ann at the library on Wednesday evening."

"I'm not sure if my wife will let me bring her out, but I'll do my best. She does love story time."

"Gee, could you spend a few minutes with me describing the man that you and Sally Ann referred to? I'd like to make sure we are keeping an eye out," Mead said. "I'm sure he's long gone by now, but we'll keep watch."

JACK AND GRETCHEN sat with Gee while he did his best to describe the man he'd seen approaching Sally Ann. Unfortunately, the description fit half of the men age thirty to fifty years who lived in Rosebud Falls. Even the green and white tractor hat was common as they'd been given away at the fair.

"We should get a police artist to do a sketch so we have something to go on," Jack suggested.

"We don't have a police artist," Mead mumbled.

"I'll find one," Jack said. "Well, Gee, are you hungry? Why don't we have lunch?"

Gee accompanied Jack and Gretchen LaCoe to a diner on Main Street where the after-church crowd was already gathering.

"THANK YOU FOR coming to my aid this morning," Gee said as they ate the daily special. "But… How did you even know I was in jail? Who asked you to represent me?"

"Your presence in town has not escaped the notice of some important people. We've been on notice for some time," Gretchen said.

"Families?"

The lawyer couple turned to each other in silence for a moment, as if they were communicating with a higher power. Gee knew that was silly, but he'd always wondered how married people seemed to communicate without speaking. Eventually, they returned their attention to him.

"The Families," Jack said. "It took me a long time to get comfortable with the concept of the Families. I'm an outsider—like you. I married into the town and into the Families. Gretchen is Heinz Nussbaum's daughter."

"Oh. Wait. LaCoe. One of the quartet is your son, isn't he?"

"That's Cameron," Gretchen said. "But to the point, if you'd just walked into town a vagrant, the Families still would have taken notice. And frankly, I'm not sure which one got interested in you first. We were contacted anonymously almost a month ago and paid through a blind trust. Our instructions were simply to provide whatever legal aid you needed."

"So, I get two lawyers for the price of one?"

"And the price is free," Jack laughed. "Gee, we don't have loyalty to any particular Family, in spite of Gretchen's connection. We don't know who asked us to look after you, so there is no conflict of interest. You didn't choose us directly, but we are the only lawyers you will ever need in Rosebud Falls."

New Owners

"THE FAMILIES HAVE never interfered in our business before."

"It's a new world, Axel. Don't look at it as interfering, but as expanding your horizons."

"You can't just dictate what we should publish," the editor said. Who did they think they were? *The Elmont Mirror* had always been an independent voice in Rosebud Falls. *His* voice.

"I wouldn't dream of it. In fact, I will do all in my power to protect the rights of our *individual* reporters. I want them to claim their own biases. In other words, no more stripping bylines from articles, Axel. The fact that we will also contribute occasional articles that support the public good is incidental."

"And will you also claim your own biases?" Axel sneered. "Will your stories carry bylines?"

"When I… or we… on rare occasions submit an article for publication, it will have been vetted and reviewed and accepted as the voice of *The Elmont Mirror.* That is what will distinguish it from other reporters. You will have the voice of Axel Hunter, the voice of Karen Weisman, the voice of Ken Probst, the voice of Kelly Murray—or I should say her photos—and the voice of *The Elmont Mirror.* The only difference between this and what you've always done is that I am the voice of *The Elmont Mirror* instead of you. You get your own bylines."

That didn't sit well with Axel. He'd run the newspaper for years and had covertly taken credit for the writing of many stories by simply eliminating bylines. This was probably something that troublemaker Karen Weisman set in motion. She'd done nothing but complain about her bylines since she came to work here two years ago. As if she'd ever be in the running for a Pulitzer Prize. This was all her fault. He'd cook her goose later.

"So, every story is to carry a byline except yours," Axel said.

"And, of course, identifying information if it comes from a news service. We're governed by that in our agreements with AP and UPI, among the other news services. I'm sure you'll do some of your best work identifying stories from the wire services that are relevant to the citizens of Rosebud Falls."

"I get it."

"Axel, I hope you won't consider this a bad thing. There are big issues that will come before the people of Rosebud Falls soon. They need to see a strong position on the part of the newspaper and know that it is approved by the Families. They trust us. And they trust the *Mirror*."

5

CITY CHAMPION

Suspicion

"I DON'T KNOW what to think, Gee. Every time I leave town, you end up in jail. Is this going to be a habit?"

"It was all a misunderstanding," Gee said nervously.

"I'm teasing, Gee," Karen laughed. "I was just trying to discover if my leaving town related to you going to jail. I mean, I could stay closer if necessary. Much closer."

"Um… How was your conference?" Gee asked. He had a vague discomfort when he thought of Karen being at the same conference in the city as Troy Cavanaugh. It was stupid, he knew. But that didn't stop the anxious knot in his stomach. After all, he and Karen had only been on two actual dates and had made no declarations about being 'with' each other. His uncertainty about his relationship was harder to deal with than his lack of identity.

"It was great! I found some allies that might be able to help in my investigation. It turns out that I'm not the only journalist trying to dig into the underground trafficking of children. That's what really makes this difficult." Karen's dedication and enthusiasm for this subject was infectious and Gee shoved his doubts aside. "There are laws against prostitution, child abuse, and slavery. But laws aren't really a deterrent if you can't catch a perpetrator in the act. As a result, the laws are used to punish the visible crimes while the much worse offenses remain hidden."

"What do you mean?"

"Laws against prostitution should protect women and men who are forced into the life by need, greed, and power. But in reality, those are the women it punishes while their johns and pimps go untouched. A parent might get turned into child protective services by a neighbor who doesn't believe in corporal punishment while another neighbor keeps an unknown child chained in their basement."

"Aren't the police investigating the hidden crimes?"

"You'd think, wouldn't you?" Karen's face fell. "We had an FBI agent come to our group to talk. Laws that protect innocent people from invasion of privacy also tie the hands of police. They need to show just cause in order to launch an investigation. There are so many leaks in the system that even following up a legitimate lead usually results in a dead end because the perp has been warned in advance and cleans house before they get there."

"How are you supposed to get a story here if the police and FBI can't crack the ring?" Gee asked. "It seems to me, the only way to expose them would be from the inside. Please don't tell me you plan to infiltrate a child trafficking ring!"

"Not me."

"Someone?"

"We're working on getting someone inside, but without a specific target, we don't know the entrances. Right now, it involves a lot of backtracking and seeing where loose threads lead. You might find it hard to believe based on television shows and popular literature, but there are actually very few journalists—or police, for that matter—who are willing to go under cover as a prostitute. Imagine how many fewer would be willing to infiltrate as a pedophile or trafficker. It involves breaking the very laws we're investigating."

"How can we uncover the problem then?"

"We'll find a way."

They sat in silence having finished their late dinner after Gee's library time. He'd been sad when Sally Ann Metzger didn't show up for the Bookhouse. *On the other hand, she's safe and wasn't spirited away to join the traffic Karen is investigating.* That thought gave him pause.

"Kidnapping."

"You did a good thing this weekend, Gee. She might never have been seen again. You did better than I did."

"What do you mean?"

"Got time for a long story? I'll make it as short as possible." Gee nodded to her to continue. "Fifteen years ago, I was a mother's helper. Technically, I was too young to babysit, but mothers of small children need help. Someone to play with their child while she makes dinner or runs the vacuum. That was me. I was a helper for a young family in the Orchard Project. My charge was just two years old and I was pushing her on a swing in the front yard. That was all I had to do. Push the swing."

"What happened?" Gee encouraged as he took Karen's hand. She squeezed his softly.

"The puppy. We were laughing and giggling with the puppy romping around the swing. He tripped me and grabbed my flipflop. He took off running around the side of the house and I chased him. It was only a minute. I picked him up and went back to the swing where little Renee was. Only she wasn't there. She was gone. I screamed, and Mrs. Lisle came running. We were frantic, looking up and down the street, in the bushes, anywhere Renee could have run off to. A neighbor heard us and called the police. It hadn't even occurred to us that she might not have wandered off." Karen started weeping and clutched Gee's hand tightly. "We never saw her again. She was gone. The police investigation gathered information indicating a white van had been parked nearby, but no one got the license number. They decided the kidnappers had been waiting for their opportunity for days. And then they just disappeared."

"Ransom? Any word from them?"

"No. That's what makes it so impossible to track these things. Most resolved kidnappings are the result of the kidnapper making contact, either to demand a ransom or even just to gloat over the fact that he won. Or they are a relative, usually a parent. But cases like this, the kidnapper never makes contact. There are no leads. He and the child just disappear."

"Karen, you're still suffering. It wasn't your fault."

"Everyone's told me that. I had counseling for years. The poor Lisle family didn't survive. Mr. Lisle committed suicide. Mrs. Lisle drank herself out of her home and disappeared. Maybe to the city. Maybe she died. But I swore then and there that I'd find the people who did this if it took the rest of my life. That's why I became a reporter and made child trafficking my special area of investigation."

It took several minutes to break through the gloom brought about by Karen's story. They awkwardly finished their meal in the little diner—made difficult by the fact that she didn't release Gee's hand. They left the diner and walked up Main Street toward the river. As they passed the radio studio, Gee noted that the broadcast desk was empty and asked Karen about it.

"There are only two regular broadcasters and a couple of high school students who cover the desk on weekends," Karen explained. "The rest of the time is network programming. Technically, WRZF is not a public radio station. It's a non-profit station but is privately owned. It buys programming from various public broadcast networks, international news outlets, and late Saturday night it even rebroadcasts the Grand Ole Opry from Tennessee. Don't ask me why."

"I heard the interview with Troy from the conference. Apparently, they are doing something right for him to win an award. I didn't know he'd be there with you."

"Yeah. He's pretty full of himself over that award. It's really just a certificate of recognition from his fellow broadcasters, but he treats it like an Oscar. He spent the whole conference trying to…"Karen stopped abruptly and turned to Gee, pulling him to a stop at the street corner. "Gee, Troy wasn't at the conference *with me*. God! I had no idea how that might appear to you."

"It wasn't… I mean, I didn't…"

"Of course you did. You're a male. And I am stupid. Listen, you need to hear this."

"Karen, you don't need to explain anything. I don't have a right to an explanation."

"Yes, you do. Because…" Karen took a deep breath and let it out. "Troy and I used to date. It was soon after I got back to Rosebud Falls and lasted until about eight months ago. We broke up right after the holidays. It would be foolish of me to tell you we weren't intimate. Of course we were. But, we broke up. I broke it up. Troy made it clear last weekend that he wants us to get together again. He's been trying for months. But it is over. Completely and finally."

"I didn't mean to make it sound like I was accusing you of something, Karen. We haven't made any vows to each other. We haven't said we are exclusive or that we are even planning to be more than the good friends we are. I'm sorry that I jumped to conclusions."

Karen laughed. "Actually, it's nice to know that you have reactions and responses that are normal, even though you don't have a memory context for them. But there is something else you should know about me before we let our relationship progress any further. I'm twenty-seven years old and, while I'm not promiscuous, I'm not inexperienced, either. One of the things I discovered about myself ten years ago is that I'm essentially monogamous. Serial monogamy, I'll grant you, but one relationship at a time. I don't step out on the man I'm with and I expect the same from him."

"But we aren't in that kind of a relationship… are we?"

"I don't know, Gee. We've known each other for a couple of months. We haven't been intimate and that's good because I could get scared if we developed our relationship any faster than we are. But I'm not exploring any other relationships while we find out where this one is going. *Capisce?*"

"Karen, you are the only woman I've been interested in since I got to Rosebud Falls. I don't know what came before that, but I don't have a feeling of 'relationship' before I got here. I have two references to my past. Bill Williams, who was at the fair running that ride, but seems to have disappeared along with the Whirl-a-Gig. I don't even know if they were real. And Rae, who gave me a book. Bill said he'd tell her I was doing well. I feel a strong connection to her, but not a romantic one. I can't explain it better than that."

"That will have to do," Karen said. "As long as we're clear about our status and intentions."

"I try not to have intentions. I'm willing to find out where this… us… leads us. I'll take it at whatever speed you suggest."

Spit on His Grave

JO RANSOM WALKED through the War Memorial Park holding her grandmother's hand. Her grandmother, Celia, made this walk nearly every day since her own mother's death in 1959. Jo, finished with college, had just moved back to Rosebud Falls and agreed to accompany her grandmother.

They approached the memorial statue in the center of the park, determination in the old woman's step. The sculptor somehow managed to contrive a pose of the seven young men assaulting Omaha Beach as if they were still the linemen of the Rosebud Falls football team. She looked at the faces on the statue as if seeking out one and spat toward it.

"Bastard," she whispered.

"Grandma! What if someone sees you disrespecting the memorial? Don't do that."

"Jo, it's time you learned the truth about your family and about that betraying man they make out to be a hero," Celia declared. She led the young woman to a bench where they could still see the statue.

"Grandma, don't get upset."

"I'm seventy-five years old. I can be upset," the old woman said indignantly. "Now listen. Those seven men left seven babies in the wombs of young women here in town. It was a scandal, yes, but an understandable one. No one wanted those boys to go to war feeling unloved. They'd already been shipped overseas before they found out their girlfriends were with child. They were not only soldiers, they were Family. One from each of the seven Families of Rosebud Falls. Noble. Honorable. They wrote letters to their Families detailing their relationships with the girls and acknowledging their sons and daughters. They asked the Families to accept their children and grant them their names."

"That's very sweet and romantic, Grandma. I've heard that before," Jo said, soothing her irritated grandmother.

"All except that one," Celia said pointing her finger. "My father, Joseph Roth, sent no letter of acknowledgement. His father, Aaron Roth, claimed my mother Maura was a loose woman attempting to capitalize on a Family name and that his son would never have mated with a common *shiksa*. He went so far as to ridicule the Families of the other six for having sons that could be led around by the nose and having their Family lines polluted. While the other six were recognized by the Families and were christened with the Family last name, my mother was an outcast, and I was simply a bastard child. I spit on his memory every day."

"Grandma, you mean we are related to the Roth Family?" Jo asked.

"What there is left of them, curse them. That old man, Benjamin Roth, my father's brother, sits in his fancy mansion by the river knowing that he is the last of his name this city will ever see. Oh, his daughter hyphenated her name and insisted that all her sons do the same. But Roth will disappear as one of the seven Families. It is the curse I give them."

The two finally stood to leave the park. Jo drove her grandmother back to the Hilltop Retirement Village. Tears flowed down her grandmother's cheeks.

"My mother, Maura, was destroyed. She died when I was fifteen. The only one who watched over her was Ohna Johansen. Ohna's daughter, Dee Poltanys became my best friend and they took me in when Mother passed away. The other five were embarrassed about how mother was treated and did their best to include us, but we had no family. Even now, I am beholden to the Poltanys Family. They built this little retirement village on the hilltop." Celia sighed and pointed out toward the West Branch River and, on the other side, the coal yard. Downtown was visible to the southeast.

"Take a last look at this cursed town and leave it forever, Jo. I tried to get my son to go, but he wouldn't leave me. He's spent a lifetime building houses for others that he could never afford to own. But you, my girl, have a college education. You can make your mark on the world. Go and don't look back. That's my advice."

Jo hugged her grandmother and promised to look in on her again tomorrow. She drove back to the park and sat on the bench looking at the memorial statue for a long time. At last, she approached the statue, spit, and left.

Harvest Schedule

"WHEN DOES THIS schedule start?" Gee asked Nathan as he tacked the work schedule to the employee bulletin board.

"Oh, this is the Harvest schedule," Nathan said. "Harvest week here is a strange concept to an outsider. We won't know exactly when it is until the foresters start the sirens and the churches ring their bells. We know it will be in September or October. Everyone participates. It's the only way we can hope to bring in all the nuts, deadwood, and timber."

"So, we're all required to serve in the Forest?"

"Gee… uh… no offense, but don't talk like that about Harvest. It's not a *requirement*. It is a *privilege* and civic duty to take part in Harvest Week. An outsider might be considered… well, an outsider if he didn't participate in Harvest. Not everyone works *in* the Forest. People have to be fed, emergency services still need to function, and essential businesses, like groceries, have to be open. But we operate with shorter hours and a skeleton staff so everyone has at least half a day every day to work the Harvest."

"I don't see my name here."

"Well, we don't know what job you'll have for Harvest. As soon as you know, I'll schedule your work hours if you have any available."

"I almost forgot about orientation."

"Don't. It's my fault you didn't get to an orientation earlier. You'd think one of us would have remembered to tell you. With school starting next week, orientations are going on all over. Schools will be on half days during Harvest and teachers are all being trained to keep their students focused on the jobs at hand. For all I know, you'll be assigned the task of setting up the park for the nightly parties. You might not make it to the Forest at all."

That thought caused a little pang for Gee. He liked the Forest. In fact, he *wanted* to work Harvest, no matter what job he was assigned. It was part of the mystique of the town. And most recently, it was where Karen Weisman held his hand for two hours as they walked and quietly talked.

"Say, don't you have to be at the courthouse this afternoon?" Nathan asked, snapping Gee out of his reverie.

"Yes. I came back here to clock out. I better get a move on."

"Good luck this afternoon."

Rebirth

"GEORGE EVARS?"

"Here, Your Honor." Gee felt like a schoolboy being called upon when the judge first said his name. They were in a conference room, not a courtroom, but there were several people jammed into the small space.

"Welcome to the community, George," the judge smiled. "Just wanted to make sure I was addressing the right person. I'm told you prefer to be called Gee."

"Yes, sir. I'm used to it."

"And Jack LaCoe, you are representing Gee?"

"Yes, your honor. Gretchen is also on the team."

"Okay," the judge said. "For those of you who don't know..." he looked at Gee, "... I'm Judge Brian Warren. In a community as small as ours, I serve as both City Judge and County Judge. Mostly I'm an arbitrator. Anything needed beyond that, we call for help. This is not a hearing, but a discussion about how the City can best help a stranger in our midst who has repeatedly shown himself a hero since the first day he walked into town. In addition to those already introduced, let me point out the others invited to this meeting. Frieda Grimm, Gee's employer on my left. Beside her, Don and Leah Roth-Augello of the Savage Credit Union. This is Karl Nussbaum of First Rose Valley Bank. And, of course, Detective Mead Oliver. We have two items at issue here. The first is that with Gee's loss of memory, possibly related to the rescue of a child in our raging river, Gee's identity was also lost. No wallet. No papers. No trace. This makes Gee, in the truest sense, an undocumented visitor. The second issue is banking related, as Gee has no place to bank his earnings. Again, I emphasize that this is not a hearing, but a fact-finding discussion to see how we can help Gee become a citizen of our city. Jack, would you like to begin?"

"The first issue I think we need to deal with is Gee's identity. There has been activity on several fronts to confirm he is who he says he is. In that regard, I'd like Detective Oliver to report his findings," Jack said. Mead cleared his throat.

"The Police Department, in cooperation with the Sheriff's office and State Police have undertaken to ascertain the true identity of the man claiming to be George Edward Evars," Mead read from his prepared statement. "This investigation has included name searches through state and national missing persons reports, a search for tax and Social Security records, and submission of fingerprints to the AFIS database maintained by the FBI. We have further submitted Mr. Evars' photograph, name, and presumed birthdate to the licensing departments of each of the 50 states to search for driver's license or other state-issued identification. Finally, well-known investigative reporter, Ms. Karen Weisman, has cooperated in providing the department with the results of her searches of membership associations, including such service organizations as Masons, fraternal organizations like Elks and Moose, and commercial memberships like AAA, Costco, and Sam's Club. Her results have returned no trace of the man calling himself George Edward Evars. However, she has also, with the approval of Mr. Evars, submitted DNA to several testing labs that are not part of the national database. This profile indicates that Mr. Evars is of mixed Northern European heritage and as much as twenty-five percent Native American heritage. It has not, however, revealed any relatives closer than five degrees of separation. We will, of course, follow up with contacting some of these distant cousins to see if anything surfaces as time and resources allow."

"Military, Homeland Security, FBI, and CIA?" the judge asked.

"Yes, your honor. All have been queried and come back blank. Some searches, like CIA take longer and they only respond if they have an interest in the person. Military branches and FBI have no match. Homeland Security, in a surprise move to us, has simply informed our office that the person in question is not of interest in any former or ongoing investigation."

"I'm surprised INS hasn't been here to haul you away, Gee," the judge laughed. "They seem to be the only ones missing."

"Your honor," Jack said, "contrary to popular opinion, there is no national law nor any law in this state that requires a person to have identity papers. He needs to have a license to drive a car, a work permit to hold a job, even a passport to get into or out of the country. But all those are situation specific."

"There is a problem with a work permit," Frieda interrupted. "We are retaining records of all money paid to Gee and have withheld income tax, Social Security, and Medicare payments, but we'll have to figure out a way to file a report by the end of September."

"That is where the INS comes in. Based on the combined evidence of the DNA tests and Homeland Security's lack of interest, we agreed to file Form I-765 with the US Citizenship and Immigration Services. They have provisionally indicated that they will issue an Employment Authorization Document. In general, a person is not otherwise required to have an ID."

"Then why are we here?" the judge asked.

"We—and that includes Gee, your honor—believe several recent misunderstandings could have been prevented if Gee could simply produce a government issued identification document. Even though it's not a law that he has to carry identification, he is required to truthfully answer law enforcement officers when asked his name and other pertinent information. Typically, this is verified by the officer through official documents. When those are missing, it becomes a hardship on both the officer and the subject," Gretchen responded. "In addition, Ms. Grimm must retain Form I-9. The EAD is only part of her solution. Gee must also produce an ID card issued by a federal, state, or local government agency or entity, providing a photograph, name, birthdate, and address. This is purely a case of helping a man more effectively fit into the community, who has already repeatedly shown his commitment to the welfare of our citizens."

"How about getting him a state ID card? The kind they issue to people who don't drive."

"It requires a birth certificate or affidavits of two people who have valid ID and will attest to the correctness of his name, birth date, and place of birth."

"We get bombarded non-stop about how many illegal aliens are in this country with drivers' licenses, Social Security numbers, and health benefits. How the heck can this be so hard?" Judge Warren said.

"People lie."

"And no one will lie for Gee," he sighed.

"Your honor, I don't want anyone to lie for me. I'd rather not exist," Gee said softly.

"I was being facetious, Gee. I'm not suggesting someone should lie for you. You're a good man," the judge said. "Let's put this aside for later consideration and talk about banking. I assume Gee needs ID to open a bank account."

"At one time it was pretty loose as long as no transaction exceeded $10,000, but the Patriot Act of 2001 put requirements on financial institutions to record a Social Security number for any account opened," Karl Nussbaum said.

"If I may, Karl," Don Roth-Augello broke in, "when the Patriot Act expired in 2011, only three provisions were renewed. Technically, we don't have to have a Social Security number attached to the account now."

"Really?"

"In fact," Jack added, "our research shows that Title 31 CFR 103.28 says,

> *Before concluding any transaction with respect to which a report is required under Sec. 103.22, a financial institution shall verify and record the name and address of the individual presenting a transaction, as well as record the identity, account number, and the social security or taxpayer identification number, **if any**, of any person or entity on whose behalf such transaction is to be effected. 103.34 indicates what record a bank must keep if no SSN is provided."*

"It's still risky," Karl said. "I just am not interested in inviting an unnecessary audit."

"I'd have to agree," Don said. "These laws tend to shift each time the wind switches from east to west."

"I don't really need a bank account for financial transactions," Gee said. "I like having cash for the most part. My purchases are small and simple. I just need a safe place to put my money so I'm not carrying it around all the time."

Karl and Don looked at each other and nodded.

"Safe deposit box," Karl said. "No matter what you put in a safe deposit box, it is not considered a financial transaction."

"There are risks there, too," Don said, "but they are your risks and not the bank's."

"What risks?"

"Safe deposit boxes are not insured. Since no record is kept of the contents, no insurance would cover them if, for example, a robbery managed to get access to the vault and could open the boxes. Or if some natural catastrophe destroyed the vault," Don answered.

"Which isn't likely, but it is a risk," Karl said. "But, even though I would love to rent you a safe deposit box, you still have to have ID. You would need to show ID and match the signature on the depositor card in order to get access to your box."

"Back to ID," Judge Warren said. "Mead, let me see your police ID, please," Judge Warren said abruptly. Startled, Mead automatically reached for his wallet and pulled out the card. Judge Warren studied it carefully. "Did you intentionally spill gravy on your shirt just before your picture was taken?" he asked. Mead blushed. Warren handed the card on to Karl and Don. "Gentlemen, would you rent a safe deposit box to Mead with this identification?" The two looked at it carefully and finally nodded.

"It looks complete. Photo ID from a government entity. Name, DOB, address, signature. I wouldn't have any problems with that," Karl said. Don agreed.

"Jack, would this solve Ms. Grimm's problem with the I-9?"

"I don't see why not," Jack said looking at Mead's ID. "It does imply, however, that Mead is employed by the Rosebud City Police Department."

"Mead, couldn't the city use someone like Gee in various extreme circumstances. Say a child falls in the river and we need a fast-acting swimmer to dive in and save him. Or a woman needs to be transported to the hospital without delay. Or a child is in danger of being kidnapped. Wouldn't it be nice to know that George Edward Evars was keeping an eye out?"

"Uh... yes, sir. But we don't have a budget..."

"Pro bono work, Mead. Gee would never ask for compensation for his heroics, would you, Gee?"

"No. I just did what needed to be done at the moment."

"I believe we should give Gee an official City ID. Photo. Signature. Date of birth. Let's think of a title. He can't actually be a policeman." Judge Warren glanced around the table.

"Based on his work at the store, he could do about anything. We call him a stock boy," Frieda said.

"Hmm. City of Rosebud Falls. Stock Boy. Certainly we can do better than that."

"Ombudsman," Gretchen said. "Or, by definition, Public Advocate. It's vague regarding what his real 'position' would be. It's like a champion for the people."

"Champion," Leah Roth-Augello repeated. "I like that. A champion for Rosebud Falls."

"Unpaid, of course," Gretchen grinned. "The perfect pro bono position."

"And since it's unpaid, there really doesn't have to be any human resources paperwork filed," Frieda added. Once the subject had changed to finding Gee a position to serve the City, the women had taken over the conversation. The men, however, were nodding as they shot ideas back and forth.

"Your honor, we here represent only a small portion of the interests of the great City of Rosebud Falls," Gretchen started formally. "But it is our recommendation that the City take under consideration the appointment of George Edward Evars, known throughout the town as Gee, to the newly created and pro bono position of City Champion to support and uphold the ideals and people of Rosebud Falls. No compensation would be offered for this position, but the Champion would be issued an official City of Rosebud Falls identification card."

"I will not act alone in this matter," Judge Warren said. "However, by the time Detective Oliver takes our Champion to the police station and issues him an ID with the title of his position, I believe I can confirm the action. Is everyone here in agreement?"

"Aye," they all answered.

"Congratulations, Gee. You've just been reborn as a citizen of Rosebud Falls."

Bank on It

"Just remember, Gee, this ID isn't going to do you a bit of good outside Rosebud Falls. You can't drive a car with it. You can't board an airplane. Since it is clearly a City ID and not a police ID, you can't carry a gun," Mead said. "Do you have a gun?"

"No," Gee answered. "I haven't really bought anything since I arrived. Oh. Except I bought a new hat at Odegard's."

"I noticed. You should probably think about getting some additional clothes. The weather's great right now, but by November we'll be having frost and freezing temps—maybe snow."

"Thanks for the advice, Mead."

"I'm just glad to have you stop by without having you suspected of anything," Mead laughed. With a fresh City ID in his hand, Gee walked south to the Savage Credit Union. Its location across Main Street from the market would be convenient for Gee.

"Gee, I suggest you keep out, say $600. I'm telling you this as a friend, not a financial adviser."

"Are you my friend, Don?" The two men laughed and Don shrugged his shoulders.

"A little too soon? Maybe one day we'll become friends. But good advice can come from acquaintances, as well."

"Why should I keep so much out? I don't have a lot of expenses and I'll get paid again in two days."

"You could wait if you want. I talked to Karl after our meeting this afternoon. We came up with another idea. You can buy a Visa gift card at the bank. We don't handle them here at the credit union, but Karl can fix you up pretty quickly. You can buy a $500 card with no ID and no transaction record. The card would allow you to make debit-like purchases. Say you want to buy some new clothes or a winter jacket but you only have thirty dollars in your wallet. You activate your gift card and suddenly you have $500 at your fingertips. It's safer than carrying cash because it can't be used by anyone who doesn't know your PIN," Don explained.

"I think I'll take that as good friendly advice, Don. Thank you for helping me get things set up today."

"Don't be a stranger, Gee."

"I'm glad you came in to talk to me, Gee. Don is right. The gift card is essentially a cash or debit card. It can be used almost anywhere a credit card can, except for certain kinds of purchases like airline tickets and car rentals. You won't need anything like that anyway. It's just a safe way to carry cash."

"When it runs out I can just add cash to it?"

"Yes and no. These things are weird. Adding funds to an existing card is usually done by electronic transfer. If you make it a bank transaction, then we need to go through all the rigmarole of ID and record keeping. I'd say it is easier to just buy another card when one runs out. You can even buy them up in advance and put them in your safe deposit box with your cash."

"Karl, is all of this legal?" Gee asked. The banker nodded.

"It's creative, but legal. Gee, if you came in here with $50,000 in cash and wanted to create transactions like this, I wouldn't even talk to you. I'd be on the phone to FinCEN so fast there would be agents waiting before you walked out the door. But we're not talking about laundering drug money here. We're talking about managing your cash while you get on your feet and get an identity established."

"Thank you. I just don't want anyone to get in trouble for helping me."

On the way out of the office, Gee spotted the red hair, blue eyes, and infectious smile of Gail Nussbaum at the reception desk.

"Miss Nussbaum, I caught your performance with the quartet at the fair," Gee said as he approached her desk. "I was truly moved by the music your little group produces. I've mentioned it to Elaine over at Jitterz, but just wanted to take the opportunity to tell you directly."

"Thank you, Mr. Gee," she said brightly. "The County Fair is just a first step to taking over the world. If there is ever anything we here at First Rose Valley Bank can do for you, please let us know."

Gee laughed and left the bank.

GAIL WASN'T SURE if there was anything important about the mystery man's visit to the bank and her uncle's friendly greeting, but she didn't let these things go by. She picked up the phone to call her cousin. It was why she was in the bank, after all—to keep track of unusual business. Cameron would want to know.

Forest Orientation

GEE SAT BEFORE Jonathon in the library auditorium with one other man and twenty-some children. He recognized several of them from his Wednesday evening story time, including little Sally Ann Metzger who made a dash over to give him a hug before her teacher got his class settled. He was surprised to see her with the first-grade class. He was sure she was in at least second grade.

As soon as the children had settled down, Jonathon started in with a song about the hickory wind.

It makes me feel better
Each time it begins,
Callin' me home,
Hickory Wind.

Jonathon's arrangement had the children clapping and all joining in on the chorus and calling out 'Hickory Wind.' Then Jonathon started telling the children about the Forest and how this year they were all old enough to help harvest nuts and would get their first chance to attend the big Harvest Festival. The way Jonathon talked about it, it didn't sound like work at all. He talked about nuts falling from the tree sounding like a rainstorm and wove in stories about how important the trees were to everyone in town. It was almost religious.

When the presentation was over, Jonathon came down off the little stage where he'd been showing slides and a movie clip of harvest. The black and white movie looked like it had been shot on 8mm film sometime in the '50s and later transferred to video. Jonathon had an array of leaves, nuts, and pieces of wood that he allowed the children to touch and sniff. He warned them again to never put any part of the hickory in their mouths.

"I'M WAYNE SAVAGE," the teacher standing next to Gee said by way of introduction.

"Gee, George Evars, but just Gee is fine."

"Nice to meet you. This is my first day with the kids. School starts Monday, but since I needed orientation, we arranged to have my class orientation at the same time," Wayne said.

"You're new in town?"

"Yes. Just took a job teaching first grade. The uh… culture here is pretty shocking for a newcomer," Wayne admitted.

"Have you walked in the Forest yet?" Gee asked.

"I confess that I just arrived last week and between finding a place to live and getting my classroom ready, I haven't had much chance to explore. I've heard about it, though."

"When you get a chance to walk in the Forest, you'll appreciate why the town loves it. I was a little confused by all the excitement, but it's a magical… no, I should say mystical place. Just remember not to take anything out of the Forest with you. It's against the law."

"I heard him say that. You sound like you had first-hand experience."

"That's why I'm in orientation."

The children broke up around Jonathon and Wayne moved to collect his charges and get them out to the bus. Jonathon came to talk to Gee.

"Well? Did you like it?"

"It's amazing, Jonathon. I'm glad I got the kids' orientation. I'll be humming that little tune all week."

"Gram Parsons and the Byrds from way back in 1968. You should hear the Nussbaum Quartet arrangement. We wrote mostly our own lyrics to be right for the kids and picked up the tempo."

"I think an adult orientation might have been overwhelming."

"We dumb it down for the adults," Jonathon laughed. "They simply can't take in as much information as children can. I think the foresters spend more time corralling and correcting adults during Harvest than helping. But we try to keep it fun. Which brings me to you. How would you like to have fun during Harvest?"

"Jonathon, you know I'll do any job you give me. I'm almost as excited about my first Harvest as those children are."

"I'm going to make you a shaker," Jonathon said.

"I'm all ears."

"You'll need to come out to the Forest for a further orientation. Doing anything tomorrow?"

"I usually take a walk in the Forest on Sundays."

"I'll meet you at ten and do your job orientation then."

Legitimacy

"HELLO, COUSIN," KAREN whispered to the young woman sitting in the park. She sat next to her and stared up at the statue of the Seven Heroes. It wasn't like they were the only ones who enlisted in the Second World War. Or even the only ones who were killed. There was a plaque of names on the back of the memorial, and it had been added to with soldiers killed in Korea, Viet Nam, and the Middle East.

"Uh… Excuse me? Do I know you?"

"Mmm. Probably not. You might recognize my name, but we've never met. What do you get out of coming down here every day to spit on the memorial?"

"I don't… How do you know?"

"Your grandmother has been coming here every day for sixty years. It's the worst kept secret in Rosebud Falls. They even started organizing rides for her when she moved into the retirement home. Everyone turns their back when she spits on the memorial. And now you."

"I didn't know the story until she told me last week. What a foul thing for him to do."

"Yes. If he'd done it." Karen listened to the catch in Jo's breathing as what she said sank in.

"What do you mean, 'if?' My grandmother is seventy-five years old. That bastard is the only one who didn't recognize his child and her mother."

"I love when the illegitimate child calls her father a bastard."

"I think I've heard enough."

"Not if you want a part of the Roth fortune. The part that rightfully belongs to you."

Jo sat back on the bench and looked at Karen expectantly—cautiously—waiting for the story.

"My great-grandmother, Miriam Roth, was the sister of your great-grandfather, the well spat-upon Joseph Roth," Karen began.

"After whom, by the way, you were named even over your grandmother's protests. That makes us third cousins if I counted correctly. The current patriarch of the Roth family, Benjamin, is 91 years old and hasn't been seen outside his house in five years. My great-grandmother would have nothing to do with her younger brother. He has no sons. Isn't that remarkable? Our common ancestor, Aaron Roth had two sons and a daughter and not one of them sired or bore a son. So, Leah Augello decided to hyphenate her name to Roth-Augello and, after getting her husband to convert from Catholicism to Judaism, further managed to get him to change his name so the Roth appellation would survive. Our family comprises fools, Jo Ransom. You are as much a Roth as our cousins, the incompetent sons of Leah Roth-Augello."

"You are," Jo snapped bitterly. "That bastard never acknowledged my grandmother as his child."

"Ah, but he did," Karen whispered. "That's what this is all about. Not our great-grandparents, but their father."

Date Night

GEE MET KAREN in the park after his orientation. "I won't be able to get together tomorrow," Gee explained. "I've been assigned a Harvest job and need to go to the Forest for training."

"What job have you been assigned?"

"I'm supposed to become a shaker."

"Oh, my."

"Is that bad?"

"No. It's wonderful. Very prestigious. It just means that every woman in Rosebud Falls will swoon for you. You'll be getting lots of offers, Gee."

"Um… You know what we talked about last Sunday… about dating and focusing on each other? That still holds for me, Karen."

"Mmm. I like that and I'm just teasing. A little. It's true that shakers get a lot of attention and I might get jealous a little. But I trust you. We have a long way to go in our relationship. I'm sure we'll have little ups and downs, but more than anything else, I trust you."

They took a long walk by the river and turned back on Main Street.

"I... don't feel much like battling the crowd at the ice cream parlor," Karen said. "Especially since I have ice cream at home. Would you... um... like to come to my place for a dish of ice cream?"

"Really? I'd love to... sit and talk with you... some more."

"Just talk and ice cream. You know?"

"I get you."

"THIS PLACE IS a mansion, Karen!"

"It's kind of posh. I rattle around here by myself. Maybe I should open it up as a boarding house. I mostly just use the kitchen and sitting room. And my bedroom upstairs. Sorry about all the plastic covering things. I just haven't had the motivation or time to make it more livable." Karen dipped bowls of ice cream in the kitchen as Gee stared through the open passage to a living room larger than the Panzas' entire house.

"Karen? How...?"

"My great-grandmother. She passed away this spring and it turned out that I'm her only heir. Believe me, in addition to the furniture, this house comes with a lot of baggage."

"So, you are a Family heir?"

"Let's not dwell on that, okay? But... um... speaking of Families..." She handed him his ice cream and led him to a comfortable sitting room with well-worn furniture. They sat at opposite ends of the overstuffed sofa and faced each other. "I think you should know more about some of the local politics."

"Politics is a subject I tend to ignore. I just want to be a good person."

"Good people are well-informed. There will be news on Tuesday after Labor Day that threatens to turn things topsy-turvy. You don't need to take a side, but about everyone else in Rosebud Falls will. There will be a ballot measure announced to annex roughly another square mile on the south side of the City. That square mile includes Savage Sand and Gravel and Calvary Tabernacle. Neither of those two entities can vote, but between the work force at the quarry and the members of the church, there will be a lot of opposition."

"Why annex it?"

"There is a segment of hickory woodland in the annex that has grown wild for over a hundred years. At the turn of the twentieth century, it was maintained and harvested the same as the rest of the Forest. But it was outside the city limits and was mysteriously withdrawn from management. It's been fenced off ever since."

"Why wasn't it part of the original City?"

"That's almost two hundred years ago. It's part of the legend of the eighth Family. And the mystique of the Savage family, who all but disappeared fifty or sixty years ago."

"Savages?" Gee mused, thinking of where he'd recently heard the name. Of course, he'd rented a safe deposit box at Savage Credit Union.

"The quarry. The Savages were stone-cutters. In addition to three hundred acres of unmanaged forest, the area holds a rich bed of rose limestone. Over the years, they've cut most of the usable stone out and the company is contemplating clear-cutting the rest of the Forest to open up more area for quarrying. They mostly just ship sand and gravel now."

"That would be terrible! They can't just cut all the trees down."

"You see? You are already as passionate about it as the Families."

"I can't imagine one of the Families proposing a clear-cut."

"I just hope it is not more sinister than that. The land isn't owned by the Savages, but they have a mineral rights lease. If the area is annexed, however, the city can proscribe certain kinds of exploitation." Karen sighed. "In the two months between the announcement and the election, I'll be doing a lot of investigation into Savage Sand and Gravel and trying to figure out how that church got established there. Things just don't add up."

"Will you be safe? I worry that my partner puts herself in danger."

"Am I your partner, Gee?"

"I didn't mean to imply…"

Karen set her bowl aside and took Gee's as she scooted over on the couch next to him. Gee caught his breath as she leaned in.

"We're progressing, Gee. We've known each other two months. We're not ready for life-long commitments today, but I think we're ready for our first kiss."

She brushed her lips softly across his.

KAREN WENT QUIETLY about her nighttime ritual, the taste of Gee's lips still on her tongue. Their first kiss. They'd held each other's eyes for several minutes before Gee stood and carried their empty ice cream bowls to the kitchen. She walked him to the door and he kissed her again before he left. She almost asked him to stay.

The doorbell rang and she thought perhaps he just couldn't stay away. She bounced down the stairs, pulling a light robe around her.

She knew she should check the peephole before answering, but her hand turned the bolt of its own volition and she flung the door wide.

"Karen…"

People Like Us

"WERE YOU WAITING on the street until he left? Are you stalking me?" Karen demanded.

"It's not like that, Karen. I didn't want to interrupt anything."

"Then why are you here?"

"I love you. You know that. We're good together."

"Troy, we were good together as long as we didn't get out of bed. It's over."

"Don't throw me over for that outsider, Karen."

"It was over long before that outsider ever got to town, Troy. I told you then and I'm telling you now. It's over."

"You don't know anything about him. He might not even be who he says he is."

"Don't. Don't even try to tear him down. We've known each for two months. Even if it isn't his real name, I know who he is. In here, Troy. In my heart."

"I love you, Karen. Marry me." Karen looked at Troy with her eyes wide. *Surely, even Troy Cavanaugh can't be this dense.*

"They don't make wedding vows for people like us. What are you going to promise, Troy? To forsake all others until I'm out of sight?"

"She was a mistake. A one-time thing."

"You missed my warning label, Troy. 'Does not play well with others. Dangerous to small pets.' You had your chance. Now, please go away."

"Karen…"

She closed the door, thankful that at least he hadn't stepped inside. She threw the bolt just as he rattled the handle. Back in her room upstairs she splashed water on her face, washing away unwelcome tears of anger.

Anger that she could no longer taste Gee's kiss.

6

SWEET HOME

Unforgiven

"THIS IS the body of our Lord Jesus Christ, broken for our sins. And this is his blood, shed for their remission," Pastor Beck intoned. The elements sat on his desk as he blessed them. He stirred the cup, adding a measured amount of Lustre Plus to the grape juice. His use of drug variations over the past ten years had greatly enhanced his ministry and his success rate in taming the wild and undisciplined children who were sent to him. The weekly communion service with a trace dose left his congregants more open to the Word as well.

He spared a glance at the recalcitrant child kneeling naked at the rail in his private office. This one would learn. The rebellious mind would be wiped clean in the blood of Christ and the child would know only obedience. He dipped a piece of bread in the cup and stepped in front of the child, careful to avoid dripping the juice.

"Open and receive the cleansing power of God." The child obeyed and Beck shoved the soggy wad into the child's open mouth. The first dose was always the riskiest and Beck relaxed now that it had been administered. "Now let your mind be emptied of all and be prepared for the Holy Spirit's baptism."

Throughout the afternoon Beck continued to give small doses to the child as he systematically destroyed all sense of self-identity. It was exhausting work, but God was his strength and would see him through.

Deacon and Dr. Jones were in the kitchen where he could call to them if he needed assistance, but it was best if no one witnessed his method. The doctor was a chemist, not a medical doctor, but could take care of things should the child prove unable to handle the drug.

Beck knew he sinned, but it was to make the child holy. To take the child's sinful nature upon himself was a heavy burden, but God would not take this cup from him and Beck would not pass the responsibility to anyone else.

As the child's mind melted under the influence of the drug and the preacher's words, Beck alternated punishment and comfort. He built fantasies in the child's mind—a new reality. He issued a new name. He redefined good and evil. He used the child as a vessel for his lust and God's blessing. And in the end, a child awoke broken to His divine will.

----⊲◆⊳----

THE DOCTOR LED the child away to lodge with the others who were being renewed. In the camp, training would continue, and additional monitored doses of the drug would be administered to be sure the training set.

Pastor Beck continued to kneel naked at the altar as Deacon Stewart sat in an armchair, patiently waiting until the minister had overcome his guilt. Deacon could tell immediately that the reprogramming of the child had been successful. The sale would more than compensate for Beck's guilt.

"Must I do more today?" Beck asked wearily. He rose and put on a robe before sitting behind his desk.

"No, Lance. You've done well," the Deacon said. "God will surely be pleased with your faithfulness."

"I hate them, you know," Beck answered vaguely. "They come to me fouled from life on the streets, with unfaithful parents, abandoned in orphanages. They come to me with murk covering their minds and I must take it all upon myself. I hate them, for *I* am convicted of their guilt. I will never forgive them. They have made me into what I am."

The Deacon nodded in sympathy. However Beck had to justify his actions made no difference to him. The result was obedient little slaves and there was always a market for the 'purified' souls he sold. As far as

Beck knew, they were treated and returned to their homes. Whatever. The preacher left that up to the camp board.

"We have another problem," Deacon said. "The aborted rescue of the child at the fair may have resulted in identifying our messenger. We needn't worry about the little girl—she was a target of opportunity—but the man who stepped in could create problems. He is the only wildcard we have to deal with at the moment."

"And Judas went out and hanged himself," Beck muttered.

"Yes. I believe we can arrange for him to remove himself from the field."

Homecoming

"Gee! How did your extra training for the Forest go?" Wayne asked when he saw Gee in the stands for the football game. Karen squeezed Gee's hand as the new teacher joined them.

"It was great. Wayne, this is my… friend, Karen. Karen, Wayne is a new first grade teacher here."

"Nice to meet you, Wayne. You were in orientation with Gee?"

"Yes. I was with twenty-five children who don't know quite what to do with a big scary man as their teacher. At the moment, I'm riding on a wave of awe like Poseidon of the Seas."

"A classicist! The poor children of Rosebud Falls. They could become educated," Karen quipped.

"They'll survive. I'm not so sure about me. So, spill it, Gee. What task are you being assigned for Harvest?"

"I'm going to be a shaker," Gee said. "Jonathon started me out climbing poles at the forester's headquarters. It took most of the day. Full orientation on safety equipment and then practice on a tree. I had a blast. I haven't climbed a tree since… in… I know I've done it, but it was a long time ago." Gee stopped and tried to puzzle out his knowledge of having climbed a tree. Karen squeezed his hand and reached into her bag for a pad of paper and a pen.

"Did you climb for fun or for work?" she asked just loudly enough for Gee to hear her over the noise of the stands. The game was about to start.

"It was definitely fun, but I don't know if I climbed trees for a job. What kind of job would that be? Forester? Lumberman? Arborist? I enjoyed climbing trees, but none of those names seem to fit," Gee said. Karen wrote down the notes. Wayne watched them with interest and she put away the notebook.

"I've never heard of a school having its homecoming football game so early," Wayne said. "It really surprised me that it was the first game of the season."

"It's been that way for years. It's because of the uncertainty of Harvest," Karen answered. "Both schools use the first game of the season as homecoming. Crosstown rivals. The same game is homecoming for both of them since they both play on this field. The rest of the season they rotate home and away games so there's a game here nearly every Friday until Thanksgiving."

"Flor del Día?" Gee asked, looking at the scoreboard. "Is it a Spanish school? Or Catholic?"

"Quite a history. It started as the Soldiers' and Sailors' Children's Home after the Civil War, but swiftly changed to a reform school. No one was happy about that, so by World War I it was just considered an orphanage with its own school. There was a big boom in private boarding schools after World War II and even though it maintains a high percentage of orphans, it is the children of wealthy New Englanders who pay the bills now. There was a big schism over the teaching of religion in the school that resulted in the little church school in South Rosebud breaking off from it. But that has never been big enough to merit consideration for sports. It's more like homeschool combined with extended Sunday School. But Flor del Día is selective. No *orphan* has ever been turned away, but those who board as outsiders must meet rigid academic and social qualifications. They have to fit into Rosebud Falls."

"Who pays for the orphans?" Wayne asked.

"The Families all take a share, but particularly the Cavanaughs," Karen said. "Oh, sorry. You're new here. When someone says 'the Families' they mean the seven founding Families of Rosebud Falls. Cavanaugh, Roth, Poltanys, Nussbaum, Meagher, Savage, and Lazorack. If you go back far enough, probably everyone born in this town is related to one of the Families within a few degrees of separation."

"Hey, your last name is Savage, isn't it, Wayne?" Gee asked. Karen's head snapped toward Gee's friend.

"Yes. Not related though, I'm sure. Look! He's going to intercept that!"

THE ROSEBUD FIREFLIES overcame the Flor del Día Bitternuts in the last few minutes of a lively game.

"Wayne, I'm always interested in capturing a little bit about new arrivals in town, especially when they are in a place of importance like our school. Would you consent to an interview sometime soon? Just a human interest piece." Wayne took Karen's offered card.

"Be careful what you agree to," Gee laughed. "This is our seventh interview."

"Gee," Karen said softly, "I think we decided this was our third date."

"That really puts it in a different perspective, doesn't it?" he responded.

"I'll give the interview idea some thought," Wayne said. "I really need to focus on lesson-planning and getting the kids ready for their first Harvest right now."

"Of course," Karen said brightly. "Just give me a call when you can."

The Victim

GEE PLANNED TO spend as much time over Labor Day weekend with Karen as he could. He was in love. He'd known it since the first night he spent in Rosebud Falls, but now he was certain. After the game Friday night, they had returned to Karen's house 'for ice cream' but had spent the better part of two hours simply making out on the sofa. It was difficult for both of them to stop and for Gee to go home. They planned another date for Saturday night and a walk in the Forest for Sunday.

He went to the market Saturday morning to help prep for Harvest week. No one knew exactly when Harvest would begin, so the town spent the first week of September getting ready. At the store, he began the cold job of thoroughly cleaning and restocking the dairy cases.

Gee moved on to roll the fresh goods from the bakery to their cases. Commercial breads were all stocked by the vendors, but Grimm's small bakery produced artisan bread, cookies, cakes, and doughnuts. The bakers were always happy for Gee's assistance in stocking and it was especially welcome on Saturday morning. Though Rosebud Falls was slow in waking up most weekends, by ten o'clock, the store would be full of people doing their weekly shopping and wanting morning snacks.

"Gee! I need bacon and a side of beef," Rupert said, coming up to him. Gee turned around. It was unlike Rupert to be sharp with him. He saw the butcher slightly stooped over with a hand on his hip. "I twisted my back and I can't lift it," the older man said.

That explained a lot and Gee hurried to get the cuts from the meat locker for Rupert. The locker was cold, but not freezing. Gee decided to get the beef for Rupert first, as the butcher would want to work on that while Gee sliced bacon.

"Sorry I was snappy," Rupert said. "It just kills me to not be able to lift my own carcass."

"It's not a problem, Rupert. Is there anything else I can do to help?"

"Get the bacon sliced while I start working on this. When you're done, I'll show you how to cut filets. The Cavanaughs are having a family gathering on Labor Day and ordered six twelve-ounce cuts. Loren's been around a long time and knows his beef almost as well as I do. He wants the strips to serve the younger generation and rib steaks for a couple of the cousins who play sports. We'll do mostly steaks this morning." Even though he was obviously in pain, Rupert was regaining some of his easy-going nature as he moved about the butcher shop. Gee wondered if it was the result of pain medicine or simply that Rupert was in the environment that he loved.

When the steaks were all prepared and a few more cuts were ready for the display case, Rupert asked Gee to return the remainder of the carcass to the locker. "I'm just not up to dealing with shoulder and rump today," he said. Gee loaded the remaining sections of beef on a cart and wheeled them to the locker, hanging what he could and making sure anything shelved was on protective butcher's paper. As he left the walk-in refrigerator, he was startled by Rena's voice.

"You came for me!" Rena stumbled as she walked toward Gee.

RENA RECOGNIZED THE man sent to her with the drug. She'd seen him before and even suggested to Pastor Beck that he seemed like a nice man and might be a good mate for her. The pastor had shaken his head sadly and told her that Brother Reef had taken a vow of celibacy, kind of like a monk. Then he'd given her communion and she'd forgotten about him until he met her as she walked to work Saturday morning.

"We thought you might need a refresher and this is something new from the doctor," Brother Reef said. For some reason, she was never quite able to focus on the man's face. "It's a step above what you've had before. You should try it now." She didn't hesitate to pop it in her mouth and listen to the monk's instructions.

Rena began a sultry walk toward Gee, only stumbling slightly over the crack in the concrete floor that seemed deeper than the last time she walked here. She should have waited to take the drug until she got to the restroom like she usually did, but he'd said to take it now. The high and the fantasy it induced overwhelmed her almost immediately. And then Gee was there and she needed to talk to him about standing her up at the fair. She walked toward him, releasing the top button of her shirt.

The button felt too large for the buttonhole, so she tore at her blouse, determined to attract Gee to her. Others crowded around in her mind. Former fantasies she could not disconnect from.

"No! Not you! Wait your turn!" she screamed at them. Lustre was never like this before. She could always control the fantasy. But now, all her imaginary lovers pressed in on her, threatening to overwhelm her. She felt Gee reaching for her as she stumbled forward and lashed out again—biting, scratching. All the fantasies of her life rebelled and attacked her as one. She desperately fought them.

SOMETHING DIDN'T LOOK right to Gee. He was used to seeing Rena at least a little high, her glassy-eyed grin as she looked at everything around her. But this time her pupils were fully dilated and her breathing seemed stressed.

"Rena, are you all right?" Gee asked. Her response was mumbled, and she reached for the decorative buttons on her pullover blouse.

"Rena? You need to sit down and wait it out. Do you need help?" He reached out to steady her and she suddenly ripped the top of her blouse. It wasn't far, but it was all the indication that Gee needed that this was not one of Rena's normal highs. He reached for the wall phone by the meat locker door.

"This is 911. State the nature of your emergency, please."

"This is Gee Evars at Grimm's Market and Meats. One of my co-workers is having some kind of fit. She's unsteady on her feet and her pupils are fully dilated. She's hitting at empty air and is mumbling. The words I can catch don't make sense." Rena shouted at him to get away but swung wildly while she was still several feet from him.

"EMTs have been dispatched. Has she taken any drugs that she might be reacting to that you know of."

"She's often high on something. This is worse than I've ever seen her. Ow! She's hitting me! And the wall and…"

"Try to comfort her with words and see if she can settle herself down."

"Rena, it's me. Gee. You're okay. You're safe here. No one will try to harm you. You're okay," Gee said as he backed away from her flailing arms. She was singly focused, though, and kept tracking Gee. She swung and scratched him across the face. "Ow! Rena, stop it. This isn't working."

"Help is on the way. Can she be safely restrained?"

"I can try, but…" Rena jumped on Gee, knocking the phone from his grip.

"I'll kill you!" she screamed. "I'll kill all of you!" Rena hit the wall with her head as if she had been thrown there and flailed against the air with her nails scratching at nothing. Without further guidance from the emergency line, Gee took a deep breath and moved in to try to restrain Rena so she wouldn't hurt herself or him further. She struck at him again and raked him with her nails.

Gee managed to get one arm around her and pin her right arm against her side. Rena was completely out of control now and threw herself from side to side, elbowing Gee behind her. When he managed to get both arms pinned to her side, she threw her head back and smashed into his nose, screaming.

"Gee! What is the meaning of this?" Rupert yelled.

"Help! Rape! Help!" Rena screamed. That was all the signal Rupert needed and he smashed a cola bottle against the side of Gee's head.

Emergency Room

"JUST LIE THERE and don't try anything." The voice sounded familiar. Gee raised his hand to feel his head and found that handcuffs held him to the bed rail and straps crossed his chest and arms. He opened his eyes to find Detective Oliver staring down at him. The left side of the detective's mouth was drawn back in a snarl that caused his left eye to squint.

"What…? Is Rena okay?"

"Do you mean did you rape her? Rupert Grimm put an end to that. That girl is in bad shape."

"I wasn't raping her. She was having a fit. I tried to help."

"Rupert said when he got to the room you were grabbing her and she was fighting you while yelling for help. Fortunately, EMTs arrived just as she passed out. They settled her onto a backboard. Doctors will know how much you hurt her soon."

"Mead, I was trying to help. I was on the line with 911 and they said to try and restrain her."

"You were what?" Mead bellowed. He stood up abruptly and stepped outside the room with his phone to his ear. Ellie gave the detective a shove out of her way to enter through the emergency room curtains.

"How are you feeling, Gee?" she asked grabbing his wrist to take his pulse. She felt the handcuffs. "Mead! What do you think you're doing?" Before Gee could answer, Mead stepped back into the cubicle with his phone still to his ear and a look of disgust on his face.

"What a cluster…" he stopped and shoved his phone in his pocket as he reached for his keys. "Why hasn't the doctor been in before now?" Mead demanded.

"Doc did triage as they were brought in and determined that Gee was just knocked out and would recover. That girl, on the other hand. Gee saved her life."

"What happened? Is she okay?" Gee asked.

"She overdosed," Ellie said.

"We got two emergency calls within a minute or two of each other. Different operators. One dispatched emergency aid from the fire department with an ambulance. The other dispatched two patrol cars to stop an assault and rape. The woman who called police said you were raping the girl."

"Is she okay?" Gee insisted, not really caring about why he was in the hospital or had been handcuffed to the bed.

"She's going to recover. Dr. Poltanys is still with her. They hit her with Naxalone and then started treatment for hallucinogens. They're still trying to get a positive ID on the drug," Ellie said.

"Drugs. Here in Rosebud Falls," Mead said disgustedly. "I guess our days of being a sleepy little burg with no big city problems are over."

"You mean being a desert full of sand for the community to keep its heads buried in," Ellie snapped. Mead grimaced.

"Gee! I can't believe this. Please tell me you didn't!" Karen exclaimed as she barged into the cubicle. She spotted Mead. "Has he been charged with something?" Mead shook his head.

"A screw-up between 911 operators," Mead said. "Two calls at once with different emergencies and police and paramedics who got caught in the middle. Ellie says Gee saved another life."

"And paid for it," Ellie said. "He's pretty banged up."

"Oh, thank God. I knew it couldn't be true," Karen said as she rushed to Gee and put kisses on his forehead. He tensed when she brushed his nose. "You're hurt!"

"He was trying to restrain a girl who was having seizures and she got a few good licks in. The officers got in a few more," Ellie scowled.

"His lawyers are going to have a great time with this one," Mead groaned. "Our whole emergency response system is going to get reviewed."

"They'll be here shortly. I called them from the car as I was on my way," Karen said.

"How did you know?" Gee asked.

"I called your house to tell you I needed to run out of town and couldn't get together tonight as we planned. Nathan was in a mad panic. Rupert told him you were a rapist and to get your things out of the house and away from his daughter. Marian was wailing in the background. I got the police blotter and found out you'd been brought here."

"I guess I'm homeless again," Gee sighed.

"You'll *never* be homeless again, Gee," Karen said vehemently. "I want… I want you to live with me. I've got all that room in the house. I told you I thought I should open a boarding house." Gee looked at Karen's tear-filled eyes and lifted his head to softly kiss her lips.

"Mead, have you arrested our client?" Gretchen LaCoe demanded as she entered the curtained cubicle. It was getting crowded. Jack, trailing a step behind his wife, came directly to Gee.

"Gee, I advise you not to say anything until we know exactly what is going on, do you understand?" he said softly. Gee nodded.

"Just another misunderstanding," he said.

"Why do they all revolve around you?"

"Excuse me, but can I get close enough to examine the patient?" Dr. Poltanys asked sarcastically. "Or should we have a cake delivered to celebrate our resident hero."

"I just tried to help," Gee said. He was embarrassed that tears were leaking from his eyes. This had been more horrifying than diving into the river. Poltanys didn't try to chase anyone out of the room, but the curtains bulged outward as they moved back to give him space to examine Gee. He checked Gee's eyes, the knot on his head, and the bruises and scratches on his cheeks, hands, and neck. He pressed lightly on Gee's ribs causing another wince. "So, what do you remember?" Poltanys asked.

"Everything, I guess," Gee said. "Up until I was knocked out and then woke up here with Detective Oliver growling at me."

"What's your name?"

"George Edward Evars. Most folks call me Gee."

"Where do you live?"

"683 Joshua Street. At least I did until they kicked me out."

"Where are you from?"

"I'm from…" It was like walking into a fog. The answer seemed to be just ahead, but he couldn't grasp it. He shook his head and then grimaced. "I remember everything back to the day I jumped in the river."

Poltanys nodded. "I was hoping Rupert Grimm had arrived at a solution to your memory problem. Why is he restrained?" Poltanys started removing the belts across Gee's chest and arms. He was still wearing the rubber apron he'd used while helping Rupert.

"Initially, it was to keep him from waking up and going for his head or cuts," Ellie said. "Then Mead…"

"I did not order restraints," the detective said. "I removed the cuffs our arresting officer placed on him. The restraints are your idea."

"I suppose that was because our other patient identified him as her assailant and rapist," Poltanys said as he began loosening the straps. Mead reached for the handcuffs. The doctor looked up at him. "As well as a list of thirty-two other men and seventeen women." He looked around the cubicle. "Including everyone in this room."

"She's mental," Mead sighed.

"Drugged," Poltanys answered. "We've seen it before and have submitted blood samples to the CDC. We've never had a case like this one. I think it's a new variant of the drug Lustre. I've been tracking it for several weeks, but most cases seem to just be disoriented or sometimes a little nauseous. Those we've interviewed profess they think it's harmless and just enhances their fantasy lives. The most common place we've seen it is among online gamers who think it makes their gaming more lifelike."

"We have that here?" Oliver spluttered.

"Most that I've been consulted on have been in the city, but we've seen one or two here in Rosebud Falls. Lustre's chemical makeup is a cross between opioids and mescaline called RDH. This dose was different—stronger—than we've seen before."

"Would you be willing to serve on a task force, Dr. Poltanys?" Gretchen asked. "I'll talk to Judge Warren and get a select committee together. We need to know how deeply this has wormed its way into our community. Detective, you'll represent our police force, of course," she said looking at him pointedly.

"Of course," Mead sighed. He looked resigned rather than enthusiastic.

Going Home

GEE AND KAREN stood on the front porch of the Panzas' house and rang the bell. His backpack and sleeping bag lay next to the door on the porch. Nathan opened the inside door but did not release the chain.

"Everything is on the porch. You don't need to come in or ever come back," Nathan said angrily. "I can't believe you're out of jail! How could you attack that vulnerable girl?"

"I didn't."

"Rupert saw you!"

"Rupert saw Gee attempting to keep an overdosed girl from harming herself," Karen broke in. "He wasn't attacking her."

"But…"

"He was on the line with 911 and following instructions when Rupert clocked him. The LaCoes might advise bringing charges against him."

"No," Gee interrupted. "Rupert acted on what he saw. I'd be thankful if my friends came to my aid like he came to Rena's."

"I know, Gee, but this treatment is stupid. You'd think *friends* would have more trust."

"Maybe we acted… hastily," Nathan admitted. He unfastened the chain and opened the inside door but did not move to open the storm door. "But the shock of hearing Rupert. He's in bad shape."

"He shouldn't be upset about what he did," Gee soothed.

"It's not about what he did. Be thankful he didn't have one of his knives on him. But when he swung at you, his back went into spasms so badly he can't stand up."

"His back was hurting all morning," Gee said. "I'm sorry it got worse."

"Onyx got him home. She'll take care of him."

"So…"

"We need some time," Nathan said. "Marian and Devon cried themselves to sleep. The stress of having you always arrested or in a hospital or riding to save someone's life is just too much for our little home. Can you… Is there any way you can give us a few days?"

"You have a place to stay, Gee," Karen said softly. "Truly."

"Uh… Do I still have a job?"

"I'll talk to Frieda and make sure your job is secure. Maybe though, take Monday off. It's a holiday."

Gee nodded, picked up his pack and turned to leave with Karen. Then he turned back to Nathan.

"Please. Tell Marian… And Devon… I'll miss them… you all."

"KAREN, ARE YOU sure you want to invite me into your home?" Gee asked as they pulled into her drive. "It's not like when I first got to Rosebud Falls. I have cash now. I could rent a room… Maybe at the Fairview."

"Grab your bag and let me show you your room," she answered. He followed her into the house and up the stairs to a fully furnished room. His attic bedroom at the Panzas' would have fit a couple of times in this room. It had a private bath off one side.

"This is far more than I need," Gee stammered as he looked down at his backpack. He had added a few things in the two months he'd lived in Rosebud Falls, but his pack still felt light.

"In my grandmother's mansion are many houses," Karen misquoted the Bible. Gee looked at her curiously. "My mother was Jewish, but my father was Lutheran. I learned to hate them both."

"Ouch."

"I know. That's a little harsh. I didn't… don't hate them. It's just that religion seems like such a waste. Still, I know one or two who actually live what they preach, and they are good people. What would you like to do for dinner tonight?" she asked, abruptly changing the subject.

"I thought you needed to cancel our date tonight. And here you've spent half the day coming to my rescue," Gee laughed. "Again. You can go ahead with your plans."

"Canceled them. A little disappointment, but I can make it up next weekend. I'll be out of town next Saturday night, so we'll have to make the most of our Friday night date."

"Are we going to have a Friday night date?"

"I hope so. So… Dinner?"

"Let's try that Italian place on the south side of town."

"Pizza?"

"No, the one across the street. What is it? Picolino?"

"I'm glad you chose that one and not the chain restaurant next to Walmart."

Gee thought for a few moments, lost in an existential crisis. He didn't respond at first when Karen called his name. He developed a knot in his stomach and felt vaguely disoriented. He sat on the edge of the bed.

"Gee! Are you all right?" Karen was getting frantic. He raised his hand to her.

"I'm... I think I'm fine. I just suddenly got dizzy and felt lost," he explained.

"Maybe we should go back to the doctor."

"I'm fine now. Really. I don't think it had anything to do with getting hit in the head. I do have a little headache from that, but like Doc Poltanys said, I'll take an aspirin."

"If you're sure," Karen said hesitantly. "I'm going to be watching you, though." Gee looked up at her and smiled.

"Karen... Really... You can't imagine how good that makes me feel."

They kissed until Gee pushed her away slightly and touched his nose gingerly.

"I think I need that aspirin."

"Oh! I didn't mean to hurt you!"

"I think if I had to suffer like that every time we kissed, I'd want to cut the frequency to maybe fifty or a hundred times a day."

"We don't kiss fifty or a... Oh, you sweetheart! Let's get you an aspirin and go to dinner."

HE WAS LIVING with Karen. Perhaps that was overstating the situation, but they *were* sharing a house. He tried not to dwell on the few awkward moments before they parted for bed the previous evening. They hadn't really wanted to separate and go to their own rooms, but Gee knew they weren't ready to tumble into bed, no matter how attracted they were to each other. He tried not to infringe on her normal daily routine, but they ran into each other frequently. Starting with breakfast.

Karen made coffee and sat across the breakfast nook table. Gee sampled the coffee hesitantly and broke into a broad grin.

"A privilege of the Families—having Birdie's coffee."

"You give too much credit to an accident of birth. It's all about money and the Families aren't the only ones who are rich. Most people can treat themselves to an occasional *cup* of Birdie's best Blue Mountain coffee, but it costs $25 a pound to buy it in beans. That's not in most people's grocery budget. With wealth comes addiction."

"Addiction? I know that caffeine is technically an addictive drug. Birdie's coffee is no more than that, is it?"

"I don't think so. But people with a caffeine addiction can get their fix from Folgers. This is special. You stop at Birdie's almost every morning for a cup of this, don't you?"

"Yes. Funny, it never takes more than one cup. I suppose if it were a real addiction, I'd want more each day. I wonder…"

"Are you wondering if that is what happened to Rena? Addicted to her drug and stepped up the use too much? I wish we knew. Dr. Poltanys seemed to think it was a new, stronger variant rather than a higher dose. We need to know more about Lustre. Where does it come from and how is it escaping government notice? Is it always available at the same price or do the dealers keep soaking their marks for more and more as time goes by? What is it doing in our town?"

"That's exactly what I'm wondering. Maybe I can talk to Rena about it when we get back to work," Gee mused.

"Maybe you should let me talk to her. We don't know how she'll respond to you. Or me either for that matter. I was on her list of assailants."

"Well, what do you think is happening?"

"Legends and lore. Let's pack a picnic lunch and go for a walk in the Forest," Karen said, abruptly changing the subject. "I want to tell you all about it, but some of it is pretty unbelievable."

"Like a strange guy with no memory showing up in town and moving in with you?"

"Yeah. A lot like that."

Picnic in the Forest

"I LOVE COMING out here," Gee said. "It's always so peaceful. Kind of settling, like if I'm in the Forest, everything is right with the world."

"As long as you consider the world to be Rosebud Falls, you are probably right," Karen laughed softly. "If everyone who lives in town were here in the Forest—which most will be when Harvest starts—there would only be a density of about three people per acre. The Forest covers a third of the city and the wild woods extend south of town another mile."

"It's really a small town, isn't it?"

"Yeah. Not much of a ripple in the fabric of civilization. To those who live here, it is a world of its own," Karen said. They set out their picnic after walking along a path next to Silver Lake, farther north in the Forest than Gee had been before. Across the lake, they could see scattered houses on an otherwise barren plot of ground.

"It's so quiet out here."

"Most people only go to the conveniently-reached parts of the Forest. Even though the lake is attractive, this part of town is as remote as Rosebud Falls gets." Gee poured glasses of wine and toasted his companion as she talked.

"Tell me about the legends."

"Look at all the nuts." She picked up one that had fallen nearby. "A veritable smorgasbord for animals preparing for winter, don't you think? But listen. Not a squirrel, not a chipmunk in the Forest. Very few birds. No insects. Why do you think?"

"The pamphlet and orientation warned that the nuts were toxic. Are they poison even to wildlife?" he asked. Karen nodded.

"The only thing out here is the trees. In the wild woods there is a lot of underbrush and accompanying wild life, but the foresters have cleared everything except the hickory from the part that is inside the city limits. Technically, the nuts are a thin-shelled hickory, most closely related to the bitternut. But something in the soil has leached into the trees and turned them into lethal weapons of nature."

"It seems strange that they are protected and preserved. Harvested."

"I found interesting things among my great-grandmother's papers when I inherited. She was the family bad girl. Rebellious. A real hellion in the 30s and 40s and even worse when her brother was killed on D-Day. Her father doted on her, though, and gave her the mansion where we live now. Her younger brother, Benjamin, is ninety years old now and still ashamed of his big sister. Aaron, their father, moved in with his daughter in '72 and left Ben the big estate on the river. Aaron gave him the house, but Ben discovered it was devoid of the Family papers. Aaron brought all the records with him to his daughter's house. The will was very specific. I inherited the house and everything in it. So, I started sticking my nose in everything."

"You're good at it. And it's a cute nose," Gee said, kissing it.

"You are distracting me from the legends." She leaned in and they kissed passionately, forgetting all else for the moment. "You know the room I gave you is only temporarily yours, don't you, dear?" she gasped as they parted. Gee nodded. He was just a guest in her house until he got settled. "When we become lovers, we'll only need one room," she continued. "And we *will* become lovers." The conviction in her voice was matched only by the intensity of her next kiss. For a long time, the two lay on their blanket, softly petting and cooing to each other as the depth of their relationship dawned fully upon them. Perhaps not today or this week, but Gee was certain that they *would* be lovers… mates.

Eventually, they lay in a tight embrace, at peace with the future. Karen whispered the legends to Gee.

"Why don't we leave Rosebud Falls and move out west where no one knows us and we don't have to deal with Family politics?" Karen said abruptly. Gee felt his gut clench as if he'd been struck.

"I… We… Karen… That's just… I can't…"

"It hurts to even think about, doesn't it? I don't know how or where or when, but you are one of us," Karen said. "According to my great-great-grandfather Aaron, the forefathers believed the land—the Forest—somehow changed them. The Families are inextricably bound to the Forest. It's not *unheard* of for a Family member to leave and seek his fortune elsewhere, but in all Aaron's papers, I've only found one instance of the head of a Family leaving town. I know the Lazoracks and Cavanaughs and Savages have all been into the wild woods south of town, but it is really still part of the Forest, even if it is outside the City."

"And you think that because I feel uncomfortable when you talk about leaving that I'm one of the Family?"

"I believe that whatever binds the Families to the Forest has caught you as well. I left town to go to college and stayed away for seven years. Since I returned two years ago, it's become harder and harder for me to leave town when I go to conferences or to investigate something in the bigger cities. I can hardly wait to return. I think you are either related to one of the Families, or the Forest has claimed another."

"Is it scary to you? I mean, contemplating that you might never leave town again?" he asked.

"No. Now that I've found you… Now that I believe you are part of me… Somehow, the idea of never leaving town again is strangely comforting."

Family Holiday

"WE'VE BEEN HAD," Clark Cavanaugh declared. He'd been pacing around the Family barbecue all day, but Loren held his son off until the others were out of earshot. "The whole annexation is going to blow up on us."

"Calm down, Clark," Troy soothed his older brother. "I doubt it's as bad as you think."

"You should talk, with your window on Main. This is what's causing all the bad 'feelings' you've been having," Clark seethed. "You already failed your task. You were supposed to corral Weisman and get the Families hooked together. Now she's with the City Champion and nobody seems to be able to control him."

"That's all beside the point, Clark," Loren Cavanaugh sighed. His oldest son was competent at the Forest bookkeeping, but he wasn't much of a strategist. He glanced across the yard at his cousin Coretta and her brood. If her granddaughter, Jessie, married Jonathon Lazorack, the unification of the Families would move forward without his sons' participation. "What is the evidence that we've 'been had'?"

"I've been researching this because something didn't seem right to me," Clark said, calming down. "Troy isn't the only one in the Family who gets feelings. I couldn't put my finger on it because it's been so gradual, but now I know. The annex includes 105 households. It will add nearly three hundred souls to our population. But over the past five years, the land ownership has changed. When we started, there were sixty-seven landowners. Over the past five years, that number has dropped to forty-one landowners. Half the parcels in the annex have changed hands in the past five years and the number of owners has gone down by twenty-six. Someone has been buying up land in the annex. That means one of the Families is buying influence. More shares of the Forest once the annexation goes through."

"I don't see how that even compares with the problem of Savage Sand and Gravel. How many employees do they have in the City and the annex? And the church members?" Loren said, perusing Clark's spreadsheet.

"Don't think that doesn't worry me," Clark replied. "I've been watching SSG stock. I even bought a few shares. It used to be traded regularly. Publicly held. Not NYSE but traded in the OTC market. Trades have been declining for two years. It's almost impossible to buy SSG stock today. For a microcap, the price is through the roof."

"So, they've been preparing for the annexation, too," Loren sighed.

"The only thing that doesn't worry me about them is that they won't have a vote in the Forest. SSG doesn't own the land. They only lease the mineral rights. I think they've been bought up. Maybe a hostile takeover underway by someone who doesn't know the circumstances."

"So, what's our stance now, brother?" Troy asked. "Are you saying we should oppose the annexation?"

"No!" both brother and father exploded at the same time.

"We watch for opportunities and exploit them," Loren said. "There might be a developing situation that benefits us. And we keep working toward Family unification. Maybe you should pay attention to Laura Lazorack, Troy."

"The gravesitter? I don't think so," Troy moaned. "I don't like trying to poach another man's woman. And she is plain weird. They've been engaged for five years."

"Look at it this way, brother," Clark sneered. "Jude Roth-Augello doesn't have any more common sense than you do. It should be an even match."

Headlines

"ANNEXATION OF SOUTH Rosebud Moves Forward," read the headline on the front of Tuesday's *Mirror*.

Under the State's Home Rule provision for small municipalities, Rosebud Falls and the unincorporated section of Elmont County known as South Rosebud will vote on November sixth to unify under a single banner. The annexation of South Rosebud will provide the community with City services, including police and fire protection, water, sewer, and electric. The City of Rosebud Falls will also gain the benefits of a wider tax base and access to the area's natural resources. A planned community along Aldo Lake is also proposed. The annexation requires a double majority, that being a majority of votes in the current City and a majority of votes cast in the annexed district.

"How did this get so far without coming to our attention before now?" Deacon demanded of his board members. He had spent twenty years manipulating the company and the board of SSG so that they could claim ownership of the property in addition to mineral rights. He was certain he could prove adverse possession but bringing City government into the mix would complicate matters. And additional oversight would threaten his other operations. He'd lose control of the wild woods.

"It looks like the whole thing was planned by the Families," Matt Hogue replied. "We have no influence when it comes to dealing with them and their meetings aren't part of public record."

"It still had to get through the State Legislature."

"It was part of the Home Rule agreement that allowed various small municipalities limited right of eminent domain to extend utilities and infrastructure." Matt was the legal voice for the company and the only one Deacon addressed.

"Which means?"

"Which means that once South Rosebud is annexed and becomes part of the City of Rosebud Falls, we can expect all the wild woods to be expropriated and transferred to City ownership."

"We need to stop this. Dead."

Living Together

"I'm DREADING GOING to Palmyra Saturday," Karen said as they cuddled on the sofa Thursday evening. Gee had returned to work on Tuesday amid apologies from the Grimms and Panzas. He had, however, turned down the invitation to return to his room at Nathan and Marian's. Karen was pleased and hadn't let on how worried she'd been that he would leave. She felt comfortable with Gee living in her home. Their schedules were very different but getting together in the evening for a glass of wine or cup of tea and talking had become the highpoint of her day.

And Gee was... doing things... in the house. It was subtle. He rose earlier than Karen to go to work, and Karen worked late in the evening to meet press deadlines. Both in the morning and the evening, Karen noticed the kitchen was spotless. No matter what she cooked for herself or how many dishes she left in the sink, it was always clean when she woke up in the morning and when she got home at night.

Gee started gradually expanding their living space, as well. When he moved in—*less than a week ago!*—she was living in the kitchen, sitting room, and her bedroom. Even in the sitting room, most of the furniture was still covered with sheets. Now, all the furniture in the sitting room was uncovered, vacuumed, rearranged, and clean. Even the lightbulbs had been replaced so they all worked.

Best of all, though, he was waiting for her when she got home at night. They sat on the sofa and talked about their days. And made out. *Me, necking!* She'd had many boyfriends and lovers, but never one she wanted to live with. Gee was... different.

"So, you'll be gone Saturday night?" Gee asked.

"Yes, I'll be back late on Sunday. Think you can stay out of trouble that long?" she laughed.

"Hmm. Maybe I should just lock myself in the house while you are gone. There are lots of little projects I could do."

"You're doing too much. Don't feel like you have to fix our whole home."

"Our?"

"You live here now. I hope... I hope you aren't in a hurry to move out."

"I'm not sure how these things progress. I don't know if I've ever done this before. I know that being here with you is… more than comfortable. It's… like I found where I belong again. I don't mean the house. I mean here. With you. I think…" She put a restraining finger against his lips.

"We're getting there. Soon. Kiss me."

They kissed. This was where they belonged. Together.

"Shall we go to the football game tomorrow night?" he asked.

"Yes. The Rosebud Fireflies are home this weekend. Maybe we'll see your friend Wayne there and you can arrange a guys' night out on Saturday."

"That sounds like an invitation to investigation. You want me to find out if he's related to the Savages and why he is really in town," he laughed. "It's a good idea. I'm sure he'll be at the game."

They kissed again and went upstairs. He turned left. Karen turned right and went along the hall to the bedroom her great-grandmother had set aside for her long ago. She glanced back at Gee as he entered his room.

Soon.

Plotting

"How many shares have we accumulated?"

"Forty-seven thousand."

"That's like nothing."

"It's given us an inside track to what's going on."

"I don't know. They've managed to keep shareholders locked out of real information over the years. I've requested all financial records in advance of any shareholder meeting. By law, they have to comply."

"In advance just means an hour before the meeting. Who did you choose to represent us?"

"I chose, Levi Dunkel, the lawyer from Palmyra. I expect they will give the shortest possible notice for the meeting and he'll have to get here quickly. How about property purchases?"

"We've managed to acquire thirteen over the past five years and all our tenants are favorable. I've asked them, however, not to put up political yard signs. I'm afraid it would make them targets. We're not the only ones who have been buying, though. Fifty-five properties have changed hands in the past five years. We only got thirteen."

"Who got the rest?"

"That's the question, isn't it?"

7

THE NUT

The Meaning of Life

THE WEEK after Labor Day was stressful as Gee attempted to return to a normal relationship with his coworkers. Oddly, Rupert was easiest to work with. Clubbing Gee had been understandable and Rupert's apology simple.

"I'm just glad you care so much about your employees," Gee said.

"Get a slab of bacon and get it sliced," Rupert responded. That was all that was needed for the two to be back to normal.

Onyx flushed in embarrassment each time she saw him. She was the one who dialed 911 and screamed that a rape was in progress. But she quietly stepped aside as he came to the deli each morning and moved the heavy kettles of soup. "You did the right thing," Gee said softly as he finished his task. She breathed a deep sigh and returned to work.

Nathan was the most difficult. Gee thought of him as his closest friend and his actions had been… personal. They avoided each other most of the week, Nathan leaving a note with instructions for the day on the bulletin board and twice calling Gee over the intercom to assist in a particular area of the store. Marian brought Devon to the library Wednesday night and stayed nearby. She thanked Gee for helping get Devon's jacket on after the reading time and then left.

To compensate for his feelings of lost friendship, he threw himself into cleaning at Karen's house each day after work.

HE PICKED UP his pay envelope Friday afternoon. Frieda silently held out the envelope of cash. Gee hefted it and raised an eyebrow at the unexpected bulk. Frieda shrugged dismissively. "Let's just call it worker's comp," she sighed.

Across the street at the credit union, he presented his City ID and was taken into the vault to retrieve his safe deposit box. When he was alone, he opened the pay envelope. His normal pay of $300 in crisp $20 bills was attached to a hand-written paystub. In addition, there were fifty $100 bills.

He sighed and put the bundle in the box with the rest of his cash, now increased to over six thousand dollars. He pulled five of the big bills from the half strap and put them in his wallet.

KAREN WOULD NOT be home until nearly time to go to the football game, so Gee wandered alone until he reached Jitterz. Something tugged at him to enter the coffee shop—perhaps just the need for companionship after a stressful week. He stood inside the shop staring at the menu board for so long that a young couple asked to go ahead of him while he decided what he wanted.

Elaine made drinks for the couple, took their money, and stood waiting for Gee.

"I've got this, honey. You can go home," a large dark woman said, moving up beside Elaine.

"I don't want him to think I'm impatient," Elaine said softly. "He's always nice to me."

"You've done a good job. Go home and rehearse. I hear you're singing in Palmyra this weekend."

"Yes ma'am. I'll see you tomorrow." Elaine hung her apron and headed out through the ice cream shop where she paused to order a cone.

"Mr. Gee, why don't you have a seat. I'll bring your drink to you," the owner said. "Violet! I need you to watch for customers for an hour. Just keep an eye out."

"Yes, Momma."

Gee heard the exchange but was still reading the board. Birdie Lanahan stepped around the counter with two cups in her hands and motioned Gee to a comfy chair with a small table next to it. He sat on the left and she set the cups down before sitting opposite him.

"Now tell Birdie your troubles, Mr. Gee," she said.

"It's nothing, Miss Birdie," Gee said, finally grounding himself in the warm steeping tea before him. "I wonder sometimes if I had friends… you know, before I came to Rosebud Falls. It seems I'm not very good at making them or keeping them."

"Oh. Feeling sorry for yourself. Drink your tea." Birdie watched as Gee took a few more sips. It was cooling rapidly in the thin cup she served. He set the cup back on the table.

"I have a remedy for the blues," he laughed. "All I need is to go home and wait for the love of my life. I can't feel sorry for myself when I'm with Karen." Birdie picked up his cup and began swirling the tea leaves around the bottom.

"I see. True, you have few friends. But you are important to many people. The Forest is in your cup. Be forewarned—it is as dangerous as it is soothing." Gee looked at the woman. Troy had told him she was a Voodoo sorceress. She was looking into his teacup. "You have love and heartbreak in your life. Maybe with the same person and maybe with others. You are puzzled and think you must find the solution. You are the solution. Discover what the puzzle is."

"Are you seeing that in my teacup?"

"The tealeaves. The smell of the room. The cut of your hair. You are a friend," Birdie concluded, "especially to the children."

"In the library," Gee smiled.

"Even children you don't know yet. Maybe they will be yours."

My own children? With…? Gee thought about his time with Devon, with the children in the library, with precocious Sally Ann. He could see himself with children. Lots of them. When he was with children, he felt almost the same as walking in the Forest. Happy. Content.

Birdie swirled the tealeaves in his cup again and looked at them before setting it down to face Gee.

"You may not have friends, but you are not alone, Mr. Gee. When you face the devil, you will find friends have your back."

Birdie picked up the teacups and took them to the kitchen, leaving a befuddled Gee. He made his way to the First Rose Valley Bank to purchase another gift card and then went home to wait for Karen.

His Passion

"Hey, can we join you?" Gee asked as he and Karen made their way to seats.

"Oh, hello, Gee. Karen. Please. Take a load off," Wayne responded.

"You look tired," Karen said. "Doing okay?"

"Two weeks into the school year and the little imps are running me ragged. My new home isn't habitable yet. I'm still trying to figure out Harvest responsibilities. I'm doing fine," Wayne sighed. "How are you?"

"I'm surprised you are even at the game with all that going on," Gee laughed.

"I was… informed… that it wasn't wise for teachers to not show up for football games. Even first grade teachers! Is there anyone in town who misses a high school football game?"

"You'll find slightly fewer come to the Flor del Día games. But we still have a good turnout. It's all part of the city preparing for Harvest and then celebrating it," Karen said. "It's not the same for basketball in the winter or baseball in the spring. Only football attracts so many."

"I have to admit, I've never seen a football stadium so big in a town so small. I have colleagues teaching in schools four times this size that don't have as good a stadium."

"Say, Wayne, I was wondering if you have plans for tomorrow evening. My lovely… girlfriend has to be out of town tomorrow and I'm looking for something to do," Gee said.

"You're lucky to have a girlfriend," Wayne sighed. "Maybe if I get out more, I'll meet more eligible candidates. I guess it depends on how far I get on my house repairs tomorrow. I have some broken windows to re-glaze and shingles that are damaged. I'd like to get the whole place ready to paint before we go into the Harvest chaos that I'm told we'll face."

"Would you like some help?" Gee volunteered. "I work at the market until noon, but I've no plans for the rest of the day."

Wayne considered Gee and glanced quickly at Karen. She was intent on the game as the two men talked. He nodded.

"That would be great if you have the time. I don't know many people in town I'd ask for help."

"I hear you."

"YOU HANDLED THAT masterfully," Karen said as they walked into the kitchen for a dish of ice cream.

"Handled what?"

"Getting an inside track on Wayne. Volunteering to help him tomorrow. It will be hard work, but you should be able to find out details about where he's from and why he's really here. I can't help but believe he is in some way related to the Savages of Rosebud Falls," Karen said.

"Karen… I'm not investigating Wayne. I know… You have a lot going on and a lot of suspicions about people's involvement, but I like the guy. We have a lot in common, being new to town and both being involved with children."

"I don't mean to come off sounding like I want you to spy on him. I mean… I do," Karen sighed. "I have the same kind of feeling about him you do, but my mind continually wants confirmation of what I believe."

"Like why you continue to place online ads to find out if anyone knows me?" Gee laughed. Karen straightened from where she was leaning against him.

"Am I infringing on your privacy, Gee? Do you want me to stop trying to find who you really are?"

"I don't mind if you keep investigating. But, you should know that I don't care. If you find something that needs to go to the police, take it to them. Don't even bother telling me I'm going to be arrested. If my past life reveals that I've done something, I'll pay the penalty. It's… Birdie said something when she was reading my tealeaves today."

"Birdie Lanahan read your leaves? I didn't think you'd be into that kind of thing."

"She just gave me a cup of tea and then started in about who I am and who my friends are. Mostly, it was what you would expect from a fortuneteller. But between what she said and what you are doing, I see one thing clearly. You are trying to solve the puzzle of my life. Who I am. Where I came from. But you are sitting beside what you are looking for. I *am* the solution to the puzzle. I'm the only one who can give meaning to my life. It can't be found in my past. It can only be found in my actions and my passions."

"What are your passions, Gee?" Karen whispered.

"You, Karen Weisman. You are my passion."

THEY KISSED AGAIN at the top of the stairs before Karen turned to her room. She hesitated at the door to see Gee still looking at her. She mimed a kiss and left the hall.

Gee went about his nightly routine, shaving and showering before finally crawling into bed. He stared toward the ceiling in the dark, thinking of the miracle in his life named Karen Weisman. She completed him. He had no need of memories to know that he was in love and that he would be forever hers.

The door opened and in the dim light of the hall, he saw Karen silhouetted, a diaphanous robe only slightly obscuring the shape of the woman beneath.

"Karen…"

"Is it too soon?" she whispered. In response, he simply pulled back the sheet and held out his arms.

HE WOKE UP alone and for a brief moment wondered if he had dreamed the night with Karen. Her light scent on his pillow quickly disabused him of that notion.

In the kitchen, he found her happily singing as she broke eggs for breakfast. The aroma of freshly brewed coffee filled the air. Her hair was neatly brushed out and she was dressed in jeans and a T-shirt.

"I love you," he said from the doorway. Karen spun and rushed to him, her smile lighting up the room.

"My lover, my lover," she whispered between kisses. "My beloved loving lover."

"When I woke up alone, I thought it might have been a dream."

"If it be thus to dream, still let me sleep!" Karen quoted. "For me, my dreams have come true."

They kissed again and she pushed him toward his seat in the breakfast nook. When he was settled, she handed him his coffee.

"I know you have to go to work this morning, but I thought we could have breakfast together. I don't normally make more than coffee and toast for breakfast, so I hope this is okay."

"I don't mind cooking for you. You don't have to get up early for me," he said.

"It just seemed like the most… domestic… couple kind of thing… best that I could do to show you I love you. Especially since I need to go to the city today and won't be with you tonight. I'll miss you more than I can ever say."

"You'll be careful, won't you?"

"Of course. I don't go without protection. But my source says she's found a lead—a young girl who simply showed up on the streets. She's been protecting her until she can find a way to help her."

"I'll worry about you. If there is anything I can do…"

"Not today. Help your friend. Have a good time tonight. Relax and know I will be with you soon."

Repairing the Past

PEAR STREET WAS a crowded and narrow one-block street between Mill Street and Orchard Avenue. When the railroad was being built in the early 1800s, the Orchard Project had housed hundreds of Irish laborers in small 'shotgun' houses along streets named for fruit trees. The streets of the Project ran haphazardly between and among the houses. The original structures had no bathrooms, just a string of outhouses lining back alleys. Next to each outhouse on the alley was a coal shed and as part of their wages, the residents received a full shed of coal each fall to last them through the winter months. The Meaghers were proud of how well they took care of their laborers and housed their families.

After the railroad was completed, many families moved, and the houses fell into disrepair. Some collapsed altogether. The surviving houses gained new life in the 1930s when water towers were built to collect rain water and siphon off groundwater. The City was modernized with water and sewer lines replacing the outhouses and wells. The Orchard Project became, if not a desired location, at least an acceptable one.

Wayne's 'new' home was the epitome of the shotgun house, eighteen feet wide and forty-odd feet long with a narrow stairway leading to a second story addition. The house was nearly the width of the lot and set back twelve feet from a broken sidewalk. The yard, overgrown with weeds, was barely large enough for the covered stoop and a rusted swing set. Gee found Wayne scraping paint from the front of the house.

After greetings, Gee immediately reached for Wayne's toolbox and began removing the first of the windows that needed glazing. Wayne had everything necessary for the project, but admitted he'd never actually glazed a window.

"Have you done this before?" Wayne asked as Gee set the first window back into place. It had been scraped, primed, glazed, puttied, and refit. "You worked like a professional at this."

"I… uh… I must have done this at some point in my life. My hands remember how to do it, but my head doesn't remember having done it," Gee said as Wayne helped him remove the next window in line. No matter how fast Gee could work, this job would take another day to complete.

"I heard you had memory problems," Wayne said. "Not that I've been checking up on you. I just mentioned your name in the faculty lounge once and stories came flooding out. You've got… a reputation."

"Well, whatever the reputation is, it's only two months old."

"Yeah. You made quite a splash when you got to town." Wayne looked at Gee and tried to keep a straight face. Both men laughed, and Wayne went back to his task of painting the trim on the front of the house. Gee continued with the windows.

That joke never seemed to get old among the denizens of Rosebud Falls.

———⋖◆⋗———

WAYNE AND GEE worked until dark and sat on the stoop with a beer. The upper story and front windows had been glazed and set. All the trim in front had been painted and the siding scraped and primed.

"What time would you like to start tomorrow?" Gee asked.

"Tomorrow? Really? You'd come back to work like a slave again?" Wayne laughed. "Uh… nine," he added.

"Well, I think I can do those windows in the back. They're the worst. Looks like it was easier for kids to throw stones at the front and back of the house than at the sides."

"True that. If I get the front painted and the lawn mowed tomorrow, the place will no longer look derelict and I can continue painting. As long as the rest of it is primed before snow flies, I'll be good for the winter."

"The windows are all single glazed. Do you have storm windows to put up outside?" Gee asked. Wayne shook his head.

"None on the property. I figure I'll make a stop at Jacob's Home Improvement after school this week and order aluminum storms. That could wipe out my housing funds but they have a deal where you can get them installed free if you finance them through the company. Eighteen months to pay. I suppose they make as much from the financing as they would for installation," Wayne mused.

"Well, we need to get them all glazed, painted, and measured this week then. I've got time. I like to be home when Karen gets home, but that isn't until late tomorrow. I usually have dinner and just tinker at maintenance around the house."

"Speaking of dinner, a laborer is worth his pay. Let's head up to the Pub & Grub and get a burger and beer." He finished the bottle he was drinking, and Gee walked the couple miles to the tavern with him.

Bar Brawl

"TIM-MAY! RAVEN! WHERE the hell is Timmy? We've got dishes piled from hell to kingdom come," Sherry, the bar owner, screamed from the kitchen door.

"He's not coming in," the waitress sighed. She set burgers and fries on the table in front Gee and Wayne. They grinned at each other and dove into their food. "His girlfriend hauled him off to wherever it is they go off to," Raven called back to her boss. "I don't know when he'll be back. Not tonight, I'm sure."

"He's supposed to let us know so we have a sub in here when he's gone," Sherry said as Raven took a Lite from the big bartender to the table near the door.

"I know, but... When he gets excited, his brain doesn't connect right," Raven sighed as she leaned against the bar. "What am I supposed to do? He's twenty-seven and the judge says he's competent enough to be independent. Hah! Like that will ever happen."

"Honey, you need to talk to that judge again. We all know Timmy'd be lost if he didn't live with you. Where else would he live? Twenty-seven years old and he still thinks he's in high school," Sherry said to her friend and waitress. "And I don't think that woman is good for him. He's been worthless for two weekends in a row. Last week because he thought he was going away with her and this week because they're gone."

"I know but I... Karen's the only one who stayed his friend after the injury. More than a friend. I don't know where she takes him, but he always comes home happy."

Gee's head came up with a sudden awareness of the conversation taking place a few feet from him. The waitress's son. With Karen. Cancelled last weekend. Gone this weekend. He couldn't be mistaken. They were talking about *his* Karen out of town with another man.

GEE COULDN'T REMEMBER having ever had the kind of knot in his stomach that was forming. It was nearly as painful as when he thought about leaving Rosebud Falls. Only this thought was of being separated from Karen. *Is this jealousy?*

Karen had nearly twenty-eight years of life in Rosebud Falls, less the time she spent at college and working in the city. Gee had only a little more than two months. How could he expect to know everything about a person in that time? The waitress, Raven, had said that Karen was the only one who stayed Timmy's friend after the injury. Gee wondered what kind of injury and why everyone else abandoned their friend.

Finally deciding that he was being irrational and needed to trust the woman who had told him repeatedly this morning that she loved him, Gee snapped back to the reality of the half-eaten hamburger in front of him.

———◁◆▷———

"Hey! Gee! You still with me, bud? You just went a long way away," Wayne laughed. "Hey, did you remember something?" Wayne had ignored the idea of Gee's amnesia, but when he went all still like that, it looked like he was caught in a mental labyrinth for some moments. Gee focused on his friend and smiled.

"A weird sensation, but no new memories," Gee admitted. "It was all about my reality here and now. I keep remembering that I only know a little bit about Rosebud Falls and the people in it. When I learn something new, I have to figure out how it fits with the rest of the picture. Sometimes I pick up a puzzle piece and I can see where it should go, but it doesn't fit right. It's confusing."

"I should think so. I... uh... have a similar kind of thing happen, even though my memories are all intact. I tend to jump to a conclusion before I know all the facts. It's hard sometimes." The two men returned to their burgers and became lost in the food as the bar got noisier.

"Hey, big man! You're back in town," called one of the Saturday night carousers. "Where you been this time?"

"Savannah," was the reply. "Don't ask me any damn thing about this trip. I just pick up the stone and deliver it. Then I pick up a load from somewhere else and bring it back here. If anybody got these de-spatchers coordinated, half the shipping costs in America would be cut."

"You got that right. I was out in my rig through Ohio headed west. I'm following a log truck because on that stretch there just isn't any room to pass. Must have been fifty to a hundred logs tied down to that flatbed. I don't know if he's going to a lumber mill or a paper mill. Who cares? But I've followed him for well over twenty-five miles when another logging truck passes us going the other direction. Same kind of load. Same size logs. Now why doesn't somebody figure out that there's already a load of logs two hundred miles back the way I came and another load two hundred miles ahead and just use the damn logs where they started? Stupidity!"

"Yeah, I feel like I'm just driving the same load around all the time. Back and forth. I swear the trailers never get unloaded. I drive one to Miami or Mobile or Toronto, and the next time I'm there, I pick up the same damn trailer and haul it back here. I marked a couple slabs once—subtle-like, you know? Sure enough, four weeks later, I hauled the same slabs back to SSG."

If Gee's reaction to the news of Karen and Timmy had been sudden, Wayne's reaction to the loud conversation behind them was just as unexpected.

—◁◆▷—

"WAYNE? HEY, I thought I was the only one going blank here. Want another beer?" Gee asked.

Wayne looked up at the puzzled expression on their waitress's face.

"Yeah. I think that would be good. Let's have one more and then walk back to town."

"Glad you boys are walking. I hear the police are punishing one of the new guys, McCarran, by making him patrol for drunk drivers on Saturday nights. He's not in a good mood," Raven said. She turned to the bar and ordered two more beers for the friends.

"Hey! You!" a big fellow from the table of truckers yelled. He pushed back from his table and knocked his chair over backward. Everyone in the bar turned to look at the ox-like man, but his eyes were focused on Gee. "I know you. You're the SOB who attacked and raped my wife. You're done here. I'm gonna put you in your grave."

"You're drunk, Larry," shouted the big bartender. "Sit down and shut up or get out."

"The hell. This little punk walks into town and all of a sudden he owns it. He rapes my sweet little Roxanne and gets off scot-free. He's gonna pay for it now."

"I'm warning you, Larry," the bartender said as he started around the bar.

"You must be the husband who beat his wife and shoved her out of his truck in a parking lot so he wouldn't be seen taking her to the hospital," Gee said softly. "Some courageous man."

Larry was through talking. He lunged at Gee, not waiting for him to stand from the table. Gee blocked the meaty fist aimed at his face and grabbed the wrist. The giant roared, but Wayne grabbed the opposite wrist. As if communicating silently, both men kicked at Larry's unstable legs as they twisted his wrists. Larry flipped over the table and landed on his back on the floor. Gee grabbed his beer bottle to stabilize it on the table and then raised it to Wayne. They found the bartender next to their table staring down at the big truck driver. Sherry was a second behind him as she burst through the kitchen door with a baseball bat in her hand. Larry struggled to get his wind back and sit up.

"You! Stay!" Sherry screamed at the downed man. She shoved him back on the floor with the end of the baseball bat. The big bouncer put a foot on Larry's chest. "You two, get out," she snapped at Wayne and Gee. "Don't come back until at least the first of next month. You're banned until then." Without saying anything, Gee and Wayne stood and placed twenty-dollar bills on the table. Gee added another ten just in case it didn't cover a decent tip. They headed for the door where flashing red lights could already be seen pulling into the parking lot.

"Use the kitchen door. That will be McCarran out front," Raven said, propelling the two men gently through the back. "And watch your back. Larry never fights fair and you've just warned him that you're dangerous. He's a bully. And he holds a grudge."

"Why isn't he in jail?" Gee asked.

"Mac will take him in to dry out tonight," Raven said, "but Larry works for Savage. The police won't hold him any longer."

House Numbers

GEE SPENT A restless night in the empty house. It was the first time he'd been alone in it since he moved a week ago. He'd had no difficulty being alone at the Panzas' but It seemed wrong to be in this house without Karen.

At six in the morning he gave up trying to sleep and prepared for his day. After his shower, he heated a wet towel to wrap his face before lathering his beard and stropping the razor. Looking in the mirror, Gee examined his face. The bruising and scratches from last week's encounter with Rena had mostly healed, but his nose was still sore. After the lather sat on his face sufficiently, he began the careful process of scraping his beard away with the straight razor. The morning ritual was comforting. It served to balance him. Since coming to live in the mansion, Gee had been shaving twice a day, in the morning when he got up, and in the evening before Karen got home. She always enjoyed touching his smooth face, it seemed. Gee certainly enjoyed it. And Friday night… he was especially glad he had shaved.

He dressed and headed toward the town center by six-thirty. Jitterz wouldn't open until eight o'clock on Sunday morning, but Louie's Café next to the antique store at 8th and Main was open at six every morning. Argos, grandson of the Louie who had started the café, was as eccentric as the old man whose name it bore. His door opened at precisely six o'clock every morning. How long the café stayed open ranged from an hour to ten hours, depending on the clientele and Argos's mood. He had a love for fishing and if the weather looked right, he was likely to serve coffee and doughnuts to the first half-hour crowd and then head for the lake.

Gee sat at the counter and ordered ham and eggs with dark rye toast. The food had been served when Wayne sat down beside him.

"Up early?" Gee asked.

"Didn't sleep well," Wayne answered.

"Same."

"Well, we can sit here gabbing all morning or get an extra hour of daylight in on the house."

"Eight o'clock."

"What?"

"Jitterz opens at eight o'clock. I'll buy you a cup and we can go to work from there."

———⊲◆⊳———

"THAT WAS AMAZING coffee," Wayne said as they started for the tools they needed. Gee chuckled as it had been his own response when Troy first introduced him to it. Wayne helped Gee remove the windows that needed work in the back of the house and then went to the front to begin painting.

They worked until three o'clock and Gee professed that he was starving and would have to take off soon. Wayne was chagrined at having not taken a break, but the day's labor had allowed him to finish painting the front of the house.

"I shouldn't have kept you so long without food," he said. "I was in a zone and never even thought of it."

"I understand. It seemed like no time at all until I had those back windows finished. Then my stomach grumbled, and I realized how long we'd been working."

"I'm going to do just one more thing," Wayne said as he finished cleaning his brushes. "Help me line these up and we'll take off." He held up brass numbers for the door and Gee helped line them up, holding them as Wayne tapped in the brads that secured them. "My new address, my friend. 436 Peach Street. Home sweet home."

Revelation

GEE GRABBED A slice of pizza and a soft drink from Gino's Pizzeria. It was four o'clock Sunday afternoon. Karen might be home. Or she might not be home until late. She hadn't said. He wanted to rush home and hold her in his arms. But he knew his emotions were rocking back and forth between elation and trepidation.

I don't step out on the man I'm with and I expect the same from him.

The memory of Karen's words washed over him. After Friday night, there was no question in Gee's mind that he and Karen were in a relationship. And relationships were built as much on trust as on faithfulness. Karen took her friend Timmy to Palmyra. It was as important for Gee to trust her as it was for her to be true.

A satisfied sigh came from his lungs as the tension washed out of him. All he needed was a walk in the Forest.

He drank in the sounds and smells of the Forest as he walked, taking a long route home. He'd felt a connection to the trees since his first walk here with Karen. She'd told him—warned him?—that whatever binds the Families to the Forest had claimed him as well. He was comforted by the thought. This strange—could he say enchanted?—woodland felt like his true home. It sank its roots into his soul.

The area around the grandfather tree Jonathon told him would be cut this fall was already being prepared for the closing Harvest formalities. Spectator areas were designated with ropes. A platform for dignitaries stood at one side of the clearing. Gee sank down and leaned his back against the old tree as he let himself absorb the magic of the Forest.

A nut fell next to him. Gee picked it up and examined it. With only a little pressure, the four-petal husk fell away from the shell. He rolled the remaining nut in the palm of his hand, feeling the glossy smooth texture of the shell.

I wonder what would happen if I ate one? Would I die immediately? Would it make me sick first? Take a day to die? A week? Would I recover? What is the mystery held inside this shell?

He tested the strength of the shell between his thumb and the first knuckle of his forefinger. It cracked, surprising Gee. He'd expected the shell to be thick and tough, but it was actually rather fragile. Opening it, he looked inside, using his pocket knife to pry the tender meat carefully from the shell. He kept it intact as much as possible, but where it broke apart, he could see the blood-red flesh. It felt slightly oily in his fingers. It was fascinating—terrifying—and Gee half-expected a forester to step out at any moment to arrest him for breaking a nut in the Forest. He quickly buried the husk and shell in the sawdust mulch under the tree.

Then, without thinking further, he popped the nutmeat in his mouth and chewed.

It was bitter. He wandered off toward the creek and scooped up a double hand of water to wash it down. Then he dipped his head in the water and drank more deeply.

He didn't feel sick. He didn't notice any effect at all. He wondered if the story of poison nuts was something the Families made up to conceal and hoard the fruits of the Forest. The tree gave him a nut and he ate it. Gee thanked the grandfather tree as it reached out to help him to his feet. He took time to listen to its story of growing to this great age—of what it had seen in the Forest. He followed the tree's roots, noting how it touched the roots of the other trees around it, sharing its great knowledge, and how they, in turn, touched the roots of others.

As Gee wandered through the Forest, he saw that the roots also touched people. In fact, everyone in Rosebud Falls was part of the Forest. Some were no more than a leaf or twig or even a breeze in the branches. Others were deeply rooted. Still others, bore fruit—nuts—and planted

new trees. Gee could see how he himself was a part of the Forest. He and
the Forest were one. The Forest had brought him to Rosebud Falls.

The man who emerged from the Forest was the same man who
entered, but his mind was gently altered. He was at peace. He was here-
now and that was all that was necessary.

Gee went home.

———————◁◆▷———————

"WILL HE BE all right? Please say he's okay."

Dr. Poltanys sat heavily in the chair next to Karen. "I honestly don't
know. He's unconscious. There's been no change since you found him
sprawled on the floor inside your front door. But antidotes… They aren't
as effective when the drug has had that long to enter the system."

"What drug? He was drugged?"

"His blood shows a high concentration of RDH. It's the same
chemical that we find in patients who have used Lustre. The same thing
we treated Rena for last weekend. But we had Rena in treatment within
half an hour of when the drug was administered. It's hard to tell, but I'd
guess the drug had been in Gee's system for as much as two, maybe three
hours before you found him. The fact that he's not dead gives me hope.
The fact that he has such a high concentration in his bloodstream…
I don't know what the outcome will be." Poltanys put an arm around
Karen as she collapsed against him, weeping.

"Can I… at least be with him?"

"It's not exactly… I shouldn't even have spoken to you about it… but
he lives with you. Until his attorneys get here, you are the closest thing
we have to a next of kin. Come on." He led Karen to the room where
Gee lay, oxygen cannula in his nose and an IV running to his left arm.
She rushed to him and grasped his right hand.

"Please. Please come back to me," she whispered. It had been a difficult trip to Palmyra. The interview abruptly ended as her subject panicked and fled. Timmy had abandoned her to play with his girlfriends
and she found herself alone in a seedy hotel. She barricaded her door.
In the morning, her contact had berated her for letting the girl she
was interviewing run away. *What was I supposed to do? Chase her down?*
Timmy hadn't appeared until mid-afternoon and it took forever to get

back home. And when she opened her front door, she found Gee, face down on the floor. "Please. Please. I need you. I love you," she repeated.

---------◁◆▷---------

"KAREN?"

"Gee! You're awake." She reached for the call button by his head.

"Yeah. What an incredible dream. We were… It was so real I thought I'd wake up with you in my arms. Why are you crying, Karen?"

"You don't remember?"

"We *did* make love. But that was Friday. I was waiting for you to get home and hoping…" Gee pushed himself up. "Where am I and why do I have tubes running all over?"

"You're in the hospital, Gee. You overdosed on Lustre," Karen said. Julia entered the room and quickly began assessing Gee's vitals—pulse, blood pressure, and temperature.

"Adam will be here in a minute. He was on the first floor," the nurse said.

"What's going on?" Gee asked. "Why am I in the hospital. The last I remember, I was waiting for Karen to get home. It's morning?"

"Good to see you awake, Gee," Dr. Poltanys said as he entered the room.

"Vitals are all within the norm, doctor," Julia said. Poltanys immediately checked Gee's eyes and removed the nasal cannula.

"Breathing okay, Gee?"

"Yeah. No problem. My nose is a little dry and sore."

"Typical when you're being given oxygen. Tell me what you remember."

"Again? Uh… The first thing I saw when I walked into town was the bar… the Pub and Grub. I…"

"Gee, about yesterday. Last night. What day is it?"

"Since it's light outside, it must be Monday. It was already dark when I got home last night."

"Home?"

"To Karen's house. That's where I live now."

"Okay. So, what happened when you got home?"

"I went in to wait for her to get home. Then I woke up here. What happened."

"Where did you get the drug?" another voice asked from the doorway. Gee looked around the doctor to see Detective Oliver.

"What drug?"

"Let's backtrack," Poltanys said. He scowled at the detective. Gee's lawyers, Jack and Gretchen LaCoe, pushed into the room past Oliver.

"You can't question him without us present," Jack said to Oliver.

"I just want to know where the drug came from," Oliver nearly shouted.

"I didn't take any drugs!" Gee called back. He coughed and Karen offered him a sip of water.

"Somehow you got the drug in your system," Poltanys explained. "No one here is accusing you of drug abuse. Someone may have drugged you. Just relax and tell us who you were with yesterday."

"I spent the day with Wayne Savage working on his house. About three we called it quits and I walked over to the pizzeria for a bite to eat. I figured Karen would be late, so I decided to go for a walk in the Forest on the way home."

"Did you see anyone? Meet anyone?"

"Grandfather." Everyone in the room seemed to move in closer.

"You met your grandfather?" Oliver asked. "You know who you are now and have relatives?"

"Oh. Sorry. I mean the grandfather tree in the Forest. The one they plan to cut this year. I sat there and talked to him for a while. I was working some things out in my head. He's nice. He gave me a nut to eat."

"Gee, are you saying you ate a nut in the Forest?" Poltanys asked.

"Oh shit! I suppose I'm going to get arrested and fined for taking something from the Forest," Gee moaned.

"Oh, my God," Karen breathed. "You ate a nut. And you're alive."

"Mead, you and I need to leave now," Jack said. He looked at his wife and Gretchen nodded. "This is above our paygrade. We're not Family. They are."

"This isn't…"

"We'll find out what we need to know later. You'd better call the Judge," Jack insisted. He pushed the detective out the door, reaching for his phone at the same time.

"We have two issues," Poltanys said. "Three. I still need to test Gee and get another blood sample to confirm that the drug is out of his system and he's okay."

"And I need to call Dad to talk to the Families," Gretchen said. "Heinz has to let them know."

"And we need to get the annexation passed," Karen said.

"Why are you concerned about that?" Gee asked. He was still feeling quite euphoric.

"You ate a nut. Sometime after that—long enough for a walk in the Forest and get home—you passed out and were comatose when Karen found you," Poltanys explained. "When we tested your blood, we discovered the chemicals found in the drug Lustre. You just provided a missing link we've suspected but were unable to confirm. Lustre is made from our Rose Hickory nuts."

"And all the Rose Hickories are under the control of the foresters except the ones in the South Rosebud annex," Karen concluded. "And Gee. Only the head of a Family ever survives eating a Rose Hickory nut. It's how challenges to leadership are settled."

"Uh… Dare I ask how your weekend was?" Gee said when Karen finally got him home. They burst out laughing as the tension drained from them. It had been a long day at the hospital, even after the doctor had cleared Gee. Dr. Poltanys' father, Jan, showed up as the representative of the Families to talk to Gee about his experience.

"Above all," Jan had said, "we need to keep this quiet. If anyone discovers that someone ate a nut and survived, we'll have a rash of daredevils trying to prove they can do it, too. That would mean deaths. You can't imagine how unique you are, Gee."

When Gretchen LaCoe, Jan Poltanys, and Judge Warren had finally left, Gee was exhausted and hungry. Karen picked up sandwiches and soup at the Hilltop Deli on the way home and the two went straight to the kitchen to eat.

"Even before I got home to find you unconscious on the floor, the weekend was a disaster," Karen said. "I went to Palmyra because Janie called. I planned to go last weekend, but there was the little incident of a girl claiming my boyfriend raped her." Gee touched his nose. It was still sore from Rena's violent reaction when he tried to restrain her. "Anyway, Janie is a sex worker. She's a bit older than most and I think she keeps working so she can help the younger girls. This runaway showed up in town and Janie took her under her wing. The girl had a story of being a sex slave for years. In a transfer of ownership, she'd seen an opportunity to run and took it. How she escaped is one of the things I was trying to discover when she suddenly saw something or someone out the window and just ran. I looked out but couldn't see anything that looked spooky."

"Did you find her again?"

"No. Janie said she didn't come back and she's really pissed at me for letting a vulnerable girl out of my sight. And to make it worse, my... um... friend..."

"Timmy?"

"I knew you'd hear his name if you went to the Pub and Grub. I can explain, Gee."

"You don't need to."

"But..."

"I'm not very experienced in relationships. At least not that I can recall. I'm not used to the surges of wonder that course through my body when I think of you. I'm not used to the desire I feel for you. And I do have momentary pangs of insecurity and even jealousy that I can't explain. And when I heard his mother call you Timmy's girlfriend, that hit me pretty hard. I didn't know how to deal with it."

"I'm not his girlfriend," Karen said. "That was over years ago."

"You're his friend. But what he is can't matter to me. You told me that you love me and we became lovers. All I need to do is trust you. That's what I was contemplating on my walk through the Forest. In a way, it was what the grandfather tree was communicating when he gave me a nut to eat. His message was clear. 'Trust me.' Well, I ate the nut. I fell into a coma, as Dr. Poltanys described it, though I remember vivid dreams. And then I woke up with you holding my hand. I don't need explanations. I love you, but more importantly, I trust you."

Tears ran down Karen's cheeks as she listened to Gee. "How can I ever show that I am worthy of that trust?" she whispered. "I love you. I want to be open and have no secrets from you. So, understand this, when

I tell you about Timmy it is not to justify myself, but to simply open myself more fully to you so you know who I really am."

Gee leaned forward and kissed his girlfriend. "Why don't we get more comfortable than sitting at the kitchen table," he suggested. "Wine in the sitting room?"

"A glass of wine would be nice. Why don't we drink it in bed?"

"TIMMY RAVEN WAS my classmate in high school. A friend because in a school our size you have to figure everyone is at least an acquaintance. But he was way out of my league. A great athlete. Very popular. Very handsome. I was a bit of a geek."

"Hard to imagine," Gee said, stroking her hair.

"First football game of the season, against Flor del Día, our star quarterback, Timmy, was knocked unconscious. No one could understand how an injury like that could cause such extensive damage. He never really recovered, did not develop any further. He's still got the mind of a high school student. Short term memory is poor, but long-term, before the injury, is sharp. He remembers how popular he was and the kind of person he was. But his friends abandoned him after the injury. He wasn't the same. He no longer looked forward, only back."

"He's still like that?" Gee asked. Karen nodded.

"Even then I already had a reputation for sticking my nose into other people's business and calling it reporting. Something about the injury didn't make sense. Why so severe? So, I stole his helmet and pads. I had money and my great-grandmother's backing, so I took the equipment to a lab in Palmyra to have it tested. Our team's new football equipment wasn't up to the standard of most toys sold for little children. When I released the report in the newspaper, it was discovered that the coach and athletic director had purchased the new equipment and taken a huge kickback. They were prosecuted."

"And you became public enemy number one because you exposed them."

"Yeah. I was as much outcast as Timmy by then, so I sort of adopted him. I took him to prom. I gave him my virginity. I stood by him when all our other friends walked away. Now, he's supposed to function as my bodyguard when I go into the city, but he's become so popular among the girls that as soon as he can get free, he runs off with one or more and I don't see him for the rest of the weekend. He was really frustrated when I cancelled the trip last weekend, so this time he took off almost as soon as we got to Palmyra and I ended up alone and barricaded in a cheap hotel room until I could collect him the next day and come home."

"You're still a good friend to him, even though he abandons you."

"It's not his fault. His mother tries hard, but there are some things that an eternal teen needs that a single mom just can't cope with. I'm worried that one day I'll take him to the city and he'll just disappear into the underground like so many others."

New Kid in Town

"As you expected, I've been made."

"That was even faster than I anticipated."

"There are still things in town with the Family name on them. That's why I'm here, isn't it?"

"You know why you are there. We're going to retake the Family business."

"I haven't made much progress on that. I've been more concerned with trying to get settled."

"We have time. The lease doesn't expire for another year."

"I know it seems like a long time, but the City is moving to annex the whole area. In a couple of months, the leases could be voided by the City. It seems I've barely had a chance to breathe. School. House hunting. This Harvest thing."

"You'll enjoy Harvest. It's one of the things I've missed most."

"Why did you ever leave?"

"My grandfather wanted me out of town while I could still go. Said he wanted me to be able to make up my own mind. It was a brave move and ultimately killed him. When I come back it's unlikely I'll ever leave again."

"Are they that evil? They'd force you to stay in town just because you are head of one of the Families?"

"It's not about the Families. It's the trees. Even now I can feel them tugging at me. Grandfather said it was a curse that the head of the Family could never leave. Maybe it's true. But the trees have a hold on the Families, just as much as the Families appear to have a hold on the Forest. It's a symbiotic relationship. The Families take care of the Forest and the Forest takes care of the Families. One can't just abandon the other."

Wayne listened to his grandfather and felt the same sense of wonder he'd known all his life. Gee had described the Forest as mystical. His grandfather certainly believed so. But Wayne had a job to do. He needed to take control of the company and figure out why this fanatical church had a such a strong interest in it.

"So, I need to locate all the shareholders and get their proxies without alerting anyone that they are about to face a proxy battle," Wayne sighed.

"I've got the shareholder list, but a lot of them are shell corporations who hold the stock. There are five million shares. We own twenty percent. Six hundred thousand shares were put in blind trusts for the war orphans. The most important thing for you right now is getting settled in and learning who is trustworthy. Just remember that the person in power is not always the one pulling the strings. Watch for figureheads."

"You've never steered me wrong, Grandad."

"Now tell me about your new friends. Karen and Gee?"

8

SHAKE IT!

Partners

"GEE, DO you think we're moving too fast with this?" Karen asked as they entered the office of LaCoe Attorneys at Law Wednesday afternoon. "I'll back off if you think we're rushing."

"After this weekend and realizing that I'm medically a ward of the City, I appreciate your willingness to step up to this." Gee pulled her to the side of the room, out of hearing of the receptionist. "How can I think you are rushing things, Karen? I'm in love with you. If I thought you were ready, I'd ask you to marry me." Karen looked lovingly up at Gee and placed a light kiss on his lips.

"You should start working on a proposal then," she whispered. "Until you figure that part out, though, this partnership is a quick and quiet way to handle all kinds of things—not just medical power of attorney."

They turned back to the reception desk and were met there by a stunningly beautiful young woman. It took Gee a moment before he recognized her as the third female cousin in the Nussbaum Quartet, the beauty queen Krystal.

"Put your tongue back in your mouth, Gee," Karen laughed. "Have you met Krystal Nussbaum? Krystal, this is my partner, Gee."

"I've seen your name floating around," Krystal said pleasantly. "It's nice to meet you."

"I heard you and your cousins sing at the fair this summer. Absolutely enchanting," Gee said.

"Thank you. We'll sing at Harvest, too. I'm glad you liked it," she said.

Gretchen LaCoe emerged from her office.

"I see you've met my niece, Gee. It's a family business, you know." Gretchen smiled and shook hands with Karen and Gee.

"Is your son on staff, too?" Gee asked.

"Oh, yes. Upset that we didn't offer him a full partnership as soon as he passed the bar. I think he expected Jack and me to simply retire and leave the practice to him."

"He really raced through college and law school," Karen said. "You must be very proud of him."

"Of course. Jack has the paperwork ready, so let's go right into the conference room." They went into the room and found Jack at the table with stacks of papers in front of him. He rose to shake hands and then they got right down to business.

"This agreement between Karen Weisman and George Evars is to establish a legal partnership. The stack of paper is thick, so I'll go over the basics and you can both read what you wish. Execution of these partnership papers, will place some intellectual and physical property into joint ownership. In addition, you will assume medical power of attorney for each other. Gee, this is a great advantage to you in several ways. You'll become a signer on a bank account, for example, that is already open in Karen's name. Without you having to provide anything other than your City ID. There will be a lot of paper-signing this afternoon but most of it is on the part of Ms. Weisman as she has the most at stake at the moment and needs to put certain safeguards in place. Is this clear?"

"Uh… I kind of feel like I'm not contributing anything to our partnership, Karen. How did you get all this put together so quickly?"

"I started the process the day after Labor Day… after you moved in with me. We've talked about this, Gee. You'd already given me insights and proposed avenues of research that I hadn't thought of, and you did it without pay or remuneration. I wasn't going to push it, though, until you ended up in the hospital Sunday night. Think of it as giving you a stake in the work we want to do."

"And with ownership of the partnership stated as joint tenants with right of survivorship," Gretchen added, "it also protects Karen from any claims that could be made by your relatives or heirs, should any be discovered, in the case of your demise. You should consider the fact that you are making an agreement based on unknown information at this time. You don't know if there are heirs or relatives out in the wide world with whom you would want to share your work and the money you are putting aside, Gee. So far, searches for your identity have all been focused on the United States. It is *possible* that you have these relatives and heirs in another country—say, Canada."

"I have considered that," Gee said. "I can only act and react as the person I am today and not as the person I might previously have been."

"That's what we love about you, Gee," Gretchen smiled.

"Well, shall we get to signing papers?" Jack said.

"Do you have time for dinner before you go to the library to read to the children?" Karen asked when they finally left the law office.

"I think so, but not Chinese. I don't think I could hold chopsticks in my fingers after all that signing."

"You? I had dozens more papers to sign than you did."

"I had no idea that intellectual property rights were so complicated."

"If it weren't for my employment history, there wouldn't have been quite so much. I write for hire, which means that when one of my stories is published in the newspaper, it belongs to the newspaper as the copyright holder. I'm paid a wage for that work. Where it becomes a bit grayer is who owns my research before I write a story. If I've done that research on company time, it belongs to the company, or at least the company could stake a claim to it. Some companies—and Alex Hunter would be all over this—would hold that I am paid a salary and therefore all my time is company time. Jack and Gretchen negotiated a new employment agreement and went over it with a fine-tooth comb. I have no idea how they managed to convince Axel, but it's in keeping with new policies on bylines and content ownership. They determined that work I started before my employment with the *Mirror*, and which had never been in their office, was my sole possession. All my notes on child trafficking, for example, are in the study at home and I started that research file while I was still in high school."

"So, we seem to be covered. What's my first assignment, boss?"

"Feed me! Then go read to your little munchkins at the library. That shows me you are committed to the betterment of our children."

"*Our* children?"

"Oh! Um... You know what I mean." Karen blushed. "But maybe one day."

"GEE!"

"Dee!" he responded to the three-year-old who launched himself at Gee from several feet away. The hug gave Gee a warm feeling. He looked over Devon's head and saw his mother coming toward him. She was smiling.

"Hello, Marian," Gee said. "I hope you're doing well. I do miss seeing you and Devon every day."

"Things are improving. Thank you so much for understanding, Gee."

"You know I want only the best for you and your family."

"Thank you. I was wondering... um... I shouldn't ask favors, but... Could you walk Devon home tonight after story time? Like you used to? I was thinking... I could use the time..."

"Of course I will," Gee said happily. "Devon likes the stories I read to the older kids as much as the ones I read to the toddlers. Don't you, Dee?"

"Stories!" he clapped.

"Thank you, Gee," Marian whispered. "The... uh... stroller is in the cloakroom."

"See you later," Gee said as he settled into the beanbag where he read to the children. Half a dozen more children gathered around and Ms. Tomczak brought him his first batch of books.

THE SECOND READING hour was about to begin, and Devon was nodding off in Gee's lap as the older children rushed in. There was a lot of chatter as the first- and second-graders arrived.

"Hi, Mr. Gee," Sally Ann said as she approached.

"Hi, Sally Ann. How is school going?"

"Boring. Mrs. Zimmer is nice, but all these other kids are..." She broke off suddenly. "Daddy says I shouldn't make disparaging remarks about others. Isn't that a cool word? It means saying bad things." She lowered her voice to a whisper only Gee could possibly hear. "So, I shouldn't say the other kids are dumb." She rolled her eyes and Gee laughed.

"No. You definitely shouldn't say that."

"Mrs. Zimmer is a giant!"

"That could be considered a disparaging remark, Sally Ann. Adults often look very big to children. Our perceptions change as we get bigger ourselves."

"I think it's cool. She's *way* taller than Mr. Savage." Gee had to stop and consider that. Wayne was perhaps an inch or two shorter than Gee, but even then, it was unusual for a woman to be that tall.

"Well, let's get started with our reading."

Proxies

"OPA, DO YOU have shares of Savage Sand and Gravel?"

"Now why would you be asking about that?"

"There is a Savage back in town."

"I've heard."

"He's trying to collect proxies for all outstanding shares he can get. I think he's planning to retake the company. It could be important for us."

"How so?"

"SSG holds the Savage Forest shares. They've abstained from every decision in the past twenty years—ever since that guy, Stewart, took control. But with the annexation, their power could threaten how the whole Forest is managed. We need to be ready to oppose or support the new Savage. Over the past few years, I acquired a few shares for the quartet and plan to give the proxy to Wayne Savage's attorney."

"A few shares?"

"Seven thousand one hundred and thirty-seven. We started in high school."

Heinz Nussbaum looked at his grandson for a long time, trying to read his intent. It was obvious on the young man's face. He intended to become The Nussbaum when Heinz was ready to pass the torch. Heinz had eight grandchildren in four families. But Cameron had created an alliance with his cousins that went far beyond singing together. He wanted to run the Family.

"And if I trust you with this?"

"*Opa*, I will always do what is right for the Family and the Forest."

"*Enkel*, I believe you, but it is complicated. If so much as one of your seven cousins challenges you, do you know what that means?"

"I'll have to show what a good negotiator I am," Cameron chuckled.

"You will have to eat the nut."

"What?"

"Do you know why I am head of the Nussbaum Family and not my cousin?" Heinz asked.

"Your cousin died."

"He died in the challenge. The Forest chose. My grandfather said I should be the next Family head. My father, you know, was killed on D-Day. My uncle protested that I was a bastard and his son was legitimate. My cousin agreed and formally challenged me."

"It sounds like some medieval duel. You can't seriously tell me you killed your cousin Georg," Cameron exclaimed.

"The challenge is to eat a nut from the Rose Hickory."

"They're lethal. Unless treated with the antidote immediately, there is enough poison in them that they will kill within an hour or two."

"And the death is very painful. Georg died. I did not."

"Every Family head goes through this ordeal? Why weren't we told about it?"

"The ordeal is only undergone when someone challenges the named heir. All the Families withhold the information until the possible heirs are old enough to understand. And it's never spoken of outside the Family. We don't want a hormonally charged fourteen-year-old deciding to prove what a man—or woman—he is by going into the Forest and poisoning himself."

"*Opa*—Grandfather—if that is what it takes to ensure our Family survival, I will eat the nut."

"Let us hope you don't need to."

⸻◈⸻

"BRYCE SAVAGE WAS a fine man. I regret that I didn't know him more than as the grandfather of my friend, Paul. P-à-l was the way his Family spelled it. Our family heritages go back in this community for two hundred years, but each family still tends toward traditional names. Just like us," Heinz said. He'd poured a glass of schnapps for his grandson and the two men settled into chairs in Heinz's modest study.

"Until me," Cameron laughed.

"It's becoming less common in your generation, but I'd wager that you will consider German names for your children," Heinz laughed. "But, the Seven Heroes dying in battle left seven orphans behind. Most, like Pàl and me, were accepted fully into our Families. Some, like Coretta Cavanaugh Sims, were accepted, but as separate from the main family line—sort of black sheep, or the bastard children they were. And Celia Eberhardt was not accepted by the Roths at all. That infuriated Bryce. So, he reorganized his company, Savage Sand and Gravel, and took it public. As a part of the move, he created trusts for each of orphans. Those trusts consist of one hundred thousand shares of SSG stock. The income is given to the orphan or his heirs. I didn't find out about the trusts until I took over as head of the family. Henry Lazorack knew about them, but I don't know if he ever told David. To my knowledge, no one has ever exercised the right to vote their shares."

"Then we could gather the proxies for those trusts together and have some influence in the company," Cameron said enthusiastically.

"I don't think you should hold the proxies," Heinz sighed. "It's not that I don't trust you, nor that I don't think you would make good choices. It's exposure I'm worried about. The shares are all held by private trusts. To expose the fact that the trusts benefit members of the Families would mean that people would start questioning what else we own and how we manage our own resources. It's too risky."

"What's the alternative?" Cameron asked. "We need to take part in this."

Heinz quietly contemplated the problem. He was seventy-five years old and had managed the Family since the morning he woke up from a nut-induced coma to find his cousin dead beside him. Then he smiled. The answer was as obvious as the Forest's selection.

"We have a City Champion."

Sirens

GEE CLOCKED OUT on Friday at noon, splitting his fifth workday between Friday and Saturday. He was climbing the steps to Frieda's office for his paycheck when he heard sirens—not police sirens, but the piercing sirens of a weather alert from fire stations and public facilities all over town. He opened the door to Frieda's office and stuck his head in.

"It sounds like we have a tornado warning, Frieda. We should head for shelter." She smiled at him. That was a first. Gee couldn't remember her ever smiling unless it was at her grandson.

"Listen," she said, holding up a finger. The sirens went silent and then three short blasts rang out. After the sirens had the short blasts, they all picked up the general alert sound again. "They'll do it three times. The weather sirens followed by three short blasts."

"Testing the system? I haven't heard them do that before."

"Welcome to Harvest, Gee," Frieda said. "They'll repeat it every fifteen minutes for the next two hours." She handed him his pay envelope just as the sirens fell silent a second time to repeat their three short blasts. "Nathan tells me you've agreed to be a shaker. You won't be back to work here for ten days. Let me remind you that when you made that agreement, you entered a binding contract to work until Harvest is over. Don't be late for your first assignment at seven tomorrow morning."

Gee stood with his mouth slightly open as the words sank in. 'Shakers are on duty until the last nut falls,' Jonathon had told him. Gee had agreed without realizing how long the hours might be. Frieda flicked her fingers at him in her normal sign of dismissal and he left the office.

As the last series of blasts from the siren died, cheers rose from the aisles of the market and people began celebrating.

It was time for Harvest.

THE CELEBRATION CONTINUED outside. In the parking lot, people honked their horns in one long and three short toots. He ran across the street to put his pay in his safe deposit box and discovered a party atmosphere in the credit union.

"Gee, how are you today?" Don asked with a smile. "What do you think of the beginning of Harvest?"

"It came as a surprise. Did everyone else know in advance?" Gee asked as he spotted tellers with wreaths on their heads.

"We all knew it was coming, but no one knew when. There was a lot of speculation as to whether it would be now or next weekend or the following one. But that kind of guessing occurs every year. It's entirely up to the foresters to declare when the nuts are ripe. Sometimes they even let slip that it will on one date and then sound the sirens a week late or a week early. The Families don't even know the date in advance," Don said. "It keeps the tourists off balance, so they can't reliably schedule their time here. The second weekend of Harvest, things get really crazy as tourists show up."

"It seems like a lot of celebration for a week of picking nuts," Gee sighed. "I guess the best thing is to just go with the flow."

"That's the way to do it. The trees and nuts have been harvested for over 150 years. Somewhere along the line, someone suggested that if they were going to work that hard, there should be a party to celebrate when it ended. That extended to a party when it began. Now there is a party every night. Go with the flow, but remember you have to be on the job when and where you're assigned. You've made a commitment to the Forest."

"'Thanks for the advice, Don."

"There will be rewards, too. Shake well!"

Gee headed up Main Street toward Karen's house wondering at the continued festive air. Workers were unfurling banners across Main Street that said, 'Welcome to Harvest.' Flags—a picture of the nine-leaflet compound leaf of the hickory and a cluster of nuts emblazoned on them— flew from nearly every storefront and street light. The City was transforming before his eyes. The bells had begun to ring from the Lutheran Church and were answered by the smaller churches in town. He could hear the responding peals from the Catholic church farther south.

"So, what do you think of your adopted home now?" Troy Cavanaugh asked, stepping out of the doorway of WRZF and bumping into Gee. None too gently. "Sorry about that," he said.

"I love seeing everyone so excited," Gee said, thinking nothing of being jostled on the crowded street. Though not close, he counted Troy among the friends he'd made in Rosebud Falls. They played basketball on Sundays. For the past two weeks he'd been telling stories of the Harvest in bygone eras.

Gee saw Karen emerge from the office of the *Mirror* across the street and began to pick up his pace to go meet her. He felt a hand tighten on his shoulder and turned to see Troy looking at her.

"You may think you've got her in the bag," Troy growled at him. "But you're just a convenient tool for her. You don't have what she wants. You aren't Family. Just remember, you're disposable." Gradually, the grip loosened on his shoulder and Gee stepped in front of him to confront Troy. "Hey, I hope you have a great Harvest," Troy continued as if he'd said nothing before. "I get double duty, broadcasting from a booth next to the river and gathering deadwood for an hour or two after lunch. I thought I'd be a shaker back in my younger days but can't do that and still be the Eye on Main."

"Thanks, Troy."

"No hard feelings, man. Just a moment of regret."

"No problem, Troy." Gee crossed the street to join Karen.

"What did he want?" she demanded when Gee caught her hand in his and turned her up Main.

"Karen… Sweetheart…" She looked up at him and smiled. "The past is the past. We only have today."

"You are so good for me, Gee," she said brightening. "Come on. Everyone's off work this afternoon. Let's make love and then get ready for tonight."

"Football?"

"The Forest Walk," she said excitedly. They hurried home.

Strategy

"Did the notices go out?" Deacon asked his legal counsel.

"Before the last siren died," Matt answered. "The Board passed approval of the seventy-two-hour shareholder notification over a year ago and it was ratified at the last annual meeting. Technically, we could have the meeting any time after two o'clock on Wednesday, but the nine a.m. Thursday time will all but guarantee no local shareholders will attend. They'll all be too busy with Harvest. Per the same rule change, the Board of Directors holds the proxy for any unvoted share."

"We're home free, then. We should begin immediately with the position statement opposing the annexation and strong suggestion that all employees oppose it. Second, we adopt the Forest motion and inform the Families that we will oppose all efforts to take over the wild woods. Make sure it is worded in such a way that as the representatives of the Savage Family holdings, we invoke our sovereignty over the lands we manage. Finally, we'll move to the Board re-election. I want the whole meeting done in thirty minutes so no one has time to mount an opposition."

"Even if the Savage who has come to town wields the Family shares, we have him beaten," Matt said. "I'd suggest a tender offer for all outstanding shares. We've been planning the takeover for years. We should hit it all at once."

"Can we put the tender offer on the table before Board re-elections?"

"I don't see why not."

"Let's get this done."

Forest Walk

"I bought these for you because I knew you'd be clueless," Karen laughed after they'd made love again and had dinner.

"Clueless. That's me," Gee laughed. "I feel like I've been turned loose in a little cove of the ocean. As soon as I think I know my way around the cove, I find an opening and discover there is a big bay just beyond what I know. I'm sure that when I'm comfortable in the bay, I'll discover an ocean—or something bigger."

"Whatever you find, you'll still be swimming," Karen laughed. "Here is your shirt and hat."

"You bought me clothes?"

"Sort of a uniform. The tan shirt will mark you as a shaker. And I just thought this hat would look good on you. Now, go get dressed and I'll be out in fifteen minutes."

GEE FINISHED SHAVING and felt his face to make sure there was no stubble. He thought he might have his cheek against Karen's tender skin again this evening. The tan shirt fit perfectly, and he set the hat—a sort of slouch style with one side of the brim pinned up against the crown— jauntily on his head. He waited in the sitting room for Karen.

Her appearance took his breath away.

She wore a pink pullover sweater with a wide neck that let it slide over one shoulder. Her full skirt extended to mid-calf and she wore ankle boots with a low heel. A wide brimmed deep pink sunhat and knit shawl completed the outfit.

"Stunning," he breathed. "Simply stunning. I'd never have imagined you in pink."

"Neither would I until I was assigned to hospitality," Karen laughed. "I'm kind of fond of it though. It's like being a different person during Harvest."

Gee threw his denim jacket over one shoulder as Karen took his arm and they walked into the cool evening air to join the increasing throngs moving toward the Forest. Occasionally, they still heard horns tooting out the Harvest sequence in the parking lots or along Main Street, but as they neared the Forest, things got quieter. People greeted each other, joined in quiet conversation, and simply strolled through the dark peace of the Forest. Karen, like many others, carried a flashlight, but left it turned off. There were few obstacles as they followed the paths among the trees.

An increasing glow led them to a tree surrounded by lanterns. Beneath the tree a colorful canvas spread extending beyond the full canopy of the tree.

"The grandfather tree," Gee said. "He gave me my nut."

"He's the center of the closing ceremonies and will be felled around the first of November," Karen explained. "There are a few others scattered through the Forest that have been marked for timber as well. The old timers know every tree in the Forest, so they'll head straight to work, but I'm sure Jonathon will lead you to your first tree. Your ground crew will work ahead of you to spread the catcher beneath your next tree. As soon as you move, your pickers will gather the nuts."

"The catcher? This canvas?"

"Yes. And also, the crew responsible for stretching it ahead of your arrival and gathering it up when your pickers leave. Back in the old days, they just shook the nuts on the ground and the pickers had to hunt for them among the leaves and mulch. Someone came up with the idea of spreading canvas drop cloths under the trees, so it would be easier to see and collect the nuts. That evolved into custom-sewn canvas catchers."

"They're beautiful."

"Another gradual evolution. The children started drawing on the canvases and eventually had contests to see which class could decorate the nicest catcher. They got sponsors among the businesses who buy the canvas and paints for the kids to work. Even a few professionals compete. Judging is on Memorial Day at the end of the school year."

"The whole mystique of the Forest just increases each time I'm out here," Gee sighed. "I feel at home out here."

Karen hugged herself to his side. Gee placed his arm across her shoulders to keep her warm. Once they had left the pool of light cast by the lanterns around the tree and headed into the darker Forest, he paused and drew her to him for a romantic kiss. They saw many other couples engaged in the same activity.

"Statistically, there are more births in Rosebud Falls in June than any other time of year," Karen giggled. "Something about Harvest makes people… more amorous."

"I empathize," Gee whispered. Karen came into his arms again and their lips met.

"So do I."

Shaker

JONATHON MET GEE at a quarter till seven and checked his gear—gloves, hardhat, whistle, and goggles.

"The nuts are only an inch to an inch-and-a-half wide and weigh about ten grams. But a lot will come out of the tree at once. And there is an occasional loose limb. Hence the hardhat," Jonathon explained.

"So, things will be falling on me," Gee said. "Hope none of it is too big!"

Jonathon donned a hardhat and goggles like Gee's and issued the rest of the equipment, a harness with a flipline, a ladder, and a long pole wrapped in foam rubber. "One of the main things is to keep your pickers from getting under the tree while you're shaking. Seems we have at least one kid crying before ten in the morning because they got hit by too many nuts or a dead branch came down. Still, almost every time you shake, you'll find one standing under the tree with an umbrella over her head and giggling like crazy."

"Kids will do anything once."

"Let's take your equipment and find you a tree," Jonathon laughed. "Since you are a novice shaker, I've got you assigned a region not far from our coordination station on this end of the Forest for today. We'll get you started and your pickers and crew boss will arrive about eight o'clock. You should have one tree ready to pick by the time they get here. The catchers move ahead of you to spread the canvas for your next tree. There are over 30,000 trees in the Forest, so once we start, we work hard and long."

"The nuts are already falling," Gee commented as one hit the ground in front of him. He thought about the nut grandfather tree had given him until Jonathon drew him back to the task at hand.

"We've had crews out for four days gathering the ground fall," Jonathon said. "And after the Harvest, there will be gleaners sweeping the Forest until snowfall to be sure we get the late fallers and anything that got covered by catchers. We gauge the time to hold Harvest based on the number of nuts per hour that fall naturally. If we waited for them to all fall naturally, it would take three weeks for the tree to clear and we'd have to be out picking every day. We want to get Harvest over in a week so the whole town isn't tied up for three solid weeks and we don't want to import labor. So, we need to shake the remaining nuts off the tree."

"What happens if it rains?" Gee asked.

"We keep picking," Jonathon responded. "But we do it carefully."

Some younger trees could be shaken by hand while standing on the ground, but a full-grown tree could be a hundred or more feet tall with a three-foot diameter trunk.

"With trees the size of these, the amount of shaking necessary with a machine would damage the tree. So, we climb. We've made sure each tree has a path for your extension ladder. Get up high, rope yourself to the tree so you don't fall, and then keep climbing. Reach as high as possible to shake the upper limbs with the pole. Once the top nuts start to fall, they cascade down the tree. Upper nuts shake lower ones off the branches. You should be able to reach up about seventy-five or eighty feet. Don't beat at the limbs. Sort of stir them with the pole. You'll be glad you have the hardhat."

Jonathon sent Gee up the ladder and stood back. It took Gee a few minutes to get secured with his flipline and comfortable enough that he could lean back and use both hands to shake the tree with the pole. Once he got a rhythm going, the nuts started to fall. They popped and clattered against his hardhat.

Gee worked his way around the trunk using branches and the flipline to support himself. This extended his reach by several feet as he leaned back against the safety harness. The tree rained nuts for nearly half an hour before the fall tailed off to a mere trickle.

"Good work!" Jonathon called. "Come on down and meet your crew." Gee made his way back to the ladder, detached his flipline, and came down. He collapsed the extension ladder and moved it away from the tree, nuts crunching underfoot. His crew was an entire second grade class with two teachers and an old woman driving a small tractor and trailer.

"Gee!" a small bundle of energy flung herself at him.

"Sally Ann! Is this your class that will be picking my trees?"

"Yes! This is my teacher, Mrs. Zimmer."

Gee looked up at the woman. She was, indeed, as tall as Sally Ann had told him—at least an inch taller than he was. Her bright green eyes and honey blonde hair were striking.

"Sally Ann has told the class a lot about you and your reading hour at the library. "Of course, she did this as a means of telling me how inadequate my story-reading skills are." Mrs. Zimmer cocked an eyebrow at Sally Ann, who blushed and hung her head. "Perhaps we need you to read to our class one day," she laughed.

"I'd be delighted. Just let me know, Mrs. Zimmer."

"Colleen. I'm only Mrs. Zimmer to my students in school. It's nice to meet you. Children, let's get those nuts gathered. There are prizes for the most baskets gathered in the day, but remember, the baskets have to be full and Mrs. Sims will be keeping tally at the wagon. Ready, set, go!" The kids rushed to the tree with their baskets and began gathering the nuts Gee had knocked from the tree.

"Wow! That was great!" Gee said, looking up at where he had climbed. A few nuts still fell.

"Gee, this is your crew boss, Coretta Sims," Jonathon said. "Finest crew boss in town."

"Jonathon, you are just trying to butter me up so I'll put in a good word with Jessie," the old woman said. "He's been after my granddaughter since they were fourteen," she laughed turning to Gee. "You look like a fine shaker, young man. This is your first Harvest, Jonathon tells me. It's my seventy-fifth. I wouldn't miss it for the world!"

"That's impressive, Mizz Sims."

"You call me Coretta. We're going to get along just fine. I was carried to the Forest on my mother's back like a papoose before I was a year old. Haven't missed a Harvest since. Get another tree shaken down before these kids are finished here. And young man," she said, taking his gloved hand in hers and looking him in the eye. She winked. "Save me a dance at the party tonight and I'll introduce you to Jessie."

"Co-ret-ta!" Jonathon moaned. She cocked an eye at her future grandson-in-law and smirked.

———◁◆▷———

The Catcher said to his Shaker,
Shaker why don't you sing?
You've got a shaker pole and a big ripe tree.
Now listen to those hickory nuts rain (on me!)
Listen to those hickory nuts rain!

Gee's catcher crew—the ones who spread canvas under the trees, held his ladder steady, and folded canvases from trees that had already been picked—were also his chief cheering section. He discovered how much singing helped keep the kids focused on their three-hour shift before another class arrived to take their place. He was a little disconcerted when he realized the Shaker song was based on Pete Seeger's rendition of 'John Henry.' The steel-driving man had burst his heart trying to out-drive a steam drill. Of course, that part wasn't in the children's version of the song. Gee later discovered there were more ribald lyrics used by some of the teens.

> If I was a shaker,
> I'd shake it in the morning.
> I'd shake it in the evening,
> All over this land.

The crews were not slow to adapt almost any song lyrics to keep the work flowing. His catchers were all dressed as clowns and were there as much to keep the kids entertained and inspired to stay ahead of Gee's progress spreading canvases and supporting his climbs. During breaks, Gee found that catcher costumes varied by crew. There were four catcher crews that were high school cheerleaders and kept the crews from the sports teams motivated. Another crew adapted gospel tunes. There was even a crew that chanted army cadences. Whatever would motivate the shaker and pickers on their crew to keep working.

> Hickory nuts keep fallin' on my head,
> But that doesn't mean my eyes will soon be turning red.
> Cryin's not for me…

Over a hundred crews, worked under the guidance of the forest ers. Most crews included a shaker, three catchers, ten-to twelve pickers, and a crew boss. The elementary school crews, however, comprised entire classes of twenty to thirty kids and their teachers. After their shifts, the kids went back to school activities so they didn't get too tired in the Forest.

THE WORK EXHAUSTED Gee. He climbed trees all day and swung the shaker pole through the branches, gently knocking the ripe nuts loose from their tenuous hold on the branch. The sound of the nuts raining down on the catcher stayed in his ears long after he had finished the last tree for the day at nearly seven o'clock when the light was fading. A twelve-hour work day! And through it all, old Coretta Sims had stayed with him, recording the tally of each child (for prizes) and swapping out loaded wagons for empties as the haulers came through the Forest. She managed the change over of four groups of children.

When he'd stored his equipment, Coretta pointed at her clipboard and got right up in Gee's face.

"We're short of our quota today, Gee," she said. "The pickers could have taken another tree in every shift, but you were slow. We can't have that. I never fall short of my quota and I won't start now."

"I'm sorry Mizz Sims. I thought I was working quickly. It was my first time, so I'll do better tomorrow." The old woman laughed at him—a full round joyful belly laugh.

"Oh, no you won't, Gee," she said through her laughter. "I know all the excuses and tomorrow the excuse will be that you are sore. Oh, and you *will* be sore! We always expect the first couple of days to be a little slow. By day three you will be up to quota. After that, we'll start gaining back what we lost the first two days."

"I was afraid you were mad at me, Mizz Sims."

"If you call me that one more time I'll get your shaker pole and start shaking *your* limbs! I'm Coretta. If you can't get your lips to form that word, then join the children in calling me Grams. Calling me Mizz Sims is the only thing that will get me mad at you, young man. But a crew boss has to put the fear of God into her shaker. Understand?"

"Ma'am, whether I'm afraid of God or not, I'm certainly afraid of you," Gee said, joining her laughter.

"Let's get some food and you can get home for a nice long bath. Here, I brought you this box of bath crystals. Don't eat them or drink the water. They're made from the hulls of the nuts. But, oh, they are so relaxing. You'll feel better in the morning."

"True," Jonathon came up to them as they entered the big tent where dinner was being served for the crews. "I was going to suggest you get some bath crystals. Glad Coretta thought of it."

"Of course I thought of it. Gee, if this lug of a forester would step aside, I'd like to introduce you to my granddaughter, Jessie. She's also a shaker." She playfully pushed Jonathon aside and pulled her granddaughter toward them.

"Happy to meet you, Miss Jessie," Gee said extending his hand. She took it easily.

"The same, Mr. Gee."

"Just Gee."

"Then just Jessie," she giggled.

"Now, Jessica, Gee is a fine young man, not so much older than you. He looked good climbing those trees today. You might want to test his limbs for strength yourself," Coretta said. Gee was about to object to the stockyard presentation to her granddaughter but caught the teasing tone of the old woman.

"Grandma!" the scandalized young woman cried. "Jonathon is right beside me."

"Now why would you care about him?" Coretta said rolling her eyes like a teenager.

"Grandma, he's my nut man," Jessie said, grabbing hold of Jonathon's arm and leaning against the relieved young man.

"Well, he'd better do something about getting a ring on your finger then before someone better comes along. I was sixteen when my nut man claimed me as his bride and we've had sixty years without finding a reason to regret it. You're both twenty-five. How am I ever supposed to hold my great-grandchildren if you don't get busy and produce them?"

"I think that's a good idea, don't you, Jonathon?" Jessie said softly. "We could have the first one on the ground in June with everyone else."

"Really, Jessie? Are you ready?"

"Get Judge Warren to bring us the papers tomorrow, Jonathon. We'll join the Harvest wedding."

AFTER CONGRATULATING JESSIE and Jonathon and getting food from the long buffet set up in the River Park, Gee made his weary way home. He ran water in the bathtub and gratefully sank into the pink-tinged foam created by the crystals. Every muscle in his body ached.

———⊲♦⊳———

"GEE! GEE! WHERE are you?"

He startled himself awake in the lukewarm water at the sound of Karen's frantic voice.

"Gee!" Karen burst into his bedroom and saw him through the open bathroom door. "Gee? Are you okay?"

"I'm fine, Karen. I just dozed off."

"I expected you downstairs and then I couldn't find you and I was worried that you'd been injured in the Forest and no one told me or that I'd find you drowned or…" She finally paused as she stood in the bathroom doorway looking at him.

"Karen? I'm in the tub." The light foam of the crystals had long-since dispersed.

"I… oh! Yes… Um… I'll… I see… I'll… just go… um… get ready for bed," she spluttered as she staggered from the room.

Gee quickly rinsed off in the shower and grabbed his sweats. Before he left the bathroom, though, he stopped to lather his face and scrape the day's growth from his chin.

———⊲♦⊳———

KAREN WAS SITTING up in Gee's bed with two cups of tea steeping on the bedside table. She looked up at Gee when he entered the room and immediately blushed.

"Oh, my God. I feel like such a twit," she laughed. "We're lovers and I still… I walked right in on you in the bathtub and got embarrassed! I haven't felt… embarrassed… around a man in… ten years. Suddenly, I feel like a teenager who's never seen a man before."

"I don't remember what it feels like to be a teenager," Gee whispered as he sat and pulled Karen next to him. She pressed her face against his shoulder. "I don't remember a lover before you. Does it feel like your heart is beating here, in the hollow of your throat just above your collar bone? Does it feel like tears are just about to spring from your eyes and you're afraid your nose will start dripping and the person you are looking at will be disgusted and start hating you? Does it make your hands shake and feel sweaty? Do you feel caterpillars crawling up and down your arms and neck? Are you afraid you'll panic and run, but you can't move

your feet? Is that feeling like a teenager or just being in love?" Karen
nodded and raised her face to look at him. Her eyes sparkled, and her
mouth turned up in a smile.

"How did you know?"

"I think I must feel like a teenager, too," he said as he closed the distance to her lips.

Invasive Species

IT WAS DIFFICULT for Gee to drag himself out of bed in the morning.
Everything hurt, and Karen was holding him tightly. The six o'clock
alarm gave him just enough time to shave, dress, and make a cup of
coffee before heading out to meet Jonathon.

He arrived to find Jonathon looking no better than he did, sipping
his own cup of coffee as he waited for Gee.

"Uh… You look like…"

"Don't I know it," Jonathon said. "Looks like you didn't get much
sleep either."

"I'm sore."

"It's like that after the first night," Jonathon grinned. "Especially if
you have a girlfriend." Both men laughed and headed to the next tree to
get it shaken down before Gee's pickers arrived.

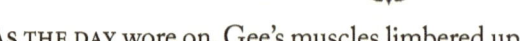

AS THE DAY wore on, Gee's muscles limbered up and he was able to work
progressively faster through the day. He soon found the rhythm, helped
along by the songs of his catchers. As soon as he was securely fastened
to his flipline, he hauled his shaker pole up by the safety rope and began
rattling the nuts off the tree.

He was the highest he'd climbed in an older tree when he heard frantic pleas from below him and turned to see Sally Ann running toward
his tree. Gee unsnapped his safety harness and slid down the ladder as
rapidly as gravity could take him. The little girl rushed to his arms.

"Gee! I saw him! I saw the bad man. He was watching us over there."
She pointed to the tree the children had been picking and he saw her

teacher, Colleen Zimmer starting toward them. Gee didn't hesitate. He reached into his shirt and pulled out the emergency whistle each of the shakers and foremen had been issued and put it between his teeth. Holding his hands over Sally Ann's ears, he blasted an emergency signal from the whistle and repeated it. Mrs. Zimmer began to run toward them and he saw the other teacher and Coretta stop the other children from joining the rush. There was a procedure for emergencies and Coretta knew it well. The children were assembled into rows and rollcall was taken, just as it would be in a fire drill at school. It was more the familiarity with the drill and its ability to calm the students than it was necessary to see that they were all present.

Jonathon and three other foresters ran to the clearing from different directions, converging on Gee's whistle. Mrs. Zimmer was demanding to know what was wrong as Gee handed Sally Ann to her and asked her to wait until the foresters arrived.

"Injury?" Jonathon asked immediately, moving to the little girl.

"No. Possibly worse, Jonathon. At the fair this summer, a man attempted to kidnap Sally Ann. She saw the man in the Forest a few minutes ago, watching her class."

"We got a bulletin with a sketch last month," one of the foresters said. "If this is true, we need to get it circulated through all the teams."

"Especially the ones with children," Gee added. "Rena's sketch was derived mostly from Sally Ann's description, and I was amazed at how close it came to my own recollection. If she says she saw him again, I believe her completely."

"We'll get the alert out and notify the police," an older forester said. "Jonathon, stay with this group of children and keep an eye peeled. Samuel, organize a forester with every group of children under the age of sixteen. I'll take care of the police." The older forester turned and jogged toward the organization tent and the other two foresters headed immediately out, talking on a handset to the other foresters. Jonathon closed his eyes for just a moment and exhaled a deep breath. When he opened his eyes, he emerged as the happy and playful forester who had given orientation to the children at the library. He conducted Mrs. Zimmer and Sally Ann away from Gee's tree and back to where the other children were still standing in their rows.

"Kids! What's the best kind of wind in the world?"

"A hickory wind!" The kids shouted in response.

"And what did the hickory wind give us?"

"Nuts!"

"A hickory wind knocked down all these nuts. If we want the hickory wind to return, we should pick up what it gave us. Who's going to have the first full basket."

"Me!" they all shouted.

"Ready, set, go!" Jonathon yelled. The kids scattered on the catcher canvas as Jonathon went to one side of the circle and directed the two teachers and Coretta to opposite corners. Gee caught his breath and climbed the tree.

"A WORD, GEE?" Detective Oliver said softly as Gee filled his plate from the buffet that evening.

"Of course, Mead," Gee said.

"Did you see the guy?"

"No. I was focused on Sally Ann. She was shaking like a leaf. He was long gone before I looked up."

"I was hoping to confirm her description."

"Not the same guy?" Gee asked.

"No, apparently, exactly the same guy. Her description of him only varied in what he was wearing. I took her to see Rena and she drew almost the same picture as she had the last time, but with a different hat and a plaid shirt."

"Well, that's good isn't it?"

"I don't have a lot of experience in this, Gee. Rosebud Falls is a peaceful place. I've had more to do since you got to town than in the past ten years. But you would think that a kid's description would vary a little, wouldn't you? Or an artist's drawing? I have to admit, Rena's talent as an artist is way better than I ever expected. But, it's almost like she's repeating something she made up," Mead puzzled.

"Unless she saw exactly the same man both times," Gee answered.

"Sure you didn't see anything? You know, from up there?"

"Sorry, Mead. I'd help more if I could. I'll be more watchful."

"Okay. Well, enjoy your dinner. We're going to circulate the sketches to everyone we can. With that many people looking out for him, maybe it will make him a little scared to come into *our* Forest."

"How is Rena, by the way? I haven't seen her since… the incident."

"She's in rehab. Doing better, she says, but isn't ready to face the world."

"I hope she mends. I can't help but worry about her."

"Mmmhmm. Better stay clear for now. Doctor says it's best to let her set the pace."

"I'll be very late tomorrow night, sweetheart," Karen said as she lay her head on Gee's shoulder. She'd listened in varying degrees of agitation as Gee told her about Sally Ann spotting 'the bad man' and what Mead had suggested about her describing the exact same thing.

"Adults simply don't give credence to children," Karen said. "I'll make sure the sketches run in Tuesday's *Mirror*. As I started to say, I'll be late tomorrow night. With Axel on nighttime security, I get the responsibility of putting the paper to bed."

"You are always a little late on Mondays. Somewhere in my background there must have been a daily newspaper because it seems odd to me to have a paper that is published Tuesday through Saturday," Gee laughed.

"It's not uncommon in this region. It lets most of us work an almost-normal Monday through Friday job. And having a Saturday edition allows us to get in all the regional high school sports scores from Friday night," she answered.

"I guess it makes sense in its own little world."

"There isn't usually much to do during Harvest. The paper is mostly stock stories. We keep a couple of slots open if something develops, but most of the layout is completed way in advance. But with Axel gone and me in charge…"

"…while the cat's away…"

"Tuesday morning's lead story will be about the stalker in the Forest even though it will be old news by then. But inside, the Families will wake to chaos as I reveal the missing heir of the Seven Heroes."

"You want to tarnish their reputations?"

"No. Just the opposite. In my great-grandmother's papers, I uncovered evidence that the oft maligned Joseph Roth actually *did* recognize his bastard child and that his father hid the letter and insurance payment from Joe's heirs. My great-great-grandfather was a royal ass. The LaCoes will file the papers with Judge Warren Monday afternoon. We're suing the entire Roth Family—including me—on behalf of the heir for her share of the Roth fortune and property."

"And that means the other Families will have to support the suit based on their own recognition of the orphans," Gee mused, pulling Karen closer to him.

"Mmm. I hope so. It will right an injustice from long ago and I want to do it while Joseph's daughter, Celia, is still living."

"I hope it doesn't backfire. Maybe I should come down to walk you home when you're working that late." Gee had an uneasy feeling about what Karen planned, though he agreed that the injustice needed to be righted.

"Don't worry. I'll have my bodyguard," Karen said simply. "I trust him."

Praise for the Worthy

"VERY GOOD, BROTHER Reef. All you need to do is keep showing up and disappearing. You don't need to actually snatch anyone. You can always take a camper if you need relief. That's what they are here for."

"Yes, sir. Thank you, sir." They were the only words he ever said. Such a good, obedient servant.

"Take some of the children into the wild wood and have them gather nuts for our lab. You know how to reward them for their service."

"Yes, sir."

"Should you run into any problems, here are a few tablets. You know what to do."

"Yes, sir."

9
CONSCIENCE OBJECTION

Family Business

MEAD CIRCULATED copies of the sketch to all shakers, foremen, and teachers on Monday. Two whistles sounded in different parts of the forest as suspects were spotted by over-vigilant workers, but it took only a few moments for police to dismiss the men without even taking them to the station. One had been black and the other barely five feet tall and 200 pounds. People were on edge.

It strained the limited resources of the police department. Off-duty sheriff's deputies were stationed at the elementary school to cover traffic. Many parents who could arrange their volunteer and work schedules joined their children's classes in the Forest. Gee saw Dale and Ruth Ann Metzger with Sally Ann's class on Monday. They nodded politely to him and went back to watching the children and scanning the surrounding Forest. Gee found that he, too, was scanning as he climbed.

———⊲◆⊳———

WHEN HE FINISHED for the day, Gee was surprised to find Judge Warren waiting for him to stow his tools.

"You're doing a mighty fine job of shaking those trees," Warren said. "Coretta speaks highly of you."

"She's a gem. And the kids all love her."

"She is at that. I've always considered her my aunt, though we aren't closely related. We'd probably have to go back a few generations to find a common ancestor, but all the war orphans considered themselves to be brothers and sisters," the judge said.

"You... Certainly you aren't old enough to be one of the war orphans."

"No. Of course not. My mother. That's why I still think of Coretta, Celia and Heinz as my aunts and uncle. My mother was born Dee Poltanys. The four of them remaining are as close as any group of siblings you will ever find."

"What happened to the other three?"

"Henry Lazorack was killed in a fall last Harvest. Ewan Meagher was lost in Viet Nam. Pàl Savage left the town with his grandfather back in the mid-fifties and hasn't been seen since. Personally, I think we'll find soon that Wayne Savage is now the heir to that family. But that's why I've come to see you, Gee. I find we have need of a champion."

"Hmm. I think this is the first time I've been approached in advance. It seems like I'm usually just in time to find an emergency," Gee mused. "What can the City Champion do for you?"

"Join me for dinner. Not here at the buffet. Let's go to Louie's."

"I thought he was only open in the morning."

"Oh, the café is closed, but Argos promised a good meal and a quiet place to talk. Would you like to invite Karen?"

"She has to put the paper to bed tonight. You should assume, though, that anything I hear, she will hear later tonight."

"Unlike some of the Families, I trust her."

GEE HAD LISTENED to nearly an hour of history, some of which he'd heard before, but now had additional context for the dedication of the four remaining war orphans, including the fact that there was a trust for each of them. Each trust held one hundred thousand shares of SSG stock. The trustee wanted to give Gee the proxy for their shares and have him attend the annual meeting.

"Why me, Judge? This seems like Family business to me."

"Yes, I suppose so. But it is about the City and the Forest. We believe the annexation may hinge in part on the shareholders' meeting. And it's more than that, Gee. It's true that we don't want the Families exposed as shareholders of SSG, but you are part of the Forest. It claimed you when you ate the nut. Without having a Family name, you are still recognized as an equal by the heads of the Families," Judge Warren said. "I can't even begin to tell you how that astounds me."

"Judge, I don't want to interfere with Family matters."

"Believe me, not all the Family heads are in complete agreement. It upsets a two-hundred-year tradition. But in spite of the fact that Heinz is in the dual role of head of Family and war orphan, and Collin Meagher is batty as they come, the war orphans have selected you to represent them on behalf of the Forest."

"What about David Lazorack. Wasn't his father a war orphan?"

"Yes. David chose to abstain from the vote. But he told the trustee to give you his proxy."

"And you just want me to go to the meeting Thursday morning and vote my conscience."

"That's all we ask, Gee. Take the proxies not as a representative of the Families, but as Champion of the Forest." They sat in silence as Gee mulled over the request. It seemed simple enough. It was unlikely that voting six hundred thousand shares would truly affect the outcome, but it seemed reasonable to do it.

"Wait! I'm supposed to shake trees. I can't take time off to go to the meeting. Harvest!"

"Cameron LaCoe has volunteered to fill in for you, and his three cousins will work as catchers and entertainment. He was a shaker in high school and is happy to get back in a tree." Judge Warren lowered his voice, even though it was only the two of them in the dining room at the back of Louie's Café. "The truth is, this was all Cameron's idea. He's the one who found out SSG was going to give short notice for its annual shareholders' meeting and uncovered the information about the orphans' trusts. His grandfather talked him out of being the point man and after a little consideration, Cameron agreed that you were the right candidate."

"Okay then. I'm in. I'll get back to the Forest as quickly as I can after the meeting."

"Good. Then I can give you this, which is the signed proxy from the trust funds for six hundred thousand shares. I suppose it's a drop in the bucket of five million outstanding shares, but at least it is a voice. Now I can focus on the shit that will hit the fan in the morning," he laughed.

"What?"

"I know what Karen is working on tonight," Warren said. "I signed the lawsuits this afternoon."

THE STORY IN Tuesday's newspaper and the suit filed before Judge Warren by the LaCoes on behalf of Celia Eberhardt Ransom were the talk of the Forest. Everyone had an opinion and as Gee listened, he discovered that even those who had no apparent Family ties knew the story of Celia Eberhardt and her mother being shunned by the Roths. The prevailing opinion was that she should get her revenge on the Family and have her share of the wealth.

Five elders gathered at Benjamin Roth's riverside home Tuesday evening. Jan Poltanys sat on Ben's right with Leah Roth-Augello on her father's left. Filling out the table were Heinz Nussbaum, Loren Cavanaugh, and David Lazorack. None was happy to be away from Harvest.

"What are you going to do, Benjamin?" Heinz demanded. The old man scowled back. Benjamin Roth hadn't been out of his mansion in five years, exercising his right as the eldest to hold Family meetings in his home. He was a spindly old man who forced himself to use a cane and walk instead of being wheeled around in a chair. But he had turned over nearly all the Family holdings to his daughter's management.

"*Nekeyve!*" the old man spat. "My sister raises her whoring head again even from the grave. This is her fault. If she had these papers as proof of our father's treachery, she should have exposed them as soon as he was dead. Instead she let our children inherit her mess." Benjamin scowled at the silent figures around the table and finally lit on his daughter. "If there is anything left of our Family's honor, it is up to *you* to redeem it. But understand this. The young Ransom girl and Karen Weisman have as much family claim to our share of the Forest as your sons, Leah. Eventually, someone will have to eat the nut."

Everyone was silent for a few moments.

"Well, Leah?" Before she could answer his question, Benjamin stood and tottered out of the room. "Good night. I am tired."

"He's right," Leah sighed. "Our Family name is disgraced. The cloud has been over our head since the beginning. It was stupid of my grandfather to think he could keep it secret. I talked to Karen before she wrote the article and filed the suits. As much as I did not want to agree with her, I couldn't find fault with her reasoning. The disgrace was brought on by our common ancestor. Every Family has its skeletons, and you are all secretly praying that Karen or someone like her doesn't discover and expose them. It is up to us and our children to set things right. I'll offer to settle with Celia Eberhardt and her granddaughter."

"Just like that? You seem pretty content to give up your family's holdings based on a newspaper article," Lazorack said.

"Oh, we'll get verification, affidavits, and maybe even a DNA sample. But in the end, I'll settle. What do you think she'll need to be happy? A million? Two? A house. It's a drop in the bucket compared to what we are about to achieve with the annexation."

"She is one of us," Heinz said softly. "Seven orphans, one from each family. Dee Poltanys, Coretta Sims, Henry Lazorack, even Pàl Savage, and I have all done what we could to see that Celia was treated respectfully. We all mourned together at Henry's passing. I think Ewan Meagher would have married her if we hadn't lost him in Viet Nam. I'll talk to Dee and Coretta. I think I can speak for them and say we'll commit to matching your contribution to Celia and Jo, Leah."

"I'll see that Coretta is compensated adequately to contribute. I know she'll want to," Loren Cavanaugh said softly.

"The same with Aunt Dee," Jan Poltanys said. "She built that retirement home so she and Celia would have a place to live."

Eyes turned to David Lazorack, who shifted uncomfortably in his chair.

"Okay. You're right. My father would have wanted this. In his memory, I'll contribute, too," David said.

Proxy Fight

THE SCANDAL AMONG the Families, especially the Jews, fit Deacon's plans just fine. They always thought they owned everything. He was reasonably certain that no one had time to pay attention to a corporate meeting with Harvest and the public relations hassle the Families would endure. The reporter had played right into his hand and public notice of the shareholders' meeting had been buried on the last page of the newspaper just below an article on the use of hickory tree sap as a treatment for arthritis.

He was surprised at the number of people in the room when he walked in on Thursday morning. Old man Meagher was there, of course. He was a perennial pain in the ass, but he'd been mentally crippled when he ate the nut years ago. He owned ten shares of common stock, which was the minimum needed to speak at a meeting. Deacon knew he would speak and had one of the board members ready to escort the old man out of the room when he was deemed a nuisance.

It bothered Deacon that there were people he didn't know at the meeting. SSG was a publicly held company, but there were fewer shareholders than in big corporations. Most of the stock in the company had been doled out as options to high-ranking employees and Deacon had a substantial portion himself. His seventy-five thousand shares represented one-and-a-half percent of the issued shares. The same number of shares of IBM stock would be worth twenty-five times more but wouldn't be noticed in their one hundred fifty billion-share pool. Investing in a microcap stock had great advantages for a small investor.

He called the meeting to order, asking Pastor Beck to lead them in an invocation that God would guide the decision-making process for this great company.

"Minutes of the last annual meeting were approved by email, so we can proceed directly to the first item on our agenda," Deacon said. "As you all know, the City of Rosebud Falls has manipulated a State law granting limited home rule and is making a land grab for South Rosebud. This is the area for which SSG holds the mineral rights. It has been the foundation of our business for a hundred and fifty years. We have filed for an injunction against the City to stop the proposed annexation, but our District Judge has delayed taking action. We are appealing, but to maintain our viability as a profitable corporation, we must turn our attention to campaigning against the annexation and encouraging the residents in South Rosebud to vote against it. This company policy, approved by the board, is hereby placed before the shareholders for a vote. All those in favor indicate by saying yes." A normal, somewhat muffled vote of yes came from those who assumed this was just a formality. "Those opposed indicate by saying no." There was a shout and loud chorus of voices raised in the negative. The voices were led in a chant of "No. No. No," by none other than Collin Meagher.

"Are we going to start with this already, Collin?" Deacon sighed.

"I object, your dishonor!" Collin said. "This is a shareholder meeting and votes must be taken by share, not by voice. I demand a share count as is my right as a stockholder in this company."

Deacon turned to his counsel and Matt just shrugged. "Might as well get it over with," the lawyer said. "As soon as he realizes that he's outvoted either way, he'll give up on the other votes."

"Very well, Collin, we will vote by share. You understand that after all shares present and accounted for are voted, the board will vote the remaining shares by perpetual proxy. If that is understood, I will begin. As chairman, I have no vote in a voice vote, but as a shareholder, I cast my seventy-five thousand shares in favor. Your turn, Collin." Deacon looked at the old man. At one time he'd been a force to deal with, but after his heir disappeared, the old man had eaten a nut in hope of a heavenly revelation of the child's location. What he got was an addled brain. It had been one of Deacon's best moves.

"I see your seventy-five thousand and raise you five thousand opposed," the old man snarled.

"It isn't poker, Collin. You can only vote the shares you own."

"And I own eighty thousand shares," the old man said. "I have every certificate with me. I've been collecting them for fifteen years with every penny I could scrape up." He held up a sheaf of stock certificates and shook them angrily at Deacon.

"That's well and good," the shocked chairman of the board responded, "but there are five million outstanding shares and that leaves four million eight hundred forty-five thousand shares yet to be voted."

"I'm Levi Dunkel, and I hold the proxy for forty-seven thousand shares of Class A common stock," said another man. "I join Mr. Meagher in casting my votes in opposition."

"Let's have order. If you have shares to vote, form a line at the microphone, state your name and your vote. Then bring your shares and proof of ownership or proxy to the secretary," Deacon shouted at the room. "This is all a colossal waste of time."

A dozen small shareholders rushed the microphone and declared their votes in favor of the company policy. It looked like a lot of people voting, but the total votes were far less than what had already been cast by the two rivals.

"My name is Rex Russell. I hold the Savage Family proxy for one million shares, plus proxies for sixty-two thousand other principals' shares of Class A common stock. I vote in opposition." He approached the secretary and presented his documentation. There was a loud round of applause as the opposition surged far ahead of those proposing a policy of non-annexation. At last, Gee approached the microphone.

"Excuse me. I'm not very experienced with this. My name is Gee. I mean George Evars. I am City Champion for Rosebud Falls. I hold proxies for six hundred thousand shares of Class B common stock that I vote in opposition to the policy." There was applause once again as it began to look like there was a chance that the opposition would win. Rex Russell and Levi Dunkel were huddled together as Gee presented his credentials to the secretary.

"Very well, you've all had your fun. By my tally, that brings the current vote to one million seven hundred twenty thousand votes in opposition and one hundred twenty thousand votes in favor. Mr. Secretary what is the total number and position of the unvoted shares?" Deacon snarled.

"Mr. Chairman, the board holds perpetual proxy for all unvoted shares, that number being three million one hundred fifty-three thousand shares. The board votes those shares in favor." The secretary sat down, leaving the room in stunned silence as Deacon grinned at them.

"Point of order, Mr. Chairman!" Rex Russell said from the microphone. Dunkel and Mr. Meagher flanked him.

"What is your point?"

"Before you announce the final tally, may I direct you to Article Five of the Articles of Incorporation, section two, Definition of Classes of Stock. I quote, 'Class A Common shall have one vote per share. Class B Common shall have ten votes per share.' Mr. Chairman, Mr. Evars voted six hundred thousand shares of Class B stock. He has, thereby, cast six million votes in opposition," Rex finished.

"He what?!" Deacon glared at Matt who was frantically trying to find a copy of the company charter, articles, and bylaws.

"It seems, in fact, that Mr. Evars wields a clear majority of fifty-seven-point-seven percent of the total voteable shares. I move that to simplify and streamline the meeting, remaining questions be turned to him for decision."

"This is preposterous!"

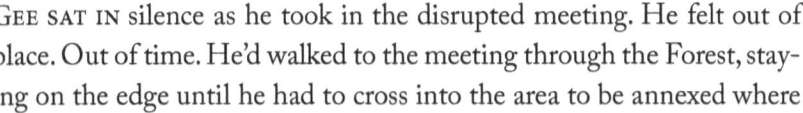

GEE SAT IN silence as he took in the disrupted meeting. He felt out of place. Out of time. He'd walked to the meeting through the Forest, staying on the edge until he had to cross into the area to be annexed where SSG headquarters was located. He'd felt detached since entering the building and fought to anchor himself.

You are not alone. I am holding you in my hand.

Gee recognized the presence in his mind. He wondered if he was having a flashback to the delirium he felt upon waking after eating the nut. The Grandfather Tree held him in its hand and peace began to flood through Gee's mind.

"What will happen when you are cut for timber? How will I know this peace ever again?" Gee asked aloud.

Then you will hold me in your hand.

"YOU!" SHOUTED PASTOR Beck, leaning in to face Gee. "You spawn of Satan! You have had every opportunity to serve God's higher purpose, but instead you reject his grace at every turning. You subvert his message and buck against the traces when he bids you yield to him. Now like Satan before you, you shall be cast from the heights of glory to find your soul in the lowest levels of perdition, there to be gnawed upon by demons for all eternity. You may think you are exalted, but you shall fall."

"That's encouraging," Gee sighed. "As long as I don't have to listen to you."

"You'll have to leave now, Preacher," Rex said as the other major players of what had been the opposition moved to talk to Gee.

"I am a stockholder and have every right to be in this meeting," Beck declared.

"Fine. Sit down and shut up. This is no longer the party you thought you were attending." Rex turned to Gee as the other lawyer pushed the preacher aside. "Mr. Evars, you gave us an unexpected boon today. We planned to come in and make a statement that we were here and would be challenging the management of the company. We'd even planned a hostile takeover if necessary. You made that unnecessary. The Savage Family wants to thank you."

"Wayne?"

"He's one. But it seems that you now control SSG by proxy. While Carl Stewart is trying to put his ducks in a row, we thought we'd better consult with you as to your goals," Rex said.

"I don't have any. I was given these proxies and told to vote my conscience on behalf of the Forest. I did not even know what was on the agenda, nor that my proxies controlled the majority of the votes," Gee said. "I just want to protect the Forest."

"Then let's try to bring our goals in line with yours so we can present a united front. I don't think that's going to be difficult. Our goal is also protecting the Forest, but our strategy is to clean house here at SSG and make sure it is not standing in the way of annexation. The company doesn't have a vote in the general election, but it does have a vote in the Forest management, supposedly exercised on behalf of the Savage Family. We have the opportunity to move quickly where we thought we would have to take weeks or maybe months. We'd like to nominate a new board of directors and elect them with your vote. Of course, you would be on it."

"No. I have no interest or desire to be on the board of directors. Let's see who else is on your list."

By the end of the annual meeting, Deacon Stewart was no longer Chairman of the Board and CEO of Savage Sand and Gravel.

DEACON WAS UNHAPPY about how the meeting had progressed. No one had ever voted the trust fund shares that had so much hidden power. As far as he knew, the six different trusts did nothing but collect the modest dividends on the shares and reinvest them. Perhaps there was a distribution, but after the check was delivered to the trusts, there was no further information available. No one even knew who the beneficiaries were.

As he thought about what he and his worthless corporate counsel had missed, he began to smile. If he had missed something so significant, what had the rabble who took over the company missed? The smile became a chuckle.

"What can you be so happy about?" Matt asked as they headed to their luxurious former offices. No one had followed them, so he anticipated purging his files before he was escorted out of the company. That at least might protect them from prosecution.

"Oh, I just realized," Deacon said to his co-conspirator, "I'm about to become a very wealthy man."

Best Man

THE NUT HARVEST was slowing down and the party was spreading through the Forest and along the river. Most of the trees left to pick were younger and took less time to shake with teams working closer to each other than in the more mature parts of the Forest. As fewer shaker crews were needed, people were reassigned to sweep the Forest for deadwood and to follow the foresters gathering pruned limbs.

Tourists arrived, booking all the available motel rooms and the area campgrounds. Part of the attraction was the opportunity to participate in gathering the poisonous nuts—to actually get to touch them. Visitors who did not participate in the 'gleaning' were confined to the marked paths through the Forest. Those who volunteered were issued a one-peck basket and given a full orientation on the importance of not letting any of the toxic nuts get into unwary hands. When a volunteer filled a basket with nuts gleaned from areas that had already been picked, he or she was given a free pass for the banquet party on Saturday night.

No matter how many warnings were issued, there were reports of people ingesting the nut meat. Generally, paramedics were able to reach the stupid person in time to administer an antidote and transfer him or her to the hospital. Recovery was accompanied by misdemeanor charges.

Shakers and crew foremen who were no longer picking trees joined the foresters to help control the masses moving through the Forest and to see that no Forest products left with the visitors.

Thursday night, booths and displays were set up in the park on both sides of the river. Furniture, beads, lotions, bath salts, coffee, smoked meats, craft projects, stains, t-shirts, toys, and handcrafts were displayed. Vendors who had genuine Rose Hickory products of any sort had an official Rosebud Falls flag on their booths. But many more regional craftsmen gathered to sell artwork, glassware, pottery, and jewelry, even if not made from the local hickory. As Harvest neared its end, the festival grew. In addition, magic acts, music, dancing, and other forms of social entertainment were available all along the river.

"Only Friday and Saturday to go," Jonathon said as he walked with Gee and Coretta Sims toward the park Thursday evening. A bouncing and excited Jessie Sims ran to meet her fiancé.

"Two more days until these two finally tie the knot," Coretta laughed.

"Forty hours!" Jessie shouted.

"You cannot imagine how difficult it has been on this old lady to manipulate them into getting together," Coretta continued.

"Grandma, you only had to let us go. We were like magnets," Jessie laughed. "Did you tell him, Jonathon?"

"Haven't had a chance yet. Gee, we'd like you to take part in the wedding ceremony Saturday. Would you be willing?" Jonathon asked.

"Really? I mean... of course. Uh... What would you like me to do? And when is it?"

"The ceremony is at one o'clock Saturday afternoon," Jessie said. "Judge Warren said there were six hickory couples this year."

"Hickory couples?"

"It's what they call couples who marry during Harvest," Jonathon explained. "The wedding and closing ceremonies will be held at the grandfather tree. All the other trees will be harvested by noon Saturday.

The Judge will perform the ceremony for the couples who want to get married beneath the last tree."

"It makes for a cheap wedding," Coretta laughed. "The newspaper runs the announcement on Friday morning so the whole town knows who is getting married that day. I've seen you with your young lady," Coretta said, digging an elbow into Gee's side. "You should check the newspaper tomorrow morning to see if your name is listed in the weddings!"

"What? They... She... It takes... I mean..."

All three laughed at Gee's loss of composure.

"Don't panic, my man," Jonathon said. "I've seen some hurry-up weddings at Harvest, but I've never seen one where both partners weren't aware it was going to happen." Gee breathed deeply and then sighed.

"Not that it would be a bad thing, you know," he said. "Um... What would you like me to do?"

"Shake it."

"What?"

"The foresters met last night and agreed that we'd like you to shake the last tree. It's an honor, not just for you but for all of the couples, and it's the last official event of Harvest," Jonathon said. "The rest of the weekend is a party."

"Why me? I'm a newcomer. There must be dozens of shakers who would like to do this. I mean, I'm honored and all."

"I honestly don't know, Gee. The forty foresters met at midnight with the boss. That's my dad. We had the list of all this year's shakers. We each wrote the name of the shaker we thought should do the last tree and the ballots were counted. The top vote-getters were up for a second ballot. It only took two rounds for one shaker to get a clear majority of the votes. That shaker was you. And, just so you know, it wasn't a close contest. On the second ballot, you had thirty of forty votes."

"I hardly know what to say."

"Just say you'll shake the last tree in honor of our wedding," Jessie said.

"I will."

The Great Commission

"God sent me, and I send you. Lustre is the Holy Spirit in you. Who you forgive is forgiven; *and* who you damn is damned."

"Yes, sir."

"That man has upset God's natural order. He is damned. God calls for his utter destruction in a most public and dramatic way, so that all may know the wages of sin."

"Yes, sir."

"You may have the little girl as your reward."

"Yes, sir."

Proposal

"Mmm. What a nice welcome home," Karen murmured as her lips left Gee's. It was late and she was surprised he waited for her before going to bed. "What inspired your passion tonight?"

"You are all the inspiration I need," he answered. "Guess what I found out? I've been chosen to shake the last tree!"

"I know! I'm so proud of you," Karen said and kissed him again. She pulled back and looked at his puzzled face. "Oh, dear. I didn't mean to spoil your surprise by sounding like it was old news. I'm sorry."

"How did you know? I only found out this evening. Jonathon told me and then I had to go eat with the foresters as they congratulated me. I didn't think anyone else knew."

"The banns are published tomorrow in the paper. They're not really banns; we just call them that for fun. But all the people involved in harvesting the last tree are listed in a big article in the *Mirror*. It includes the choice of who will shake the tree, who will pick, the names of the couples to be married, the Judge, the names of all the foresters, teams, and even the servers at the tables. Almost the whole paper tomorrow is dedicated to listing the people who have done their part for Harvest. The story leads with the location of the last tree and the names of those involved in the ceremony and wedding. Then the paper is filled with name after name of everyone who has helped and what they've done."

"Of course. Coretta told me the names would be listed in the paper tomorrow. It just didn't occur to me that you would see it first," Gee laughed. Even if it was not a surprise, Karen was still overjoyed with his selection as the shaker. "Uh... Darling... My name isn't mentioned in any of the other lists, is it?"

"What? What other lists? It is in the list of shakers when they are all recognized by job. What do you mean?"

"Oh, I just wanted to know in advance if we were listed in the names of those getting married," he deadpanned. She looked up at him as her eyes widened and she gasped.

"I could run back to the newspaper office and stop the presses!" she exclaimed. It was Gee's turn to gasp in surprise. Karen laughed at him. She settled back into his arms as they leaned against the headboard and sipped the chilled chardonnay Gee had ready for her.

"I missed part of the day shaking today, but Cameron and the Quartet were a big hit with my pickers."

"As editor of the day, I got that story as well. 'The man who engineered the sudden takeover of Savage Sand and Gravel, and then went to Harvest.' You are becoming a folk hero."

"I had no idea what I was doing. And, honestly, I don't think the people who sent me to do it knew how it would play out."

"Who *did* send you?"

"Judge Warren put the proxies in my hand, but he mentioned Cameron LaCoe as a driving force. And I have a feeling that neither one of them knew that they'd handed me control of the company. It certainly came as a shock to the other people who were voting at the meeting."

"And now Wayne Savage will be the new CEO," Karen said as she sipped her wine. "You know that none of those former board members are going to let this go without a fight. They're all members of the same church. Deacon Stewart is a ruthless businessman, but his employees are loyal to a fault."

"Um... Wayne won't be the CEO," Gee said. "There were a lot of phone conversations during the meeting. I really just rubberstamped the decision that the new powers wanted."

"The announcement said that The Savage would return to chair the board of directors," Karen said as she puzzled out the situation.

"As I understand it, Wayne's grandfather, Pàl Savage, will be here tomorrow."

"Do they know? Oh, my! Another war orphan returns to Rosebud Falls. If I had known that, I would have written a different headline. How perfect!"

"I spoke to him briefly on the phone," Gee said. "He sounds like a good man. I expected him to tell me how he wanted me to vote. After all, it is technically his company, I guess. But he just asked me to be a caretaker of the votes and to exercise my proxies when I felt the company strayed."

"Here's to the man who shakes my world," Karen said, softly lifting her lips to his.

"To the woman I only dreamed was here for me," Gee responded. "Perhaps next year we can be listed together on the wedding page."

"Would you really... want to...?" Karen began as they set their glasses aside and kissed more deeply. She looked up into his eyes for assurance.

"Jonathon and Jessie were childhood sweethearts. They've known each other all their lives. Grew up together. Fell in love at fourteen. Now they are getting married. You are my childhood sweetheart, Karen."

"We didn't grow up together," she whispered as she lay her head on his chest.

"Maybe not in the traditional sense, but you are one of the first people I met in my new life. You are where my memories begin. You are the woman I've grown up with over the past months. You are the only woman I remember ever loving."

When Karen looked up at Gee again, her eyes were moist.

"You really do love me."

"I love you, Karen Weisman. Will you marry me and build our lives together?"

Until the Last Nut Falls

THERE HAD BEEN no sign of the bad man since Sally Ann spotted him on Sunday and with Harvest nearing an end, parents were beginning to relax. Several school crews joined Gee and Coretta for shorter shifts on Friday so all the kids could have one more chance to pick with him. Most of Gee's work was on the ground or step ladders now, shaking trees that were only about twenty-five feet tall. These smaller trees were nonetheless loaded with nuts. They were pruned each year and new growth went into nut production rather than tree height.

A dozen shakers went through the orchard of small trees like locusts. Even the sound that was created as thousands of nuts hit the canvas catchers beneath the trees created an insect-like buzz that never let up. Twice as many picking crews were needed just to keep up with the progress the shakers made.

Jonathon and other foresters helped keep the pickers moving by singing and chanting with them, starting contests, and randomly giving out prizes to the kids. Older kids and teens often teamed up with younger classes to keep the laughter going and the young ones enthused. As Friday drew to a close, Gee looked forward to a relaxing evening before the final batch of trees was harvested in the morning. He filled his plate from the buffet, his shaker shirt being the only meal ticket he needed.

"I'm sorry, Gee," a small voice said beside him. He turned and saw Rena standing by his bench as the Nussbaum Quartet set up on stage. She was changed, her hair a single medium brown color that matched her brown eyes. The makeup that made her eyes look like a raccoon was gone and she had a clean, slightly freckled complexion. There was much less hardware decorating her body as well and Gee could see several empty piercings.

"Rena," he said softly. "Are you feeling better?"

"Much better, thank you. I could have really hurt you or someone else if you hadn't wrestled me down. I'm sorry it wasn't fun wrestling," she sighed.

"You needn't think about that, Rena," Gee answered. "I'm just glad you are doing… better."

"I'm in treatment. It's not so much a chemical addiction as an emotional one. They let me out tonight to attend the party and I get to attend church Sunday because I did those sketches of the kidnapper. My…

uh… chaperone is right over there… in case you were worried." Gee followed Rena's gesture and saw a woman who didn't look much older than the addict. "I keep having flashes of the wonderful fantasies I had! My shrink calls them post-hypnotic suggestions. It's apparently a lot like doing mushrooms."

"Where do you get it?" Gee asked. Rena glanced around furtively. For a moment Gee was afraid she was going into a panic attack.

"They'll kill me for telling," she whispered. "Please don't let anyone know I told you. Please!"

"Told me what?"

"It's the monk. Not Pastor Beck. He's so kind. But that monk. Gee, the sketch I did…"

"It was incredibly accurate and will help the police catch him."

"It's him. As soon as Sally Ann started describing him, I knew it was Brother Reef. He's the one who brought me the drug at the store and told me God wanted me to have you. It wasn't an accident, Gee. He sent me after you."

There was a long pause as Rena's words sank in. Why would anyone from her church want to hurt him? And to give her drugs. He'd have to talk to Karen.

"I'll see you around, Gee," Rena said. "Liz says it's time to get back. Wish I could stay to hear the Nussbaums sing, but I know that if I get healthy, I'll be able to hear them again another time. Please don't tell them I told you. Please?"

"Get healthy, Rena. We're going to find the people responsible for poisoning you. I won't let them hurt you."

She left with her chaperone and three minutes later, Gee was caught up in the blending tones of the quartet's voices as they sang on stage. He simply hoped he could fulfill the promise he'd just made.

"THEY'RE PRETTY COOL," Wayne said as he caught up with Gee after the concert. "I'm surprised to see you out here this late. Figured you'd be home asleep by now."

"It's tempting. I usually try to stay awake until Karen gets home about ten. I… kind of like the time we spend together at night."

"I can appreciate that. Uh… Speaking of which… If Karen still wants to do an interview, tell her that I'm available. I guess the word is out that I'm a Savage."

"It would be hard to keep it a secret after yesterday's shareholder meeting."

"There won't be any major visible changes to the public for a while, but the board of directors has been replaced. The SEC papers will be filed on Monday."

"This is big news for Rosebud Falls," Gee said.

"If Karen wants to talk, I'll fill her in on as much as I can until my grandfather gets to town. I'd rather the news come from me than have Carl Stewart do a hack job on it."

"I'm sure Karen will be looking you up tomorrow."

"She won't have to look too far. I plan to attend the closing ceremony and mass wedding tomorrow," Wayne laughed.

"Yeah. Well, I'll be the nut in the tree."

GEE AND KAREN sat on the sofa as she ate from the plate of food he'd brought her from the festival. He told her about his conversation with Wayne.

"I think the world is about to end," Karen sighed.

"How so? I thought you would think of this as good news."

"Oh, I do. But how many coincidences can we endure without seeing a sign of some sort."

"What's got you tied in knots, sweetheart?"

"I love it when you call me that," she said as she lifted her lips to his. "Okay, so a man with no memory walks into town and becomes a local hero. He saves children, abused women, and drug addicts. He becomes the City Champion. His arrival coincides with the announcement that the City is annexing a southern suburb. At the same time, after sixty years absent, a Savage shows up in town. The two men become friends and both seem to have a great affinity toward saving and helping children. Let us not forget that your trusty investigative reporter exposes an old fraud and instead of covering it up, the Families concede the injustice and all join together to both recognize our cousin Celia and to give her and her heirs a fortune with which to start their new lives.

"While walking in the Forest one day, our hero eats a highly toxic nut, survives, and is *instantly* accepted by the heads of the Families as an equal. He is then given the proxy for the controlling shares of SSG and joins forces with other discontented shareholders—including Savage, Meagher, and, if my sources are correct, Leah Roth-Augello—to oust the current board of directors and install a new CEO, reversing the company's stance on the annexation and putting the wild woods one step closer to Forest management. Our hero is then asked to take on the prestigious role of Wedding Shaker for the closing ceremonies of Harvest. And if that weren't enough coincidences, the hardnosed investigative reporter attempting to identify who this stranger in our midst is, falls head over heels in love and can't wait to marry him. It's too much. It must be a sign that the world is coming to an end. At least the world of Family control over Rosebud Falls."

"Overwhelming?"

"Who are you, George Edward Evars? Who has taken control of our City, our Forest, our Families, our children, our largest company, … and my heart? Who are you that I find myself blindly trusting you and offering every bit of my being to you?"

The couple sat in silence, knowing that no answers to Karen's questions were forthcoming. All these coincidences. The carnie, Bill, had told Gee that there was always a one hundred percent chance of a coincidence occurring, but what made them significant was awareness. Gee did not have answers to the questions, yet according to Birdie Lanahan, he *was* the answer. Simply being here-now. There were still so many unanswered questions.

"And then there is Brother Reef, the bad man," Gee said. "He shows up and disappears and shows up and disappears. Is he part of the church or is he simply using it as a convenient cover. Is he a religious at all? Where will he show up next? I'm waiting for the other shoe to drop."

"Brother Reef? You have a name for the kidnapper?"

"I talked to Rena tonight. Her chaperone brought her out to dinner. She said the kidnapper was the same person that brought her the drug. He is a known entity at the Calvary Tabernacle."

"Call Mead Oliver."

"It's almost midnight."

"Call him now. He can decide when he interviews her, but he should have every minute available to him to make that decision."

"I promised Rena I wouldn't let them know she told me."

"Then don't. Mead Oliver trusts you as much as I do."

"When he doesn't have me in handcuffs."

"He'll listen if you tell him that you just overheard that the suspect had been seen on more than one occasion at the church. Do it, Gee. Do it now."

Gee made the call. Mead wasn't happy to be roused from his sleep, especially by Gee. But what Gee said lit a fire and the detective got little sleep for the rest of the night.

"GEE?" KAREN SIGHED.

"Yes, my love."

"Tomorrow is the last day of Harvest. You'll be finished by mid-afternoon and not working for the rest of the festival."

"I'm looking forward to it."

"It's Saturday. I don't have to work Saturday night because there is no paper on Sunday."

"That's wonderful. We can walk around the festival together."

"Yes. There is nothing else on the agenda until the parade Sunday afternoon."

"I suppose I need to march with the other shakers."

"Mmmhmm. But I was thinking that since things were so relaxed and celebratory tomorrow that maybe…" She looked up into his eyes and saw his smile. "Maybe we could choose one room and… *really* move in together." He scooped up his giggling girlfriend, housemate, roommate, fiancée in his arms, and carried her to bed.

Person of Interest

"GOOD MORNING, BROTHERS. How may this humble servant of God help you this early morning," the pastor said upon opening his door. Mead scanned around. The place was a mansion. How did a humble servant of God ever afford such a palace?

"Are you Lance Beck, minister at Calvary Tabernacle?" the uniformed sheriff asked.

"Yes, yes. And you are?"

"I'm Sheriff Brad Johnson. I'm being observed today by Detective Mead Oliver of the Rosebud City Police," said the sheriff. Mead had been briefed before they started this and was only along as an observer. Pastor Beck and the Calvary Tabernacle were outside the city limits and thus not under his jurisdiction. Until the area got annexed. Then it would be a different matter. But for now, he would just observe his county counterpart. "We are looking for a man that has reportedly been seen in your congregation." Mead noticed oily sweat break out on the preacher's forehead.

"Oh, dear. Not one of my flock. I pray for the souls of those who come thirsting for God's Word, but, alas, some fall by the wayside and the fowls of the air devour them. Some fall on stony ground where the sun withers them away. And some fall among thorns and are choked and yield no fruit. Let us pray for the redemption of this poor soul."

"Reverend, we're here to identify and locate this suspect. You can pray for his soul after we leave. Can you identify the man in this picture?" The sheriff held out the sketch, cutting the preacher's prayer off before it began.

"Hmm. Let me get my reading glasses," Pastor Beck said, leaving the two officers on his front step.

"What do you think?" Sheriff Johnson asked.

"He's buying time. I think he already knows who we are looking for," Mead answered. "The question is whether he'll come back to the door or if we need to get a warrant."

"He'll come back. He knows that simply ignoring us will bring the suspicion directly to him. The real question is whether he'll throw the suspect under the bus to save his own skin." The sheriff cocked an ear. "He's talking to someone. Maybe on the phone. I only hear one voice." Mead poked a finger in one ear and scrubbed vigorously to figure out why he couldn't hear what the sheriff heard. "Here he comes," the sheriff said.

Beck opened the door and reached for the drawing. He hemmed and hawed, turning his head from side to side.

"He looks familiar, but I don't believe he is a member of our flock."

"I'm told he answers to the name Brother Reef," Mead suggested. The sheriff shot him a look, but Beck shuddered.

"Oh. Oh, yes. I can see the resemblance now that you mention it. It certainly couldn't be him, though."

"Why not?"

"Well, for multiple reasons," Beck stalled. "First, you see, he isn't a member of our church, though when he passes through town he sometimes stops to worship with us."

"Passes through town?"

"Yes. You see, this is why I don't believe he could be your suspect. I haven't seen him in church for several weeks. I would have to say he is a little… I *do* hate to be unkind, but… let's say soft in the head. He's a simpleton. I've never heard him say more than 'Amen' in all the years he has wandered through. Homeless, I believe. Kind of considers himself to be a monk or hermit. Loves children and they seem to adore him. Always willing to lend a helping hand, no matter what the job. A kind and gentle man. I consider him harmless. But, like I said, just a fellow-traveler on life's weary road. Not a member of our church. Certainly not a suspect in any crime."

"And you have no idea where he might be at the moment?"

"We don't often see him in the winter. He's probably started his migration south," Beck said. He mopped his forehead with a large handkerchief.

"Should you happen to see him, please pass on our cards and let him know we'd like to talk to him, just to eliminate him from our list of suspects," the sheriff said. He and Mead both held out cards that the minister took.

"Yes, of course," Beck said. "And I do hope you find the kidnapper and bring him to justice."

⸻◁◆▷⸻

"He sure knew a lot about the guy for never hearing him say more than 'amen.' Did you record everything?" Mead asked.

"Yes. We pretty much have to record everything these days. I'm surprised you aren't wearing a body cam."

"I am, but we're out of my jurisdiction. And since I'm not a uniform, I have a little more leeway," Mead said. "But the reason I was asking was that I don't recall us ever mentioning what Brother Reef was suspected of. Yet the preacher just told us he hoped we found the kidnapper."

"The picture was in the newspaper this week," Sheriff Johnson answered. "Along with the note that he was wanted for questioning in a case of attempted kidnapping, so I suppose the preacher could have read it. But there was something else I noticed."

"What's that?"

"He went to get his reading glasses so he could see the picture, but he never put them on."

10

FALLING FOR YOU

Before the Fall

GEE ARRIVED to start shaking in the morning, only to find all his picking crews waiting for him. Around him, other shakers and their crews converged on the last remaining area of the forest to pick.

"We've got all *little* trees this morning, but there are a lot of them," Jonathon said. "They shake fast, but the picking takes just as long, so all the crews will be working."

"Your pickers are waiting for you, Gee. You've worked with over a hundred children this week and they all adore you," Coretta added.

"I've scarcely had anything to do with the children," Gee laughed. "I'm always in a tree and they are picking under the previous one."

"Oh, but the shakers are the most inspiring people at Harvest. To see a big, strong man leap into the branches makes my heart flutter. I married my shaker," Coretta said. "One of the couples being married today includes a shaker and her forester." She giggled like a little girl. "It's a wonder she ever waited for him!"

"Coretta!" Jonathon moaned. "This is embarrassing."

"The first time Jonathon tried to be a shaker, he fell off his ladder," Coretta explained. "Jessie stripped off his gear and put it on herself in a matter of seconds. He was still lying on the ground when she started knocking nuts out of the branches."

"We kind of traded places. Heights make me dizzy."

"She might have been the wedding shaker today except that she can't be up in the tree and get married at the same time," Coretta laughed.

"Okay, so shall we get some trees picked?" Gee asked as he finished strapping his own gear on.

"Yes. The catchers are out spreading canvas under the trees as we speak and will be moving stepladders from tree to tree to stay ahead of you. One of the catchers will hold the ladder as you climb."

"Anything else I should know about this that's out of the ordinary?"

"Just be your usual fun and entertaining self," Coretta said. "Anytime you call out to the kids, they'll respond. Sing! Laugh! Knock the nuts out of those trees!"

And so he went to work.

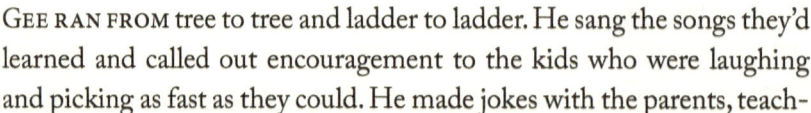

GEE RAN FROM tree to tree and ladder to ladder. He sang the songs they'd learned and called out encouragement to the kids who were laughing and picking as fast as they could. He made jokes with the parents, teachers, and foresters who surrounded this final section of orchard as they worked their way toward the wedding tree.

At noon, the last nut had fallen, and the kids, parents, foresters, foremen, catchers, and spectators cheered.

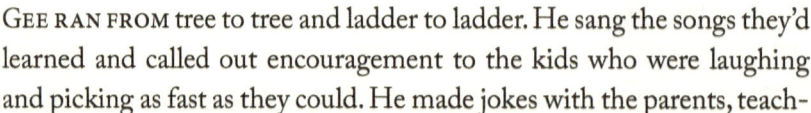

"AND NOW WE come to the last tree," a voice said over a loudspeaker system near the wedding tree. Gee looked around and saw Jonathon's father, David Lazorack, on a small platform just beyond the tree's canopy. "The closing ceremonies here at the wedding tree will begin at one o'clock. Please abide by the rules and stay outside the roped area. We will resume in one hour."

Karen met Gee at the foresters' coordination tent.

"Look at you! You're soaking wet!" Karen laughed. "Come in here, big strong shaker man." She took his shirt and worked his wet undershirt over his head. Then she led him to a basin with warm water and began washing his chest.

"Karen, it's uh… You don't have to… uh… I mean… I can…" Gee stammered, his body involuntarily responding to Karen's gentle washing.

"I can't let you go out there and charge up your ladder looking all sweaty and bedraggled," she giggled. "And I'm certainly not going to let any of the other volunteers wash your sweaty pits. Here, put this towel over your shoulders and lean over the basin so I can rinse your hair." Karen laughed about Gee's discomfort and told him she'd caught the last half hour of his shaking and it was no wonder that all the kids loved him. She let him towel dry.

"I couldn't do this part," she said, "but I brought you your mug and razor. Do you want to shave?" Gee looked at his reflection in the little mirror over the basin in the tent and stroked his chin.

"I guess I'd better. Just make sure no one comes bouncing into the tent while I have a razor at my throat, okay?"

Gee lathered and Karen held his belt while he stropped the razor. His practiced fingers made quick work of his stubble as Karen watched in fascination.

"And that's why your face is always so silky smooth when I come to bed at night," she whispered after Gee had rinsed the remaining soap off and dried his face. She stroked his cheek and closed in for a kiss. One hand stayed on his face while the other ran through the soft hair on his chest. Finally, she took a deep breath and stepped away from him.

"Here's a clean shaker shirt and your hat. I'll pack your Dopp kit." He pulled on the shirt and smiled patiently at Karen as she buttoned it. He tucked it into his pants and returned his belt to its loops as Karen placed the hat on his head.

Gabe Truman, one of the older foresters, collected them and led Gee to the staging area to explain the process.

"I'll see you after the ceremony," Karen said. She gave him one more kiss on his smooth cheek and left to find her place in the crowd.

"Okay, so here's how the order goes," Gabe said. "David Lazorack will welcome everyone and do opening remarks. He'll recognize the volunteers by group and then turn it over to Clark Cavanaugh. Clark will go through the numbers. How many tons of nuts, cords of deadwood, and expected board feet of lumber to be cut for this year's Harvest. Jack LaCoe, who chairs the festival committee, will take up space for a few minutes and bluster about how this was the best festival ever and invite everyone to the parade tomorrow."

"You don't like Jack much," Gee said matter-of-factly.

"He's fine. But… he's an outsider. Married Gretchen Nussbaum and got into the Family, but he'll always be an outsider."

"Like me," Gee said. The forester looked at Gee as though just realizing that he wasn't born in Rosebud Falls. He pursed his lips as he considered this a while.

"You're a strange one, that's true," Gabe said. "You've been in town around three months, but… as far as anyone knows—including you—you were created whole that day you walked into Rosebud Falls. Then the Forest claimed you. Most people don't know about the nut, but the foresters do. No one thinks you're an outsider now. You wouldn't be going up that tree today if they did."

"There were ten foresters who didn't vote for me," Gee reminded him. The forester laughed.

"That's all they told you? The ten who didn't vote for you voted for Jessie Sims. They thought it would be a great joke to make her shake her own wedding tree." They shared a laugh. "I've been a forester out here for forty years. We have our own sense of humor. Now, back to the ceremony. When LaCoe is done rambling, he'll turn the show over to Judge Warren. The judge will call forward the couples to be married and their witnesses. 'Do you? I do.' That kind of thing."

"I think Coretta is more excited about that than even Jessie and Jonathon."

"She was married under a wedding tree close to sixty years ago," Gabe laughed. "Once the couples all kiss, they'll spread around the tree with big umbrellas over them. You'll come running up the path, grab the rope on your shaker pole and climb up to the perch. Attach your flipline, just like usual, and pull your pole up. Your responsibility is the same as it was in the rest of the Forest. Be entertaining and shake the tree. Nuts will cascade down and bounce off the umbrellas. It's the hickory blessing. After the cascade starts, others will open umbrellas and join the newlyweds under the tree. Just keep shaking and singing until the last nut falls. Now let's check your harness and safety gear. You still need your goggles, gloves, harness, and flipline."

The ceremony began. Clark finished his assessment of the year's harvest. Jack LaCoe was mercifully short, simply welcoming all the tourists and inviting everyone back again next year. Judge Warren was introduced, and he called the wedding parties forward. While the couples and their witnesses moved into place, a bagpiper played somewhere deep in the Forest. Gee watched the simple but moving ceremony with a sense of joy for his friends.

"I now confirm the marriages of those here presented," Judge Warren intoned. "Ladies and gentlemen, take your spouses to the wedding tree and open your umbrellas."

As the couples fanned out around the tree, leaving a good space for Gee to approach his ladder, he tightened the chinstrap on his hat and ran toward the tree. Ten feet from the foot of the ladder, he did a front flip that landed him a step away. The crowd applauded his antic as he fastened the pull line for the shaker pole to his belt and began climbing. At the top of the heavy-duty extension ladder, Gee shifted to tree limbs and continued climbing to the place where Gabe had told him he would find secure limbs to rest on.

Gee tossed his flipline around the tree and fastened the carabiner to his safety harness. Turning to look away from the tree, he began hauling up the shaker pole. With the pole in hand he took one more look at the crowd below before yelling out, "A Hickory Wind is…"

Gee stopped short as his eyes locked on movement near the children who would gather the nuts. A man moved deliberately toward them and Gee saw Sally Ann just a few steps ahead of him.

"That's him!" Gee yelled out. "Sally Ann! Behind you! Mead, arrest that man. It's Reef!" There was a shift among the spectators in the direction Gee was pointing with his shaker pole, most wondering at the shaker's unusual behavior. Foresters and police, however, were moving. Gee twisted again to keep his eye on the man and felt a sudden snap away from the tree as his flipline broke. Screams sounded all around the clearing as Gee hit his shaker pole, caught between two limbs halfway down the tree. He could feel his ribs crack as the pole gave way and flipped him over.

One-point-two seconds later, Gee hit the ground, fleetingly wishing he'd worn his hardhat.

After the Fall

BROTHER REEF UNDERESTIMATED the power of a child.

Sally Ann's scream when she saw the 'bad man' riveted her classmates so they missed Gee's spectacular fall from the tree.

"Get 'im!" Sally Ann yelled at her classmates. Reef easily caught and restrained the fifty-pound dynamo when she launched herself at him, but when multiplied by thirty, he was quickly bowled over. By the time Mead and two foresters had reached the scene, Reef was crying out and pinned down by the second grade class. It took a blast from Coretta's whistle and a shouted "Form up!" from Colleen Zimmer before the children backed off enough for Mead to cuff the man and turn him over to two uniformed policemen to transport to jail.

That was when Sally Ann noticed the ambulance wasn't coming for the bad man, but that Gee was being loaded into the back, accompanied by a doctor and nurse.

"No! Gee!" cried the girl. She tried to run after the ambulance but was caught by her father.

"He'll be okay," Dale Metzger comforted his daughter. "We'll go see him in the hospital. He just fell… um… coming to help you."

"I want to see Gee!"

"Honey, I'm sure he's very proud of you," Ruth Ann said. "Though that was a very foolish thing for you to do."

"Come on," Dale said, "We'll have to go back to the school to get our car and then we'll head to the hospital. We need to sign you out with your teacher."

JONATHON AND JESSIE were closest to Gee's fallen body and rushed to his aid, yelling for a medical team. With a crowd like this, EMTs were only a minute away, fighting their way through the panicking crowd. They strapped Gee to a backboard and the crowds parted. Dr. Poltanys and his nurse sister, Julia, intercepted the EMTs at the ambulance. They rode with Gee as the ambulance sirens screamed to clear a path out of the Forest.

"LET ME THROUGH!" Karen screamed. "That's my fiancé!" People near her in the unyielding crowd finally turned and tried to clear a path to the scene, but by the time Karen got through, the EMTs had already moved him to the ambulance. Like Sally Ann, Karen ran after the wailing siren.

Strong arms grabbed Karen as she stumbled—Jessie on one side and Wayne Savage supporting her on the other.

"I have to get to the hospital," Karen cried. "I have to see him."

"This way," Jessie said, leading her past the tree in the opposite direction.

David Lazorack, without any equipment, was already at the top of the ladder and swinging to the first limb.

"Dad! Get equipment and a spotter!" Jonathon yelled.

"Go!" his father yelled back. "Gabe is on his way. That flipline was cut, it didn't break. I'm going to find out what cut it." Gabe, the old forester who had helped Gee prepare for the ceremony, raced across the clearing and hit the bottom rung of the ladder with a spring that belied his age.

"I've got this," Gabe yelled as he climbed to meet David with safety gear. They roped themselves together and climbed. Jonathon pulled up in a golf cart and Jessie seated Karen in it.

"What's going on?" Karen cried. "I have to get to the hospital!"

"We had this waiting to take us through the Forest to our car," Jessie said. Wayne steadied Karen in the back as the cart lurched forward. "It will be faster to go through the Forest to our car than to get through the crowd."

Karen could only sob as Wayne held her, the image of Gee falling from the tree seared into her brain. It seemed to take forever.

JONATHON HAD TO pull over for the flashing lights of a police car while he was still two blocks from the hospital. Karen recognized Detective Oliver's car with Judge Warren riding shotgun as it sped by. Jonathon was upset and frustrated when he was directed away from the emergency access by a uniformed policeman.

"Unless you are bleeding, you need to go to the parking lot," the officer shouted. "We can't get another vehicle into the drive here." The emergency room entrance was blocked by vehicles with flashing lights crowded into the access area. Jonathon pulled up in the adjoining parking lot as close as he could get and waved his passengers out of the car while he went to park it. Jessie and Wayne supported a stumbling and crying Karen as they rushed toward the emergency room doors.

Inside, the hospital was almost as chaotic as outside, though no one seemed to be injured. Judge Warren and Mead Oliver were standing near the door into the heart of the emergency room arguing with a nurse who stubbornly refused them access. Sheriff Johnson pushed his way through the doors behind Karen and rushed to join Mead and the judge. Karen frantically tried to get the attention of the receptionist as another officer came out of the emergency room.

"He's dead," the officer flatly addressed the detective.

"No!" Karen screamed. Wayne and Jessie caught her as she collapsed between them.

------------⊲◆⊳------------

"How could you let that happen?" Mead yelled at the police officer.

"What the hell?" Warren said at the same time as he looked over toward Karen. An emergency light flashed over the door as Nurse Ellie rushed through and over to the unconscious woman.

"You were there when we put him in the car, Detective," Officer McCarran said. "I was on my way to the station when I saw him go into convulsions in the back seat. That's when I radioed for backup and changed course for the hospital. As soon as Officer Jacobs arrived we opened the back and got the prisoner onto a cart. Dr. Gaston was here on duty and pronounced him DOA as soon as we got into the emergency room."

Judge Warren spun away from the police and strode across the room to where Ellie was holding a glass of water to Karen's lips.

"Dead? No! He can't be dead!" Karen wailed as she regained consciousness.

"Karen! Karen, listen to me!" Judge Warren was kneeling over her as Ellie tried to grasp what was happening. "It wasn't Gee! It was the prisoner who died. Karen, listen. Gee is all right," Warren pled. Then he looked at Ellie. "Isn't he?"

"Gee is in surgery with Dr. Poltanys," Ellie said. "Julia is assisting him."

"Surgery?" Warren asked.

"I can't say much, but the doctor had to cut his chest to pull a broken rib away from his lung," Ellie said.

"I need to go to him. I need to be with him," Karen pled.

"I can't get you into surgery, Karen," Ellie said. "I don't know if you can even be admitted to the recovery room."

"Karen has Gee's medical power of attorney," Jack LaCoe said as he paused inside the door. He caught the exchange and addressed both the judge and nurse. "That is as close to next of kin as we can get and should be all that's necessary to get her in to see Gee as soon as possible."

"Good. Drink some water and sit, Karen," Ellie said. "If you feel faint again, put your head between your knees. We'll get you to the recovery room as soon as Gee is out. I'm being beeped by Dr. Gaston. I need to go." Wayne helped Karen to a seat while Jessie got a bottle of water from the vending machine. Jonathon came into the waiting room and spotted them.

"What a mess out there. Even after I parked, they started stopping everyone coming into the emergency room to verify there was a reason to be here. It looks like half the town is out there. I even saw the little girl who spotted Reef earlier in the week. She's crying like crazy, but the police won't let them through."

"Ms. Weisman, I'm sorry I blurted out the words I did without looking to see who might hear me," Officer McCarran said as he came up to the little group. "I hope you are aware by now that Gee is in surgery and it was the suspect who died. I apologize for causing you unnecessary stress."

"You're forgiven," Karen struggled to say. "Thank you."

"If there is anything I can do…"

"Yes. There is," Karen said rapidly. "There is a distraught little girl and her parents out there. Her name is Sally Ann Metzger. Please go out and reassure her that Gee is all right. If you can get her family in here, that would be appreciated. I know Gee will want to see her."

"Karen, you have enough to deal with. Let us handle the little things," Jack said. "I'll make sure the Metzgers are treated well. Gretchen will stay here with you to run interference. Gee will be okay."

"He will be. Won't he?" Karen was still babbling and looking for assurance. "I'll die if he isn't okay."

---◄◆►---

"THANK YOU FOR getting me here so quickly," Karen said to Jonathon and Jessie. "Um… You should go and um… start your honeymoon."

"Oh, we started last night," Jessie giggled. Jonathon turned red. "We can wait for round two until we know for sure how Gee is."

"Waiting is always the hardest part," Wayne agreed. Jonathon's phone buzzed and his face lost color. He spun to locate Mead talking to the Judge and a doctor and rapidly crossed the waiting room to him.

"Dr. Gaston, as our county medical examiner, I want you to get an autopsy underway immediately," Judge Warren said.

"We don't have family information or permission," Mead protested.

"I'll have a court order drawn up as soon as I get to the office," Warren said.

"I can tell you what we're going to find," Dr. Gaston said. "Ruptured organs. Appendix for sure."

"Jacques, get the body down to the morgue and document every-thing, but keep it under wraps. All information regarding the cause of death is to be suppressed until we know what we're dealing with."

"Detective Oliver," Jonathon said. The men turned sharply to him.

"Not a word of this to anyone, Jonathon," the judge snapped. Gaston turned and headed back into the emergency room.

"No, sir. I didn't hear a thing. But my father just sent me pictures from the tree. Gee's flipline was cut. Falling wasn't an accident." Jonathon held out his phone with the pictures his father had just sent. "That's a fifteen-inch sharpened blade you see in this picture. Dad says Gabe got cut on it when he reached around the tree with the line and they suspect there was a drug on it. Gabe is woozy and they're bringing him here."

"Tell Gaston to put the perp on ice and get back up here ready to receive another injury," Warren snapped at the overwhelmed receptionist.

"Gee must have tossed his flipline around the tree and fastened it without ever knowing it was against a blade. After all the thrashing around he did up there pulling up his shaker pole and then pointing out that bastard, the line was severed enough to break," Jonathon concluded.

"I'll need to get someone up there to collect the blade as evidence," Mead said. "Damn it, I don't have enough officers!"

"Get backup from Sheriff Johnson," Warren said. "Also release word that this Brother Reef was wanted on suspicion of attempted kidnapping and two counts of attempted murder. There is no newspaper until Tuesday, but if you put it out on the police blotter, there will be plenty of busybodies listening to get the word out."

"AH, THE RECEPTION committee or fan club?" Dr. Poltanys said as he stepped into the waiting room after finishing with Gee. Gabe Truman had already been taken into an examining room by Dr. Gaston.

"How is he? Is he awake? Can I see him now?" Karen said. She started to step around the doctor but he held up a hand to delay her.

"He's in recovery. You'll be able to wait in his room and I expect he'll be there in about fifteen or twenty minutes. Julia will show you where. I've never had so many nurses competing to tend to a patient. I think my mother is even hovering around recovery."

"So, what's the prognosis?" Warren asked.

"Gee has two cracked and one badly broken rib, a dislocated shoulder and bruises over most of his body. After x-rays, we moved immediately to surgery because the broken rib was impinging on his right lung. I was afraid any shift would cause a puncture if I didn't go in and set it. Now that it is set and wired in place, all we can do is let it heal. I also managed to put the shoulder back in place. Apparently, he tried to break his fall by keeping hold of the pole and the force pulled the ball out of the socket. It probably saved his life. If he'd fallen the full seventy feet without anything to break the fall he'd have ended up much the same as your grandfather did, Jonathon."

"Any damage to his head?" Judge Warren asked. Poltanys let out an uncharacteristic laugh.

"With Gee, how can you tell?" There were several unsuppressed titters. "He seems his same old self. He was awake during x-rays. He looked at me and said, 'The first thing I remember is seeing the Pub and Grub.' I think he was trying to be funny."

"May I go see him now?" Karen pled.

"Go to recovery and Julia will tell you when. I need to look in on Dr. Gaston and the other injury now. I understand we lost one."

"Not a great loss," Judge Warren said. "Gaston will tell you about it."

Recovery

THERE HAD BEEN a long line of well-wishers, who had been limited to three or four at a time and for only five minutes each. At least one representative of each Family had come to deliver their Family's get well wishes. Ellie and Julia took turns controlling the stream of visitors and no one was allowed to stay longer than the nurses would permit. Jonathon and Jessie were the first to come by his room.

"You should be off on your honeymoon!" Gee said. His friends hugged each other.

"It's not like we're leaving town. We'll do that after the parade tomorrow," Jonathon said.

"We have a special place we're going in the Forest tonight," Jessie said, looking up at her new husband adoringly. "The perfect place to start our family."

"Jessie!" Jonathon hissed. It was apparent that Jessie could get Jonathon to blush every bit as easily as her grandmother could. The red in his face began to subside when he turned back to Gee. "We brought you this. It was supposed to be presented after the shaking and we had it on our cart. I told you there were rewards to be had in the Forest." Jonathon held out a rod of polished hickory, five feet long. "You picked this up in the Forest the first day I met you. I had it made up into a walking stick by Luke Zimmer. It might not be the exact same stick, but it's the thought that counts. Traditionally, the wedding shaker receives a gift from the married couples and we all agreed to give you this."

"This is beautiful, Jonathon. I won't get arrested for carrying around, will I?"

"You're safe." The couple thanked Gee again and left for their somewhat delayed honeymoon.

GEE QUICKLY DISCOVERED how many other friends he had as they dropped by to wish him well. Mead Oliver stopped to say that Rena Lynd had positively identified the deceased suspect as the man who had provided the Lustre Plus that put her in the hospital. That gave police another set of crimes to pin on the dead man. They immediately released a bulletin that Brother Reef had been wanted for distribution and sale of a controlled substance and for attempted murder by overdose. The charges, of course, could never be pressed, but it would help to quell any sympathy for the dead man.

The LaCoes told Gee he was fully covered for his medical expenses under the Festival policy. They assured both Gee and Karen that the medical power of attorney had been accepted on both their behalf and assured Karen that as far as the hospital was concerned, there was no issue regarding her access to Gee in the same capacity as a spouse. She gripped his hand a little more firmly and felt his responding squeeze.

Judge Warren, of course, had stopped briefly, and even Gabe Truman had come up to Gee's room after he was treated for a mild poisoning from the cut he suffered.

It was two tiny voices, however, that brought a smile to Gee's face. "Gee!" Devon rushed across the room and struggled at the edge of the bed to reach Gee's hand.

"Dee!" he responded.

"Honey, Gee is hurt so be very gentle," Marian said as she crossed the room.

"Hello, Mr. Gee," the slightly more mature voice of Sally Ann called for his attention.

"My two favorite reading buddies!" Gee said reaching out for their hands. His right arm still hurt, but his left could function.

"The kids have been frantic to see you," Ruth Ann said. "I'm so thankful Marian and Nathan showed up to help calm things down. Sally Ann's entire class was lined up in formation outside the hospital singing hickory songs for you."

"Thank you for bringing your daughter in to see me, Mrs. Metzger. And Marian, you can't imagine how much it means to me to see my little buddy. My left side is okay as long as we don't try to wrestle. Can you lift him up over here so we can talk? And Sally Ann, come right here beside me. You can sit on the edge of the bed if someone will lift you up."

"Are you sure?" Marian asked. She picked the toddler up and placed him under Gee's left arm. Dale lifted his daughter so she could sit on the edge of the bed next to them.

"All better?" Devon said as he settled in and gave Gee a little kiss on the cheek. "Read?"

"That helped, little buddy. But I don't have a book in the hospital to read to you."

"The bad man wanted to hurt us, Gee. He wanted to hurt all the children," Sally Ann said fiercely.

"I'm glad you helped the police, sweetie," Gee said thoughtfully. "I just hope you won't always feel that you need to strike out. Bad things in our world can't always be helped by hitting them."

"I know that, Mr. Gee," said the bright little girl. "Mrs. Zimmer promised to help us understand."

"Then listen to your teacher and know that we all love you. We're doing our very best to make sure our town is a good place for you to grow up," Gee said.

"Are you hungry?" Nathan asked as he entered the room. "The dinner they're serving down by the river is unbelievable. I volunteered to bring you… um… both a plate."

"Nathan, you're a life-saver. I was afraid we were going to have to eat hospital food tonight," Gee said. Marian helped Karen clear the tray table and set out an array of great-smelling food. "Oh, man! Those ribs look great. I might need help eating them."

"We all just wanted to make sure you were okay," Ruth Ann said. "Nurse Julia allowed us two extra minutes on her stopwatch so the children could take their time, but we'll have to go to avoid her wrath."

"I'm not that big an ogre," Julia said from the door. Ellie entered the room behind her.

"I guess you won't be able to work for a while with that shoulder and ribs," Nathan accurately surmised as he gathered his son from under Gee's arm. "I just want you to know, Gee, that your job is waiting for you when you're ready to come back. We… I… miss you… down at the store."

"I'll be back as soon as I can lift those soup kettles," Gee laughed and then caught his breath. "Oh! It hurts to laugh."

"Yeah. You'll die the first time you sneeze," Ellie warned him.

"Devon and Sally Ann, it's time to say night-night to Gee. He needs to eat now," Marian said.

"Love you, Gee," Devon and Sally Ann both said as their parents led them to the door. Karen moved the tray table to where Gee could reach the food.

"We all love you, Gee," Marian assured him.

"Out. All of you!" a commanding presence said from the door. "This patient has had enough visitors and needs to get some rest. That includes you two," she said pointing at the nurses. The head nurse who stood in the door was five and a half feet tall but towered over everyone as if she were six feet or more. Her green eyes blazed in a near match to the color of her scrubs.

"I'm not leaving," Karen said defiantly.

"Don't you need to get this poor man toiletries, clean clothes, and pajamas? We frown on couples sleeping nude together in the hospital. Unless it's a doctor and a nurse, of course." Her severe demeanor broke at last and a smile creased her face. "I assume you do plan to spend the night, don't you, Karen?"

"Yes, Mrs. Poltanys."

"Then go get the things you need and I'll keep your fiancé company for a few minutes. I've heard my husband, my son, and my daughter all talking about him but haven't yet had the honor."

"Yes, ma'am," Karen said. "I'll be right back, honey," she said as she kissed Gee lightly on the forehead and then almost ran for the door.

"Uh... Hello," Gee said as the nurse held two fingers to his wrist and looked at her watch. "I'm Gee."

"Yes. We haven't met because I'm on a nice regular day shift and you tend to arrive in the middle of the night or on weekends. But I've heard much about you." Gee looked at the older woman. Pale blonde hair hid any sign that she might be graying, but Gee estimated her age to be near sixty. Her high-set cheekbones reminded him of someone and he struggled to remember if he'd met her before. "I'm Sofia Poltanys. You've met both my son and daughter here at the hospital. It's all I can do to keep them corralled. They would create havoc on their own, but not in *my* hospital."

"You own the hospital?" Gee asked. Sofia laughed out loud.

"In a manner of speaking. I'm the head nurse and ne'er doctor nor nurse dare cross my path," she said in mock severe tones. "Especially not if they are my children."

"I've heard only good things about your children and my experiences here bear that out."

"Well, it looks like you'll live through another misadventure," she said.

"Thank you, Mrs. Poltanys."

"Just Sofia, dear. I only require my children to address me by title."

"They call you Mrs. Poltanys?" Gee asked.

"No. They call me 'your majesty'," she laughed.

KAREN LEFT GEE only long enough to pick up toiletries and fresh clothes for them. She intended to stay in the chair next to his bed all night, but Gee had other ideas.

"It really didn't hurt to have Devon next to me," he whispered. "If I can slide over a couple of inches, I'm sure it wouldn't hurt to have you next to me."

"Really? You want me there beside you?"

"Now and always, Karen."

"Is Sofia gone?"

"I think so. She said she only stopped in to restore order in her hospital. She was a little scary at first."

"Everyone is afraid of Sofia Poltanys. She's just... in authority," Karen laughed.

She helped him slide over and crawled onto the bed next to him. Before settling down, she leaned over to kiss him softly. He winced as the kiss became deeper and she pulled away.

"This isn't exactly what I had in mind when I suggested we move in together today," Karen whispered as he placed his arm around her shoulders. "But here in your arms is where I want to be. Where I want to live. I love you, Gee."

Dragon of the Apocalypse

"BROTHERS AND SISTERS, yesterday was a tragic day in our community. The events during the City's Harvest have left many of us feeling frightened and insecure. Our children are wondering what the world has come to. This is a time for us to put our trust in the Lord and ask his guidance," Pastor Beck intoned as an introduction to his sermon. He had spent much of the night working on this sermon and knew that he needed to mold his congregation into a force. Ever since the shocking ouster of the board at SSG—all members of Calvary Tabernacle—the Lord had laid a burden on his heart that he needed to carry and rise above.

"A kind and quiet man entered the Forest yesterday. He was mercilessly attacked and brought low. And today we mourn the passing of Brother Reef. Many of you have already heard baseless rumors and accusations against this gentle soul. I want to tell you, the enemies of God will spread lies about Brother Reef for no other reason than that he was a true believer. I know for a fact that the police were looking for him. But 'Why?' you may ask. In the early hours yesterday, I spoke to the County Sheriff and a City detective. I was assured by these officers of the law that they wished to speak to Brother Reef to *eliminate* him as a suspect in unnamed crimes.

"Yet, when Brother Reef died—*while in their custody*—there was a flurry of accusations and justifications for their unseemly actions. In truth, he should never have been in their hands at all.

"You see, there was another involved in these false accusations. I have met this soulless being and when I looked into his eyes, I stared into the great abyss. On the very day this man first appeared in our community, I pled for his soul, but already, the dark minions of hell had surrounded him. They call him a hero—a champion—but we know the signs of the deceiver, do we not?"

"Amen," voiced one of the more vocal of the congregants. He was soon joined by the voices of several others.

"Has this servant of darkness ever once praised our Lord for putting him where he could be used for good? No! Instead he accepts the accolades of the people. He has trapped—dare I say, enslaved—the children of the community. Think on this. At the very moment he accused Brother Reef in the Forest yesterday afternoon, God cast him down from his exalted perch! But the damage had already been done. Even as he fell, he mustered his tiny army to attack Brother Reef."

"No!" shouted a woman near the center of the sanctuary.

"I say yes!" Beck responded. "Can you imagine one of *our* precious little ones as part of an unholy mob, attacking and bringing down an innocent as if they were hounds after a stag?"

"No! No!" the congregation was getting worked up and Pastor Beck continued to whip them into a frenzy.

"It was only the Prince of Darkness who could change innocent children into a pack of wolves, with eyes glowing like demon spawn. And yet, the parents of the City praise his name while he turns their children into ravening beasts.

"Our church… Our faith… The very essence of Christianity is being attacked in Rosebud Falls. The City would strip from us the resources we need for our Youth Reclamation Camp. The City would build a wall around our enclave and silence our voices. You might be thinking, 'Oh, we are a tiny church. We don't count in the great scheme of things. We are helpless. We can't do anything.' But I tell you, you are Joshua's army camped beside the City of Jericho. You must shout out against the evils that surround us and blow the trumpets of righteousness. For the City has put its trust in a false god.

"For generations, citizens have believed in the faithfulness of the city fathers, the Seven Families, to protect and defend the community. But those we trusted have become seven heads of the dragon of the apocalypse and they are led by Lucifer himself. As it is written:

"Woe to the inhabitants of the City and of the Forest! for the devil is come down unto you, having great wrath, because he knoweth that he hath but a short time. … And the seven-headed dragon of the Families is wroth with the church, and have come to make war with the remnant which keep the commandments of God, and have the testimony of Jesus Christ. … He that leadeth

into captivity shall go into captivity: he that killeth with the sword must be killed with the sword. If you have an ear, then hear the Word of God."

The congregation rose to sing 'Onward Christian Soldiers' and left the church ready to do battle with the great Satan.

Grand Parade

GEE MOANED AS he worked his way out of Karen's car at the high school Sunday at noon.

"I'm not sure this is such a good idea. I walk back and forth to the market every day, but now, even walking from the car to the stadium feels like too far. I really don't think I can march in a parade, Karen."

"They won't make you, sweetheart. Here's your new walking stick. Let's just say hi and then we'll go find a place to watch from." Gee leaned heavily on the stick in his left hand and walked with Karen protecting his right side toward the staging area a hundred yards away. In less than a minute, he was puffing shallow breaths, nearly hyperventilating. He just wanted to sit down.

"Yay, Gee!" a group of kids screamed as they ran toward him. Gee tensed, and Karen moved in front of him to slow down the onslaught. A whistle-blast brought all of them to a sudden stop and the members of his crew organized themselves into their fire drill attendance formation. Coretta took the whistle from her mouth and smiled at Gee as Colleen Zimmer brought a golf cart towing a trailer to a stop in front of him. On the trailer was a luxurious leather throne.

"We got the most comfortable ride we could manage for you," Colleen said. "We thought at first that we'd get you a recliner, but we were afraid you would have difficulty getting out of it. This chair has good cushioning and even has one of those levers that helps old people get out of their chair."

"Oh boy. Now I've joined the ranks of old people," Gee said. He was careful not to laugh, but let Colleen see the mirth in his eyes.

"We borrowed it from Coretta," she whispered. At that, Coretta's whistle blew, and the kids were released to gather around the trailer as Gee settled into the chair. A hastily lettered sign on the back said, 'Wedding Shaker.' The cart was decorated with baskets, leaves, and Rosebud flags.

"I never use this chair," Coretta said. "My son thought it was a good idea for me to protect my fragile old bones. Ha! After the parade, we'll deliver it to *your* home to use while you recover."

"That's so thoughtful of you, Coretta," Karen said. She kissed Gee softly on the cheek. "I'll see you at the end of the parade, love. Here's your staff. Now you can pretend to be King of Harvest."

"He won't pretend," Sally Ann piped up. "He *is* the King of Harvest."

ONCE THE PARADE started moving, it was to be an hour long, led by the Rosebud High School marching band and half a dozen convertibles carrying the Harvest dignitaries. The convertibles were followed by Gee's throne, surrounded by the happy chanting children.

The ambush struck just as the parade turned north on Main Street in front of the Rexall Drug Store. Congregants from Calvary Tabernacle stood along the parade route chanting, "No Annexation!" But when Gee's wagon arrived the demonstration turned nasty.

"Beelzebub!"

"Murderer!"

"Leave our children alone!"

Gee was nonplussed, but the children marching with him moved up beside his wagon and the crowd began throwing nuts at them.

"Demon-spawn!"

"Hellions!"

Gee started to stand, but the movement of the wagon knocked him back into his seat. A policeman manning the barricade that prevented traffic along the parade route was on his radio as he moved to intercept the surging crowd, pelting the children and Gee with nuts. Two motorcycle policemen who were escorting the front of the parade peeled back along the column with sirens howling.

Seeing the coming confrontation, the congregation redoubled their efforts to spend the tiny missiles on the parade and then fell back, scattering away from the route. Coretta blew her whistle, bringing order to the panicked children.

"Pickers! Collect those nuts! The hickory wind just brought us a windfall! Just like in the Forest, don't leave a single nut on the ground. Fill your hands and bring them to the baskets on the cart." The children went to work immediately as the police cordoned off the Rexall parking lot and blocked any more attacks.

Gee began singing as loudly as his injured ribs would let him, "Hickory nuts keep falling on my head…" one of the children's favorite picking songs, and they joined in, drowning out the few catcalls that continued from farther away. A troop of foresters trotted up along the parade route from farther back and helped the children sweep up the nuts that had been thrown, joining in the singing.

The parade was delayed only a few minutes as the street was cleared of all nuts, but the singing continued along the route all the way to the fairgrounds where the parade finally ended.

Most people along the route had no idea what had occurred at the south turn, but joined in singing along with the children, the high school band, and the other floats that followed Gee's crew. By the end of the three-plus miles to the fairgrounds, all but a few of the hardiest kids had taken seats on the hay wagons following Gee's cart. Many spectators walked along the river trail back to the main festival instead of following the parade to its end. Colleen drove the cart with Gee in his chair to Karen's home where the rest of the Zimmers helped unload the chair and move it inside.

Gee pled exhaustion and struggled upstairs while Karen talked to Colleen Zimmer and found out what had happened on the parade route. At last the Zimmers left and Karen ran upstairs to find Gee sound asleep fully clothed in his own bed.

"You poor man," she said as she sat and stroked his hair. She removed his shoes and made sure he was comfortable. Gee didn't stir. Karen kissed him softly and whispered, "I love you." She went back downstairs to her office. "They want to play with hellfire. We'll see how they like it when it rains down on their heads."

Golden Parachute

"YOU EXPECT PEOPLE in this company to follow a man in a dress?" Deacon snarled when he walked into the conference room Monday morning.

"It's a kilt." Pàl Savage stood at the end of the Rose Hickory conference table in the executive board room. "Of course, you knew that, so we'll just assume your comment is part of your normal lack of consideration for other people, ideas, concepts, and morality. Sit down, Mr. Stewart."

Stewart sat at the end of the table opposite Savage. His attorney, Matt Hogue, sat to his left. He moved immediately to take control of the meeting without waiting for Savage to introduce the others at the table.

"My attorney has prepared two documents and we're here to determine which will be served," Stewart began. Savage sat back and crossed his arms, waiting for the former chairman of the board to present his spiel. Stewart took his lack of objection as a sign of the old man's inherent weakness and inability to run a company. Stewart turned to Matt to make the presentation.

"The first document is a tender offer of ten cents per share for all outstanding shares of Savage Sand and Gravel by Deacon Carl Stewart. This is a complete buyout and takeover. All shares are to be tendered no later than midnight on September 30 or be forfeited. This offer is to be approved by the board of directors and notification sent to shareholders within twenty-four hours," Matt began.

"A little undervalued, I'd say," Savage offered vaguely. "The second document?"

"The alternative is to face lawsuit for fifty million dollars, the amount of the severance package guaranteed to Deacon Stewart in event of his dismissal. This will, I am sure you realize, result in the imminent bankruptcy of Savage Sand and Gravel. In the end, Deacon Stewart will still acquire all the assets of SSG which amounts to the same thing as accepting his tender offer, except that shareholders will receive nothing for their shares. I think you can clearly see that it is to the advantage of the shareholders, whom you profess to honor, to accept the tender offer."

"I see. And exactly why are these two options on the table?"

"My contract states that in case of involuntary termination, I will receive the sum of fifty million dollars," Stewart gloated. "There is no way around it."

"And exactly when were you involuntarily terminated?" Pàl asked.

"What? Your cronies replaced me at the shareholder meeting on Thursday. That's why you are sitting in *my seat* at the head of this table today," Stewart shouted.

"No one has terminated you. Yet."

"But…"

"You were *elected* chairman of the board, not employed as chairman. In fact, the corporate bylaws specifically state that board members shall not receive compensation or remuneration beyond reasonable expenses for their participation. While your employment contract states such important things as your exorbitant salary, earned vacation, and sever-ance package, it says nothing about the actual job you will do in the company leaving it as 'duties to be assigned.' No one in authority over you, which means the board of directors or me as chairman of the board and CEO, has relieved you of either your position as president or your job responsibilities. Without a termination of employment, your two documents have no standing in law or in fact." Pàl sat back and stared at the two men.

"That's ridiculous. Your puppets at the annual meeting already stated that when you were elected as chairman of the board, you would also take over as chief executive officer," Stewart said.

"I have gone over the corporate records and budgets for the past five years," Pàl said. "Other than some questionable line items in the budget and expenses, I find no indication that you have failed as an operations officer. Therefore, unless you are resigning from the company, which would cancel your golden parachute, I see no reason to immedi-ately replace you as president and chief operating officer. I believe the term of your contract expires at the end of next year, approximately fif-teen months from now. There is no clause mandating extension of the contract or any of its terms. Should we discover during that time that you are not performing according to expectations as president and chief operating officer, you have my word that we will find an *appropriate* position for you… somewhere."

"You can't box me in like that!"

"I'd suggest you check this with your attorney, who, by the way, does not have a similar golden parachute and has been replaced as corporate counsel. He may wish to discuss future employment possibilities with our new corporate counsel, Rex Russell."

The two men stared at each other for a full minute, but Stewart was defeated in this round. He stood to leave.

"I will need your confirmation that you will perform the duties that have been assigned to you," Savage said. "I believe you have built a loyal employee base and would hate to see a general walkout and loss of their jobs."

"I'll let you know by the end of the day."

11

Return to the Fold

Headings

Headlines

FOR THE first time, Axel was happy with the new rule requiring reporter bylines, and that he had a new owner who would make the tough decisions. Unable to reach Karen all day, he had taken the call from Savage Sand and Gravel and had interviewed Pàl Savage. The story was much different than the one slipped through the mail slot in the mid-afternoon.

"Do we go with the interview or the supposedly official press release?" Axel asked. The young man reading over the stories pushed back in his chair.

"The press release confirms two salient points from the interview. First, the board of directors was ousted. Second, Pàl Savage has returned to run his company," Cameron said. "None of the rest of the press release has anything other than innuendo. Go with the story of your interview with Pàl Savage, but simply indicate that the press release confirmed details. Be sure you spell his name correctly. There's a grave accent over the 'a'. You can put in parenthesis that most in Rosebud Falls pronounce it the same as 'Paul.' Otherwise, your story is good."

"Now what about this piece from Karen Weisman?" Axel asked. Cameron returned to the screen.

"She certainly is a mama-bear when it comes to Gee Evars, isn't she?" the young attorney who now owned *The Elmont Mirror* laughed.

"I think she has it right, but I want her name on it. I'll write an 'official release' as a sidebar that simply recounts that there is an ongoing investigation being conducted by both the police and the sheriff's office. I wish I knew her 'confidential sources' and could confirm them. If I could, I'd validate the story on behalf of the Families."

"How did she get an anonymous source inside the church and access to the Coroner's report?" Axel asked. "If there's one thing I do know about her—aside from the fact she's been a pain in the ass ever since she came to work here—it's that she always has legitimate sources. Your parents make sure of that."

"Yes, but that is not available even to me. The information is under attorney-client privilege and as an officer of the court, my father can simply attest that the sources were valid. Put it on the front page, but below the fold. There must have been a hundred cameras that caught that fall and I would love to know how she got this photo of the blade in the tree. I just don't want people to see that picture on the newsstand when they glance at the paper," Cameron said. "I think you made all the right choices here, Axel. Thank you for checking in with me."

"Mr. LaCoe, I admit that I was upset when you took over and changed policies, but I also confess that you've been fair," Axel said slowly. "What worries me is that we've always maintained a politically neutral position and we seem to be... becoming more biased."

"I appreciate your concern, Axel. Really. But in a time of war, the media can't be seen as supporting the enemy. It has to take a stand."

"War?"

"The events of Saturday and Sunday were acts of terror against the City, the Forest, and our people. Make no mistake about it, Axel. The preacher and members of that church have declared war against the Families, and we will not let up on them until they surrender. Or are destroyed."

"Terrorist Disrupts Closing Harvest Ceremony," Gee read from Tuesday's newspaper. "Isn't that a little strong?"

"You think I should have used the politically correct conservative line and said a mentally ill man succumbed to pressures in his head and disturbed the peace?" Karen asked sarcastically. "I could have ended the piece in the next sentence by saying, 'Our thoughts and prayers are with those who were inconvenienced.'"

"I was more concerned about you and what this could do to your standing among the Families," Gee said softly. "Karen, don't you know how much I worry about you?"

"Yes, I do, love. But the story wouldn't have been published without Cameron's approval. Even with my byline."

"Cameron? The baritone in the quartet?"

"The son of your lawyers and suddenly heir-apparent to the Nussbaum Family leadership," Karen corrected him. "And the new owner of *The Elmont Mirror*."

"He is?"

"He doesn't know I know, so please don't just blurt that out in public. Technically, the newspaper is owned by the Rosebud Free Writers Trust, a trust that was recently transferred to four cousins and of which Cameron LaCoe is the trustee."

"Wow! Is Cameron trying to take control of the Families?"

"Strangely enough," Karen mused, "I have a lot of faith in him. He has much more to lose in this rodeo than to gain."

"What does that mean?"

"Old research. It's not important right now. Finish reading my brilliant writing. You sound so smart when you read my words," she giggled.

He scowled at her from the 'old person' chair where he sat. He wanted to complain about his enforced immobility, but when he tried to move, his ribs made him thankful for the chair with a lift.

> *A white male, approximately thirty-five years old, planted a sharp blade in the Harvest wedding tree, intent on causing injury or death to the shaker who climbed it. Police indicate that the incident is still 'under investigation' but confirmed that the blade held clear fingerprints that match the suspect. The blade was further coated with the drug Lustre Plus, a known hallucinogen that could easily have caused the shaker to 'feel like flying' if he had been cut by the blade instead of having his safety line severed.*
>
> *The suspect has also been linked to both distribution and heavy usage of the drug and is suspected in two attempted kidnappings*

which had put him on the Rosebud Falls' Police Department Most Wanted list.

The suspect was apprehended by police, thanks to the quick thinking and action of children in second grade, waiting to gather the nuts under the wedding tree. While in custody and being transported to the county jail, the prisoner suffered a rup- tured appendix and was pronounced dead on arrival at Poltanys Memorial Hospital.

A court-ordered autopsy revealed a previously unknown side-effect of prolonged use of the drug. The outer walls of several of the terrorist's organs had thinned to the point that imminent death was almost certain. Affected organs included the heart, liver, kidneys, spleen, and even stomach.

Gee looked up at his girlfriend, setting aside the newspaper for a minute.

"How did you get hold of the autopsy so quickly?" he asked.

"I have sources," Karen said. She held her lover's eyes with hers and eventually looked away. "Honestly, I think it was intentionally leaked. Did you know that all police bands are recorded and are a part of the public record? For some reason, Dr. Gaston chose to radio his findings to Detective Oliver rather than calling him or delivering the written report in a secure manner. When asked for confirmation, Dr. Gaston said that it was a common practice to use the police radio to communi- cate findings before the official report was drafted. Detective Oliver flew into a well-staged snit over the use of an unsecured channel and swore that such a breach would never occur again."

"There goes a reliable source," Gee chuckled. Karen walked over to him with a sultry sway to her hips and kissed him softly.

"I haf other vays," she declared. "Keep reading."

Victim blaming raises its ugly head. According to a witness who asked to remain anonymous, Pastor Lance Beck 'whipped his congregation to a frenzy' prior to loosing the mob on Sunday's Harvest Parade. After hearing their pastor, a known affili- ate of the dead terrorist, compare injured shaker George Evars to Lucifer, the Seven Families to the seven-headed beast of Revelation, and the children who apprehended the terrorist to

demon spawn, congregants assaulted Evars (known as Gee to all
in Rosebud Falls) with insults and a hail of acorns thrown at the
shaker and the children accompanying him on the parade route.

"Acorns?"

"I conceded that it wouldn't be a good idea to let the public know that the assailants had access to hickory nuts," Karen replied. "I can't believe Alex called and asked me to accept the change. Those imbeciles actually tried to blame the children!" Karen exploded. Even though she had written the words, she acted almost as if it was the first time she had heard them.

"Who was on the inside? That must truly gall the minister," Gee said.

"Rena went to church Sunday."

"Oh no. It must have been very hard on her to come to you with that story. I know that even though she associates Brother Reef with the church, she really likes her pastor," Gee said. "It makes me sad."

"It wasn't Rena," Karen said. "She is still in treatment and was accompanied by her chaperone. Liz was shocked speechless and called me first thing Monday morning. There is a lot to be discovered in that church and I plan to get to the bottom of it."

Gee finished reading the story and put the newspaper down. He nodded thoughtfully and then turned to Karen. "This isn't going to end it, you know."

"I know."

"And calling them 'outsiders' with no relationship to the City is going to call attention to the Families."

"Yes and no. I have positive ID on fourteen of the protesters and none of them live in the city limits nor in South Rosebud. They have no vote in the election but are campaigning to stop the annexation. I'm not going to let up. Next week, I'll hit them again. The City has not been mobilized by the Families since the Seven Heroes. Calvary Tabernacle may very well face protests itself."

"Be careful, my love. Your byline on this story paints a target on you."

"I love you, Gee. I'll be careful."

The Prodigal Returns

"THIS MEETING OF the War Orphans is now called to order," Heinz said as he rapped the deck of cards on the table. The women rolled their eyes as he began to deal.

"You'd think that he'd get tired of that line after seventy years," Dee Poltanys Warren said.

"Good old dependable Heinz," Celia sighed.

"Who made him chairman, anyway?" Coretta asked. "How are you doing, dear?" she said, ignoring Heinz and turning to Celia. "This has to have been an exciting week for you."

"It's taken a little wind out of my sails," Celia said. "But nothing has really changed. You have all been my friends, my brother and sisters, regardless of how others viewed me."

"How are you going to spend your millions?" Heinz asked. "Round-the-world cruise? That's what Gerta's after me about. She says I should make Cameron my heir and resign as family head."

"I could be convinced if you were all going," Celia said. "But why would an old woman go off around the world alone?"

"You'd attract someone, dear. Strong, handsome…"

"Forty years younger," Dee interrupted Coretta.

"Younger that what?"

"Heinz," all three women chorused.

"Did you know Leah came by?" Celia asked. "She offered to drive me to the Jewish cemetery so I could spit on her—our—grandfather's grave instead of the war memorial?" The four laughed at the ridiculous situation. "I've directed her to put it all in Jo's name. I have everything I've ever wanted. I don't see a reason to need new wills and codicils or what have you."

"You've always had us," Heinz said softly.

"And I love each of you," Celia smiled. "I just wish Henry, Ewan, and Pàl were with us, rest their souls."

"Speaking of which," Heinz said, glancing at his watch. There was a light knock on the door of the retirement home card room.

"Ah, our weekly card bunch is here. You see, Mr. Savage, we are not a stuffy place where you get confined to your room. This is a retirement village, not a nursing home," the staffer said.

"I don't know. These folks look awfully old to me," the man said grinning as he stepped into the room.

"Pàl?" Dee exclaimed. "Pàl Savage?" The four card players all stood and Heinz stepped back so the women could embrace their one-time play fellow.

"What are you doing here?" Celia asked. "I mean, I'm so glad you are here, Pàl. But why?"

"I came to celebrate with you," Pàl said. "And to help my grandson navigate the tricky waters of Rosebud Falls."

"And to take over Savage Sand and Gravel," Heinz added.

"Sit here between Celia and Dee," Coretta said. "I'm married."

"Which is why she sits by good old safe and very married Heinz," the elder Nussbaum laughed. Pàl took the proffered seat.

"Are you responsible for engineering the takeover of SSG?" Dee asked.

"I helped. But the real work was done by Wayne and his silent partner. That's why I'm really here. Neither of them needs to be in the spotlight about this."

"There wasn't anything in the paper about a partnership or about Wayne at all," Celia said. "It just said a well-orchestrated shareholder revolt."

"Well, we hoped to show that there was dissension among the shareholders. The truth is that my grandfather engineered the takeover sixty years ago, before we left town."

"How so?" Coretta asked.

"I'm told that you all receive a distribution from a sealed trust," Pàl said.

"There were times when that was the only thing that kept me going," Celia answered.

"Well, the trust was set up at the same time that Savage Sand and Gravel went public as a corporation," Pàl said. "Your trusts were funded with one hundred thousand shares of SSG stock that my grandfather set up."

"No!"

"Someone found out what was in the trusts. That someone arranged for this very nice man, about the same age as my grandson, to vote the proxy for those shares at the company's annual meeting. Heinz?" Pàl said.

"My grandson," Heinz admitted. "He came to me with the information and I suggested that the City Champion vote the shares."

"That sounds good, Pàl, but I can do the math. Six hundred thousand out of five million shares, as the paper cited, isn't enough to control the company by itself. Was it just enough to put you in the majority?" Dee asked.

"That is where my grandfather hid a surprise. For sixty years, your shares lay silent until Mr. Evars voted them at the meeting last Thursday. We'd hoped to hold enough shares to influence the company policies. What we discovered was that the shares *granda* set up for you were of a class that could control the company. So, in spite of having only five million shares, there are ten million four hundred thousand votes, and between your trusts and my shares, we control seven million of those votes. That's what changed the game last week and brought me back to Rosebud Falls."

"Are you back to stay, Pàl?" Celia asked softly. He smiled at her.

"As I told that nice young staff person who was showing me around, I'm thinking this might be a good place for me to retire. Florida is nice and sunny, but any state where the unofficial state bird is the vulture is no place for old people."

"You haven't lost any of your old sense of humor," Coretta laughed.

"Yep. As bad as ever," Heinz said.

"Should we do something about the proxies for our shares?" Coretta asked. Her brow was creased in worry. "I like that nice young shaker, but should he really have so much power?"

"If we each take control of our own shares, we stand the risk of being divided again," Heinz said. "When Cameron brought the shares to light, he wanted to hold the proxies. I told him no. I don't think the power should transfer to one of the Families."

"I agree," Pàl said. "In fact, I am turning the proxy for my million shares over to the City Champion as well. He has nothing to gain or to lose, no matter what comes of the company. He has no ownership. As long as he is controlled by his connection to the City and the Forest, he will make good decisions."

"We need Gee to talk to David Lazorack and to Collin Meagher," Heinz said. "If we five are agreed to maintain the proxy as is, we would still have less than a majority if they withdrew from the alliance."

"Hmm. I think I will talk with my grandson-in-law," Coretta mused. "My interest will pass to his wife as David's will ultimately pass to him. And he is a good friend of our City Champion."

"If we have business out of the way," Celia said, "can we just spend time catching up with Pàl? When did you start wearing a kilt?"

Scholarship

"THERE'S GOING TO be a rally before the football game tomorrow night," Karen said. "The Nussbaum Quartet will perform, so even though you missed their second performance during Harvest, you'll get another chance tomorrow."

"Ahhh, that's great," Gee moaned. He wasn't sure if he was responding to her words or the gentle massage of his shoulder with the liniment. He'd had a long soak in the bath salts Coretta had given him after confirming with Dr. Poltanys that it wouldn't hurt his stitches. He'd never had so many stitches in his life as since he came to Rosebud Falls.

Hmm. That was a new data point. He'd had stitches before, but not as many or as frequently as since he got to Rosebud Falls. When he told Karen his discovery, she reached for her notebook and jotted it down.

"What's tomorrow's news today?" he asked as they cuddled in bed together after his massage.

"I've let that preacher know that I am following up on the events during the Harvest parade with a full investigative report on his background as a minister and as a youth deprogrammer. I asked nicely for an interview, but he declined. I discovered, however, that in two other communities where he operated in the past, he was accused of kidnapping. The accusations didn't stick as the parents of the teens involved held that it was their right to commit their child to the pastor's care for conversion therapy."

"What happened to the kids?"

"One committed suicide. The other, after having been cured of his homosexuality, returned to his parents' home and was reported to have married a neighbor girl when they turned eighteen."

"That drug, Karen. Lustre? Can it be used to control a person?"

"That's a truly frightening prospect, Gee. People blindly obeying commands. They'd be like…"

"Slaves."

"Slaves that could be used for anything."

"Assassins. Nut-pickers. Sex slaves."

"HEY, GUY. HAVE a seat. Karen, you look lovely as always," Wayne said. He was in a good mood and looking forward to the game, but also to the introduction he was about to make. "Gee, Karen, I'd like you to meet my grandfather, Pàl Savage." The older gentleman reached over to take Gee's offered hand.

"It's a pleasure to meet you in person, Mr. Savage," Gee said. "I'm sorry I haven't been up to accepting invitations the past couple weeks."

"Wayne has told me much about his two friends and I've been following your stories closely since I arrived in town. You are both very influential," Pàl said.

"Influence is Karen's bailiwick. I just jump—or fall—into ridiculous situations without thinking," Gee said.

"Perhaps you don't know how much that raises your level of influence," Pàl laughed. "Ms. Weisman, I would very much like to talk to you about your impressions of the current… ah… political environment here in Rosebud Falls."

"Please, just Karen," she said. "I'd be delighted to have a discussion, though I, too, doubt my level of influence. Especially lately."

"Ah, Karen, that is not what my friends say. Though they seem to believe you could have accomplished such things with a little less panache, they all agree that you are the person responsible for helping a very dear old friend of mine."

"Really, Mr. Savage?"

"Please, if you are Karen, I am Pàl. The difference between the English and Scottish pronunciations are so small as to make it a moot point."

"Thank you, Pàl. I'm glad I could help in whatever way I have."

"You set Celia Eberhardt's mind at rest at long last," Pàl said. "And through your actions, made her granddaughter very wealthy. I hope you will not withdraw your influence from young Jo. She admires you greatly."

"I think she's extremely sweet."

"We continue to need your help, Karen."

"What can I do?"

"In two weeks here in Rosebud Falls, I have become even more concerned about the activities of my former board of directors and CEO," Pàl said. "You have been stirring a hornets' nest with your continued pressure on the church located near the quarry. Among the hornets are the former CEO, who is also the chairman of the board of deacons for Calvary Tabernacle. I find that all the former board members of SSG were also members of that church. That seems… out of the ordinary for a publicly held company to me."

"I share your unease. I have long believed that something is going on there that is not quite right. For example, how did the church become situated on that plot of land in the first place?"

"A matter for further investigation, don't you think?" Pàl said. "But I believe our conversation this evening must come to an end as we enjoy the festivities about to begin."

───────◁◆▷───────

THE MUSIC OF The Nussbaum Quartet washed over Gee. It was special—vibrant. None of her cousins were quite the musician Elaine was, but their support made her voice twice as powerful. Karen gripped his hand, apparently just as lost in the music.

"Isn't it great to have The Nussbaum Quartet back with us for this rally?" newspaper editor Axel Hunter asked the cheering fans. "And who is the team of the evening?"

"Fireflies!"

"That's right," Axel continued. "The *Mirror* has always been a strong supporter of Harvest and of our two local schools. As a result, we want to recognize the students of Rosebud High School and invite its senior class officers to the stage. And, even though their team is in Manchester tonight, we also have the senior class officers of Flor del Día here with us. These two school are formidable foes on the gridiron. But in the Forest, they take it to a whole new level of both competition and cooperation." The class officers of the two schools approached from opposite ends of the platform and shook hands in the middle.

"It is a new tradition that we are starting tonight to have two scholarships awarded. Each scholarship is for one thousand dollars and will go to the senior chosen by his or her classmates as most valuable harvester. Remember that without the nearly 700 students of these two schools, our Harvest would last until snow flies. Flor del Día, who will receive the scholarship as MVH for your school?" Axel asked the student on his left.

"Thank you, Mr. Hunter. Flor del Día is honored to participate in the annual Harvest. Rosebud Falls is home to our student body. We live practically *in* the Forest and students walk there every day. One of those students has been a harvester every year since she arrived at Flor del Día as a seventh-grade orphan almost six years ago. The student body is happy to announce its choice of Norma Smith as our MVH and recipient of this scholarship," the student concluded to enthusiastic applause.

"And now turning to Rosebud High School. Who has been elected as your most valuable harvester?"

"Mr. Hunter, you will see two cousins leading the Fireflies on the field tonight. They are co-captains of our offensive team. Center Viktor Nussbaum is a senior and James Nussbaum is a junior and our varsity quarterback. They proved as fast a combination in the Forest as they are on the football field and the student body had no difficulty choosing Victor as our senior MVH," the student announced.

"So, Viktor Nussbaum will receive the thousand-dollar scholarship."

"No, sir," the student representative continued. "Viktor has respectfully declined the scholarship. He has a full-ride scholarship at Rutgers next fall and he has said his family would never want him to receive money that was better used by someone else. Viktor requested, and the student body ratified his decision, that the thousand-dollar scholarship be presented to the MVH from Flor del Día to double her award."

The crowd erupted as the quartet rose in volume behind the group on stage. The student wasn't quite finished.

"We are crosstown rivals on the gridiron, but we are all partners in the love of our Forest and our commitment to Harvest. Will you accept this additional scholarship on behalf of your MVH?"

"On behalf of Norma Smith and Flor del Día, we accept the scholarship and your friendship. Thank you, your school, and your MVH for this consideration. May we always be trusted friends... except on the football field!"

After the applause died down and the class officers shook hands again, Axel continued as the quartet stepped back up to their microphones.

"It's the amazing spirit of this town and its willingness to reach across borders and that makes us what we are," Axel said. "That's why *The Elmont Mirror* is officially supporting the annexation of South Rosebud so we can extend our community, our services, and our spirit. Now let's stand for our National Anthem and get ready to play football!"

The crowd stood to join Elaine's beautiful voice in the anthem.

"FORGIVE ME FOR this presumption, Gee," Pàl said as the group walked to the gates after the game. Gee was still using his hickory staff as he walked, but it was more to keep people from getting too close and jostling him than for real support. Karen protected his injured right side, holding his hand.

"What is that, Mr. Savage?"

"I'd like you to take this."

"What is it?" Gee said, hesitantly taking the envelope Pàl held out to him.

"It is the proxy for the Savage Family one million class A shares of SSG stock."

"But you're here! Why would you want me to act as proxy for your shares?"

"When my grandfather took the company public, he set trusts up with a hundred thousand shares of class B stock, one that would benefit each of the other war orphans. No trust was set up for me because he held one million shares that I would inherit. You hold the proxy for the six trusts. It's only appropriate that you hold mine as well."

"But surely, they'll all take control of their own now," Gee said. "They didn't give me permanent control or anything."

"Now that I have added my voice to theirs, they are unlikely to retract them. All the seven ever wanted was to bring Rosebud Falls together and protect the Forest. Now, I'm confident that we will succeed."

First Family

"SURPRISE!" JESSIE SAID. "We're back!"

"Already? You guys didn't take a very long honeymoon," Gee said.

"Really? It seemed like forever," Jessie sighed as she stepped aside so Gee and Karen could come into her in-laws' home.

"Jessie! I can't believe you got bored with him already!" Karen laughed.

"Are you kidding? That part of the honeymoon was great! But we could have done that in the Forest and not had to travel all the way to Niagara Falls. We have a waterfall right here in Rosebud Falls."

"Aww. That's sweet," Karen said. She glanced at Gee. "You know, I'm beginning to feel the same way."

"Gee. Karen," David Lazorack said as Jonathon brought the couple into the spacious sitting room where his father was mixing drinks. "Welcome to our home."

"It's good to see you, Mr. Lazorack," Gee said.

"Mmm. I feel better now that I see you are healthy. Karen, my apologies for having been abrupt with you the last time we met," David said.

"I understand the stress Harvest puts on you, David," she said. "I just hope this year's events don't force any changes on our annual celebration."

"It's almost inevitable," he answered. "We'll try to make the changes as subtle as possible, but I foresee as much as doubling the number of foresters we have in the next year. Ah. Here's Rebecca. Becky, I don't think you've been properly introduced to Gee Evars. And I think you know Karen Weisman. Gee, my wife Rebecca."

"It's a pleasure, ma'am."

"It's nice to see you again, Rebecca."

"I hoped to meet you after the wedding, but circumstances prevented things," Rebecca said. "I'm so glad to see you up and recovering."

"Mom! Dad! We're here!" a woman's voice rang from the kitchen.

"In here, Laura," Rebecca responded. A young woman with dirty blonde hair, dark rimmed glasses, and a perpetually sad expression on her face entered, followed by a thin man with black curly hair and a tightly-cropped black beard. "Gee, I'd like you to meet my daughter Laura and her fiancé, Jude Roth-Augello," Rebecca said. "I'm sorry, Karen. I should include you in these introductions, but I know you already all know each other. Laura and Jude, meet Karen's friend, Gee Evars of tree-climbing fame."

"I'm afraid tree-falling fame is more like it," Gee laughed as he reached for Jude's outstretched hand and then turned to Laura. Tears sparkled in Laura's eyes as she tensed up and, for a moment, Gee thought she was going to strike him.

"Why did you live?" she demanded. "Why didn't my grandfather live?"

"Laura," David said softly. "It's not Gee's fault that Dad died."

"Sorry," Laura said glancing at Gee but focusing on Karen. "Too much dying."

"Well, let's go into the dining room now that everyone is here," Rebecca said brightly. "Dinner is ready. Laura, would you help me set it on the table, please?"

"YOU ARE WIELDING a great deal of power in our city, for a newcomer," David said to Gee. "And I understand you want more."

"I don't want *any* power," Gee protested. "What gave you that idea?"

"David…" Rebecca started.

"Sorry," David said. "My daughter gets her shortness of temper and willingness to jump in with both feet from me. I don't set a very good example." He lifted a spoonful of the thick stew to his mouth and paused before setting it back down. "My father died in last year's Harvest in much the same kind of fall you took. He had been pushing to get the annexation initiative on the ballot last year and the drive basically fell apart with his death. A carabiner broke. There was no sign of it having been tampered with, but I had all the equipment he used sent in for examination along with several other sets to spot check them. Not all carabiners are created equal. The ones on my father's rig were an inferior quality. So much so that they were tested for fifty pounds breaking strength and Dad weighed close to two hundred. The carabiners on all the other rigs tested at a standard five thousand pounds of breaking strength."

"That doesn't sound accidental," Gee said. "Any more than having a blade up there to cut the flipline does."

"They've become very popular over the past decade as decorative snaps for attaching wallets, keychains, and toys to belt loops or strollers. Cheap brittle alloys are imported from China. But unless they are treated with an anode dye, you can't tell the difference between the types at a glance. Repeatedly climbing, fastening the loop, throwing himself back to stretch his shaker pole up into the branches. Eventually, one of the links gave out. He was murdered, but the police haven't been able to tie a suspect to his death. Now they want to blame it on the same guy who cut your rope. Maybe they're right, but perhaps he's just an easy way to close the case. I'm sure of one thing. It was done to stop the annexation."

"Why is it so important?" Gee asked.

"The trees down there are crying, Gee," Jonathon broke in. "All you need to do is walk into the wild woods and you know they are hurting. The understory is overgrown and is choking out the hardwood. The nuts are small and diseased. The leaves yellow and fall a month before the Forest. We need to get down there and help those trees."

"Who owns it? SSG?"

"It's not exactly clear," David said. "SSG manages the whole area. That includes the quarry, the wild woods, and the lake. They have mineral leases, but there might be more. They fenced it all off and blocked us from access years ago. So, we need to know your intentions, Gee. How are you going to wield your votes within that company? My father was one of the war orphans. The trust that contains one hundred thousand shares passes to me and my heirs, Jonathon and Laura. If you continue to hold our proxy, how will you use it?"

Gee contemplated the issue and turned to Karen for encouragement. She squeezed his hand and nodded.

"When Judge Warren handed me the proxies, he said to go to the meeting and vote my conscience for the City and the Forest. When I went to the meeting, I didn't know what the issues were or how much 'power' as you say I wielded. I just voted for what felt best for the Forest. I don't see that ever changing," Gee said.

"Laura. Jonathon. This affects you as much as me. We've talked about this trust since Dad died. Are you in favor of letting Gee manage our vote?" David asked. Laura nodded her head.

"Yes," Jonathon said.

"Then you'll have our proxy," David said. "Protect our Forest."

"Excuse me," Jessie broke in. "Now that the Lazorack Family has made its decision, my grandmother, war orphan Coretta Sims of the Cavanaugh Family, has authorized me as her heir to confirm that Gee has the proxy for her trust and will continue to have it for as long as he defends the Forest."

"Jessie?" Gee said.

"Coretta says." That was her final answer.

———◁◆▷———

"I'm exhausted," Karen said. She and Gee got home about the same time Wednesday evening. Gee had used his hickory stick to help him walk the two blocks to the library to read to the children. Ms. Tomczyk was surprised but excited to see him. There were more children present for reading than there had been before Harvest. She got Gee a chair instead of his usual beanbag and the children weren't allowed to climb all over him as they usually did, but they all had fun reading.

"Me, too," he sighed as they settled into bed. The walk home after reading time was far more exhausting than getting there. "I might have overdone it a little, but I really needed to see the kids tonight. Look at all the cards and notes. They brought them thinking they'd have to leave them at the library to be delivered to me. Ms. Tomczyk asked me to bring them back after you'd seen them so she can display them in the library along with a picture of me at reading time."

"It's so sweet. Those kids really love you," Karen said leaning over to kiss him softly and discovering that even with the exhaustion, his cheek was shaved smooth. "So do I."

"Mmm. So what did my own Lois Lane super-reporter expose today?" he asked after their kiss.

"Oh, I got to go talk to the heads of Families today," she said. "Loren Cavanaugh and Benjamin Roth, of course, referred me to Clark and Leah, who both made strong statements in support of annexation. I had a lovely talk with Heinz Nussbaum, who gave a polite nod at the annexation and said it sounded like a good idea. He's such a teddy bear."

"That's three and we talked to Lazorack and Savage over the weekend."

"Collin Meagher doesn't have a phone apparently. I... I'm not sure I can go down there. Too many bad memories. So that left me with Jan Poltanys."

"That's Dr. Poltanys' father, right?"

"Yes. There has always been at least one Poltanys involved in medicine. The family is a major contradiction."

"How so?"

"Well, first of all, I think the brainpower in the Poltanys Family exceeds all the other Families put together. And Jan is no exception. The Family is always a big supporter of medical research. Second, medical work is only a part of the family's social involvement. They built that entire Hilltop Retirement Village. Your favorite building, the library, had four principal donors. Roth donated the land, Savage donated the stone, Meagher donated the labor, and Poltanys donated the books. The Family is interested in everything having to do with social activism and improving people's lives."

"I don't see any contradictions in that."

"No. It's when you figure out where their money came from and continues to come from that a contradiction arises. There are huge seams of bituminous coal a hundred miles north of us. The Poltanys family opened the coal mines that fueled the cities to the south for over a hundred years. The canal west of town was built to transport coal and various other ores to Rosebud Falls where it was offloaded from barges and then loaded onto coal trains from here to the city. The first century of the hospital's existence, they probably treated more cases of black lung disease than anything else. In addition to the coal, Poltanys shipped their sick workers to Rosebud Falls. Underground mining is hard and dangerous, but Poltanys shifted their operation to strip mining before the war, opening huge gashes in the environment."

"Wow. So, hospital, retirement home, library… It all sounds like guilt money."

"I'd like to think so, but Jan Poltanys is a soft-spoken and thoughtful man. We are invited to join the Family for dinner Saturday."

"We are?"

"It seems that you have continuing business with each of the war orphans or their beneficiaries. I'm campaigning for the annexation and you are there to confirm their proxies." They settled down for sleep and Karen turned off the light.

"Sounds like Poltanys is a good man to have on your side," Gee yawned.

"How about me? Can I be on your side without putting too much pressure on your ribs?" He wrapped his left arm around Karen and pulled her snuggly against his side. Any discomfort was worth it.

Dinner with the Poltanys Clan

"I'M SORRY IT has taken so long to invite you to a social event, Gee, Karen," Jan Poltanys explained in greeting them at the door of his remarkably modest home. Located on the south side of the hill crowned by the Hilltop Retirement Village, the house was only about twenty years old.

"I'm flattered that you invited us, Mr. Poltanys," Gee said.

"Please, it's just Jan."

"Lovely to see you again, Jan," Karen said. "Thank you for agreeing to talk to us."

"Well, there was some concern about a doctor and some nurses having a social relationship with one of their patients, having nothing at all to do with a golf course," Jan laughed. "I had to explain to them that if we truly followed the non-fraternization rule, none of us would have any friends. Come meet the rest of the Family."

"Gee," Adam Poltanys said as he joined his father. "It's good to see you. Any trouble finding the place?"

"None at all, Adam," Gee said, intentionally not using his doctoral title.

"I believe you know my daughter, Julia, and my wife, Sofia," Jan continued introductions.

"Hello, Julia. Nice to see you wearing something other than green," Gee chuckled. He turned to Sofia and bowed as deeply as his ribs would let him. "Your majesty."

"Jan, I've just adopted this young man. I may make him my heir," Sofia said haughtily. The family laughed and entered the great room where Gee saw several familiar faces. Jan took him around to introduce him as they had drinks.

"I believe you know Judge Warren," Jan began.

"In this gathering we don't use titles," the judge said. "Good evening, Gee. Please call me Brian among friends. This is my wife, Geraldine and over in a corner somewhere with Zach's Derek, you'll find my twins, Leslie and Stefan."

"Uh… Yes, sir… Okay. Are you related?" Gee asked, looking between Jan Poltanys and Judge Warren.

"Let me introduce my mother, Dee Poltanys Warren," Brian said.

"It's a pleasure to meet you," Dee responded. "I'm the Poltanys version of a War Orphan. My father and Jan's father were brothers. Jan's father was much younger and did not get caught up in the disaster of the war. So, yes, Jan and I are cousins, even though I'm old enough to be his…"

"Beloved auntie," Jan answered. "Your twelve years on me doesn't qualify you for motherhood. Oh, let me introduce you to my other son, Zach and his family. He's my designated heir unless one of the others wants to challenge him."

"Not likely," Adam called.

"Zach, I think we've met on the basketball court, though it seems a long time since I've played now," Gee said. "I've come to believe the Family heads carry a heavy responsibility in Rosebud Falls, though I am not completely clear on all it entails."

"That's why we all try to groom an heir as early as possible," Jan said. "That's Zach's role here. He'll take over as Family head should anything happen to me."

"Hopefully, not for a long time," the young man said. He was relaxed about his role. "Dad shows no sign of any of Grandfather's ailments, so I hope I'll be at least his age before I have to take over. Right now, I want to be able to take my kids to Disneyland and maybe travel once around the world. We've become too ingrown, parochial in our isolation. We need to expand our horizons for Rosebud Falls."

"And there you have the younger generation's assessment of what's wrong in the world today," Jan laughed. "And it's a good assessment. We tend to think our world in Rosebud Falls is the only world there is."

"And Karen, that brings us to you," Zach said.

"Really? How so?" Karen asked. She'd rejoined Gee after a short conversation with Julia.

"The other Families, Cavanaugh, Lazorack, Roth, even Savage, will tell or have told you about how annexation would be a benefit to both the City and the residents of South Rosebud. Most of the benefits you'll hear are financial," Zach said. "The estimated benefits don't outweigh the extended burden of fire, police, and medical services and the fact that we will need new road extensions into that part of the town in order to deliver those services. Zoning ordinances might change and if so, might affect the residents. They should expect their relative isolation will end with more development."

"So, you are opposed to the annexation?" Karen asked Zach and then turned to Jan for confirmation. Jan remained neutral and turned back to his son.

"No. We are in favor of annexation but not for financial reasons. Those will be a wash. Dad?" Zach smoothly turned the family positioning over to his father.

"It's the right thing to do," Jan said. "We want to weigh all our decisions in some objective scale that balances benefits and costs. But it simply doesn't work that way. South Rosebud should have been considered a part of Rosebud Falls from the beginning. I believe Family disagreements have harmed the unity of our City for long enough. You, Karen, did a great thing in righting a wrong against Celia and Jo Ransom. It was embarrassing—perhaps for your Roth Family the most, but for all the Families who said and did nothing all these years. It was wrong for South Rosebud to have been excluded from the original City. It is time to right that wrong."

———— ◁◆▷ ————

AFTER DINNER JAN asked Karen to excuse Gee for a conference and she was quickly hustled away by her friend, Julia. Gee joined Jan, Zach, Judge Warren, and Dee Warren in Jan's study.

"Now that you've had your bit of family lesson, we wanted to discuss something else with you," Brian said. "We... I made you Champion for Rosebud Falls when we decided to get you an ID. When I presided over that meeting with your lawyer, employer, bankers, and our police detective, I had no idea what would ultimately come of it. Now we're finding out."

"During Harvest, you were given the proxies for six hundred thousand shares of SSG stock," Jan continued. "When Brian gave you those proxies, he did not know—nor did any of us—that we had handed you a controlling interest in the company. Frankly, none of us individually knew what was in the trusts for the war orphans. Bryce Savage set up these trusts and everyone thought it was a great act of altruism, but the trusts are in the care of First Rose Valley Bank. The only thing any of the beneficiaries knew was that they received an annual distribution check from the trust."

"That includes me," Dee added. "And Celia Eberhardt and Heinz Nussbaum, and Coretta Sims and Henry Lazorack. When Ewan Meagher was killed in Viet Nam, the trust passed to his half-brother, Collin Meagher. Bryce Savage was a good man and was committed to the idea that the Families had to come together. When they wouldn't listen to his counsel, he took his company public and left town, taking Pàl and his mother, Natalie, with him to see the world. But still, none of us knew that the trusts he created were funded with a hundred thousand shares of stock in SSG."

"Now that we all know, we need to revisit the decision to give you the proxy for voting Mom's share of the company," Warren said.

"I don't know why people think I am a good choice to hold these proxies. I didn't know why when you handed them to me during Harvest and told me to vote my conscience, Judge. Why would you want me to hold a controlling interest in SSG?" Gee asked.

"I want the best for my home, my family, and my City," Dee said. "Gee, to our knowledge, you are the only person not of a Family and not treated immediately with an antidote, to have eaten a nut in the Forest and lived. You could bring us all together."

"I've received a renewal of the proxies for Lazorack, Cavanaugh, and Savage," Gee said. "I will tell you the same thing that I told them. Whatever power or leverage this proxy gives me, I will use for the health and protection of the Forest and the people of Rosebud Falls."

"That's good enough for me," Dee said.

"We'd like you to keep the proxy for Mom's shares," Warren confirmed.

"I would expect you will hear from Heinz Nussbaum soon and probably from Celia Ransom," Jan said. "I don't know how to tell you to go about contacting Collin Meagher. He's… unpredictable."

All We Like Sheep

"I'M SO SORRY, Pastor. I thought I was bringing a lost sheep to the fold. I didn't know she was using our services to fuel hatred of our church to outsiders," the young woman pled. She had mustered all her courage to visit the preacher at his home on Sunday afternoon. Released from treatment only the Friday before, Rena had immediately returned to the comfort of her church, this time without her accompanying chaperone, Liz. Before she left the center, Liz had pled with her not to return to the fold, filling her head with lies about Pastor. Rena had finally realized that her chaperone had been the source of the hateful stories in the newspaper.

"Precious child, you didn't know. Your heart was right. Come, sit with me in my study." Rena entered the massive house on the lake looking at the view from the study with a sense of wonder and awe.

"So beautiful!" she breathed.

"It is a refuge," Pastor Beck said. "I carry the burden of the souls of our congregation—indeed all of Rosebud Falls—on my shoulders. Sitting here with the Lord gives me strength to carry on. He provides in… unexpected ways. It is one of his many blessings." Instead of sitting behind his massive desk, the preacher led her to a sofa and sat beside her, putting a comforting arm around the girl. "Now tell me what has happened in your life these past weeks so that we can pray and discover how to make things right between you and our Lord."

Rena unburdened her soul in the arms of her minister. She had been so lonely in the rehab center without her fellowship. They had pumped her for help in identifying Brother Reef and she'd been confused, believing the man to have been a threat because they told her he was. But she had borne no ill-will for the strange man, blaming herself for taking too much of the drug he offered or not understanding his instructions. She had genuinely liked Gee and thought he might be her future mate, unaware of the faults Pastor Beck pointed out.

And then, Sunday morning, the pastor's sermon had been so filled with love that she had been moved to visit him.

"All we like sheep have gone astray; we have turned every one to his own way; and the LORD hath laid on him the iniquity of us all," the preacher had quoted. Then he pled with the congregation—admittedly a little smaller this week than previously—to return to the fold, to confess their sins, and enter the loving arms of forgiveness. It was especially important to seal their doors against outsiders who would distort their message and persecute them. Rena was overwhelmed with the conviction that she had been the one to bring persecution upon her church and she wept in her pastor's arms as he held her close and petted her.

But Rena's pain went much deeper and Beck was a master at ferreting out her darkest secrets.

"No one will ever love me, Pastor. I should leave so I do not bring greater shame on our church." She looked up at him to plead for forgiveness and instead found his lips clasped to hers.

"I will love you, Rena," he said, his voice seeming somehow coarser than she had heard before. "I will take care of you."

"Oh, Pastor! You'll marry me?"

"Oh, sweet child, how I wish it could be so. But we must always be mindful of the frailties of our brothers and sisters. I will provide for you in every way, protecting you from the world and fulfilling your deepest desires. But for now, you should live in the youth camp where we can keep you away from those who would continue to hurt you. Come, kneel at the altar and let me purge your mind of unholy thoughts and unite with you in God's loving forgiveness."

12

Desperate Measures

The Grandfather Tree

GEE ARRIVED at the wedding tree just before the appointed time
of nine-thirty Monday morning. He was showered, shaved, and
dressed in the crisply pressed shaker shirt Karen had laid out for him.
He wore his forest hat and carried his hickory stick.

Jan and Zach Poltanys greeted Gee as soon as he arrived and escorted
him to a gathering near where the podium had been during the festival.

"Gee, I'd like to introduce you to some of the other Family heads,"
Jan said. "I think you know Leah who stands here for her father,
Benjamin Roth. David Lazorack is over with the foresters getting ready
for the felling. This is Heinz Nussbaum. Heinz, Gee Evars, our City
Champion."

"I know you've met others in my family, but on behalf of all of us,
welcome to Rosebud Falls, Gee," Heinz said, shaking Gee's hand. "After
the ceremony today, I'd like to invite you for lunch with me to meet the
rest of the clan."

"Uh... Thank you. Your daughter, Gretchen, alerted me to expect an
invitation. I'm looking forward to it."

"This is Loren Cavanaugh," Heinz said, turning to another of the
older men gathered near the tree. "Loren, you've never met Gee, have you?"

"Good to meet you, Gee. I don't get out as much as I used to. I've
been hiding behind my sons, I'm afraid."

"I've met Troy. We play basketball Sundays... when I'm not all banged up."

"Indeed. Don't take him too seriously. It's hard enough keeping his head from swelling with that window on Main Street. You worked with my cousin, Coretta during Harvest and Jessie speaks highly of you."

"I'm happy to say that Jessie and Jonathon have become two of my best friends," Gee said. David Lazorack left the tree to join the Family representatives as the mournful sounds of a bagpipe found their way through the Forest.

"That's a sound that hasn't been heard at Harvest in too many years," Heinz said wistfully.

"It's good to have him back," Loren agreed.

"Didn't a bagpipe play at the wedding?" Gee asked.

"Yes. It was our first clue that Pàl Savage had returned," Heinz said. "I believe you've met Pàl. We would've had quite a reunion after the wedding if things had gone a bit differently."

The pipes drew nearer and Pàl strode into the clearing, resplendent in his Black Watch tartan. The foresters stood back as he circled the tree three times, finally letting the last strains of the music fade. Pàl walked over to the Family representatives as the foresters got the equipment in place.

"Welcome back, Pàl," Heinz said. "That is quite the get-up. You look like your grandfather."

"When we left Rosebud Falls, *Granda* took me to Scotland to get me in touch with my roots. I took to the pipes pretty quickly and joined the Black Watch Pipe and Drum Corps. I'm just glad my unit wore a glengarry rather than a bearskin," Pàl laughed, tapping his hat.

"Pàl, your true roots are right here in Rosebud Falls," Heinz said softly.

"Yes. But like you, my old friend, there is something about keeping our ancestral heritage alive that makes it easier to understand our heritage in the Forest."

THE CANVAS CATCHER surrounding this tree had not been removed after Harvest. While not the wedding shaker, Jessie *was* the climber who would trim branches and lower them to the ground before cutting the trunk into segments. Sawdust and any remaining nuts would be kept in the canvas catcher. When everything was prepared, Jessie snapped her harness on. Gee glanced at it.

"Don't worry, Gee. We replaced all the fliplines with cable core lines. And the other climbers have been all over the tree this week to make sure it is clean and trimmed," Jessie said. "This will really be mostly for show until we start bringing down the sections. That's what that baby's for," she said pointing at a crane. When everyone was ready, Jessie started scaling the tree.

Every bit of the tree was either millable or would be used for firewood. Even the root ball would be dug out. Jessie wore cleats—something not used during the nut Harvest to avoid damaging the trees. A forester tossed her a rope which she looped over a higher branch and then tied to the one she would cut. After pulling her chainsaw up, she made two quick cuts, one from the bottom and one from the top, and the first ten-inch-thick limb swung away from the tree and was lowered gently to the ground. Half a dozen foresters hauled the twenty-foot branch away from the base of the tree and began trimming while Jessie moved to the next limb and repeated the process.

It took nearly two hours to fully limb the tree. Jessie was strapped around a part of the bole that was no more than eight inches across and eighty feet high when they moved the crane up. Orange stripes painted on the tree at twenty-foot intervals showed where the sections would be cut.

"The first section is always the hardest to bring down," Loren Cavanaugh said as he stepped up to Gee. "She can't climb high enough to get the crane hooked at the top of the trunk. That means the first section will flip when it's cut through. On a forty-foot tree, of course, we can use a bucket truck and tie off wherever we want to, but this part of cutting a hundred-foot tree is the most dangerous."

Jessie tightened the crane line above her cut mark and fired up her fourteen-inch chain saw. She made her first incision as carefully as a doctor, some twenty feet below the top of the tree. The second cut went in at a slight angle from the opposite side.

"Rose Hickory is one of the densest woods there is to cut, weighing in at about fifty-five pounds per cubic foot. That section of tree Jessie is cutting weighs nearly half a ton. They get heavier from there on down," Loren continued his information.

Everyone held still as a loud pop echoed above the sound of the chainsaw. Jessie jerked her tool free and the saw died immediately. She slid ten feet down the trunk, stopping her descent with her cleats. The crane pulled up and away from the tree as the top flipped upside down. Jessie hugged the tree with her face tight against the trunk as the limbs from the upper section slapped back against the other side. The crane kept moving and swung the section clear of the tree to lower to the ground. Amid the cheers, Jessie's loud, "Woo-ooo!" with her upraised fists echoed over them all.

"You okay, darlin'?" Jonathon called up to her. The tree she was now strapped to was no more than a straight pole rising eighty feet in the air.

"A little bruised, but nothing you can't kiss and make better later, baby!" she called back. The foresters applauded, and Jessie went back to work to prepare the next section.

Lunch with the Nussbaums

GEE MARVELED AT the view from Heinz Nussbaum's deck overlooking the river and railroad. The deck and patio, wrapping around three sides of the immense home, showed the dark side as well as light of Rosebud Falls. To the west, Gee could see the coal yard and railroad cars that would take the cargo south. While no longer used to heat homes and provide energy for power plants, the coal was a staple in steel mills and foundries. It was still loaded on Poltanys barges in the north, transported via canal to Rosebud Falls, and transferred to Nussbaum railcars for the trip farther south. It seemed strange that such a magnificent home would overlook the coal yard.

"My grandfather said it was to keep us humble," Heinz said as he watched Gee taking in the sight. "He said we created the mess, so we should have to live with it."

"You created it?"

"The coal yard was the result of a deal with the Poltanys clan intended to keep Rosebud Falls beautiful," Heinz elaborated. "There are seven locks on the canal to bring the barges a hundred miles to here. But it would take three more to get from the West Branch to the south end of Rosebud Falls. So, instead of continuing the canal with locks, we created this transfer point. The same could have been said about the railroad. We could have built bridges and trestles and the Meaghers would have laid tracks all the way to the coal fields. But we compromised. The railroad never crosses the river. Tracks to here. Canal to there. The lives of the seven Families have been filled with compromises. It's what we do to keep the balance in the city."

"That's… educational," Gee said, not sure what Heinz's point was.

"You have to look the other direction," his host continued. They walked toward the other end of the deck and looked out over downtown Rosebud Falls. "We aren't big, but we have our own beauty—our civic pride, if you will. The downtown has some sore spots. We don't have quite enough businesses to fill all the storefronts. We fought against Walmart moving in, but we could only keep it outside the City Limits. People are loyal to our local businesses, but the competition is a strain. Look at the falls sparkling over there. And beyond, our Forest. You see, the coal yard and the railroad were another kind of compromise. We sacrificed the beauty of this side to preserve the beauty of that side. Compromise."

"There are some things you can't compromise," Gee said. "You don't compromise the Forest, for example."

"Ah, but we did. I don't think anyone knows the real truth of why the wild woods are not part of the City—part of the Forest. Someday, I suspect, Miss Weisman will dig deeply enough into her ancestor's private papers that she will uncover what the mystery is. I could not find it in my Family papers. Before World War I, it seems that all the Nussbaum Family records were simply accounts and shipping records. That's when we got into banking and beautification of the downtown. But at least now, we are moving to rectify the past and bring that section into the City."

"It must be difficult on some of the Families. Change always is."

"True. But there is a new generation. Ben Roth's daughter. My grandchildren. The heir to the Savages. The new guardians of the Forest, Jonathon and Jessie. The doctors and nurses at the hospital. This generation doesn't know compromise," Heinz finished. "And they are our future. They are our children, Gee, and they need a champion to protect them."

"The title was given to me with tongue-in-cheek, so I could have a valid ID, Mr. Nussbaum. Don't take it too seriously."

"I don't stand on formality when I am begging a man to help me," Heinz said. "Please talk to me as your friend, Heinz."

"Are you my friend?"

"I hope you will think so when I continue," the old man sighed. "Your friend—fiancée?—has made a target of herself with her newspaper attacks on that church. She has been vocal in her support of the annexation. She has exposed some of her own Family's dirty laundry and gotten it cleaned up. If you can't think of yourself as Champion for the City, think of yourself as champion and protector of your future wife. Whatever you need from my family, the legal support of my daughter, the financial support of the bank, shipping and trading records, access to the other churches, even a little soothing music, we will provide for you."

"I'm not a miracle-worker," Gee objected. "I've just happened to be at the right place and at the right time to help a couple of people."

"That's all we're asking, Gee. As one of the war orphans, I'm asking you to continue as proxy-holder for the trust that benefits my family. You've exercised the proxy to the benefit of the City and Forest once. Just continue to vote your conscience. Cameron?"

"Gee, I've acquired a few shares for the quartet over the years. We'd like to give you the proxy for our seven thousand four hundred thirty-seven shares," the young attorney said. Then he returned to his cousins and they sang.

Approaching Normal

"GEE! YOU'RE BACK!" Nathan shouted when his friend came through the market to the employee room.

"Do I still have a job?"

"Of course you do, my man! How are you feeling? You look like you're still leaning on that stick," Nathan said.

"I am. I guess I'm not quite ready to lift the soup kettles, but Doc said the exercise I'd get stocking shelves would be good for me… if you can use me, that is." Gee looked around and sighed. "To tell the truth, I'm going a little stir-crazy. After I finally managed to stand up from my chair by myself, I couldn't wait to start getting out of the house."

"Well, we can sure use you. I hired a high school kid to work a bit after school, but he needs guidance. Maybe you could switch to a later shift for a few days and show him the ropes," Nathan said.

"I didn't get here until almost noon today. I waited and left the house with Karen in order to convince her that I could walk this far without exhausting myself. She wants to drive down to pick me up when I'm finished," Gee laughed.

"I'm truly sorry that we forced you out of our home," Nathan sighed. "I'm so glad you ended up with a true friend and love." He hesitated as if he was going on with an apology, but Gee shook his head.

"How about if I start in the canned goods aisle. Has anyone been helping Mrs. Resnick reach things from the top shelf?"

"Everyone!" Nathan laughed. "I've already got a cart loaded for stocking."

"Mr. Gee," Ryan said when he'd put on an apron. "It's nice to see you back."

"Thank you, Ryan. So, it's you they hired to replace me?"

"Not replace. No one could ever do that! I'm just filling in for a little extra cash. I've got a girlfriend, you know."

"Nothing taxes the wallet like dating."

"Especially when your parents have cut you off," Ryan growled.

"What? Why?"

"The Moffats and the O'Rourkes have been feuding for seventy-five years just because they opened competing drugstores after the war," he explained. "Even though the O'Rourkes sold the Rexall years ago, the families still insist the other is somehow evil. Shannon and I were forbidden to see each other and when we refused, both families cut off our allowance to keep us at home. So, we got jobs."

"Hmm. I guess you don't have to be one of the seven Families to have family problems," Gee mused. "How are you doing?"

"Well, we don't have a lot of time together. I think that was part of the plan. But the opposition of our families has made our relationship stronger. Um… Thank you, by the way."

Gee didn't need Ryan to explain why he was being thanked, remembering his advice to the teen about buying condoms. He smiled.

"Say, I understand Rena got out of rehab. Has she come into work yet?"

"I saw her on Saturday and heard her tell Mr. Panza she'd be back Monday morning. I haven't seen her, though."

Family Dinner

"WE'VE BEEN SUMMONED," Karen said as she looked at the card. "A formal invitation, no less."

"What? Summoned by whom?" Gee asked. They'd taken their evening glass of wine and the stack of mail to bed with them after Gee returned from a fun night at the library with the children.

"The patriarch of the Roth Family is holding a dinner Saturday night, to begin at sundown. 'Benjamin Roth requests the honor of your presence at a Family dinner Saturday, October 20, at the close of Sabbath.' Simple, to the point, and beyond refutation. I'm sorry, my love, but we are going to dinner at the Roth mansion Saturday night."

"I'll try not to be too awed," Gee laughed. "I doubt his mansion has anything on this one."

"Oh, my poor naïve man. You have no idea how ostentatious a Family mansion can be. Great-grandmother settled for a small city home. That's this one. I believe we might be the only one of the 'cottages' that was built on less than an acre." Karen shook her head sadly. "The Roth Estate covers over ten acres along the river. The old man rattles around in it like a pebble in a coffee can."

"Why doesn't Leah and her family live with him?"

"When she married Don Augello, Benjamin nearly cut her off entirely. It wasn't until Don converted and hyphenated his name to Roth-Augello that Benjamin even consented to seeing his grandchildren."

"Why would he invite us… me?"

"He is the only one of the Family heads that hasn't had the pleasure of your company. I'm sure he wants to see what the fuss is about. He's getting old—ninety-one, I think. Each time there is a Family gathering, everyone expects him to name his heir. At the moment, the only one he would dare to name is Leah, but he's afraid the dynasty is dying."

"We'll go and see him," Gee said softly. "He will see that you are by far the best choice."

"Ugh! Why would I want to be head of the Roth Family after the disgrace they visited on Celia Eberhardt and her mother?"

"Perhaps because you brought the disgrace to light. No good deed goes unpunished."

"Is that why you end up in the hospital or jail every time you help someone?" Karen laughed.

<hr />

KAREN WAS PUZZLED when she walked into Axel's office and found Cameron LaCoe sitting behind her editor's desk. She had learned long ago that the newspaper was owned by a trust managed by the Nussbaums, but they'd always stayed far away from the office. The summons on her desk had been in Axel's handwriting.

"Cameron?"

"Hi, Karen. I just wanted to tell you what a good job I thought you were doing in keeping the heat on that church," Cameron said.

"Are you the editor now?"

"No. I'm the publisher. Traditionally, the publisher hasn't taken an active role in managing the paper, but when the trust was signed over to my cousins and me, we decided there were some practices that we did not want to continue. The elimination of bylines, for example, and ownership of content. How do you like your new contract, by the way?"

"I admit that when I read it and your mother went over it with me, I thought it was too good to be true. I own all my source material? You have *first* rights to my stories but ownership continues with the author? That's certainly not common."

"Becoming far more common now that republication covers an online universe. You *do* note that our first rights include an online version of the newspaper should one evolve—and it will. But there are too many opportunities for reporters to earn more from their work. We're a newspaper. A story is only good while it is new. A clever reporter should be able to come up with all kinds of ways to resell her stories—repackage them even. Like creating a lengthy exposé—say a book—about the practices within this church you're investigating. Don't you think?"

"Cameron, are you encouraging me to take the battle a step further than I have?" Karen asked with some amusement in her voice.

"I know that you have what it takes to do it," Cameron answered. "I don't know if you'll want to. That's up to you."

"Well, thank you for the vote of confidence and encouragement," Karen said, preparing to leave the office.

"Karen, that isn't what this meeting is all about." She stopped at Cameron's words and turned back to the young attorney.

"The other shoe?"

"Maybe. Axel asked me to handle this part because there has been some animosity between the two of you. Understandable. I'd like you to take point on election coverage. You have been needling the church with your investigative material. Don't stop that. But we have a lot of election issues that are being inadequately covered. We have nineteen days—thirteen issues—before the election. Including Election Day. We have a congressional race. We have City Council elections. We have school board elections. None of those are being covered and they all have a bearing on what we most want, the annexation vote. You're doing a good job driving that, I want you to take on the rest."

"Who do you want me to support?" she asked warily.

"You are the investigative reporter," he responded. "Tell me who the paper should support."

"Really?"

"It's a new world, Karen. You are in a position to shape it."

◦◊◦

"MY, MY," KAREN breathed as they pulled up to the Roth mansion Saturday night. "Uncle Ben is really going all out. Look."

"What?"

"That's Celia and Jo Ransom getting out of Leah's car. This could be an interesting night," Karen said.

"He won't be nasty to them, will he?" Gee asked. He'd not yet had the opportunity to meet the war orphan of the Roth clan, but just based on Karen's research he was predisposed to favor Celia and her granddaughter.

"No. Leah has really been very nice and is helping get them accepted. I don't think she's leading anyone into a trap. Let's see what's going on."

WHEN THEY ENTERED, Gee was introduced to Leah's sons, Joseph and Jude. The youngest, Levi, was away at medical school. Joseph grinned lecherously at Jo but pulled a very young woman with bright eyes forward to introduce as his wife, Judith. Gee was shocked at the apparent disparity in their ages. Judith looked like a teenager and he was certain Joseph was in his thirties if not forty.

Gee had met Jude, Laura Lazorack's fiancé. He was a polite but slightly aloof man. His dark beard was not quite full enough to be identified as Orthodox, but he had long curls hanging at the side of his ears and wore black rimmed glasses that made him look scholarly. He and Laura politely greeted the guests.

"My youngest son, Levi, won't join us," Leah said. "He has sworn never to return to Rosebud Falls. I believe he thinks he would be trapped into becoming the family patriarch."

"He wouldn't," Judith spoke up. "Joseph will lead the family." She was haughty, and it was obvious that Joseph didn't share her expectation. But it was her mother-in-law whose eyes she held. While they waited for a response, Jude pressed a small cap into Gee's hand and pointed to how to wear it at the table. Gee complied.

"Dear, no matter how ambitious you are and how clever, no one in their right mind would trust Joseph to manage the family fortune," Leah sighed. "Don't worry. You'll have your own little empire to rule, but you will never live in this house. Ah, here comes Dad." The old man, Benjamin Roth, tottered into the dining room scowling at everyone and shaking off the hand of his assistant. He made his way to the head of the table, helped by his cane. There was a quiet shuffle as each person took a place at the table, standing behind his or her chair. Without waiting to be introduced to anyone, Benjamin stretched a hand out toward the table laden with food for their dinner.

"*Barukh ata Adonai Eloheinu melekh ha'olam shehakol niyah bidvaro,*" he said.

"Blessed are You, Lord our God, Ruler of the universe, at whose word all came to be," the family responded and Ben sat heavily in his chair.

After the formal blessing, food was passed, and the conversation was similar to any other family. Leah asked about Laura's family and whether her brother had returned from his honeymoon. Gee noticed that the youngest person at the table, Joseph's wife Judith, dished food and helped with Benjamin's plate.

"Is there anything else you need, *Zeyde?*" she asked obsequiously. It was obvious she was not taking Leah's word on the line of succession.

"It is time to officially welcome our newest family members," Leah said. "Our lost sheep have been found. Here is to Celia and Jo Ransom. Welcome to the Family." Everyone raised their glasses, including the old man, though he never looked up at Celia, sitting to his right. Celia insouciantly lifted her glass and tapped it against his, startling the old man. He looked up at her and she raised an eyebrow at her.

"*L'chaim,*" he finally said.

"To life," she responded. The old man actually grinned at her. He reached for an envelope he'd dropped beside the table when he entered the room. Judith scrambled to get it for him.

"Let me get that for you, *Zeyde,*" Judith exclaimed, rushing to pick up the large brown envelope at his feet.

"Oh, suck up to your husband, not to me," he growled at her as he took the envelope. "I believe this is yours, Celia." Aside from the few words of the blessing and the toast, they were the first words he'd spoken during the meal. The chastised girl had a tear running down her cheek and leaned against Joseph. "You have my regrets for a life wasted. May your granddaughter live long to enjoy the blessings herein."

"Benjamin, I know you helped provide for me after mother died. I don't hold you responsible for what your father did," she answered softly.

"To the third and fourth generations," the old man sighed glancing at his grandsons. "Too soon old and too late wise."

"Yes... *Fetter*," she said, surprising him once again.

Don leaned over to whisper in Gee's ear, "That means uncle."

The old man straightened and brought everyone's attention to him.

"About the next head of the Family..." he stated boldly. Judith clutched her husband's hand so hard he grimaced, but neither he nor his brother met his grandfather's eyes. "Jo or Karen?"

"What?" Leah exclaimed. Even she seemed taken by surprise.

"Understand, there is only one person in this room proven acceptable to lead the Family, and he is not related," Benjamin said, scanning the room. He paused on Don, but the banker simply smirked and shook his head. "If George Evars marries Karen Weisman, that is the succession. He has eaten the nut and the Forest accepted him."

"If all it takes is to eat a stupid nut, I'll eat it," Judith declared.

"And you would die." Silence fell on the table as they all looked at Joseph. "*Meyn libe*, only a Family member can survive eating a nut. In every instance, a non-Family member will die if not given an antidote within half an hour. And half of those in the Family who try die as well."

"He did it."

"The exception proves the rule," Don Roth-Augello said. "If word of that got out, we would have a rash of suicides from people just like you eating the nut and never waking up. Be happy with what you have. Joseph will take care of you and you will never lack for anything."

"My grandfather," Benjamin sighed. Everyone looked at the old man. "He challenged his brother when the succession was decided. Fortunately, my father had already been born and thus an existential crisis was averted." He chuckled at his own joke, but it was not clear that anyone else understood it. "He died. His brother became head of the Family and adopted my father, Aaron, as his heir. The Forest chose."

"Mr. Roth, I can't really head your Family. I... I need to represent all the Families," Gee said. "I need to represent the Forest." Benjamin nodded.

"So. Karen or Josephine. We have not yet escaped the trial."

The old man pushed his chair back so violently as he stood that it crashed to the floor behind him. He turned and left the room in silence shuffling away with his attendant quickly at his side. Judith started to go after him but Joseph wisely put a hand on her shoulder and she stayed seated.

Jude raised his glass and the others at the table followed his gesture, waiting for his toast.

"Cousins," he said.

"GEE… UH… GRANDMA says I need to talk to you," Jo said quietly.

"Don't," he said. "Don't take the challenge. Take what you have and live your life."

"Thank you, but that isn't what I was going to ask," she giggled. "Grandma says that I am her heir to the war orphan trust and I have to make a decision. I made it long before she told me, but I want to tell you. We… *I* would like you to continue to hold the proxy for our shares of SSG stock and continue to vote your conscience for the City and the Forest."

Gee sighed and looked at the young woman feeling far more pressure than if Ben had declared him heir.

"I will do my best, Jo."

Final Proxy

"YOUR ANALYSIS OF candidates has become more pointed," Gee said as he finished reading Karen's article Tuesday morning. "It feels like you have unleashed a whole new aspect of your election day preparation."

"I got commissioned by my publisher to be the point person on election coverage and to present the candidates in an honest light," Karen said. "I never expected this, but in spite of their desire that I cover it on behalf of the newspaper, it still goes out with my byline so people can identify me easily. They're even running my photo as the special reporter for the election."

"It seems likely to make you into a target. Karen, I want… I'd feel… Please let me accompany you more. I know you can't hide until the election is over but let me be near you as much as possible."

"I don't need a protector, Gee. I need a supporter. Encourage me. Praise me. Love me. But don't hover over me."

"It's so hard. But I have to say, some of this is truly great analysis."

"What did you like?"

"The article about US Representative candidate Josh Hardin."

Hardin has said that every decision and every vote in Congress will be weighed against his belief in God and the Bible. But Hardin is quick to point out that most people don't actually understand the Bible so he will pray carefully for God's enlightenment. In other words, Hardin pledges to weigh each vote against his personal interpretation of the Bible. Not yours or mine. Not the Torah. Not the Koran. Not the Bhagavad Gita. He won't even specify which version of the Bible he will be using.

"That's good but quoting the oath of office to him and getting his response was brilliant," Gee said.

Hardin will take the congressional oath of office but reserves the right to act according to God's will above the constitution. For those who do not understand the oath congressmen, senators, and even the vice president take, it is as follows:

"I do solemnly swear that I will support and defend the Constitution of the United States against all enemies, foreign and domestic; that I will bear true faith and allegiance to the same; that I take this obligation freely, without any mental reservation or purpose of evasion; and that I will well and faithfully discharge the duties of the office on which I am about to enter: So help me God."

In other words, Hardin will swear an oath under God and immediately break that oath to the people and to God if the decision goes against his personal belief, even if that is not according to the Constitution. How faithfully can Hardin discharge the duties of this office when he has already stated that he will break his oath under God?

"Did I use any circular logic in that argument?" Karen asked. She seemed to puzzle it out again and shook her head. "No, that's what he said he would do."

"At least he's not really local. Our congressional district is so huge that his home is over fifty miles from here," Gee said, looking at the map Karen kept spread on her desk. "I worry more about City and School Board candidates coming after you."

"I'm not too worried about that," Karen said. "So far, it appears that they are all truly straight-shooting and honest candidates. They disagree on the best way to handle specific issues and priorities for the budget, but those are things that need to be worked out in any governing body. Not everyone agrees on the best way to run things. The real issue that divides people continues to be the annexation. I've already put together the next four articles that weigh the pros and cons and show exactly what each means. And everyone will hate me for anything I say that disagrees with them."

"JUST WHO I wanted to see," Birdie said as Gee walked into Jitterz.

"Going to read my tealeaves, Birdie?" Gee joshed back. He reached for the cup of coffee Elaine held out to him. "I loved your music at your grandfather's house last week," Gee said to the barista as he paid her.

"Thank you, Gee. I just wanted to get that business stuff out of the way so we could sing. That's really all that's important." Elaine smiled at him, but it was a sad smile. All Elaine's smiles were sad. Gee turned to Birdie who stood with a food box wrapped in tinfoil.

"What do you have there?"

"Food for an old man. Come and walk with me."

The two crossed Main Street at Sixth and headed south on Mill Street. It was a familiar route to Gee. He often walked this direction when he visited his friend, Wayne. At the corner of Peach Street, Birdie turned left. The half-block-long street had only one house on it, a large blocky building. Gee tentatively followed Birdie up the rickety steps to the front door where she pounded loudly.

"Hey! Old man! Come and eat some breakfast. I made French toast for you," she called through the door. She didn't step inside.

"Is that you, you old witch?" the old man who came to the door snarled. "What are you feeding me today? Eye of newt."

"Ach. That's Irish for you. You know voodoo uses only the fresh blood of a chicken. I mixed it with the eggs and dipped your bread in it." The old man shuffled onto the porch and sat in an Adirondack chair without acknowledging Gee. Birdie gave him the plate of food and he dug into it hungrily.

"Who knew chicken blood tasted like cinnamon?" The old man chuckled.

"You. You're only crazy when it suits your purposes. Who do you think you're fooling?"

"You. You're only voodoo when it suits your purposes. Otherwise you're as Irish as I am."

"Only if one of you Irish boys came to Haiti and knocked up my mother," Birdie said.

"I'm Irish by birth," he said. "You're Irish by spirit. One's as good as the other." The old man picked up the last piece of bacon on his plate and held it to his lips. "Who's this?" he demanded, looking at Gee for the first time. "Don't I know you?"

"Collin, this is Gee. He's our City Champion. Gee, Collin Meagher. Last remnant of the Meagher clan. You've got something Gee needs, Collin," Birdie said. The old man squinted at Gee.

"You can't have any of my newspapers. If there's a date you want to look at, I'll let you read it, but it has to go right back where it came from."

"There's newspapers in the library, Collin. He doesn't need a newspaper."

"Library newspapers!" Collin spat. "They put them on microbe film. I tried looking at it once. You can't feel the paper. You can't feel the news. Just little dots on a screen that hurts your eyes. Got to feel the news. Never be informed if you don't read the newspaper. What do you want, City Champion?" he demanded. Gee finally understood why Birdie brought him here.

"I've been visiting all the beneficiaries of the war orphan trust funds," Gee said. "The trustee gave me the proxy to vote the shares at the last meeting, but I want to get confirmation from each beneficiary that they want me to continue to vote their shares on behalf of the City and the Forest." Gee was startled when the old man began to laugh.

"That was some meeting! Six million votes. 'Let's just let Gee make all the decisions.' I laughed at that Deacon fellow all the way out of the building."

"I admired your courage in voting your shares when it seemed you didn't have a chance to succeed," Gee said.

"Did it once before," Meagher said. "Got word they were going to clear-cut a portion of the wild woods. I stumped around everywhere I could go and got a bunch of shareholders together. When they brought up clearcutting, I rallied the troops and we outvoted them. Stopped it cold. That was before they passed the change so that the board automatically held the proxy for all unvoted shares."

"Then you've long defended the Forest," Gee said.

"They stole my great-niece. Right in front of my eyes, just down the street there. Took her out of her little swing and drove away before anyone could react. And then they disappeared. I swore I'd hunt them all down and ruin them. That's why I read the newspaper. That's why I ate the nut. I see things. I know things. I'll watch them all hang from the tallest hickory."

Gee shook his head. It sounded exactly like the scene Karen had described from years ago when she was babysitting.

"You have allies now," he said. "The young Family scions are determined to put a stop to this."

"Birdie, call Violet over here," Collin said as he nodded his head. Birdie turned to talk on the phone while Collin motioned Gee inside.

Newspapers sat in floor-to-ceiling stacks all around the room. Not just *The Elmont Mirror*, but the *Wall Street Journal*, *Washington Post*, *New York Times*, and *USA Today*. Some towers looked ready to topple. Collin found a pen and pulled a stack of papers toward himself as he sat on a couple of newspapers on his chair. "The old men wouldn't help me when I begged of them. They weren't even sure I was the head of the Family," he continued to mumble as he scratched on a form. "So, I ate a nut. I had a vision. The Families are going to change. The Forest demands it." He finished copying down numbers from a stack of papers nearly buried beneath old newspaper, signed his name, and handed the form to Gee.

It took a moment for Gee to decipher the figures.

"This is a proxy for the eighty thousand shares you voted at the meeting," Gee said.

"Talk to Leah Roth," Collin said. "That lawyer who voted forty-seven thousand had her proxy." Collin didn't sound at all like the crazy old man he appeared to be. "I've sold all my land except the plot this house sits on. Every penny I put into their stock, just so I could pull it down around their heads. They call you our champion. Well, ride into the joust with that. But you have to promise me one thing, young champion. All the trees become a part of the Forest. Every one. I don't care if I ever see a penny out of this, as long as those bastards never see another nut. Not one tree, boy. Not one tree."

"Violet's here," Birdie shouted from the doorway. Gee followed Collin out of the house. Birdie's daughter gave Collin a hug.

"What is it, *Uncail?*" Gee had heard Violet speak on many occasions but had never before heard the Irish lilt to her voice that she put on for the old man.

"This man is the champion for the Forest. I've given him my proxy to vote my shares in SSG to protect it. You need to decide if you'll give him the proxy for your shares."

"I don't have any shares."

"You are the heir of the Meaghers. There is a fund that has been accumulating in your name fed by a trust that holds one hundred thousand shares of SSG stock. You'll never be able to touch the stock, but you can direct how the shares are voted by your proxy," Collin said. "It's best you build up a lot of friends before you have to take over the Family."

Violet looked like Collin had been talking in a foreign tongue. Her puzzled expression was turned first on her mother and then on Gee before she locked on Collin's old eyes. Slowly, she nodded.

"Mr. Gee, I'd like you to continue to vote the shares in my Trust according to your conscience and for the benefit of the Forest. Will you agree?" she said softly.

"I agree."

A Descending Darkness

"A CANOE? WE'RE not going to do it in a canoe!" Shannon giggled as she climbed into the craft with the blankets and basket she packed.

"Shannon? Honey, is this too... unromantic? For our first time? I mean... It seems so planned out."

"I've known for months we were going to do it," she sighed. "How long have you had those condoms?"

"Um… two months. A little more."

"And all that time, there was only one reason to have them and we both knew what it was. I think that I've had enough time to think it over and be sure this is what I really want. I love you, Ryan. Take me to the secret hideaway you found and make love to me."

"We don't need to go far from shore," Ryan said. "We just paddle a few hundred yards this way and after the fence we get to the woods. It's not as nice as the Forest, but once the annexation goes through, the foresters will clean it up in no time."

"You sound so enthusiastic. Are you thinking of becoming a forester?" The canoe glided across Lake Aldo almost silently as Ryan thought about her question.

"Becoming a forester sounds neat," Ryan finally said. "I'd like to, but… my dad, you know, wants me to be a pharmacist."

"But what do you want, Ryan?" He looked at the pretty girl in the bow of the canoe and smiled.

"You." He answered with a giggle.

"Keep paddling."

"I think the best way for me to end the feud is to become a forester and steal away the prettiest girl I know."

"Maybe they'll have home lots on this side of the lake available when it's part of the city and we can build a cottage in the Forest," she said dreamily. Ryan maneuvered the little craft against a tree root and scrambled to get out and pull the canoe to shore. Shannon stepped out without getting wet. Once the canoe was secure, they picked up their blankets and headed into the woods.

"A cottage is just what I found," Ryan said. "Only it's more like an abandoned shack near the quarry."

"A shack with you will be my palace."

GEE FINISHED THE light tasks he had at the market Saturday morning. It had been five weeks since his fall from the tree, and while normal activity was fine, he found sudden movements, lifting too much, or an unexpected sneeze were enough to send the muscles around his injured ribs into spasms. Even making love with Karen was done carefully.

The walk from the market home always seemed to improve his flexibility and the promise Karen had made of a relaxing afternoon with popcorn and a movie inspired him to a brisk pace. He had to slow a little to stop twinges from breathing too deeply, but he was more than ready to be home.

He laughed as he approached the house. Karen had spent the morning decorating for Halloween and the mansion looked haunted. She'd strung orange lights and set out tombstones next to the drive. Cobwebs masked the *porte-cochère* from the door. A creaky sound effect played when he opened the door.

"Karen? I'm home!"

No answer. Gee wondered what his fiancée was planning as a surprise. He walked through the house quickly, checking the sitting room and study where they spent much of their time. Seeing no one, he naturally headed for the bedroom. Karen was not there and did not respond to his repeated calls. He came back down to the kitchen and spotted the note on the counter.

Rena called, desperate to talk. Hiding near the quarry. I'm on my way. Love, Karen

Gee reached for his cell phone.

"THEY'RE GOING TO kill me," Rena sobbed into Karen's chest. "He didn't have to drug me. I'd have done anything for him. I love him. Then he sent me to the camp and they kept giving me the drug. I'm not me anymore!"

"Rena, honey, we need to get you out of here and someplace you'll be safe. Who did this to you?"

"They did. The church."

"Pastor Beck?"

"No! Maybe. I think Deacon drugs the communion. I don't think it's Pastor. I love him. He doesn't need to drug me."

"Come on. Let's get out of here. I don't think we're safer here than in the hospital. We need to go now, though, Rena."

"Oh, my God!" Rena screamed. She was looking over Karen's shoulder. Karen started to turn, but a strong arm gripped her around the waist and a hand held a sweet-smelling cloth to her face. The last thing she was aware of was a long, wailing scream.

SHANNON INHALED TO scream and Ryan clamped his hand over her mouth.

"Shh. Shh. Baby, don't make a sound. He'll know we're here." Shannon was hyperventilating but nodded her head. Ryan released her mouth and she gasped for air.

"He killed her!" Shannon whispered. Ryan held her close to him and tried to soothe his panicked girlfriend.

"We don't know for sure, but if we don't hurry she could die at any minute. Listen, Baby. You need to call 911. I'm going to climb down in the pit and see if she's alive or if there's anything I can do to help her."

"They'll know we're here! Everyone will know why we came out here. I'll be grounded forever," Shannon moaned.

"Shannon! Listen! There is nothing I wouldn't do to protect you, but this is bigger than us. Honey, she could be dying. We have to get help. Here. Here's your phone. Dial the number and tell them where we are. Then you can run far away. But be quiet, baby. We don't know where that guy took the other girl. Shannon, you have to do it now!"

With that, Ryan broke away from his girlfriend where they were hidden in the underbrush. They'd been on their way to the shack he knew of in the woods when they almost stumbled onto the man attacking two women at the edge of the quarry. Ryan ran to the quarry and looked over the edge. He wasn't sure if that was her in the shadows or not. Water had filled the quarry up to about twenty feet below the edge. Ryan looked for a way down and began to climb. He wasn't Gee. He couldn't just dive from there. But he could help.

"9-1-1. STATE THE nature of your emergency please."

"We... I... Just saw a murder. I think."

"We are tracking your cell phone as being at Savage Sand and Gravel."

"Yes. No. At the quarry. She... He pushed her over the cliff... and then dragged the other girl away into the woods."

"Tell me what part of the quarry," the operator said. "Do you know who it was?"

"Um... I don't know. We approached from the lake. My... my boyfriend... is... He went to try and save her. He's in the quarry, too." Shannon held her hand over her mouth to stifle her sobs. "I'm scared. Please hurry!"

"Stay on the line with me, honey. Help is on the way. We'll talk while they get here. You stay hidden. What's your name?"

"Sh... Sh... Shannon O'Rourke. This isn't how it was supposed to be!"

GEE LISTENED TO Karen's phone ring. It went to voice mail and instead of leaving a message, he redialed. This time the phone connected.

"Karen! Are you okay?" Gee shouted. Silence was broken by a laugh.

"You're too late, Champ. Your girlfriend has gone... a little nuts."

Gee heard the phone hit the ground and a crunch before it went dead.

"9-1-1. STATE THE nature of your emergency please."

"This is George Evars. I believe my fiancée, Karen Weisman, has been kidnapped and is in immediate danger."

"Do you have any additional information?"

"Yes. I just called her cell phone and a man answered. He said, 'You're too late. Your girlfriend has gone nuts.' Then he crushed the phone."

"Do you have any idea where this was?"

"Wait. She set up my phone and put some tracking app on it. Can I use it while I'm on the line with you?"

"Make the attempt. I have recorded your cell number incoming and will call you back if it disconnects."

"This is crazy. I have the app open. It says my last call was to some-where south of the City Limits. Oh, hell! That has to be the wild woods down near Savage Sand and Gravel."

"Can you send the coordinates? We have a team working to extract a person from the quarry. Is that where your locator app says?"

"Um... I see. Let me see. Does the quarry have water in it? The app says the phone was somewhere northeast of the quarry."

"We'll need the coordinates. Does the app show them?"

Gee read off the coordinates shown on the cell phone app Karen installed on his phone.

"Stay on the line."

"I can't. I have to go help." Gee disconnected and immediately punched in the number for Jonathon.

"Hey, Mr. Shaker Man! What's up with you this fine Saturday afternoon."

"Jonathon, I need your help. We need to get into the wild woods. Now! Karen's been kidnapped and is being held there."

"I'm on my way. Jessie will head straight for the fence. I'll swing by and pick you up. I know a path wide enough for a car to get to the fence. Be on the street in five minutes," Jonathon said. "Damn it! Dad's calling. I'll talk to you in five." The line went dead and immediately rang back.

Gee shoved his feet into his boots and grabbed his denim jacket as he headed for the door and thumbed his phone.

"Mr. Evars, please do not hang up. I have the sheriff on the line from near the quarry. Please stand by."

Into the Woods

Chaos reigned into the night as county, city, and volunteer rescuers invaded the wild woods. The limited rescue resources of the county had moved immediately to Savage Sand and Gravel. Wayne Savage met them at the gates and followed the firetruck, ambulance, and sheriff's car to the gravel pit. There, they found a shivering and frightened Shannon O'Rourke lying at the edge of the pit encouraging her boyfriend below.

Ryan lay on a ledge next to the water with the blankets the couple brought to the woods piled on top of him as he shivered next to a breathing but unconscious Rena Lynd. From the time of her first phone call to 911, it took over an hour before the ambulance moved out of SSG and screamed toward the hospital with Shannon, Ryan, and Rena all crammed in the back.

By that time, additional resources had begun arriving at the site to launch a search for Karen Weisman in the wild woods. David Lazorack had sent the alert to the foresters and ten had entered the land through the main gates at Wayne's invitation. Two sheriff's deputies arrived along with another firetruck. A call for a rescue dog and forensics expert was sent to state police and they were reportedly on the way as the rescuers searched in the waning light for the path Shannon said the assailant took into the woods. Floodlights from the firetrucks lit the edge of the woods a hundred feet from the quarry road.

WHEN GEE AND Jonathon arrived at the south edge of the Forest where an eight-foot chain link fence separated it from the wild wood, Jessie and David were already at work opening a passage. It was not the first time foresters had slipped into the wild woods to assess its condition, and they quickly clipped the wires used to hold their access closed. Two more foresters, including Gabe, who had given Gee instructions at the wedding tree, brought equipment—hardhats with headlamps, machetes, and gloves as the six would-be rescuers wiggled through the opening in the fence and began searching for a path into the woods.

There were multiple short paths into the wild woods, but most ended in a tangle of undergrowth. Gee's cell phone GPS showed the blinking dot of Karen's last known position but getting there was a long and painful process. An unexpected ravine cut across their path. Gee ignored the pain in his ribs as he followed Jonathon into the cut, hacking at blackberry brambles along the bottom.

When they found a small cabin, David Lazorack pulled a handgun from his belt and waved the others back. He burst through the door. The cabin was clean and empty but showed signs of recent habitation. No other clues.

"Over here," Gabe shouted. The others rushed to his side to see a path that was little more than a game trail. They followed along the trail finally hearing a dog barking some distance from them. The trail finally opened onto a clearing barely large enough for a shack surrounded by trees and undergrowth. At the same time, rescuers from the other direction broke into the clearing and the sheriff's deputies took point in bursting into the cabin with guns drawn.

"Medic!" a deputy shouted from inside. "She's breathing."

No one attempted to stop Gee from entering the cabin behind the paramedic that rushed to Karen's side. Careful not to interfere with the medic's evaluation and conversation over the crackling lapel radio, Gee lay down next to his love and softly touched her hand as he began his plea for her life.

The medic pulled a blanket over Karen's naked body and, with a fireman's help, strapped her to a backboard. They carried her out of the wild wood to a waiting ambulance. Gee joined her for the ride to the hospital.

"Please stay with me, Karen," he pled. "I love you. I love you."

13

Breaking Fences

A Silent Calling

SEEING THE woman just beyond his reach, there was only one thing Ryan could do. He stripped and dove into the water, gasping air into his shocked lungs. It took longer than he expected to wrestle the body onto the shelf of rock that jutted into the water. The ledge was a good foot above the surface and the water was deep. He had nothing to brace himself against as he pushed the girl onto the rock. But he didn't give up. As soon as they were both on the ledge, he practiced all he had been taught in lifeguard training, forcing the water from her lungs and continuing artificial respiration until he felt her thready breath and heartbeat. Shannon lay at the edge of the quarry looking down on him. She talked him through the process, relaying instructions from the 911 operator. She dropped the blankets to him. He stripped the wet clothing off the young woman and warmed her with his body.

———◁◆▷———

FOUR PEOPLE WERE hospitalized.

Suffering from hypothermia and exhaustion, Ryan was kept in the hospital as his mother sat next to him all night.

Shannon was released to her parents early in the morning after being given a sedative for shock. She had seen an attempted murder, a kidnapping, and her boyfriend nearly drown while trying to rescue a woman from the frigid waters of the old quarry. Nothing but sleep and gentle caring could heal her.

Rena Lynd was in a coma. Apparently, her arm had hit the ledge on her way into the water, shattering the radius. Shannon guessed that it had taken at least fifteen minutes from the time Rena went over the edge until she was breathing again. The 911 call confirmed that it had been longer but no one knew if or for how long she had been technically dead. Doctors were more concerned about her unresponsiveness and were unsure why she was alive at all. Blood tests showed high amounts of RDH in her bloodstream, the chemical she had spent so much time in rehab purging just a month ago. No one sat beside Rena's bed.

Karen Weisman...

"She's comatose, Gee, and I don't know if she'll ever wake up."

"I DON'T KNOW what else to say," Dr. Poltanys said as they followed Karen's gurney into the room. Aides carefully transferred her to the bed and made sure everything was correctly connected. A mask kept her breathing. Fluids were administered by IV. She was intubated to keep her air passages open and prevent her from swallowing her tongue. Gee moved to her side and held her hand as soon as the nurses had cleared a path. He looked back at Poltanys.

"What happened to her? Was she drugged?"

"In a manner of speaking. It appears she was forced to eat nuts. There were traces of the nutmeat still in her mouth and stomach. The chemical levels in her bloodstream are off the charts. Gee, I don't know why she's alive. Our best estimate is that the nuts had been in her system for at least eight hours before we got her here. There's nothing we can do. The antidote won't touch it this late in the game."

"Nuts? She ate more than one?"

"I'm pretty sure she did. Maybe as many as half a dozen."

"I LOVE YOU. I love you, Karen. Please stay with me. Come through for us."

Sunday had passed as had most of Monday with Gee sitting at Karen's side. Jonathon and Jessie stood beside him talking softly. Finally, they each laid a hand on his shoulder.

"This is an intervention, Gee," Jessie said softly. "Karen is not coming back to us with you sitting here smelling like you do. You haven't eaten since Saturday morning. You haven't bathed for longer still. Your clothes are caked with dirt from struggling through the wild woods. I think the only reason you've been allowed to stay is because Dr. Poltanys is afraid of you. Or afraid of his nurses."

"Gee, you have to take a break. You need food, a shower, clean clothes, and sleep. It's not an option any longer. You have to go home and get refreshed."

"I can't leave her. Not like this," Gee cried. "I can't leave her alone."

"I'll stay," Jessie said. "Gee, she is not alone. Neither of you are. You haven't even acknowledged your visitors. We practically had to force our way into the room with you. I will be with her and I will call you if there is any sign of change."

"The doctor says she's stable. You can't help her by making yourself sick," Jonathon said, pulling at Gee to get him to stand. Gee sighed and bent to kiss Karen's forehead.

"I'll be back soon, love," he whispered. "I'll take a shower and shave, then you can wake up and we'll have breakfast. Okay? Okay. I love you."

Gee stumbled after Jonathon as Jessie settled into his chair and held Karen's hand.

JONATHON WAS CONCERNED when Gee did not come back downstairs for dinner after his shower. He waited with the basket of fried chicken he'd picked up from KFC. After eating a piece, he decided to check on his friend.

Gee was sprawled out on the bed, a blanket pulled half over him, sound asleep.

Jonathon called his wife and told her he'd be with her as soon as he cleaned up the kitchen.

GEE WAS DISORIENTED when he woke up. He reached for Karen and she wasn't there. Opening his eyes to the empty spot beside him in bed, the events of the past three days flooded his mind and his eyes. He hurried through his morning routine, thankful that he had at least made it through his shower the night before. He carefully shaved and dressed before going downstairs in time to hear the doorbell. Rerouting himself from the kitchen to the front door, he opened it to find Wayne Savage waiting.

"Wayne. Hi. I was just…"

"…on your way to the hospital. I figured you'd be ready by now. I'll drive," his friend said.

"How did you know?"

"Word travels fast. Jonathon called me last night. He and Jessie were there until about midnight."

"Karen was alone?"

"No. Jo Ransom came in to sit with Karen. She's still there, but the poor girl is probably exhausted. I… uh… told her I'd drive her home this morning. After you get there," Wayne said.

"Jo was there alone all night? We should get going." Gee grabbed his Rose Hickory walking stick from next to the door. Somehow, he'd missed having it with him since he left the house so hurriedly on Saturday.

"Well… not exactly. I met her at the hospital Sunday. You were pretty out of it, so you might not remember all the people who were there to see you and Karen. Anyway, Jo and I got to talking and… well, we went out to dinner last night and then Jonathon called and Jo insisted on going to the hospital and I just stayed to… you know… keep her company. I left the hospital about half an hour ago to come get you." Wayne was clearly a little embarrassed about seeing Jo Ransom socially and spending the night with her in Karen's room, though Gee could not imagine why. It was exactly the kind of thing he would do himself.

"It took half an hour to get here from the hospital?"

"No. Uh… careful where you sit. There's a cup of Birdie's coffee in the cup holder. She sent along some breakfast for you. Said something about you knowing what she puts in it." Wayne turned a puzzled look to Gee.

"Mmm. French toast. Must have mixed chicken blood with the eggs."

"Gee?"

"You know, voodoo magic. Oh, this is good. I don't remember when I ate last. And she included bacon."

They rode the rest of the way to the hospital in silence as Gee ate breakfast and drank his coffee, thankful for the friends he had made in Rosebud Falls.

"I'm back, sweetheart," Gee said as he bent over Karen to kiss her forehead. He'd gone straight to his love before greeting Jo and missed the greeting she gave Wayne.

As Gee bent next to Karen, his hickory stick leaned into the bed and touched the back of her hand. Her hand grabbed the stick with such force that it was nearly jerked from Gee's grip. Karen took a huge gulp of air, her eyes flying open. She stared ahead, gasping, her hand trying to reach the tube in her throat.

"Call the doctor!" Gee yelled, fumbling for the call button by Karen's head. She convulsed and gasped for air, throwing her head from side to side. A nurse pushed Gee aside, but he could only move a foot away. Karen continued to clutch the stick that he still held.

Ellie rushed into the room and assessed the situation as she tried to calm Karen from the other side of the bed. She carefully reached across and held Karen still while she removed the tube from her throat. Karen moaned through her frantic gasps, finally calming as she looked around and eventually looking at Gee's walking stick held in her hand.

"What do we have?" Dr. Poltanys demanded crisply.

"Patient is awake and responding to her surrounding," Ellie intoned. "Intubation removed as it was causing her distress. She seems to have calmed. Heart rate is slightly elevated, but blood pressure has returned to normal."

Poltanys examined Karen's eyes, still locked on the stick.

"Karen, can you hear me? Look at me." Karen's eyes snapped up to look at the doctor. "That's good. Let me just check your pupils. A bit of a shock to wake up with a tube in your throat, wasn't it? That's better now." His voice was calm and soothing as he continued his examination of her responses. She tracked his finger as he moved it in front of her face and raised a hand to point at the mask that covered her nose. Poltanys carefully removed it. "How are you feeling?" he asked gently.

"Uh... Drunk."

"That's an interesting way to describe it. You've suffered the same kind of overdose that Gee did a few weeks ago. You remember Gee, don't you?" Poltanys said. Karen's heart rate and blood pressure monitors appeared to stabilize as she looked over at Gee.

"Love."

"I love you, Karen," Gee responded. She smiled.

"I hurt. All over."

"Let's get you something for pain. You took a pretty good beating along with everything else."

"Dragged me by the hair. Like a caveman."

"I'm sorry to say you lost a bit over your left ear. But you were punched, too."

"Hit me when I wouldn't eat the nut. Then he shoved it in my mouth and poured water down my throat. Need water."

Ellie held a straw to Karen's lips and she took a sip to soothe her throat from the rawness of the tube.

"He made you eat a nut!" Gee said. "Oh, Karen! You lived through the nut."

"Seven. He named them as I ate them. After the first one, I just chewed and swallowed. I knew it wouldn't make a difference after one. I would be just as dead." Karen's eyes squinted together as Dr. Poltanys directed Ellie regarding the painkillers he wanted administered. "I'm alive."

"You're alive, Karen," Poltanys said. The other nurse left and Ellie was back with a handheld recorder. "Karen, how many nuts did you eat?"

"Seven."

"He named them?"

"One for each Family. 'This is Roth,' he said. 'This is Nussbaum.' He cracked the nut and shoved the meat in my mouth and I ate it. I feel a little dizzy."

"That's the painkillers kicking in. Feeling better now?" Poltanys asked.

"Better. Still drunk."

"That might take longer. Can you let go of Gee's stick now?"

"Don't want to. He's still talking," Karen said. Her eyes drifted closed and she sighed. "Says I need to sleep now." With that, her breathing evened into the regular breaths of sleep.

"I'll be damned," Poltanys said. He continued to look at the young woman and shook his head. "I'd suggest you just stay with her for a while and let her hold your... that." He shook his head again. He looked at Ellie and then at Wayne and Jo who continued to watch from a corner of the room. "We are all going to try hard... not to make jokes about that." Poltanys left the room and after Ellie gave Gee a quick hug, she followed the doctor. Gee busied himself smoothing Karen's hair with one hand while his other drifted down the hickory stick to cover her hand.

"I guess that's settled," Jo said with a little giggle.

"What?" Wayne asked.

"The succession. *I'm* sure not going to eat a nut. I just... I can't believe what I just saw," Jo said.

"HE SAID... THE grandfather said... he was trying to reach me but couldn't find me until you touched me with a part of him," Karen whispered to Gee after she'd awakened and had been checked over once more. "I have to... visit... the Family trees."

"Family trees? Genealogy?" Gee asked.

"Oh. No. Every family has a Rose Hickory. It is on their estate. The Roth Family tree is next to the river in front of Ben's mansion. Poltanys is in the middle of the Hilltop Retirement Village where their original home stood. I'm not sure about the others. But every Family has a tree," Karen said.

"I saw one. Collin Meagher said the nut he ate came from the tree in his yard."

"Of course. That would make sense. The nuts I ate came from the wild woods. The one you ate, from the grandfather tree in the Forest. But every Family has a tree."

"Karen, my love, are you still feeling... um... drunk?"

"Yes. No. It's different than that. I'm still feeling connected. I'm not completely certain what is real and what isn't. I look around and see my study at home and then I blink my eyes and see the hospital. You... were a little drunk when you ate a nut, too," she said.

"I didn't think of it exactly that way, but I knew about vision quests."

"How?"

"I… Karen? I was… on a vision quest when I came here. It was…" he squeezed his eyes closed trying to recall this remnant from his past before it slipped away again. "I was to go home. To here."

"Do you remember anything else?"

"No. Just that I needed to come home. And here is home. Rosebud Falls."

"We'll figure this out, won't we?" Karen asked.

"I think we know what we are supposed to know. I don't think it was my memory. I think it was grandfather tree telling me I'm home."

Interrogation

GEE AWOKE LYING next to Karen in her hospital bed Wednesday, much the way she had joined him when he was injured. They lay with the Rose Hickory staff between them, both gripping its smooth surface. Julia was gently nudging Gee awake.

"I'm sorry to disturb you," the nurse said softly. "It's going to be a busy day and you both need to be prepared."

"Don't leave," Karen moaned. "We were just about to make love."

"Karen?" Gee whispered. "You should wake up, sweetheart. Um… we're in the hospital, not at home."

"Oh? Oh!" she said as her eyes flew open and took in their surroundings. "Um… Forget what I said, okay?"

"Must have been a good dream," Julia laughed. "Okay, you two. Dr. Poltanys and Dr. Gaston want to run a series of tests this morning to determine if you have all your faculties, Karen. You seem to fade in and out a lot. I'm afraid it's going to be a rigorous morning. Then… the DA is not satisfied with the interview you gave the sheriff yesterday. She wants confirmation that you are cognizant of your surroundings and can answer questions lucidly, then she wants the whole interview again. Preferably without talking to grandfather tree."

"This is going to be a miserable day," Karen sighed. "What do I have to do first?"

"First, you need to let go of Gee's walking stick. He needs to go home and shower and shave so he's as fresh and able as you are. You are going to get a shower and scrubs so you don't need to do the physical tests in a gown. Maybe Gee could bring some sweats back for you."

"Where are my clothes?"

"Uh… honey, when we found you, you were… naked on the bare wood floor of a shack in the woods. I don't believe anyone found your clothes."

"Was… was I raped, too?"

"Dr. Poltanys should be taking these questions," Julia said. "A rape kit was part of the standard procedure for the condition you were in, though they had a lot to deal with Sunday morning. I can tell you that it appeared you'd been violated but there was no DNA evidence."

Karen turned her head to Gee's shoulder and cried.

⸺◁◆▷⸺

"I'M SORRY WE have to go through all this again, Miss Weisman," Sheriff Johnson said. Detective Oliver had joined him for the questioning and Gretchen LaCoe sat next to her. "We're just looking for a clue. Who would have wanted you dead?"

Karen snorted. "Do you read my articles in the *Mirror*? Offhand, I'd say there are about five hundred suspects accumulated over the past two years. That's what? One out of eight people in Rosebud Falls?" They sat at a conference table in the hospital which was better than the proposed bedside interview. Karen would be far more comfortable, though, if she was dressed in a suit instead of sweats. And if Gee was with her. They'd insisted on a private interview.

"Let's start with why you were at the quarry," Johnson said. "Earlier, you said that Rena Lynd called you. Can you describe the call?"

"She was distraught. I had to ask twice who it was. She was crying that she couldn't hide any longer. She was hungry and scared."

"Did she say who she was hiding from?"

"Just 'them.' I was concerned for her safety and she wanted me to meet her at the quarry, so I dashed off a note to Gee and drove down there. The gate at SSG was open, so I just drove in," Karen said. The sheriff made a note.

"Why didn't you call the police if you thought there was a woman in distress and in danger?"

Karen sighed deeply and looked at the sheriff and detective with an eyebrow raised. "I'm an investigative reporter. My first thought is always to protect my sources. And she begged me to come alone. I falsely assumed there would be time to call in reinforcements if I discovered they were needed."

"We've always tried to have a good relationship with you and the media," Detective Oliver said.

"I know, Mead. I'll think twice before I walk into that kind of situation again."

"You say you didn't see the man who attacked you, but you were alerted to his presence by Rena. Did she recognize him?" Johnson asked.

"She seemed to. And she was frightened of him. Before I could turn around, though, he'd slapped something across my face that made me faint. I screamed… or I thought I did. Now I think it was Rena who screamed."

"Do you have any idea who it was? Did you recognize the voice? See anything about him?"

"I know who I want it to be," Karen said. "Rena told me she loved him and he didn't have to drug her. I think the only person she could have been describing is the preacher at Calvary Tabernacle. When her chaperone from rehab, Liz, spoke to me about the church, she indicated that Rena was totally infatuated with the preacher."

"Both of those, sadly, are hearsay. Unless Rena recovers and can positively tell us who pushed her over the edge, we have no evidence."

"How is she?"

"Unchanged. She had nearly as high a level of RDH in her blood as she had when she was brought in after the incident at the market," Oliver said. "Dr. Gaston said that the shock of hitting the ledge and the cold water may have helped her purge her stomach, but it was too late to purge her bloodstream. He believes the coma is a direct result of the overdose."

"So, YOU WANT control of the Family so badly that you'd go to this extreme," Leah snarled at Karen later in the afternoon.

"Leah, I didn't choose this."

"Silence, both of you," growled Benjamin as he leaned shakily on his cane next to Karen's bed. As far as Karen knew, it was the first time the old man had been outside his mansion in five years. "Leah, if you want to challenge her, you know what you have to do. As of this moment, Karen Weisman is The Roth."

"I'm angry, but I'm not stupid," Leah said. "I'll sign over all the accounts and powers of attorney you've given me as soon as she is out of the hospital."

"No, Leah," Karen said. "Please. You are managing everything on behalf of Ben, please continue to manage it on my behalf. I didn't plan for this and I didn't prepare for it. Please help me help the Family."

"Really?"

"We've known for years that you didn't have anyone to take over after you," Ben said to Leah. "I know you love your sons but putting the Family leadership into any one of their hands would mean the end of the Family. I concur with Karen. You've done a good job. This isn't about your ability, but what comes after."

"Please continue as administrator of the Family estate. I reviewed all the records after you gave me my share of the Forest and your decisions and votes have always been right on. I'll sign my one share back into the pool. I was also impressed with the way you have managed the real estate. The Family business is in good hands under your management and maybe by the time you want to retire, you will have trained me, or my heir, well enough to take over," Karen said.

"I have nothing against you, Karen. I thought at one time of adopting you and making you *my* heir," Leah said. "This was just so sudden."

"Tell me about it," Karen said.

"Gee," Leah continued, "over the past few years, I have used my own resources and those of my husband to acquire a stake in SSG of forty-seven thousand shares. At the annual meeting, my attorney discovered what a paltry influence that has. I would like you to take the proxy for my shares and continue to vote your conscience to the benefit of the City and the Forest and the Family."

"I'll do my best, Leah."

Trick or Treat

"You have to go now," Karen said. "Everything you need is in the pantry. I stocked up a week ago. I can't stand the idea of all the children coming to the house and you not being there to hand out treats."

"I can't believe there are that many children in our neighborhood," Gee laughed.

"There aren't. But I let it slip to Ms. Tomczyk that you would be handing out Halloween treats and she sort of let it out to the parents who bring their children to the Bookhouse. Um... word might have gotten around the school, too."

"Oh my. I'd better get home and get ready."

"Gee!"

"Hello, my little buddy."

"Tick-r-teat!"

"You bet. Do you have a trick for me?" Devon's eyes got big and he turned toward his Mom and Dad a few steps away.

"I sing!" he exclaimed happily. It was the ABC song and Devon got all the words right and some of the tune. Gee happily gave his little friend a chocolate candy bar.

"Oooh. You give out the good stuff," Marian said.

"What do I have to do to get one of those?" Nathan laughed. Gee reached in his bag and threw a candy bar to each of his friends.

"That's because you are accompanying my best friend," Gee said. He called the parents close. "Watch out for him. Especially around here. I don't think the attack on Karen was the last gambit in throwing the annexation vote," he whispered.

"Is this ever going to end?" Marian asked. Nathan took his son's hand.

"After Tuesday, win or lose, there will no longer be a reason for all this tension. I hope."

"Is that why you are sitting outside instead of opening the door when the bell rings tonight?" Nathan asked.

"Yes. It lets me see who is approaching and I can watch the kids on the street."

"Well, yours is the only house on this block and we aren't going to stay in this neighborhood. We just wanted Devon to see his Gee." Marian said.

"You know I'll do everything in my power to protect him," Gee said.

"And all the other kids of our City. Thank you, Gee," Nathan answered.

A group of six kids, all dressed as hickory shakers were headed up the drive.

"You've got a fan club," Marian laughed as they left.

Kids dressed as shakers, foresters, and even in their normal picker clothes seemed to be a prevalent theme among the trick-or-treaters. He was glad Karen had stocked up with a huge supply of candy bars. He wasn't sure there would be any left at the end of the night. Several kids sang the hickory song when Gee asked for a trick. One group—led by his little nemesis, Sally Ann Metzger—screamed and fell down on their shaker poles, mimicking Gee's fall from the tree. Gee repeated his warning to all the parents and chaperones who escorted kids to his door, but he didn't spot any unusual activity on the street that signaled danger.

The last group of kids to approach his house, just before he decided it was time to turn off the lights at nine o'clock, were teenagers. They were dressed in more elaborate costumes than most of the younger children wore. Gee recognized several popular superheroes and comic characters among them.

"Do you... uh... allow teens to trick or treat here?" the lead girl asked as she was pushed forward by her boyfriend. They were dressed as Wonder Woman and Captain America.

"When someone comes to my door in great costumes like yours, I'm happy to give you treats. Have you guys had fun tonight?"

"Yeah. There are only a few houses we know that allow teens. We took a chance on yours, Gee."

"Uh... Gee..." Captain America said. "Shannon and me... We were the ones who saw that girl go over the cliff at the quarry. I've never been so frightened. We figured out what our real responsibility was, though."

"Ryan figured it out and made me call 911 while he saved that woman's life. It's made us all think, though. I was afraid to act because I didn't want anyone to know that Ryan and I had run off to make love. He showed me that no matter how embarrassing, we have to set aside our personal fears to do what's right."

Gee laughed. "Your quick action probably saved two lives. Come on, guys. Have a seat on the ledge and tell me what you've all been thinking." They milled about and eventually the dozen or so teens all had a place to sit and a candy bar. Another of the teens spoke. He was dressed in a Superman outfit and Gee didn't think the muscles were padded.

"I'm Viktor, Mr. Gee. You know me and James from basketball. We… well, some of us are from Rosebud and some from Flor. But we all figured out how brave Ryan and Shannon had to be to go to the police and face the anger of their parents. We all knew they were going steady, but no one would ever out them." Shannon buried her face against her boyfriend's chest in embarrassment. "Anyway, after they did what they did, we got together and decided we needed to be brave like them. Like you."

"Like me?"

"We've all noticed. You just do what's right, no matter what. We're going to do that too," a very tall young woman dressed as Elastigirl stepped forward.

"You tell, 'im, Stretch."

"Must you do that, Dash?"

"You could only be Luke and Colleen Zimmer's kids. Right?"

"Yeah. I'm Alyson and the imbecile is Barrett."

"I've played basketball with you, too," Barrett added.

"And how are you being brave now, Alyson."

"I'm standing up."

"Huh?"

"I've always been ashamed of… my height. I've been the tallest girl in my class since kindergarten. I hate it. But I'm going to stand up straight. I'm six-one and I don't even like sports. I can't get a date and I don't care anymore. I'm going to stand up and be proud."

"Hey, wait! I'll date you. I thought you'd like shoot me down."

"You'd date anyone, Viktor. Is there anyone else in our class you haven't taken out?"

"Yeah, but um… maybe you're who I've been hunting for."

"Give it a shot, Alyson!"

"Um… well…"

"How about being my date to the dance after the game Friday night," Viktor said.

"Really?"

"Hey, we just all agreed to start being brave. I'm bravely asking you out in front of all these people. Don't shoot me down. Please?"

"Um… Okay. The dance. I'll wear flats."

"Not on my account. I love looking up to you."

"Okay, so you guys have all decided to be brave. What's that really mean?" Gee asked the kids.

"Well, what Ryan and Shannon did was brave. What Viktor and Alyson just did was brave. I guess being brave means stopping being afraid," Barrett said.

"I'm afraid almost all the time," Gee said.

"But…"

"Having courage doesn't mean not having fears but it's about not letting them stop you from doing what's right. It's watching out for each other and for your community. Let your ideals guide you instead of your fears."

"Wow. Thanks, Gee. Um… I guess we just wanted you to know that we… and there's more than just those of us standing here… We've got your back," Ryan said. Gee shook hands with each of the dozen kids, knowing that he wasn't alone as champion for Rosebud Falls.

KAREN DID NOT return home with Gee for the rest of the week. He sat with her in her room, but she didn't want to go outside at all. He picked up a new cell phone for her Thursday. He told her about his encounter with the teens on Halloween and that produced the first genuine smile that he'd seen.

"I'm getting better," Karen said. "Really, Gee. I'm just so frightened sometimes. But these kids got the right message. I'm going to do the right thing."

"God! If there was anyone braver than you two, the world couldn't stand it," Julia said as she fussed with Karen's bedside and helped her apply a little makeup.

"What's going on?" Gee asked. "This seems like exceptional service, Julia."

"Command performance," Julia answered. "Karen is going home soon, but there were some people who couldn't wait to visit you." There was a knock on the door and people started filing into the room. Gee had assumed that it would be the hospital staff who wanted to say good-bye, but Jessie and Jonathon stepped in, followed by Jo and Wayne. The Warren twins, Leslie and Stefan, went to stand by their cousin Julia. Gee wasn't sure if he was as surprised as Karen when Troy Cavanaugh brought Violet Lanahan into the room, followed by Cameron LaCoe and the entire quartet. The room was crowded, but after everyone said hi, they edged toward the walls and gave the Nussbaums room to perform. By the time the quartet had filled the room with 'The Voice Within,' a crowd had gathered in the hall, crying and swaying to the music. People applauded and went back to their work, somehow filled with new hope.

GEE LOOKED AROUND the room, touched that the group of friends had come to wish them well and lend their support. But then he noticed something else. Every Family was represented in the room. And all the heirs of the war orphans. He looked curiously at Julia and she smiled.

"Stefan and Leslie were afraid that fourteen was too young to participate, so I told them I'd stand with them," she said.

"What's going on?"

"We came to see Karen and you because we respect you and look to you for guidance. This group represents three things," Wayne said. "First and foremost, we all consider ourselves to be your friends. We all wanted to stand in one room and tell you that."

"Thank you," Karen said. "I don't think we could ask for better friends."

"Second," Troy took up the narrative, "we represent the youngest adult generation of the Families. There are some who are younger, but even Leslie and Stefan wanted to be here. We'll all be looking at a new generation soon and none of us know what role they'll play in the coming era. I look out my window on Main Street and I can see a change has taken place in this City in just the past few months. The fight over the annexation has divided us and I think we might be on the brink of losing. Karen, your voice has been pulling people together. We miss it. We need you as a representative of all the Families. After all, you ate a nut for each of us."

"I… I didn't do it to take control of the Families," Karen said. "I didn't even want to lead my own Family."

"We didn't ask you to take control, Karen," Julia said. "We asked you to represent. You and Troy have the loudest voices in our City. We want you to use them."

"Which brings us to the third reason we're here," Elaine joined in, surprising everyone. "Jo, Jessie, Jonathon, Wayne, Stefan and Leslie, Violet, and my cousins and I are the heirs of the seven heroes and their trusts. We've already given you our proxies to represent us at SSG. It's important because SSG controls the mineral and resource rights to most of the annex—including the wild woods. We don't want our grandparents and their fathers to just unite the Families. Our real trust is the Forest, and Gee, you were selected by the Forest as the head of the Forest Family. We desperately need you to unite the wild woods with the Forest so it is all protected. Maybe that's not why you thought you came to Rosebud Falls but it's why we all choose you to be our champion." Elaine took a deep breath as if it was the first one she'd take since she sang. She turned and buried her head against Cameron's chest as Krystal and Gail held the two of them together.

Lies, Lies, Damn Lies

LATE FRIDAY NIGHT, Gee was getting ready to settle next to Karen in the narrow hospital bed when her phone chimed. She was being released in the morning and reached for the phone automatically.

Karen looked at the text message and showed him the phone. He barely caught it when it fell from her hand and she began sobbing. A text message said, 'We aren't through with you yet, little girl.' Attached to the message was a photo of a house in the Orchard Project with a swing set in the yard.

"That's…"

"The house where my little playmate was abducted fifteen years ago," Karen finished. "They are threatening me with her."

"Are you sure?" Gee asked. "That's the house where Wayne lives."

"I KNOW WHAT I have to do," Karen sighed when she got home from the hospital with Gee on Saturday morning. They'd picked up a copy of the day's *Mirror* on the way home and read it with increasing foreboding. "I just hope I haven't waited too long."

"At least one of us knows what she's supposed to do," Gee said. "I still don't know how to fulfill all their hopes for the Forest."

"It will come to you," Karen said, kissing him. "I want to make love. Then I need to write. I need to tell the truth."

"MR. SAVAGE, I have a proposal," Gee said to Wayne's grandfather.

"Gee, I think we've established that I'm just Pàl. What's the proposal? You know you can just direct the company."

"I'm not comfortable with that. I want to know that what I propose is really for the best."

"That's one of the reasons we've all been so comfortable assigning our proxies to you. You now hold well-over the two-thirds majority that it would take to overturn any corporate decision. But you are not willing to exercise that power. What's your proposal?"

"I'm still pretty new at this, so let me know if I'm out of line. I understand that the land out here doesn't actually belong to Savage Sand and Gravel. Who does it belong to?" Gee asked.

"I don't know, Gee. I know that sounds strange. For all intents and purposes, I suppose we could stake a claim to it. Adverse possession. Yet, SSG really only leased the mineral and resource rights. The Savage Family only ever used them for quarrying the limestone that built our City. But somewhere along the line, the Savages acquired a trusteeship for the actual owners. Under that trust, we've used the lease fees and royalties from SSG to pay the taxes, and even sign the renewable lease. I'm not sure even my grandfather was aware of who the actual beneficiary of the trust is."

"It seems then that SSG has practical control over the land and the lease. I understand the church subleases the land on which it is built."

"And I'm going to put an end to that," Pàl growled. "They signed a fifty-year lease and it is up in two years. They'll have to move."

"Oh. Well. I don't know how to deal with that. I won't be sad to see them go. But, if SSG was able to lease land to the church, couldn't it lease the wild woods to the City?" Gee asked. "We really need to get it under management of the foresters."

"Hmm. That's good thinking, Gee. Until we can arrange something more permanent. But maybe not leased to the City. The Forest is inside the City Limits but is independently owned and operated. Mostly, if I understand correctly, it was set up that way so it couldn't be influenced by local politics. We've certainly seen enough instances of public lands being taken out of the public trust and given to developers to exploit lately. The independent ownership of the Forest protects it from changes in political and economic winds."

"So, we could lease it to the Forest?"

"Let me make some calls, Gee. I've been gone from this town for sixty years. Like you, I need advice from those who know better than I do. Let's see if we can make this happen."

"I'm glad you came in, Cameron. Frankly, I have no idea what to do with this. I'm worried we could be sued for libel."

"Did you check with Dad? I mean Jack?"

"Yes. He verified that Karen has legitimate sources who must remain anonymous for their safety. He would not, of course, verify the content of the quotes," Axel said.

"Damn, it's a whole book. What's this come out to?"

"Close to one hundred eighty column inches. We'll have to ditch nearly every story we currently have laid out," Axel sighed. He could see a long night ahead.

"No. Put it to bed the way it is and start printing."

"We won't run this?"

"We will. I want a full four-page wrapper around the whole paper with just this story. Give me six column inches in the bottom right corner of the front page to run an official disclaimer indicating what Karen went through last weekend and the results of her kidnapping and coma. I'm not going to make her into a liar, but I want it clear that she's the one who did the research. Give me a screamer in two lines at the top of the page. A three-column picture of that shack where she was found under the headline. The interior shot where she was barely covered by the blanket before the medics moved her."

Axel was shocked. They'd intentionally not run that photo in the original story of Karen's abduction and rescue. She was still unconscious at the time. A photo that size would lap beneath the fold. He couldn't remember a headline like this since he'd seen the D-Day headline in the archives.

"Get every picture you can to support the story. If we need to send Kelly out to the quarry for more, send her. I want a three-column picture that the girl took of her boyfriend rescuing the Lynd woman on page two."

"We didn't run that because he's a minor."

"I'll get permission. He's a hero. Little picture of the church and one of SSG. See what else we have. File picture of the preacher? Here's the skinny. Karen's text and as many photos as it takes to fill the four pages with nice organized subheads. No ads and no other articles. I'll have edited copy to you by the time you get the rest of the paper to bed."

Axel's evening—all night—was committed. The newspaper he'd worked at for as long as his publisher had been alive was going to start a war.

On Election Day.

⊲◆⊳

"AH, WOULD YOU mind a little walk through town? Maybe breakfast at Jitterz?" Karen asked as she stretched luxuriously in her lover's arms.

"Of course. Thinking you'll spot anything?" Gee answered, nibbling on her ear. Karen reached for her phone.

"No text messages. No word. It just seems strange that Axel didn't even call to tell me he wouldn't run the story. I'd like to see the paper."

"He's probably still reeling from shock."

They walked the mile into the downtown area, stopping in front of

The Elmont Mirror for a newspaper on the way to Jitterz. Karen held the paper up for Gee to see.

"You did it." He smiled at her. "Let's get our coffee and read about the chaos to come."

"Karen Weisman is passing right outside the window here on Main Street," Troy Cavanaugh's voice said through the speakers in front of WRZF. "Karen, will you come into the studio for an impromptu interview? And look, we have City Champion Gee Evars here as well." They looked through the window of the studio and saw Troy frantically waving for them to step inside.

"And so it begins," Karen said. She led Gee into the studio where an assistant of Troy's was quickly arranging a microphone, and chairs for Karen and Gee in front of Troy's broadcast desk.

"This is an unscheduled interview," Troy continued. "But it seems that everything happening on this Election Day is a little surprising. I have with me newspaper reporter Karen Weisman, who has just laid a bombshell on Rosebud Falls with her article in this morning's *Mirror*. With her is City Champion, George Evars, whom we all know as Gee. Welcome Karen and Gee."

"Thank you, Troy."

"Let's get right to this headline. I don't think there has been type this big on the front page since Pearl Harbor. 'LIES! LIES! DAMN LIES!' the headline says. The story is a scathing condemnation of the seven Families of Rosebud Falls, the Savage Sand and Gravel company, and the Calvary Tabernacle. Is there anyone in town you haven't called out, Karen?"

"This story has been hidden from the people of Rosebud Falls for more than seventy-five years, Troy. Even within the Families, few of us knew the truth about why the last annexation of South Rosebud failed and why it is so important for it to succeed today," Karen said.

"The story says that the Families have been protecting the citizens from the truth about the Forest for two hundred years," Troy read. "Is it a dangerous truth? That seems like a noble thing to do."

"It does, Troy. And the Family heads of that time probably did their best in setting up the structure we have. But if you read the comments the Family representatives made in interviews with me, you find them filled with City spirit, the economic value of the annexation, the benefits of extended services, and even Jan Poltanys' statement that it's just the right thing to do. They lied to us—to the people. The real reason to annex South Rosebud is the wild woods. Everyone has known for generations that the Rose Hickory nuts are poisonous. It seems like once every few years, someone just has to try one and we put up another gravestone. But what they have hidden amidst all the great benefits we derive from the Forest is that fact that these nuts can also be distilled for nefarious purposes. Specifically, the new designer drug Lustre and its evil cousin Lustre Plus are made from Rose Hickory nuts. And those nuts have been harvested from the wild woods. We must bring this area under control before environmental and drug task forces come in to terminally wipe out the threat."

"This implies—well, more than implies—that someone has been harvesting nuts from the wild woods and operating a drug lab somewhere. And since SSG owns the mineral and resource rights to that parcel, it points directly at one of Rosebud Falls' oldest employers," Troy said.

"And the church that makes itself at home there. Until Harvest this year, the directors of the company and its CEO were all members of Calvary Tabernacle, making their decisions based on the directives of the church. A shareholder revolt at the last annual meeting suddenly ousted them."

"Karen, the article goes on to say that a member of the congregation and an impartial observer have both reported that it appears the communion elements served in the church every Sunday are laced with the drug Lustre. Who is this member and observer?" Troy asked.

"For their safety, their identities must remain anonymous."

"Safety?"

"Need I remind you that both Gee and I have been attacked and another woman still lies in a coma after the events of last weekend."

"What should the people—the voters—of Rosebud Falls do?"

"There's a new order in Rosebud Falls. This is less an election than a revolution of the next generation—both Family and non-Family—claiming a birthright that should have been theirs long ago. We are cleaning house and doing what's right. That is why it is so important to pass the annexation on the ballot today. It isn't about resources, fire and police services, or a blot on our landscape. This is purely and simply Rosebud Falls claiming its heritage and protecting the Forest and the citizens. And it starts by making South Rosebud part of our city."

"I don't want to drag you back into the horrifying experience of being kidnapped and drugged last weekend, but was this the trigger for your attack against the Families, SSG, and the church today?" Troy asked. Karen took a deep breath as the horror of that night washed over her again. She shook it off when Gee reached for her hand.

"I read the sidebar to the story just as we were walking up the street," Karen began. "It implies that my experience left me feeling vulnerable. Well, as you said, I'd been kidnapped, drugged… and raped. But I went to the quarry that day because a frightened woman was hiding there. And while tortured and drugged, I still found evidence that the Families had lied about the importance of the annex and the church was complicit in manufacturing the drug. The picture on the front page of the paper today is the shack in the woods where I was found that horrid night. This was not merely someone's hideaway in the wilderness. Forensic evidence shows that the shack had been a sophisticated manufacturing facility where OUR NUTS were being processed into dangerous drugs. We cannot let this survive today's election. We must annex South Rosebud and put the ideals of Rosebud Falls to work at cleaning up this mess."

Seeds of Revolution

"AH, THE COUPLE of the hour," Birdie said as Gee and Karen finally walked into Jitterz. "Have you voted yet?"

"Next stop, Mizz Birdie," Karen said. "We needed to assess the situation downtown before we go up to the library to vote."

"Here's your coffee," Elaine said.

"Thank you, Elaine," Gee responded, paying for the drinks and a couple of breakfast sandwiches.

Birdie pulled a chair up next to where they sat.

"All hell's going to break loose," she said softly. "I hear the kids… the ones on their way to the high school… talking. I don't say anything, so they assume I don't hear anything. When they see a quiet adult day after day who never condemns or interrupts them, they tend to forget she has ears. Today, they are talking about needing courage." She cast an eye at Gee. "Your names come up. They talk about the fence that separates the wild woods from the city. They nod. They say tonight."

"They'll tear down the fence," Karen said.

"They need adult supervision. Help," Birdie agreed. Both she and Karen looked at Gee.

"I… need to talk to some people," Gee said. "Will you be okay getting to the library and then home, love?"

"IT'S GOING TO be a lot of work," Jonathon said. "I don't think they know what they're getting into. It's a mile of chain link. A couple dozen kids aren't going to just shake it down with their bare hands."

"We need to be there to help," Jessie said as she looked over her husband's shoulder at the map spread out on the foresters' conference table. "They'll follow the same path we used when we were teens. They'll go from Flor del Día across the creek and then south."

"We cut the fence here last weekend and only did a quick fix afterward," Jonathon said, pointing at a spot along the border.

"If we set up with some tools at that point, and get the kids focused on taking down the fence to the west, that's probably all we'll need," Gabe surmised. The old forester had worked in the area for forty years.

"How do you figure, Gabe?" Jessie asked.

"Removing chain link fence is hard work. It's heavy. By the time they reach the creek, they'll be exhausted. And it's a good endpoint. They can feel they opened the Forest, even though it's just three hundred yards."

"We need to make sure they clean up their mess," Gee said. "They can't just tear down the fence and leave it there. It has to be removed."

"There might be one of the small tractor trailer combinations left out there with the keys in it," Jonathon said, smiling. They agreed to meet after dark.

IT WAS AFTER sundown. They election was over. The radio had been reporting the projected results since four in the afternoon. He quietly entered the hospital room. Somehow this girl—this young woman—had come to represent the entire battle to him. He took her hand and knelt at the bedside to pray earnestly for her soul.

"Lance Beck, step away from the bed," a voice demanded from the doorway. Detective Mead Oliver stood there backed up by two uniformed police officers with their guns drawn. "You are under arrest for the attempted murder of Rena Lynd and for the assault, kidnapping, and attempted murder of Karen Weisman."

"No! That can't be. It's a mistake. I'm a man of God," Beck said as he stood. Dave McCarron moved behind him and cuffed his hands.

"You have the right to remain silent. Anything you say can and will be used against you in a court of law. You have the right to have an attorney. If you cannot afford one, one will be appointed to you by the court. Do you understand each of these rights I have explained to you?"

"No. Yes. I understand, but this is all a mistake. She is a precious child of God. I would never hurt her."

"Having these rights in mind, do you wish to talk to us now?"

"No. Maybe. I should have a lawyer. This is all a big mistake."

The preacher looked again at the comatose girl and a tear trickled down his cheek.

"I love you."

Pitchforks and Torches

GEE MOVED AMONG the high schoolers and quietly talked to them as they marched from Flor del Día to the south edge of the Forest. He was surprised at the number of kids he met. He expected a couple dozen. He saw a couple hundred.

"How did you know we'd be here?" Ryan asked Gee as they walked through the peaceful Forest. Flashlights lit their way and Gee was pleased to see that most of the kids had gloves at least. A few carried tools of various sorts.

"It's a brave thing to do. And it's hard to keep a mob like this a secret."

Foresters joined the group, one or two at a time, as they walked. Their friendly demeanor was something the kids were used to from their first orientations and the foresters were their allies in caring for the Forest. The foresters talked about the need to protect the Forest while they worked and how to most efficiently remove the fence. By the time they had walked the half-mile to the fence line, the crowd had swelled even more, and kids were surprised to find some of their parents silently waiting. Ewan Moffat and Jim O'Rourke stood near the cut mark where Ryan and Shannon led the high schoolers. The young couple walked straight up to their fathers.

"Dad, this is my boyfriend, Ryan Moffat," Shannon started. Before her father could respond, Ryan joined in.

"Dad, this is my girlfriend, Shannon O'Rourke. I hope you've both come to help us and not to object." Ryan looked from his father to Shannon's. The two fathers looked at each other and Ewan held out his hand. Jim took it.

"I think we have other things to be concerned with now," Jim said. "I have a pair of wire cutters for you, Shannon. Will that help?" The kids threw themselves at their fathers and hugged them. Then Ryan turned to the assembled crowd. He was a little shaken to see so many watching him.

"We've got a lot of hands," Ryan said. "And a lot of helpers. Just like at Harvest, we need to divide into teams. If you aren't strong enough to cut wires or carry fence posts, take the flashlights and lanterns so we can all see to work safely. Let's get cutters going first. We need a team going each direction from the place they cut through last weekend. If you've got a shovel, spread out and start loosening the fence posts. Those of you with tough work gloves and clothes, you'll have to start with the barbed wire on top of the fence. Be careful not to drop it on anyone else—or yourself. If you do get hurt... um... Nurse Ellie and..." Ryan broke off as he saw the small team of medical personnel. Gee smiled at Dr. Poltanys and his sister Julia. "...and all those doctor types are here to help. We need to roll all this stuff up and cart it out of here, so somebody start getting ready to load the trailer we found. We might need to make a couple of trips. Or more. And remember. The Forest is our lifeblood. We're here to protect it, not to harm it. And we're here to put a stop to using *our nuts* to make drugs that poison people."

With those words from their sixteen-year-old leader, the teens began to organize themselves into teams and spread out along the fence line. Word had gotten around town and Gee saw Detective Oliver standing by with a uniformed officer. Neither moved to stop the activity. Gee saw a couple of sheriff's deputies helping remove barbed wire.

Beside him, the people who came to pledge their support in the hospital stood. Karen took his hand. The other heads of Families stood behind them. Even old Ben Roth had been driven in a cart to watch the fence come down. Collin Meagher openly wept near him.

"This is how it happens," Karen whispered to her lover. Then Elaine's voice rose in the Forest as the City went to work.

No more fences, no more parting,
No more suff'ring in our heart;
We are here now. We are starting,
Never more to be apart.

THE END

WILD WOODS

Coming Summer of 2019

GEE STOMPED the snow off his boots before removing them and hopping one bare foot at a time through the open door. The effort was vain as a gust of wind blew snow in behind him. He slammed the door against the frigid blast.

Pàl Savage finally negotiated having the foresters take over management of the wild woods. There were problems on both sides of the argument, not the least of which included the cost of taking on management of three hundred more acres of woodland. The area was so overgrown that estimates ranged from five to ten years to make the wild woods a productive part of the Forest.

The young leaders of the Families came forward with a proposal to fund the reclamation effort. After the election, the next generation had become a force their elders had to reckon with. Karen had become the youngest Family head, even though Ben Roth was still living and Leah managed the Family businesses. Karen declined, however, to join the next generation rebels.

———————⊲◆⊳———————

"THE THING IS that you are working toward the future of the Families' involvement in the City and in the Forest," she said. "If I hadn't had the Roth Family leadership kind of forced on me, I'd be right there with you."

"I don't see the problem, Karen," Cameron LaCoe said. "We need the Family heads to listen or we'll never get things changed."

"That's exactly what I mean. I'm one of the people you need to convince. I think Jo Ransom should represent the Roths. Of course, you could have one of Leah's sons. It's not like the Family head appointed any of you."

"As if any of us would trust Jude or Joseph to have an idea," Jessie laughed. "Have you noticed that only three of us in this alliance have the same last name as our families?" She shoved her husband's shoulder and Jonathon held up both hands. He, Zach Poltanys, and Wayne Savage were the only designated heirs with the Family name.

"Maybe that is going to finally spell the end of Family precedence," Jonathon said. "Should I take Sims as my last name instead of having Jessie become a Lazorack?"

"I can see what Karen is getting at," Wayne said. "If we are going to act independently of the Family but still influencing it, none of us should be the Family head for as long as we can avoid it. I'm going to have to find a younger family member when *Granda* passes on. Maybe I have an undiscovered cousin."

"You could just have Gee represent you," Violet Lanahan suggested. "He holds about seventy percent of the proxies for SSG."

"Or maybe I'll just adopt that Ryan Moffat," Wayne laughed. "He's sure become a natural leader."

THE FINAL OUTCOME of the negotiations among the younger family reps, their Family heads, and SSG was that the Families would fund the reclamation project to be repaid from the profits realized by the wild woods before they were fully incorporated into the Forest.

There was just one obstacle left.

"GEE, HOW WOULD you like to become a forester?" Pàl asked at their next meeting. Gee laughed.

"The idea has been floating around in my head, but I don't want to leave and go to college somewhere to get a forestry degree like Jonathon did. I don't even know that I could get admitted to a college. I'll do as much volunteer work as I can, though."

"Not good enough. There are other ways of becoming a forester. How about if you apprenticed yourself?"

"Do you think that would work? I'll have to talk to Jonathon and see if they have a program," Gee said. He was happy working at the market, but since well before Harvest he had become more attached to the Forest. Ever since grandfather tree gave him a nut and he ate it.

"He'll agree. He agreed before we concluded the negotiation," Pàl said. "Bringing the wild woods under Forest management is contingent on you becoming a forester and leading the integration."

"Well, I like... Wait! What?"

"The Families, the foresters, the scions, and SSG have all agreed. We will place all the undesignated land in the annex—not just the three hundred acres, but all the area that has hickory trees—under the management of the foresters as a reclamation project if you will work on it."

"I can't lead that kind of an effort!" Gee sputtered. "I don't know anything about reclaiming a forest."

"Of course not. No one expects you to know everything all at once. But the foresters will take you on and train you, you'll work with them to establish a plan for the project, and you'll coordinate volunteers to work on it. Unlike your 'job' as City Champion, this one has a salary. Not one you can get rich off of, but you won't need to balance it with working at the market."

"You already decided this. Asking me if I wanted to be a forester was just a ruse," Gee sighed.

"Mmm. Yes. To be blunt. I thought it would be better if you actually wanted to do the job," Pàl said. "But the truth is that you are now identified with the Forest. It's still not general knowledge that you ate a nut but everyone saw your performance as a shaker. Everyone saw you fall from the tree. Everyone saw you walk with the teens when they tore down the fence. Even if it takes you a while to learn what is necessary, everyone looks to you for leadership."

"I'll do it." It was a simple statement, but Gee had no idea what it would ultimately mean.

ONCE GEE CHANGED clothes and had dry socks and slippers on, he headed to the kitchen. Karen would still be a couple of hours and he could get soup started. He made a short detour by the sitting room to start a fire and then happily started cooking.

It had been a cold day working in the Forest. Little had been done in the wild woods so far. Gee discovered late fall and early winter were primary maintenance times. Once the sap stopped flowing, the foresters were out pruning the trees and assessing the needs for the next season. And each day, a small team spent an hour or two cutting brush from the wild woods. Having the foliage drop made it easier to see what they were cutting but the Thanksgiving snowstorm had made it more difficult to wade into the understory and do the trimming. An hour of work with a machete in freezing temperatures was all anyone wanted to put in.

Gee had the soup heating in a slow cooker and was boiling water for a cup of tea when he heard the front doorbell ring. He wiped his hands and went to answer it.

A girl—or perhaps a young woman—stood on the lower step looking up at the house. When Gee opened the door, she took a step back as if preparing to flee.

"Hi. What can I do for you?" Gee asked. She looked half frozen in tennis shoes and a windbreaker. She was not dressed for the weather at all.

"Is… Is this where Karen Weisman lives?"

"Yes, it is. Are you here to see her? You look cold. Come inside."

The girl took another step back and looked around as if weighing her options. "Will you let me leave?"

"Of course! But you look half frozen. There is a fire burning in the sitting room and I was just about to make tea. Or would you prefer hot chocolate? Come in. Come in."

The girl visibly shivered and stepped inside only far enough for Gee to close the door.

"I'm Nina. Miss Weisman said… She said if I ever came to Rosebud Falls… She said I could stay with her."

The effort of coming inside, the sudden warmth of the room, tears, and exhaustion all seemed to catch up with the girl at once. Gee caught her as she collapsed and carried her to the sofa, feeling her cold sodden clothes. He quickly pulled a blanket over her and grabbed his cell phone.